RISE OF THE FAY

Formatting by Elaine York, Allusion Graphics, LLC
www.allusiongraphics.com

WARNING:

The following content may contain elements of: explicit sexual content, sexual assault, violence, pornographic content, death or dying, hateful/inappropriate language, homophobia/ homophobic slurs. Contents may not be suitable for children.

Reader Discretion Advised

Rise of the Fay

The Fay

Andre L. Carr

Dedication

When I was little, I always read and viewed heroes as someone I could never really relate to. The hero always seemed to get the girl in the end. This book is not like that. This is for all the boys, girls, men, and women like me who never had a hero of their own. Any of you out there who are different and struggling to overcome obstacles in life and who are always told "You can't" because of who you are and what you represent. Just know that you can, and every one of us has a hero within them. Don't you ever think for a moment that they are right — because every one of us are a force to be reckoned with.

1: AFFIANCED

THE CLOCK STARTED TICKING. I rushed up to the rock-climbing wall to begin the race against my opponent, Issac, who was across the room. Reaching up to grab onto the oddly shaped things they called jugs, I hoisted myself up. The ropes attached to my harness rippled behind me as I continued to climb. The wall must have been at least fifty-feet high. Maybe it was the wrong time to mention I wasn't a fan of heights so even ten-feet high would have given me pause. I proceeded to ascend, higher and higher with each grip of the jug, and my palms began to get sweaty. The chants of people cheering my name and Issac's as we climbed farther up spurred us to continue. I looked back at the clock...two minutes in. I could see my reflection in the mirror that covered the wall behind us while dangling from the rock wall.

The sweat on my arms was dripping off of me, and I could see my dark curls glistening from exertion from the oil in my hair, mixed with the perspiration. My hazel green eyes stared back at me with determination in the mirror. I was six-foot tall and glad for my height and arm span because it gave me an advantage in this race. My friend Ann was cheering my name and telling me that Issac was getting farther ahead. Shit. I turned back to the wall and needed to get my ass into gear. Issac was now at least ten feet above me. I started to make my way up, and the higher I got, the smaller the crowd looked down below. The sweat was both a mixture of adrenaline and anxiety, both at war with each other.

Two feet behind Issac now and I could see that the rock wall forked in half above both of us. I reached up to grab my next jug and instantly lost my grip from the sweat on my palms, causing me to drop at least a foot. Thankfully, I was able to catch myself mid-fall, but could hear the crowd down below let out a big, "Owww."

I grabbed back on to the jug and hoisted myself up higher. I began to make my way up the left side of the fork, and I could hear Ann clearly over the crowd screaming at me, "That's the wrong way. That's the wrong way."

I glanced up and noticed the glistening red buzzer was on the other side of the split.

"Shit." That's most definitely not going to allow me to win this race. But fate or dumb-ass luck was on my side because at that same moment Issac lost his footing. I couldn't backtrack now because there wasn't enough time to navigate back down and then back up the right way. So I kept going up higher on the left side, and I could hear the crowd murmuring,

"What is he doing?"

Issac got a grip and shouted out, "You can't beat me, man. Been doing this for years and not about to lose to a newb."

I replied, "Never underestimate the underdog."

You could hear the people below laughing and others saying I was wrong for not turning back. Issac was just two feet lower than I was, and I needed to make it to the other side of the fork to hit the buzzer. I shimmied to the edge of the rock wall and held on with my left hand as my right dangled. I hugged my feet against the wall and lowered down into a crouching position.

Ann yelled, "Don't you do it, Alec. Don't you dare do it."

I looked back and smiled because I had no choice, there was no other way I was going to win if I didn't take a chance. The crowd got silent, anticipation of the unknown, and I could hear my heart beating in my throat. I steadied my breathing and knew Issac was parallel to me on the other side. So I did the only thing I could do... I shifted my weight back and forth and silently counted down in my head.

Three...two...one...

I flung myself across the five-foot fork in the wall and reached for the closest jug I could grab. Just barely made it, and I could overhear the crowd going wild. Dangling there by one hand, I found my footing and continued to lift myself up.

The crowd started to clap and chant, "ALEC, ALEC, ALEC."

The race wasn't over, though, and I looked over to Issac who looked shocked that I pulled something like that off. All the years I've known Issac, I've never seen him do what I just did. Guess he just never had the motivation to take a chance.

I looked him in the eye, laughed, and shouted, "UNDERDOG."

Issac shook his head and laughed right along with me while he kept climbing. I was three feet from the buzzer, and Issac was two feet away. I kept pulling myself up higher on the wall and reached my hand up to tap the elusive button. But I was too far, and I couldn't go any farther. I could feel my arms and hands beginning to tire out, the adrenaline I'd felt only moments ago sapping the life right out of my energy reserves. I looked over and Issac was reaching for the buzzer, too. Screw it. What's one more leap of faith? Since I had my harness on, and even though we were up fifty feet in the air, it had to be safe, right? I squatted down and used every last bit of energy I had to jump up and tap the buzzer.

I slapped it, and you could hear the alarm buzzing right before Issac touched his. I started to fall, and the guys down below caught my weight before I free-fell another forty feet. I stopped suddenly and gently bounced against the wall, then continued my descent with ease. Issac was repelling down at the same speed I was and was shaking his head...I'm sure in awe of my skills, but more likely he couldn't believe I beat him and was pissed. We reached the bottom and landed on the blue mats, and Issac furiously started to remove his safety harness. Yep, definitely pissed. The group of viewers began to walk over to me, congratulating me on my win as Issac stormed off.

Ann quickly approached me. "I can't believe you made that jump, Alec. That was crazy. Finally, a worthy opponent for Issac. Maybe he will stop shit-talking everyone."

"I didn't think I would make it either. It was just beginner's luck, I suppose," I told her while removing my harness.

Another man approached and mentioned, "That was no beginner's luck, you must have been climbing for years to pull that off."

"I have honestly only been climbing for the last four months."

"Well, I would keep at it because you're good."

"Thanks. I appreciate it, but it's just for fun," I reminded him, ending his praise.

Everyone in the gym was buzzing about my leap and Issac appeared to be cooled down now but I knew I needed to talk to him. I told Ann that I would come back and to keep the fans at bay. I made my way through the crowd where Issac sat, angry and disappointed. He could hardly look at me. Issac had been a good friend of mine in high school. We'd lost touch over the years after I began living my truth, a truth that he struggled with. Our friendship rekindled when he realized that I was still the same person after the years that had passed. Issac admitted that he'd been raised to believe that my kind was to be looked down upon. Something he regretted even until this day. But four years after high school and finally getting out from under his family's influence made him see that I was still the same person I'd always been. So here we were now, still friends even though losing at something that he was extremely good at didn't sit well with him.

Issac was five foot ten with a stocky, muscular build and clear, almost porcelain skin. He had sky blue eyes and a lightly scruffed goatee. His dark hair was cropped, and most of the women who saw him fell for his charming demeanor. He sported a six-inch scar on his chest from a heart transplant he had received when he was in high school. A scar that got him more female adoration. Ann really struggled when he was out of school for months while recovering. She visited him in the hospital quite often, but he had been asleep most of the time. I never understood her going to visit as often as she did, knowing that he'd most likely be sleeping. She said she just liked watching him rest because he looked like an angel. Yeah, okay, I couldn't see it. So, because of the transplant and all the time it took for him to get back to normal, he had a tendency to overdo everything he set his mind to...he had something to prove and I think in the back of his mind he thought he had to pack as much into his life as he could because tomorrow was never promised. I totally understood it but didn't mean he had to be pissed at me because I won a race. It was his idea, anyway.

"Hey," I said with an apologetic tone. "You did good, don't beat yourself up about it."

"It's not that, dude, you kicked ass up there," Issac replied as he turned and looked me in the eye. "You know, for years we have been friends, and I've seen you do so many things that just seemed to come with ease, like you'd been doing it your whole life. I don't know how you pull it off, but you just do. The guys in school were always such assholes to you, me included if I'm being honest. You could have been a star in any sport if people were more inclusive."

"It's fine, Issac. You know I've always been the outcast, and honestly, it's never been my thing to be in the spotlight. Things ended up the way that they did, and I can't change that. I've never once looked back and wished I could do things differently, ya know."

Issac replied, "I know, man. But I feel like you could have been bigger than what you thought. Don't ever sell yourself short, Alec."

"Okay, thanks, Dad," I blushed, and that was just enough to break the tension as we both laughed.

"So, when is Liam coming back?"

My mood brightened, "I pick him up from the airport at nine tonight."

Issac asked, "How long has it been?"

"Pretty much since I started rock climbing. About four months, it's been a while since he's been gone that long, but I'll be happy to have him back home."

Ann rushed over to us and said, "Did I hear 'Liam' talk?"

I laughed and said, "Yes, he is coming back tonight, and yes, I am definitely excited."

Ann let out a squeal and started dancing with joy. "Sorry, I'm just so happy for you guys. It just gives me hope that there is still love in this world."

Then her mood went from romance to seduction "So...you guys gonna...ya know?" And she gave me a wink.

Issac and I both shouted, "Oh. My. God." And then we all started laughing. I share a lot of things with my friends, but I won't be going into the details of what I have planned for Liam when he gets back.

I noticed what time it was and jerked into action, "Well, guys, this was a fun date. I'm gonna head over to my mom's house before I get Liam. You two going to make it home safe?" I gave them a wink.

Ann yelled, "Wow, Alec. Really?"

I knew Ann always had a thing for Issac, but she was too shy to ever say anything to him. Ann was an adorable red-headed woman who was twenty-six years old like me. She was thin and stood at five foot two with pale skin, freckles, and chocolate brown eyes. Ann was a timid girl until she got to know you, then she would open up, and Jesus, it was hard to keep her quiet. Since high school, she's said that Issac is her true love, but she's just too hesitant to make a move because of how confident he was.

I laughed and said, "Hey, I'm just askin. I'm gonna head out. Be safe getting home, you two. Ann, I'll call you later to give you the updates on Liam."

Ann and Issac both said, "Bye," and I could see the other people in the gym waving goodbye to me, as well. I waved back but I didn't know them too well, so it wasn't the same as when I waved to Issac or Ann. It was just easier keeping a smaller and closer-knit group of friends. But I was honestly friendly with everyone. I slung my backpack over my shoulder and headed to my black Jeep Wrangler. Issac always told me that it was such a cliché car. I didn't care. I loved my Jeep. I got in and started it up. Before putting it in gear, I took a look in the rearview mirror to see behind me and to check my reflection.

The sweat from my exertion was almost dry now but I noticed my skin was still flushed. My hazel green eyes were calmer, my face was clean shaven, and my jawline strong. My features always got compliments. Most said I should model, while others said I should do porn. I laughed to myself every time I thought about that. Sharp facial features that balanced out the soft ones, as well. I know I looked so much like my mother, which always put a smile on my face. My voice was higher pitched than most men but with just a hint of masculinity. Even though I looked heterosexual, my voice was a dead giveaway when I spoke. Liam always told me that my voice was calming to him, and he enjoyed hearing me talk. Pulling out of my parking space, I made my way out of the parking lot. My mom's house wasn't too far from The Climber's Gym, and I knew she'd been dying to see me so we could catch up.

On my drive there, I thought of how lucky I am to have a mom like her and how much I loved her. Since I was a kid, she has always been alone. She is a powerful woman in my life and raised me and Colden all on her own. I have always looked up to her. Colden, on the other hand, was a bit of a handful. I'm not sure what it was about him, but he always seemed to have a chip on his shoulder. He consistently has a negative outlook on life. Even though we were identical twins, we were nothing alike. Many would get us confused when we were children, but most could immediately tell us apart from our mannerisms.

I was always the quiet, reserved twin. Colden was more outspoken and the 'rough and tough' twin with a short temper. Growing up, Colden and I sort of drifted apart. He started getting involved with drugs and gangs. He'd been in and out of juvie all throughout childhood, and he could never make it through a day of school without getting into a fight. It got worse when he started to fight teachers. Let's just say Colden was never a fan of being told what to do. He has been expelled from so many educational programs that my mom decided it would be easier on everyone if he stopped going. Even through everything, though, he was still my brother and I loved him. He had my back on a lot of things, and when others would pick on me — for being me — Colden would do whatever it took to protect me.

Things changed when I came out when I was fourteen. Just before high school, I was at a breaking point. The hiding, lies, shame, and covering my tracks of who I truly was became too big of a burden to bear. Colden began to get more distant with me. He soon began to side with the homophobes who were against me. He would encourage the taunting and call me names behind my back. Me being more sensitive, I finally asked him if my sexuality ever affected his day-to-day life. Colden told me that he accepted me but that he wouldn't approve of me ever getting married or having children. That was a low blow, especially coming from someone like him. A family member, my twin brother from the only family that I had. Even through all of that, I still accepted him for being the way he was toward me, too. I just wish his feelings could have been reciprocated.

Finally at my mom's house, I stepped out of the car. I shivered because my clothes were still damp from sweat and the cool breeze gave me a chill. I reached into the Jeep to grab my jacket. Not ideal to be wearing tennis shoes with a tank top, gym shorts, and compression pants during the end of winter in Toronto. I wrapped myself up in my grey track jacket and walked toward the doorway. My mom's front door opened, and she was standing in the doorway, smiling. I always found it weird that she always knew the exact moment when I was walking up.

She giggled at me and said, "Get over here, you big ape."

"Hi, Mom," I told her as I gave her a hug.

She led me inside and closed the door. Thankfully, inside she had a fire going because I was freezing. I enjoyed the cold but only when I wanted it to be.

My mom said, "Take off your coat, hun. Are you hungry? There is food on the stove if you want any. I made some salmon and rice, and there is dessert, too."

"No, I think Liam and I will get some food after I pick him up."

My mother never had much company over. I knew she had some girlfriends who would come by and visit, but for the most part, I knew I was the only person who came and visited her. Her name was Abigail Everly. Of course, she took my father's last name when he was alive. My brother and I were both Alec and Colden Everly. Or the Everly twins as people would call us. I always wondered if my mom would go back to her old last name of Langston because Dad had been dead for so many years. I just wish that she would move on from his death, but love is never easy to move on from...at least that's what she always told me.

She replied, "Oh, yeah. That's right, Liam is going to be back tonight, isn't he? I bet you're excited. He was gone for about four months...that's far too long to be apart."

"Yeah, I agree, but it's his job, Mom. I can't tell him that he can't go." Although I wish I could say that most of the time, I know that it's not feasible.

Abigail interjected, "Well, I know, but sometimes I think he should just retire from the military."

I responded, "He's not part of the military, he has the highest ranking with the Emerald Berets. Besides, he is way too young to retire anyway. Thirty years old isn't old enough to retire."

"Baby, you know I adore him for you. But I just wish you had someone with you at all times."

I laughed and said, "Mom, it's 2062. Liam is not a self-made billionaire. We manage well, and I've never been a fan of money and fame, even if Liam is the breadwinner of our relationship. It changes people and I like us the way we are. Although, I wish I could contribute more. But you know that ever since Liam left, my applications for the Peace Corps' upcoming excursions have been denied. Money is tight on my end."

"Did they ever follow-up with you about that?" my mother asked.

"They said I didn't have the 'experience' they required for those specific trips. It doesn't make sense. I've been working with them for over seven years. I have plenty of experience." Folding my arms across my chest, the disappointment evident.

"Everything will work out in the end. Maybe some time away from your job will give you and Liam more time together since he's back home now."

I doubt it.

She continued, "I'd rather you be by each other's side instead of you being alone."

"You can't play that card, you've been alone since..." I stopped myself.

I could see my mother getting a little upset. All the years my mother has been alone, she has said that even though our dad was dead, she had a feeling that one day he would walk through the doors and all the years of being alone would melt away. She walked off toward the small table near the wall, and you could see her long, dark curly hair bouncing when she walked. My mother was in her early fifties, a European mixed with Latino and Native American. That's where my skin color and hair came from. She was a stunning woman, many confused her as being my sister because she had a heart-shaped face and a very youthful look to her. Her eyes were a dark honey brown. She always told me that I had my dad's eyes. She stood at five foot eight, but her height made her look less threatening because I knew she could be aggressive, especially after raising Colden.

She opened the drawer and pulled out an old photo album. I started to roll my eyes because she loved to reminisce about the past and we'd looked through these albums on more than one occasion. She had me sit down on the couch, and she laid the old and slightly burned photo album on the coffee table in front of us. She started to open the book, and you could see some of the ashes trickle off the cover and land on the table.

She began, "I know you hate when I do this, but before you were born, your father and I were so close. I loved him so much. When he died in the fire while I was pregnant with you and Colden, I made a promise to myself that I would never look for someone to replace him."

Sadly, I never see my father's face in any of these photos except one. His hands were either always blocking the camera or his face was cut off from the photos. The majority of the photo album was of me and my brother growing up as kids. My mother continued, "You know, I've always had this feeling that it wasn't over. That our love story wasn't finished. Not in the sense that he's waiting for me in the afterlife, but more of an intuition. And that I will always forever hang on to because..."

And I mouthed the words with her, "My intuition is never wrong."

Annoyed, I asked, "Can I see the photo of him?"

She said yes without hesitation. She loved showing this one and only photo of him. She pulled out the picture from the back of the album. You could tell the photo was old as I took it from her, not just because of the slightly burned edges, but because of the quality of the picture. The photo of my father, Samuel Everly, was the only photo I've seen of him. He was a thin yet in-shape man with great skin, and a defined jawline that came to a point. My mother smiled as I viewed the photo. I didn't know anything about him, other than he was my father. He was of mixed heritage... Native American and Portuguese, and he died before I was born. She would try to tell me about him while I was growing up, but I tuned her out because he was dead. No reason to reminisce over the deceased, especially over one whom I never knew.

I set the photo aside. My mother seemed upset, and she picked up the photograph. "I'm sorry," I said, "I just don't know what to feel, Mom. I never knew him, so I don't really have feelings toward him. What did he do for work exactly?"

She replied, appalled, "He was the leading expert in the field of medicine. Your father was all about finding the next cure for any type of cancer, disease, or deformation. He was very driven, just like you."

"Well, I guess we have some aspects in common. Working in the Peace Corps could be seen as a helping hand to others. I'm no doctor, but I try to help any way that I can."

"I see a lot of him in you. Always trying to help and save others." She rubbed my shoulder and smiled.

She started going through the pages of the album again. There were photos of Colden and me as kids playing games together. I began to laugh a little because I would always win at the games that required critical thinking that we'd play. She continued to flip through, and she pointed at a photo of me winning a soccer game.

"See, you were always so good at sports, I know you never had a love for it, but you were always so competitive." I laughed and just let her keep looking.

There were more photos of me playing tennis and running track. First place in all areas. More recent pictures of me working in the Peace Corps surrounded by children from Ethiopia.

She said, "Sometimes I wonder how you became to be so great. People always asked me as if you were a superstar. I just tell them it's obviously in the genes."

"It's funny because Issac just mentioned that at the gym. I honestly just try my hardest. I don't really put much thought or effort into it."

My mother went on, "Yeah, I've never been able to explain it. I think it's...I don't know if I should say what I'm thinking."

I wanted to know, "What? What is it?"

"Well, those kids at the schools were just...pardon my French, little shits."

I burst out laughing. "Why?"

"Well, just because when you came out, people wanted to turn their backs on you. You were and still are great at what you do. And for them to turn away just because of a small part of your life didn't agree with the same small part of theirs, it just makes me angry." I could tell she was upset.

"Mom, it doesn't matter. I tried to fit in. My appetite for sports was never what I was passionate about. Like Dad, I was more interested in helping people rather than trying to show them up." I spoke honestly.

"I know, but even still. That's not a good way to raise your children, by shunning the ones who are different. I love your brother Colden, but even he made me upset because I didn't raise him to respond in that way. It's all his peers and what's said on television."

I wanted to ask her what exactly he said but was worried about what I would hear. I know me and my brother never kept in contact, but he was still my brother and I always worried about him.

"Where is Colden now?" I smugly asked.

"I don't know, honey, the last I heard from him was that he was in South America searching for something. Mind you, it was just a letter. But since then, I've written to him and he hasn't responded. Sent text messages. Sent emails. Nothing. That was nearly six months ago."

That made me curious, but it was nearly 8:30, and Liam's plane was close to touching down. I started to stand up and stretch, the pseudo rock-climbing competition had made my limbs fatigued.

"Well, I'm going to go get Liam from the airport. He should be here soon."

My mom set the album down as I grabbed my coat.

"Tell Liam that I said hello and don't be shy to bring him over for dinner. I like spending time with you."

I laughed and said I would. I put on my track jacket and headed for the door. Before I walked out, my mom gave me a hug and said, "I love you so much, you know if your dad were here, I bet he would've been really proud of you, and your brother. You know before you were born, your father gave you two a nickname. He used to call you the 'Diablo Twins'," she said with a giggle.

I nodded my head and replied, "Yeah, if he were still here, I'm sure he would be, too. As for the Diablo Twins, I'm not sure I agree with that, maybe for Colden, but not for me."

I laughed and told her goodbye and that I would talk to her soon. I closed the door behind me and had this feeling of remorse. After everything I've done and been through, all the things I've overcome and accomplished, part of me has always wondered if my father would have accepted me? Or would he have the same resentment toward me like Colden did? That's a question I've asked myself for years. My mother accepted me with open arms, just wanted whatever made me happy, but men are different. I shrugged off the melancholy. He was dead, and it was a question that would forever remain unanswered.

I headed to my car in a hurry because it was 8:35 and I needed to make it to the airport as soon as possible. I jumped into my Jeep, cranked up the heat and peeled off. The airport was twenty minutes away, and I suddenly got a notification on my cell phone from Liam. I was so excited to see my baby again. I opened the holo-message on my phone from him.

I pressed play, and a blue hologram of him hovered over the face of my phone.

"Hey baby, you'll never guess what happened. I'm on the plane, and this flight attendant has been flirting with me non-stop." He started laughing. *"She asked me, 'What is a fine-looking*

Emerald Beret soldier like you heading to Canada for?' I told her
I was heading home to be with the love of my life. And she said,
'Oh, well she is a lucky girl!' and I said, 'Yeah, and HE knows it'

He started laughing again.

"She looked at me sideways and hasn't paid me any attention
since. I'm almost home, baby. I've missed you so much, and I
have a bit of a surprise for you when I get there, so dress the
part. I'll see you soon."

And he blew me a kiss.

The holo-message faded back into the screen. I laughed and
thought to myself that Liam is just going to have to take me as I
am because I do not have time to change. I started to accelerate
through traffic as fast as I could to make it to the airport. All the
while, I was getting messages from Ann asking if Liam was here
yet and what we were going to do.

I've known Liam since high school, and it was almost like a
fairy tale. But more of a rough one at that. I was a freshman, and
Liam was a hotshot senior on the wrestling team. At the time,
Liam was in the closet, and I was one-hundred-percent out. Even
though I was out, thankfully I was never picked on. Most were
accepting, and very few others were not — mainly those who had
huge egos and played on every athletic team in the school.

Liam would always flirt with me, and I always had the
feeling that he was interested. Liam stood at six foot three and
was incredibly built. He had gorgeous dark hair and dark eyes
that all the girls swooned over...even me. He always had a perfect
tan, especially for a Caucasian boy. His muscular build and sharp
jawline almost made him look like he stepped out of an action
movie. At the time, Liam denied his feelings for me. He said that
it was just a phase. For the rest of his senior year, we kind of
drifted apart because I didn't want to ruin his image, and at the
time, I assumed he didn't want to be known as gay because of who
he hung out with.

Graduation was fast approaching, and then one day he messaged me, asking if I would attend his graduation party. But not as an attendee...as his date. Of course, I said yes, but I had to ask. "What about everyone else? Aren't you worried that they might look at you differently?"

To this day, he gave me an answer that I will never forget.

"I don't care what anyone else thinks, this is how I feel about you, and I'm tired of hiding it. It's unfair to you and me. As long as you're by my side during this, I know I will be okay." Of course, I melted. He was willing to lay everything on the line for me.

The night of the party I showed up in my best party clothes. When I approached the door, there were kids outside whispering to each other, asking why I was at Liam's house party. I looked down and went inside, refusing to let them see how anxious being here made me. I was beginning to get nervous. My heart was racing a thousand beats a minute, and my mind was jumping all over the place. Was this real, or was it just a prank? Through the crowd of new graduates, I could see Liam at the other end of the house. He looked equally as anxious and nervous. I stood there, and it was like time stopped because we locked eyes through the crowd.

Liam walked toward me and I to him. We met halfway, and Liam wrapped his muscular arms around me and hugged me. I could feel him shaking slightly. You could hear the voices of the teens around us asking, 'What the hell is going on?' Everyone knew my sexuality, and they knew that Liam and I never 'hung-out'. Liam pulled back, but still had his hands on my waist. He looked around nervously as everyone's eyes were on us. I whispered to him that he didn't have to do this. Liam looked at me and had a small smile on his face. He said, "Trust me, I do." And then he leaned in and kissed me. The whispers around us started to get louder and louder.

After we kissed, Liam looked around. Everyone's jaws dropped. Liam spoke up, "Everyone, I have an announcement."

Some people in the back murmured, "Yeah, we bet you do." Liam continued, "Most of you know who Alec Everly is." He held my arm up, and I shyly recoiled into his chest while his arm was still around my waist. He soon lowered my arm and continued, "Alec and I share a history. I know many of you don't know this about me, and I've just barely come to terms with it myself. But I'd like for everyone here to know that I'm gay. And I don't expect all of you to be happy about that. But I've fallen in love with Alec this past year, and I can't deny that anymore." People gasped, and lots of conversation began.

"Surely, if any of you have something bad to say about this... then you may leave. If any of you have a problem with us...then, you may also leave." Some people started to walk out. Members of the wrestling team began to leave, too. I felt terrible because Liam was not only doing this for himself, but for me. So many of his closest friends and teammates continued walking out. However, I was more shocked when I saw that many people stayed. Liam started to continue, "And for those of you who can accept Alec and me being together...LET'S CONTINUE THIS PARTY."

People started to clap and cheer. The music began to play, and people just drank and danced. Some still trickled out to leave, but for the most part, many people acted like nothing had changed. I reached up to kiss Liam again. We both smiled. Lots of people came up to us, asking questions and wanting to know what we were going to do next now that Liam graduated. We were young and in love, no matter what we did, we just knew that whatever it was, we would be together.

We've been inseparable ever since.

Trying to bring myself back to reality, I was pulling into the parking garage of the airport at 9:15. Shit, I'm late. Like most airports, the terminals were confusing and hard to navigate. As I exited my Jeep and made my way over to the directory, I came across a large table with blue-green lights projecting a hologram of the airport that displayed planes coming and going. I pulled up my email of Liam's itinerary, and it said he would be at terminal thirteen. I verbally requested to the computer, "Route to terminal thirteen, please." The hologram zoomed in to where I was located and drew a route to where terminal thirteen was. I voiced to the projection, "Start route, please."

The floor lit up with blue-green hologram arrows with the number 707 inside and pointed in the direction of where I needed to go. Probably the best thing the airport could have come up with in this day and age. I noticed many others were using this feature. However, each person was designated with their very own color of arrows and numbers to avoid confusion. I followed my arrows for a few minutes. Lots of people were coming and going. Some weren't even using the airport's features, and I assumed that most who traveled frequently didn't need to use them because they were familiar with the airport layout and which planes left out of which terminals. I continued my route, and I could see members of the Emerald Berets passing by with their families and loved ones.

I must be getting close. My arrows were beginning to fade into the floor so I must be close. I stopped in my tracks and continued to look ahead. Through the crowd of people, I saw him. Liam was standing there looking just as he did at that graduation party all those years ago. Although he was thirty now and I was twenty-six, we still looked like we were fresh out of high school. This time Liam wasn't in party clothes, but in a deep green uniform that was only worn by the Emerald Berets. I watched Liam look around until he caught my gaze. I could see him smiling, and I grinned back. I ran to him while he dropped his suitcases and ran to me.

We met in the middle where he wrapped his muscular arms around me and lifted me off the ground. He poured four months of being apart into that hug and I loved it. I started to laugh and jokingly told him, "Put me down, you crazy." I could feel him laughing in my chest. He set me down and kissed me. The way he held me was like he never wanted to let go of me again. My eyes had little tears in them. Liam had some in his eyes, too. We looked around, and no one was fazed by us. The people at the airport just kept moving. We both looked at each other, both started talking all at once.

"I've missed you so much, baby," Liam said, choked up. I wiped a tear from my eyes and said, "Yeah, I missed you, too. It's been so long."

Then we both mouthed, "Too long."

We burst out in laughter and I said, "I'm sorry I didn't dress better. I just came from The Climber's Gym and Mom's house."

"It's okay, you know I love you no matter what you are wearing," he said. "And speaking of love, I wanted to take you somewhere we haven't been in a while. Do you have a jacket with you, at least?"

"Yes, of course. It's freezing outside."

"Okay, good, because you're gonna need it."

"Wait...where are we going?" Liam knew I hated surprises and not being told the plan.

"You'll see when we get there," he said.

I rolled my eyes, and we started to walk away, absolutely forgetting about his luggage because we were so swept up in seeing each other again. We both laughed and walked back to get his bags. Liam knew I was terrible with directions, and he decided to lead the way. Even after all my years in the Peace Corps, traveling was something I did often, luckily enough for me, we always traveled in groups and someone else always led the way. I went on to ask him how his trip was.

"Oh, it was crazy. I've never been to that side of Canada before. The people there mainly spoke French, and it was hard getting in the rhythm of speaking in that language again."

Liam's family was rigorous about him learning both languages with full comprehension. I, of course, tried learning many languages myself. I spoke English, French, and broken Portuguese. I learned very quickly that being in the Peace Corps required that I had to learn to communicate with those I came into contact with.

I casually spoke, "Tes fesses ont l'air bien dans cet uniforme." Which means, "Your butt looks good in this uniform."

Liam let out a massive laugh within the airport and responded, "You would think so and I approve of your message."

I laughed with him as we continued through the airport and made our way to my Jeep. We loaded all of Liam's luggage into the back and I gave him the keys because I had no idea where we were going. Liam hopped in the driver's seat and said, "God, it's nice to be back in here again." Liam had a massive obsession with my Jeep. He loved that we could go off-roading with it because he didn't have the luxury of that with his car. He drove a Tesla model XIII that we kept at our house. He enjoyed the luxury of his car but also liked to let loose in my Jeep. So we had the best of both worlds.

I grabbed my track jacket off of the passenger seat and started to put it on. Liam looked at me and said, "You're gonna need something warmer than that, babe." It made me really curious as to where we were going because I couldn't remember everywhere that we had been that was within driving distance that was really cold.

"WHERE ARE WE GOING?"

Liam laughed while he rummaged through his suitcase in the back seat. He pulled out his bomber jacket with white fur on the collar and handed it to me.

He said, "You'll see."

I put my track jacket on and took Liam's bomber and put it over mine. Liam pressed the gas and started heading to our destination.

On our way there, Liam and I talked about everything that had happened in the last four months. It seemed like the time that had passed, faded away, almost like we were never apart. Over the years, Liam and I have been separated for months from time to time. With his line of work and mine, we were always traveling. Of course, with any relationship, we had our ups and downs, but we always seem to gravitate back to one another.

I started to ask, "Okay, I know you hate when I ask this, but..."

Liam knew it was coming, and he began to roll his eyes and smile.

"When are you going to be leaving again? Because I want to make sure we have as much time to spend together before you leave for another... Oh, I don't know, year."

Liam laughed, "I have never left for a year, and you know that."

"I know, but still, it's highly possible." Turning away, pretending to be mad.

Liam grabbed me and pulled me toward him. He struggled because even though I wasn't as big as he was, I was still stronger. He laughed because he also knew with all his muscle that he couldn't take me. I gave in and let him pull me closer.

"What?" I said, peeved.

"That's part of the surprise I wanted to tell you, but you have to wait till we get there, okay?" he said, attempting to level with me.

I looked at him, surprised because he's been a Emerald Beret for years and is always getting deployed. I just wanted him home. And it got me thinking...promotion? That was the only logical explanation.

"Okay, I'll wait,"

He smiled and then hit a corner and started to go off the road and up toward a mountain. I grabbed onto the handrail, screaming, "Holy shit." As Liam laughed, I shouted, "Give me a warning next time." He giggled to himself and murmured, "But you don't like surprises."

We continued on a dirt road and slowly began to decrease our speed. It was really dark outside, and thankfully, years ago, Liam installed a light bar on the top of the Jeep. He flipped the lights on and almost came to a stop. A bunch of rocks were on the trail, and Liam started to drive over them slowly as if the Jeep was crawling over them like a tarantula. We managed to get up to a high elevation, and he said that we made it. I took a look around, and we were on a small mountaintop not too far off from the city.

I looked at Liam and he had a grin from ear to ear. I knew exactly where we were. Three years ago, Liam and I were contemplating buying a house as our next step. We came up here to get away from the chaos and to talk about our future. Liam wanted city life and I wanted the country. We came up with a compromise to have the best of both worlds. Find a place that was both near the city and also near the country. After weeks of looking, we found the perfect place and settled into a three-bedroom home. Everything was decided here, by us...together.

I jumped out of the car, and Liam followed. I walked near the edge of the mountain, and the view was absolutely gorgeous. You could clearly see the entire skyline. It's hard to remember where you are until you just take a breath and look at how far you've come. I could hear Liam approaching me from behind as he wrapped his arms around me. He was always warm, and I needed his warmth because of how high up we were.

Liam spoke, "Hey, I think I left something in my jacket pocket. Can you take it out?"

He took his arms off of me, and I asked, "Yeah, what is it?" I fished into both pockets, reaching into every nook and cranny until I could find what it was. I could feel a slim rectangular case that seemed to be wrapped in felt. I pulled it out of my pocket and could see it was a black jewelry box. My fingers started to tremble because I think I knew what it was.

"What is this..." I said, while opening the box.

Inside was a 3D image of a red rose that popped out, so lovely and delicate. And in the center of the rose was a ring that seemed to be made out of pure white gold. The backdrop of the ring reflected across my face from the moonlight because it appeared to be made out of sterling silver. At the ring's core was a white gold arrow that revolved around the entire band that aided as an accent and complementary element to the most unique and beautiful ring I'd ever seen.

I turned around, and Liam was down on one knee.

"Oh my God," I mouthed as vapor from the heat of my breath drifted from my lips.

Liam was grinning at me and had some tears welling in his eyes.

"Alec Everly, we have been together for years. The best years, and we have been through so much and not a day goes by that I don't think about you and continue to picture our lives together. I'm gone all the time, but things are finally in my favor, and I know you are busy with your job, as well, but even through everything, we still pull through, no matter what."

Tears formed in my eyes wondering if this was really happening.

"Alec Everly, would you do me the honor of becoming my husband?" he asked.

I paused and said, "Wait, I want to remember this moment, okay." He snickered, and so did I. He tried to continue with a straight face, and I said, "Hey, just wait..." and I looked back at the view, and said, "This couldn't have been the most perfect time."

I turned back to him, "Yes, Yes. A thousand times, yes," I said while choking up.

He laughed and rose up to kiss me. He held me in his arms, and it was just a full circle of what I've always wanted our lives to be. It was bliss, and everything was perfect. We embraced a little longer and kissed some more. I started to laugh, and we both turned to look at the view.

I began to yell, "WE'RE ENGAGED." Over the mountaintop.

Liam laughed and said, "THIS IS MY FIANCÉ. WE'RE ENGAGED..." We both laughed, and I turned to him and told him, "I love you so much, baby, but...I think I'm freezing to death?

So maybe we should get back to the car." He laughed at me and replied, "Oh, yeah, how cold?"

"Well, I can't feel my face."

We both burst out laughing and started to walk toward the car.

We got in, and Liam took the ring and put it on my finger. Everything felt so real after he did that.

"It looks amazing on you, baby."

I turned on the cab light, looked at it and said, "I really love it, Liam. This is just amazingly perfect, thank you."

"I was so worried you wouldn't like it, and I went around asking the guys in my squad what I should get, and they were telling me all sorts of things but I knew I only wanted the best for you."

"No, I love it. It's breathtaking. Now I need to go shopping and find you a ring."

"I know whatever you get me will be perfect."

Suddenly, I started thinking about the steps of planning a wedding. We were newly engaged, and I had to let my friends and family know.

"I need to call Mom, and tell her the great news!"

My mother. Oh God, she is going to freak out, and I already know she would want to be a part of the wedding. Oh, and Ann would definitely want to be a part of it, as well. I'd have to let Issac know. And maybe Ann and Issac could go as a date and would finally realize they love each other and eventually get hitched. So many things were crossing my mind, and I just had to take a moment to breathe. I could hear Liam on his phone calling his parents to let them know the news.

I know I needed to tell my mom, but a phone call wouldn't do. I had to call Ann first because I knew how excited she would be. She always told me that Liam and I would make a cute 'husband and husband,' and I can only imagine what her ideas for the wedding would be. I pulled out my phone, "Call Ann, please." My phone began to call immediately, and she picked up after the first ring. A hologram of her projected over my screen, and her first words were,

"Are you and Liam doing it yet?" she laughed.

I burst out laughing and looked over at Liam, who had a smirk on his face, and he quickly gave me a wink. That would come later.

"No. We aren't...yet?" I answered with a laugh. "You will never guess what just happened,"

"What?" she asked. "Is he going to stay here for good?"

I looked over at Liam, and he nodded his head.

"I guess he is, which is amazing, but look."

I held up my hand and showed her my ring. She let out the biggest scream of excitement.

"Oh my God. That's incredible, Alec! I can't believe it. Oh my gosh, I have to help plan the wedding. No, like seriously, I need to help plan. I would make the best bridesmaid ever. Well, in your case 'grooms-maid?'" she said as she laughed with a little confusion.

"Yes, that was my next question. Oh, beautiful Ann. Would you please be my 'grooms-maid of hon..'"

Before I could even finish my sentence, she blurted out, "YES." Without any hesitation. I was so lucky to have her in my life. Our dorky personalities just clicked, and I didn't doubt her wedding planning skills because her house was beautifully decorated.

"So, when is the date?" she asked.

"I'm not sure, actually, it literally just happened. I'm sure Liam has a date in mind, though." He looked over at me and nodded while he was still on the phone with his parents.

"Okay, keep me updated. The sooner we start planning, the better. Have you told your mom yet? She must be freaking out now."

I replied, "No, you were the first one I called. Actually, I think I want to tell her in person."

"Okay. Oh my God, you should record her reaction. I bet she will cry. I talked to her about you and Liam before, and she's so happy that you found him,"

"Yes, I'm so damn lucky that I found him, too." I responded. "Okay, well, I'm going to let you go. I think we will head over to her place now to tell her. I'll try to remember to record her reaction."

"Okay, hun," she replied, "Wait, have you told Issac yet?"

"No, I told you that I called you first. I haven't told anyone just you, so feel special because you are my 'grooms-maid' of honor," I said as I laughed. "If you want to tell him yourself, you can." I paused for a little because I knew she had feelings for him and it was undeniably apparent. "Maybe even invite him as your date to the wedding?"

"Oh, God, Alec. Shut up. I would never... He would have to ask me," she said while she laughed.

"Okay, well, I'll let you go, talk to you soon,"

We both replied, "Bye," at the same time as if we were singing a tune.

I had so many feelings within the moment, I turned to Liam and started to kiss him on his neck. He was still on the phone with his parents. And you could hear him getting choked up with pleasure in his voice.

"Hey...I'm gonna have to...let you...go," he said as I started to kiss him more and massage his muscular thighs with my hand.

"Okay...love you...mmm, too." He slightly moaned as he hung up the phone. I couldn't help but laugh.

"Hey, don't do that, you know it's been four months, right?" he said with a smile on his face. "I don't want my mom and dad hearing that over the phone."

"Oh, yeah? Mommy and Daddy wouldn't want their big strong boy climaxing because of the things little old me are doing to you, now would they?" I needed more as I started to unbutton his shirt and rub against his pecs while kissing his neck.

Liam was a very sexual person. Although he was always the perfect officer and gentleman in public, once we got home, Liam doesn't hold back. One of the many reasons I loved him was that he believed in a give and take relationship. We both prefer to give and take. No pun intended. I knew we needed to stop, though, and I knew what that would mean for both of us because you could tell Liam was very, very excited from the simplest signs of affection. Yeah, it had definitely been too long for either of us.

"This isn't where I want to spend your first night back after being gone four months, Liam. I need you at home, in our bed, all night. Let's head over to my mom's house and tell her the good news and then we'll finish this at home, in the comfort and *warmth* of our bed because it's cold as hell in this Jeep."

Liam growled because he wanted more. But I knew he felt the same way. He started the car, and we made our way to my mother's house. Thankfully, it was a short trip.

We pulled into her driveway, and I was slightly nervous. For one, it was almost midnight. Second, this was a big step, and I wanted my family to be a part of it. My intuition was telling that she would want my brother to be a part of the wedding. It's not that I didn't want him to be a part of it — but how can I want him there when he doesn't support or condone my relationship with Liam? He apparently doesn't want me to have a family and live out the same happy and fulfilled life that many others enjoyed. Liam shut the car off and began to get out. I stayed in my seat for a few seconds longer. I just had an overwhelming feeling that something big was going to happen. He turned to look at me.

"You okay?"

I nodded my head and started to unbuckle my seatbelt and stepped out of the car. I could feel the brisk cold air hit my cheeks. The heat of my first breath came out, and I had this overwhelming and unusual feeling in my stomach. Liam walked over to me and put his arms around me and kissed me on the lips.

"Tell me...what's wrong?"

"I don't know, this is something I've wanted for us for a long time. And suddenly I have a feeling that things are about to become very complicated," I told him. "It's not going to complicate things with us, but it's just...I don't know. Maybe I'm just second-guessing my mother's response."

"You and I have been through so much, there's nothing we can't handle together. This is about us now. I'm sure your mother will be happy for us."

"That's not what I'm worried about. It's my brother. When he finds out...and I know how my mother is. She's going to want him there. And I don't want him to make a scene because of who we are and what we are celebrating."

Liam's brows furrowed, "If your brother even thinks that he has a right to speak out about what we have...oh, you better believe we will be exchanging words. He would be thrown out by me personally."

"That's exactly what I mean." As I worriedly continued. "I don't want that to happen. Which makes me not want him there, but I also do want him there, if that makes sense? He's my brother. He and my mom are the only family I have left. And I know my mom is going to throw that in my face."

Our conversation was getting a little loud, and I could see a light switch on in my mom's house.

Liam grabbed me again and whispered this time, "If you don't want him there, then he doesn't need to be there. But if he does come, we just need to give him a list of boundaries. It's going to work out either way."

We could hear the deadbolt on the front door start to unlock. Instantly, we both turned toward the door, smiling. My mom opened the door wearing her white bathrobe. You could tell she had been asleep because of the way her eyes were half-closed.

"Hey, Mrs. Everly. I'm sorry about being loud, did we wake you?" Liam said. He always had a way of smoothing things over. His good looks and charisma could charm the pants off of anyone... including me.

"What are you boys doing out here so late at night?" my mom asked. Her face went from slightly tired to happy to see us together again.

"Hey, Mom, sorry to wake you. We just came by to tell you something,"

"Come in here and get out of the cold," she said as her maternal instincts kicked in.

Liam bundled me up as we made our way into the house.

"I'm sorry that we woke you, Mom, it's just that Liam and I wanted to come over and give you the good news."

"News? What's going on, tell me. Here, have a seat on the couch." She had us take off our coats and ushered us both into the living room. We took our seats on the couch, and my mother sat in the standalone chair as if she was an executive of a significant organization.

"Well, you know Liam and I have been together for many years..." I started to say.

Liam instantly interrupted because he was too excited to tell her the news. "I PROPOSED," Liam said happily, with a big smile on his face.

My mother's face lit up with joy.

"Oh, thank you, God. I have been waiting for this day for so long. Ever since I saw you two together, I knew you were inseparable. I was telling Ann the other day that I had a feeling you two were going to get hitched. I knew it. Oh, I just knew it."

My mother's response made me giggle.

"And there is something else I wanted to say," Liam told her. "I've actually been put into the position of High Command & Chief of the Emerald Berets."

I screamed, "Oh, my God, babe. What? I didn't know that. You didn't tell me that. That's so great. Wait, so that means you're staying?"

"Yes! But we need to work out the kinks because a schedule hasn't been set in stone. I have a briefing the day after tomorrow, and I might be sent off again. Of course, I may just be here tonight and tomorrow, my schedule is always so fluid," he said. "Our timing around the wedding needs to be calculated to avoid conflict with my job. Eventually I can stay, but for now, we need to plan accordingly."

I start to get emotional because he's been working so long for a position like this, and not only that, but because everything was clicking into place. He was going to be here for good and we were getting married. My life couldn't possibly get any more perfect.

"Oh Lord, this is the greatest news I've gotten in a while. Now I'm going to be able to have some grandbabies," my mother shouted.

I broke from my tears and started to laugh, as did Liam.

"Okay, Mom, just hold off on the baby talk, at least until after the wedding," I said, jokingly. "It's a bit early to be talking about babies. Let's just get the wedding in order and then we can go down that rabbit hole."

"Yes, honey, of course. But I want some grandchildren. With your brother always gone, who knows when he will have kids. I'm not getting any younger, and I want to be able to look at your kids and see you, me, and your father within them," she said. "Speaking of your brother."

"Mom, don't," I replied, shaking my head. As I spoke, Liam turned to me a bit nervous.

"Alec, please," she continued. "He is your brother. He needs to be a part of this, no matter what his stance is on the subject. He's all the family we have left. He will be attending, and that's that." She stood her ground.

I rolled my eyes and looked at Liam. I was upset, but I also knew she was right. After all, he was my only brother. His opinion mattered, even though he didn't support us. He had to be there.

"Fine." I exhaled, looking at both of them. "But you need to keep him on a leash, both of you." This was me putting my foot down. "Mom, you need to put him in his place if he even has a hint of an attitude about any of this."

"You got it, sweetie. Oh, my God, I can't wait. And please, please, please let me help plan the wedding." My mother pleaded.

Liam interrupted, "My parents said they would be happy to pay for the wedding and help in any way." He continued. "And Ann has already said she wants to be a part of the wedding planning, too," he said as he peered over to me. He knew me too well. Ann would be on speed dial to any wedding venue in the world starting at the crack of dawn tomorrow.

"Oh, I have the best idea." My mother was getting excited. "What if we have the reception on a yacht? Oh, that would be so beautiful. Roses everywhere, with an instrumental band playing in the background. Amazing reception with the wedding vows of 'I Do' and you two set off in a small boat to a beautiful island for your honeymoon."

Liam replied, "That actually sounds really nice. I'll have to talk to my parents, and you guys can start planning. I'm happy with any date, just as long as I get to marry your son as soon as possible." He smiled with so much love in his eyes as he gazed at me.

I stood up, "Okay, then," I said. "I'm fine with any date, too. Oh, God, babe. We are getting married." The nerves settling in. "I think Colden will come around, especially with everyone being excited. It should be fine. So how can we get ahold of him?" I asked my mother. "Well, honey, I'm not sure." My mom answered with a worried look on her face. "I haven't been able to contact him for a while now."

"Have you tried calling him?" I asked.

"Yes, but it just goes to voicemail. The only thing I know is that he is somewhere in South America. Well, I think he is? That's the last letter I got from him, then he just stopped responding."

"Well, he must have an email address?" I asked. Not too many people these days sent email. Everything was sent through holograms now.

"I have his last letter here." My mother got up and went into her room.

"See, I told you it would all work out," Liam said as he stood up and walked over to me.

"Yes, I know...you were right." I agreed while rolling my eyes.

My mother came out of her room with a letter that had six postage stamps on it. It must have taken a while to get here. She handed me the message, and you could see it was sent from a post office in Santiago, Chile. I started to open it and asked my mother if it was okay if I read it. She nodded her head, and I continued.

Dear Mom,

I know I haven't been in contact that much recently. A lot has happened, and it's a lot to explain. But I think I've found something that ties into our father's death. I have a feeling that it wasn't an accident. I know you have always thought that Dad's death wasn't a mishap, and I think you might be right. I was able to track some of Dad's scientific work down here in Chile. I don't want to scare you, but I think some of his work was...well, illegal.

I believe that there is a gang that Dad was involved with. This gang has a major chain of islands under control off the coast of Chile. And the only way in is to become a part of them. You know my history, and you know how I can be. The only way for me to get more proof is to go to these islands.

I'm writing to you so this letter can't be tracked. I'll be safe. I love you so much, Mom. I will be in contact soon, please don't worry about me.

-Colden

The letter was dated six months ago. Reading it gave me some concern. Liam could see the look on my face and was curious as to what I just read. I tucked the letter under my armpit and glanced at my mother.

"See, baby, now you know why I am worried," she explained.

"What did it say?" Liam asked.

"It's a long story, but he might be involved with a gang in South America now," I replied like it was nothing new.

Even though Liam and I had been together for a very long time, I didn't want him involved in my family's history for his own good. Some things were better left unsaid. I also didn't want him to think my family and I were loons because suddenly Colden had a hunch that our father's death was possibly something more sinister.

"So we can't get ahold of him at all?" I said. "It seems the only way to find him is from this address. I know we are on a time constraint, so the sooner I leave, the better."

"We'll go together. I've been wanting to see South America since I was a kid," Liam said. "A quick, one-day trip there and back, just in time to make it back for my briefing."

"No," I responded quickly, "If I know anything about my brother, it's best if I approach him alone." My mother looked at me with concern.

"No, baby. I think it would be nice for you both to go down there and visit." My mother insisted.

I replied, "Mom, you remember the last time I brought a boyfriend around Colden?"

Before Liam, I was with another guy who seemed promising. Back in high school, Colden was more out of control then. He had no filter and said what he wanted and didn't care whom he offended. During our outing, Colden made a disgusting comment about me and my boyfriend that I didn't pay attention to. He didn't respond well to Colden's verbal attack. So he took matters into his own hands and it ended in a fistfight — and me never talking to my boyfriend again. My mother ordered me to break up with him, reminding me that family is always family.

My mother had the same look that I did. "Yes, you are probably right, baby."

"All right, I don't feel comfortable with you going off to a different country alone to find your brother who is involved with a gang," Liam said with dominance in his voice. "I trust you'll be safe, but you need to bring protection with you, at least."

"Liam. You know I don't like that," I said. "Guns have never been my thing."

"I know. And I don't care. It's me or a gun. You choose. South America has the highest homicide rate in the world. Don't think for a second I'm sending you there without a gun," he declared.

I ignored the subject and turned to my mother. "Can you find a reasonably priced plane ticket to South America? One there and back, within the same day?" I asked.

"Of course, I'm all over it." She spoke with enthusiasm as she went to get her laptop.

I turned to Liam, and he had this overwhelmed look on his face. Still stewing over the gun issue. Over the years, Liam has taken me to many shooting ranges. He taught me how to properly discharge a weapon, reload, and perfect my aim with moving targets. Shooting at the gun range was one thing, but I had no reason to carry one with me at all times. Liam was the opposite. With his profession, he always has a concealed weapon on him.

"Babe, I will be fine," I explained. "I've been to South America with the Peace Corps before, without any issues."

"Yes, but this is different," he said in anger, or was that frustration? "Have you been to Santiago before?"

"Well, no."

"Then I think you should bring your gun. Plain and simple,"

Liam purchased a Taurus 1911 .45 ACP and had it registered to me as a birthday gift three years ago. I knew how to use it, but for the most part, it just sat in our gun safe collecting dust. Liam carried a two-toned Glock .45 that was usually concealed near his lower back. He's never once pulled it out when we're in public. I could imagine why, because with his height and build, most wouldn't have the courage to stand up to him, except for me. No matter how intimidating he looked, he didn't scare me because I knew he would never hurt me.

"Okay," I said, just to calm him, but also thinking of ways to play dumb and say, "Oh, I must have forgotten to pack it." My mother came out of the room with her glasses on and laptop in her hands.

"I found a ticket there and back that's roughly CAD 400, did you want that one? It flies out tomorrow afternoon."

"Okay...well, I guess I'm taking off tomorrow," I said, slightly excited because I always liked to travel, but nervous about venturing to someplace new.

"I can pay for it, babe," Liam said, pulling out his wallet. He walked over to my mother and took the laptop from her and started to enter his information. My mother took my hand and sat me down on the couch with her.

"Thank you for doing this, Alec," she said with both sorrow and joy in her voice. "I know you and your brother have never gotten along. But maybe this will change his perspective? Maybe he will finally see that you are happy and that the love you and Liam share is one of a kind."

"I miss Colden, and it would be nice to see him again, especially under these circumstances. But can I ask you something?" I paused and started to whisper because I didn't want Liam to overhear. "Do you really think Dad was murdered?"

A moment of silence passed before she responded. "Honey, I'm not sure if it was an accident or on purpose. But things didn't add up when he passed." She paused again to look over at Liam to make sure he couldn't hear and continued. "When your father died, they refused to let me see his body. They said that the burns rendered him unrecognizable. I requested an autopsy, and they refused. I think that someone higher up in this country denied my request. And at the funeral, it just seemed off. They denied having an open casket, and the casket itself didn't make sense to me."

"What do you mean?"

"Well, your father was a very tall man. But the casket wasn't made for someone of his height. I'm not a scientist, but I was told that he died of carbon monoxide poisoning and that the leak was contained before the fire could cause severe damage." She paused to see what I thought and continued. "Don't you see? If he died before the fire started, how was it that he was burned beyond recognition? Which was it? Things don't add up."

"You are all booked, babe," Liam interrupted before I could give her a response.

"It could be nothing, honey. It happened a long time ago." I could tell she didn't mean it. If her and my brother both questioned his death, something must have been very wrong.

"Thank you, Liam. When do I leave?" I asked, trying to force a smile after what we just talked about.

"Noon."

My mother stood up, "Well, I'm sure you two want to get home and get packing. Need some rest for your flight tomorrow," she said.

I got up and gave her a hug. I whispered in her ear, "I'll find out what I can and be in touch. I love you."

"I love you, too, honey. Please be careful," my mother replied.

Liam went to go grab our jackets and walked over to give my mother a hug. My mom laughed and said, "What were they feeding you over there. I can hardly fit my arms around you."

Liam laughed and said, "Oh yeah, we're cornfed like the Americans." He continued, "I love you, Mrs. Everly, and I'll have my parents get a hold of you so you all can start planning the wedding. Have a good night."

"I will, honey. You, too," she replied.

Liam put his coat on, and I did the same. He put his arm over my shoulder and kissed me on the lips before we walked out of the door. Liam got into the car and started it. I looked back at my mom's house, having that same gut feeling like I did before. There was a tension in the air, like I might not be back for a while. I shook it off and got into the Jeep. Liam pulled out of the driveway, and a wave of exhaustion hit me. It had been a long day filled with a rollercoaster of emotions, and I was drained. Liam looked over at me and could tell I was tired. We pulled away from her house, and the car's speed turned her home into a blur from my window. Liam kissed me on the lips once again, and I smiled. The rocking of the Jeep began to put me asleep. I knew Liam would understand my exhaustion. From all the excitement that happened today, and my travels set in motion for tomorrow, I needed rest.

Liam switched on the audio system and played a relaxing song. I gradually drifted to sleep, dreaming of tomorrow.

2: PILGRAMAGE

S HIMMERS OF LIGHT WERE passing by, or so I thought
because my eyes were still closed. I slowly started to dawn
my eyes open, and I could see shards of light were being
reflected off of my ring in the sunlight. I could feel the warmth
and comfort of the covers that were over me. I raised the covers
up and noticed that my clothes were off, and I only had on black
boxer briefs. Liam must have carried me to bed and undressed me
because, as I looked around, I could see our pale grey tapestries
hanging down from our canopy bed frame. Our room had a mix of
innovative art and green plants. We designed our room together
and gave it a modern, earth-toned feel with walls that were
painted a gender-neutral asphalt grey. Our bed was facing a wall
that had an eighty-inch picture frame of the world map. Little did
people know it was actually a transitioning television. On the wall
behind our bed was a bookcase that took up the entire wall. The
case was full of books that Liam and I have read over the years
that were all placed in alphabetical order. Some of the book titles
gleamed in the sunlight that cast through the grand windows of
our room.

I looked over and saw Liam asleep. He was in his underwear,
too. I placed my hand on his chest and could feel the warmth of his
slow beating heart. I couldn't believe I was engaged to him. I felt
so...lucky. You could see Liam's jaw clench ever so slightly when
he would take in a breath. I noticed his scruff starting to grow

in and honestly favored it on him. He always looked so peaceful sleeping, and I envied his ability to sleep that way. I continued to look at his arms and chest and could see the hairs on his arms standing up. It was a little cold in our room, and I blamed myself for his goosebumps as I held the covers up admiring his body. I always found myself counting all eight of his abs when his shirt was off. I couldn't help myself around him, once his shirt came off, it was game over for me.

Liam always said he loved my body. Although my frame was slightly smaller than his, I still had definition in all the right places. He said our bodies were the perfect proportion to fit each other.

When Liam and I are together around others, it's clear to suspect that we are a couple. For one, Liam could hardly keep his hands off me. Second, I always found people catching me checking out Liam's butt. Liam and I never received hatred from others, just looks. Interracial couples were often given the side eye. No matter what day and age, I don't think people will ever end their prejudices about us. It was a stigma that would live on forever.

I moved in closer to Liam and put my leg across his. I kissed his cheek, then moved down to his neck while rubbing my hand across his chest and arms. I could hear Liam's inhales deepen as I continued to kiss his pecs. My hand glided down his lightly haired chest and abs. I smiled because Liam let out a sigh of pleasure to finally be touched by me again; he knew exactly where my hand was going. By this point, I knew he was awake because my hand was gripping and massaging his cock, and with every caress it grew bigger and bigger. At the same time, I was becoming aroused because after being apart for four months, I was finally touching him.

I straddled him while kissing every ab as I made my way down his stomach. Using both of my hands while still kissing his chest, I slipped his underwear off, revealing his long and thick 'friend' of mine. His chest hair was light, and it led down his stomach, giving his abs high contour all the way down to his happy trail. I began to kiss around him, lightly biting his inner thigh, teasing him. Liam twitched as I did so and began to gasp. I raised Liam's legs up around my shoulders, wrapping my arms around his thighs so he couldn't get away. I caressed my tongue over his crown. Liam's hand was brushing through my hair now, urging me on and pulling me into him. I finally gave in and wrapped my lips around his dick.

Liam muttered, "Ah, yes." Over and over again as I continued to pleasure him as deep as I could go.

His movements turned aggressive, which only made me swallow him deeper. Using both hands that were placed on my head, he started to push me down more and we were both moaning at this time. His moans became louder as I took him as deep as I could, over and over again. Liam tried to pull away. He was getting close and I knew he didn't want it to end that quickly. He grabbed me by my hair and pulled me up his torso so that we were face to face.

Kissing me on the lips, he suddenly grabbed me and rolled me over onto my back in an instant. His strength was such an intense turn-on as he straddled me now, pinning me down with his pelvis. My hands were on his shoulders, and I wrapped my legs around his waist. He continued to kiss me while grinding up against me. Our breathing turned heavy. I moved my hands down his muscular back toward his ass. Grabbing and pulling him into me. As he thrust, so did I. He started to ravage my neck with kisses and bites. I moaned, "Oh, fuck...yessss."

I continued to kiss him as he thrust against me. He stopped suddenly and looked over to his nightstand and looked back over to me. Quickly, he tore my underwear off. And when I say tore, he literally split my underwear into two pieces as he threw them across the room. I didn't care at this point. He wrapped his muscular arms around my waist and lifted me up as I wrapped my legs around him tighter. He slammed me into the wall, causing one of the paintings on the wall to fall to the ground.

"Oh, is that how you wanna play?"

"It's been four months, how did you expect me to play?"

I kissed him while tugging on his hair aggressively. He pulled back and started to laugh, and I lightly slapped him across the face. He let out a grunt, and his eyes narrowed.

"Seriously?"

He rammed me with his pelvis as I felt his dick flex in between my legs. He spun around while carrying me and began to walk into the bathroom. Setting me down, he opened the glass shower door and turned on the water as I walked over behind him. I placed my hands on his waist and started to thrust against his ass while kissing his upper back. I reached around while he was checking the water temperature and gripped his dick with my right hand while slowly jerking him off. He exhaled deeply and turned his head around to kiss me on the mouth while arching his back, leaning into my thrust. He reached into the shower and grabbed some lube and a condom that was off to the side.

I laughed and said, "You already had this planned out, didn't you?"

He just winked at me and smiled.

He stepped into the shower and wrapped one arm around my waist, bringing me in with him. As if I wouldn't have followed him wherever he went. He closed the glass door behind him, placed the condom on, and started to lubricate himself while admiring the water that beaded down my body. I was ready for whatever he had in mind as I leaned my head back into the showering waterfall as Liam stepped toward me and put his arms around me.

Suddenly I blurted out, "Oh shit, what time is it?" I asked, because knowing us, we would be at it for hours.

"It's ten," Liam continued. "That's why I brought you in here. We're going to be multitasking."

"Very smooth," I said, smiling.

Liam reached down to my cock and started massaging the lube into my skin. He leaned into the water to kiss me, forcing his tongue into my mouth, but it was an invasion that I welcomed. I put my arms over his shoulders as he reached around and began fingering me. I let out a small moan because not only was Liam's hands skilled, but his fingers were thick as he prepared me for what was next.

"I love you." I exhaled.

"I love you, too, baby." As he breathed in and out deeply. "Whose ass is this? Huh?" he asked, dominantly.

"It's yours, baby, all yours," I said as his fingers slid deeper into me. I began pushing up against them, welcoming the long-lost intrusion.

Liam stopped fingering me and lifted me up, pushing my back against the stone wall as I wrapped my legs around his waist. He placed me in the 'Yourself on the shelf' position, supporting my back with his arms as he began to enter me. I breathed out deliberately and gripped onto Liam tightly. I kissed his neck and ear as he slowly thrust in and out of me. I could hear him groaning in pleasure while he slid deeper into me, thrusting quicker and steadier.

"Oh my God." I moaned into Liam's ear as he held onto me tighter.

"Do you like that? I bet you missed that after four months, huh?" He continued to thrust as I pulled him into me deeper.

"Give me those four months back right now!" I wish this moment would last forever. I could feel his body tensing up as he continued to moan in pleasure. He was close, so close.

Liam started to moan, "Alec, oh shit. Alec."

"Come on, Liam, harder," I said to feed into his climax.

"FUCK..." he shouted as I embraced him while he was twitching from his orgasm.

I continued to pull him into me as he winced in delight. I could feel the heat of his breath in my ear, coupled with the steam from the shower gave me a euphoric feeling as he told me how much he loved me.

"I love you so much, I want to be married to you already," he said, exhausted from his climax. The feeling of being wanted by Liam in every which way made me feel important. Both mentally and physically.

Liam set me down and pulled me to him and said, "Come here." While he turned around and handed me a condom.

"Give and take," I whispered under my breath as I slid on a condom before he guided my dick inside of him.

The shower was still going and we were both being pelted by every drop of water that rained down on us. Liam groaned as I slid deeper into him. I rubbed his back with water as I continued to thrust into him. I could feel his arms wrap around me as he aided my thrusts into him. His face was pressed against the wall, and his beautifully arched back fed into me as his skin rippled with every thrust I gave. He leaned back to kiss me on the mouth while doing so. I could feel myself quivering, the anticipation of my orgasm just out of reach. I wanted us to come together so I wrapped my arms around him so that I could jerk him off.

I could feel the rush coming while the heat of Liam's breath was on my lips. As I grew close, I continued to thrust into his velvet goldmine until I peaked. He came right along with me for the second time. It had been too long for me and him to ever be apart like that again. And now, with his promotion and our engagement, this would only bring us closer together and more intimate than ever before.

He turned around and kissed me on the mouth. We held each other in an embrace as if the world completely stopped. Both of us breathing heavily, while kissing one another. We stopped for a moment with our foreheads touching each other, gazing into one another eyes as we smiled.

"To the first of many with my new fiancé," Liam said.

"Ditto." I smiled and held on to him a little longer. The shower continued to run, and off in the distance you could hear the clock on the nightstand ticking. Liam and I began to shower, playfully throwing soap on each other and kissing. I didn't want this moment to end, but my flight was leaving soon, and I wasn't even packed yet. Liam finished showering first because I had rubbed his entire body down with soap. I finished lathering myself up and shortly rinsed off after. I opened the shower door, reaching for the first towel I could find. I dried myself off while looking in the mirror. I don't think I've ever seen myself this happy since before Liam left.

"It's 11 o'clock, babe. We need to hurry," Liam yelled.

"Shit," I whispered to myself.

I came out of the bathroom and Liam already had clothes laying out for me. He had a fresh pair of clean boxer briefs out for me, along with a flesh-toned tank top, a light blue button-up shirt, and navy blue pants with khaki-colored casual dress shoes. There was also a light military jacket on the bed, as well. Not my ideal clothes to travel with but I was in no position to complain because we were in a rush.

I could hear Liam rummaging through the closet. He must have been packing clothes for me. I figured he would pack light because I would only be there for a day. I could hear beeping as if a code was being entered. I rolled my eyes because I knew exactly what he was doing. I soon heard a massive thud in the closet as I started to dress. I looked over to the clock, and it was 11:15 now. I began to dress faster, and I saw Liam out of the corner of my eye exiting the closet with a rolling suitcase and a military-looking pack, which I assumed would be my carry on. Liam was in his underwear, smiling at me as I threw on the clothes that he chose for me.

"Yeah, we are definitely going to be late," I said, laughing at him.

"With how I drive, I don't think so. Looking sexy, fiancé." As he winked and set the luggage next to the bed.

I continued to button my shirt and said, "Sexy? How about you take off that underwear and show me what sexy looks like again."

Liam laughed and said, "I wish, babe, but there's no time."

He walked back into the closet to pick out what he was going to wear. I put the rest of my clothes on and threw on my coat.

He stepped out of the closet shortly after wearing blue jeans, and a tan, earth-toned t-shirt. I loved how simple he could dress and still look sexy at the same time. Liam knew I loved it when he walked around with only jeans on and nothing else, something about him being barefoot and shirtless was a turn-on.

"Let's get going," he said as he threw on a track jacket and some boots.

I picked up the bag in hopes that Liam packed accordingly. With how often he traveled for work, I'm sure he packed well enough. I slung the pack over my shoulder and started to roll my luggage until I noticed how heavy it was. Liam quickly grabbed the luggage from me as if he was hiding something. I had a gut feeling of why, but I just went with it. There was no time to waste. We both made our way downstairs and crossed through the living and dining room.

Liam and I grew to become wealthy, mainly Liam because of his job. However, we never flaunted our wealth. Our house alone spoke for itself. Liam went out through the garage door, and I stopped in the kitchen, making sure I didn't forget anything. I was also getting hungry, we hadn't eaten last night or had breakfast, and heaven only knew if I'd have enough time to eat before my flight.

I found some tiramisu I made a few days ago and grabbed that first. Then I grabbed some leftover drumsticks and made my way through the garage door. Liam already had the Jeep started and the garage door open, honking the horn.

"Why are you so impatient? We'll make it with the way you drive, right?" I reminded him, mimicking his tone as I got in.

"Well, I'd rather not get a speeding ticket on the way,"

Liam threw the car into reverse and peeled out. Thankfully there wasn't too much traffic on the way to the airport and it also gave me enough time to scarf down my food. Liam seemed off... I'm sure because I was leaving just as he got back.

"I'm sorry I have to leave. But I'll be back in twenty-four hours. I promise," I said, "If I can't find him, I'll just head back. It should be a simple trip."

"Well, if anything happens you can call me. I'll be right next to my phone until you get back," Liam spoke reassuringly.

We pulled into the airport and found a parking spot in one of the garages. Liam drove so fast we made it there by 11:45. Liam jumped out of the car and reached into the back to get my luggage. I got out and put my backpack on my shoulders. I asked Liam what terminal and gate my flight was leaving from. Liam pulled out his phone, and a hologram of the terminal popped up, along with my itinerary, ticket, and personal info. I noticed that the pass read, 'Passenger will have baggage checked for firearm compliance.' I glanced at Liam.

"Liam, Really? I mean, I knew you wanted me to bring my gun, but I thought you were kidding," I said smugly. I knew he was never kidding, and I was more or less hoping he would have forgotten.

"I told you I wasn't going to have you go there unarmed," he said. "It's for the best, Alec, trust me. If something were to happen, at least you have protection without me being there. Let's get to the terminal, okay?"

"Okay, fine. Just know I'm not happy about it, and I don't have the patience to handle this right now," I said as I began to storm off toward the entrance. I could hear Liam running up from behind me. He grabbed my arm aggressively and turned me around before we passed through the glass doors.

"Listen to me. Don't be pissed at me for trying to look out for you, Alec. You think I'm going to let my fiancé go to some foreign place where he could be a fucking walking target? I don't think so. So take the damn gun, and use it if necessary," he said in a demanding tone and paused because he didn't want to hurt my feelings. I was never one to pick a fight in public, but this was something I took very seriously. People were walking into the airport entrance giving us the eye as they walked past. Liam gave them a death stare so they would continue on their way.

He looked back at me with concern in his eyes. "Look, I'm sorry, okay. Why do you have to be so damn stubborn? I just...I just can't have anything happen to you. I love you, and I care about you. Just please, don't be upset with me before you leave."

I rolled my eyes and exhaled, "I'm sorry, too. I didn't mean to go off like that. But I'll bring it if it makes you feel better," I said to calm him. "Let's just go, okay?"

"All right," Liam said as he kissed me on the cheek and put his arm around my waist as we passed through the glass doors.

We made our way through the airport without any issues and made it just in time for check-in. The person at the counter was actually a hologram of a pretty woman.

"Hello, and thanks for flying with us today. Please provide your identification, ticket, and place your luggage on the conveyer belt to your right."

I was a little worried because I knew Liam put my 1911 in my luggage. I was also slightly annoyed at the fact that we had to speak to a hologram rather than a real person. Since technology had advanced, many people have lost their employment, being replaced by machines. I handed Liam my pack and kind of walked off to view the ads around the airport. I didn't want to be around when the airport noticed I had a weapon in my luggage.

After checking in, we started walking around until something caught my attention. I saw a group of people gathering around a holographic ad for the latest invention that allowed you to be more connected to technology around you. An implant could be installed in the back of your neck. Once implanted, the wearer's irises had a white halo that surrounded them. They could now control their house, commanding it to unlock just by looking at it. It kind of gave me the creeps. Not only would the implant allow the wearer to control their home, but they could also look up information about other people around them. It was simply too much overreach into our personal and private lives, but that was just my opinion.

I think the idea of it was fresh and innovative, but then again, the eyes of the newly implanted users just seemed...off. I mean, the advertisement made them not even look human anymore. I tugged on Liam's hand and we began to walk away, but at that moment I could distinctly hear the hologram voice address me in an almost menacing tone.

"Alec Everly."

As I turned, I noticed all the people surrounding the announcement were staring at me, but then I realized that, holy shit, all of them had implants installed already. All of their eyes had white halos around their irises. It was a little disturbing because not one person said a word, they just stared at me with blank expressions. I slowly edged backward.

The ad continued in a more generic dialogue, "Don't miss out on your Capitol Optic's implant today."

All the individuals surrounding the ad were smiling at me now. Hello, even creepier. I continued to back away while mouthing the words "What the fuck?" I was so in my own world that I accidentally bumped into Liam.

He wrapped his arm around me, "What are you doing, babe? We have to get going. Your plane leaves in five minutes." He started to guide me toward the terminal entrance.

"Are you all right? You look sort of pale," he asked. He must have felt me quivering because that Capitol Optic's ad freaked me the hell out.

"Yeah, I'm okay. That ad was just so bizarre," I told him while trying to figure out how the ad knew my name.

"I'll have to check it out, then," Liam said, interested.

"Yeah, maybe you shouldn't because if you start walking around with creepy eyes controlling your surroundings, I think I might just have to end things."

Liam laughed because he knew I wasn't serious — well, I was, sort of — as he took me over to the entrance of the terminal where we had to say our goodbyes. The portal only allowed passengers in, and as much as I would like Liam to come with me, I knew it wouldn't help the situation out with Colden for both of us to show up there. I needed to ease him into our announcement about our upcoming wedding. Liam reached into his pocket and pulled out a translation device. I loved him so much, he really did think of everything.

"How do you do that?" I asked, smiling at him.

"I just know you, that's all," he said, laughing. "So this is goodbye?"

"Yeah, it's weird, isn't it? Usually I say goodbye to you. Look, as soon as I get there I will call you, okay?"

"I'll be near my phone waiting, babe," Liam said, "Are you sure you won't have me come along? Maybe we could have a quick wedding on a beach out there?" he said, joking, but he also seemed to be considering it at the same time.

"No, we can't do that...our families would be livid."

"Fine..." he said, shrugging his shoulders. He pulled me into him with his arms at my waist. "I love you... future, Mr. Brooks," he said, smugly.

"What?" Blushing, I said, "We never talked about that. Is that what you want?" I questioned with a serious tone.

It was always conventional for the bride to take the groom's last name. But since we were both grooms, I just assumed my last name would stay the same. But when he called me Mr. Brooks, it kind of made me feel like this was real and I found myself wanting his last name more than ever. Liam had a big family. Brothers and sisters, aunts and uncles, first cousins, and second cousins. I never really had any of that.

"If you agree to it, I'd like you to take my last name," Liam said proudly. "And if you don't, I would understand."

"We could always come to a compromise, too. Maybe Alec Everly-Brooks?" I asked, adding a hyphen so I would still be me but also a part of him.

"I like it. Sounds very bougie. Damn, it's twelve...time to go." Liam kissed me and I almost wanted to cry. I'd just gotten him back and here I was leaving again so soon. We embraced for a little longer before I had to board.

I could hear an announcement for terminal six saying the flight is now boarding.

"I love you," I said to Liam and kissed him on the lips. "I'll call you as soon as we land, okay."

"All right, the minute you land, you better," Liam said a little choked up.

"Okay," I said and began to walk toward the jetway. I turned before I entered and blew Liam a kiss. He pretended to grab it out of the air and place the kiss on his lips. I smiled and turned toward the jetway and walked in. I made my way onto the plane and found my seat near the window and sat down. Placing my pack in between my legs, I pulled out the white translator Liam gave me. I wasn't sure how it worked, but I could see an interface that allowed you to select what dialect you wanted to be translated.

I switched the dialect to Portuguese, and a flight attendant approached me and said, "Você gostaria de uma bebida antes do voo?"

Shortly after, the translation machine spoke in English saying, "Would you like anything to drink before the flight?"

I smiled and looked at the flight attendant, shaking my head, and I said, "No, thank you." She smiled back and continued to ask others.

I thought to myself that this could come in handy. All I knew was that I had a six-hour flight ahead of me, and I was tired just thinking about it. I was very thankful for today's technology, though, because planes were now equipped with a turbo boost. It took half the time away from any flight. I rested my head against the headrest, and I could see my seat-mate loading his carry-on into the overhead. He said hello to me and took his seat. I politely said hello back. A few minutes went by, and everyone was beginning to take their places as one of the flight attendants started to go over the safety protocols.

"So, where are you headed?" The man spoke in clear English as he turned to me.

"Santiago, and you?" I said, trying to keep the conversation light.

"Could be a nice vacation for someone. I'm going to San Antonio, Chile."

"Well, I'm not really going for a vacation, I'm actually going to search for my brother."

"Oh, wow. I'm going to Santiago first and then catching a ride to San Antonio, Chile, after. My girlfriend lives there, and I'm going to be staying with her for a little while," he said, obviously excited.

I thought it was safe to assume he had a girlfriend. He was a very handsome guy, although no one could ever be as attractive to me as Liam. I replied, "That sounds nice." I tended to keep conversations to a minimum when significant others were brought up because it invariably led to them asking about my love life.

"What about you? The Mrs. must have been head over heels giving you a ring like that," he said, eyeing my wedding ring.

I looked down at my ring and just went along with it. "Yeah, I'm fortunate to have my fiancé."

He started to pull out his phone from his coat pocket. He flipped through his photos and stopped on a picture of a beautiful woman. She had long, dark curly hair, olive skin, and a very athletic body.

"Yeah, this is her. She's gorgeous, isn't she?" he said proudly as if he hit the jackpot with her.

"Yeah, she is stunning," I said humbly. She was beautiful but obviously not my type.

"What about your wife? What does she look like?"

I could see the flight attendant from earlier was making her way back over to us.

"Olá senhor, gostaria de uma bebida antes de voarmos?" My translator started to speak in English.

The man looked over and said, "That's a neat gadget." And he turned back toward the attendant, "Sim, eu vou ter um copo de tequila por favor." And then he turned back to me and asked if I wanted some tequila, too.

"Oh, no, I'm fine. Thank you," I said kindly.

Going to a foreign place alone was enough of a high for me. I would definitely get into trouble in a foreign country if I was drinking.

"No phones," the flight attendant said with an accent.

The man apologized and began to put his phone away. I was relieved that I didn't have to show the man a photo of Liam. I wasn't ashamed of Liam. I just didn't want the rest of the plane ride to be awkward for my flying partner.

"So, what's your name? I'm Edwardo."

"My name is Alec, nice to meet you," I replied as I shook his hand. I needed to keep the conversation between us light because I would rather sleep the entire way there.

"Would you do me a favor and wake me when we get there, Edwardo?"

"Oh, yeah, sure. It's going to be a long flight, I'm a bit of a nervous flyer. Hence, the booze. But I'll be up, too anxious to sleep," he said as the flight attendant made her way back with his tequila as he downed the shot immediately. I felt bad for cutting the conversation short, but I didn't have the energy to chit-chat with him through the entire plane ride.

"Thank you," I said, as I adjusted my headrest to cradle my head.

The light for the 'fasten your seatbelt' came on, and I followed directions. I could feel the plane gearing up for taking off. Suddenly the aircraft jumped forward, and the pressure of the speed had everyone pushed back. At that same moment, Edwardo had another shot of tequila at his lips, and he almost choked as it forcefully went down his throat because of the force of the plane moving. I giggled a little to myself as he grabbed onto my forearm. I didn't pay him any mind until I began to feel his fingernails digging into my skin.

I winced a little, he then noticed and eased off a bit, but still held on, nonetheless. I didn't mind, it wasn't the first time someone next to me on a plane did that. The speed of the aircraft began to ease as we leveled off in the air. People started to take a breath as if the hard part was over. I could see Edwardo in the corner of my eye sweating bullets. The plane began to coast, and I looked over at him again and said, "So, can I have my arm back now?"

"Oh, shit." He exhaled. "I'm sorry. You are one brave son of a bitch."

"It comes with practice." I laughed. "Well, I'm going to get some sleep. We should be okay for now."

"Okay," he said while fanning himself. He called the flight attendant over and requested more shots. He'll be good and drunk by the time we get to Santiago.

I leaned my head against the window. The city looked beautiful from up above. The clouds rolled beneath us. I could see the wings of the plane wobble slightly, causing the jet to tremble. I enjoyed the hypnotic motion as it slowly rocked me to sleep.

The weather was glacial, and it was pouring rain. I looked around, and I could see palm trees swaying in the fierce winds. The sounds of waves were crashing over one another behind me. I turned around to see I was standing on a muddy beach, and the clouds that engulfed the sky were moving at an unreal speed. The waves in the ocean grew larger in scale, a tsunami was afoot as I could see the waves that touched the shoreline beginning to drag farther out into the sea. Amongst the chaotic thunder and lightning, I could see a very tall man standing on the shore wearing a white tank top and blue jeans. His shape reminded me of Liam, and part of me was afraid to approach him, but I knew what was about to happen...he would soon be consumed by a tidal wave that hungered for the entire beach. I began trudging forward, and with every step I took, I was impaled by ice-cold rain. As I grew closer, the hair on my body stood on end because of the frigid winds and fear of the tidal wave approaching. The closer I got to the man who looked like Liam, I could see heat radiating from his body. The drops of rain that hit his exposed arms sizzled into water vapor that was carried off by the winds. I reached out to spin him around and took a step back in fright. His eyes were encapsulated by a silver-hued halo, and he had an expression on his face of lunacy. I looked up just as the colossal wave was about to demolish us. Liam's hands forcefully wrapped around my neck, an attempt to choke me to death. As he smiled, he said my name over and over with a sick grin on his face. "Alec, Alec, Alec." As he choked me, I realized that I was going to die twice. Looking into Liam's eyes, I attempted to scream as the tidal wave devoured us both.

"Alec. Alec. ALEC." I jolted forward in my seat as I clawed at my neck gasping for air. Edwardo was staring at me, sweating bullets again. I apologized, thanking God it was just a nightmare. I could see through the window that we had landed. Other passengers were giving me outlandish looks as I tried to recover from that horrible nightmare. I began to regain focus, and I glanced back over to Edwardo, who was clearly intoxicated.

"I'm sorry, Edwardo. Thank you for waking me up," I said as I inhaled deeply.

"Yeah, thankfully, I did because it didn't seem like you were sleeping too well." The smell of tequila was seeping from his pores. If I were ever to meet Edwardo again, I would know his sentiment for flying was taken with a bottle of tequila.

"Yeah, I'm not sure what that was about. I'm really sorry," I repeated as I unbuckled my seatbelt and stood while reaching for my pack.

"Well, I'm feeling no pain, that's for sure," Edwardo said with a drunken smile on his face.

The booze obviously worked. I could see out the window that there was probably another hour of sunlight left. Towering palm trees went on for miles behind the airport. It looked like paradise. I pulled out my phone, and I noticed an email that Liam sent that said I had a hotel reservation at the Belmon Hotel Das Cataratas.

I clicked open the email, and a 3D hologram of the hotel popped up. You could see the floor plan of the room and a model of the hotel. It was gorgeous. Leave it to Liam to find me the most expensive hotel out here. In the background, you could see the hotel had a slew of beautiful waterfalls behind it. I noticed Edwardo's expression light up.

"Is this your hotel, too?" I laughed.

"Hell yes, it is. It looks like we are going to be hotel mates for the night."

I'm not sure why Edwardo took to me. Maybe it was the fact that I gave him some tranquility before the flight. Part of me was thankful for him because it would be nice to have a familiar face around, if even temporarily. We grabbed our belongings and made our way to the jetway. Edwardo looked back at me and said, "I know my way around this airport, and since we are headed to the same hotel, I can pay for the ride there, if that's okay?"

"That's really nice of you, but totally not necessary," I said apprehensively.

Liam would frown at me riding with a stranger. I mean, after all, I didn't know much about him except that he was here to be with his girlfriend.

"Don't worry, man. This isn't my first rodeo," he said as he stumbled down the jetway. He just barely caught himself from falling. Yikes, maybe I need to raise my friend standards.

"Hey, do you mind if I call you Ed?"

"Oh, yeah, that's fine with me. I'll call you Al. We're like BFFs...we got nicknames now," he said, slurring his words.

"Oh, God," I said, giggling because my Santiago best friend was the town drunk.

Ed managed to lead us to the correct baggage claim area. South America was a little slower with technology upgrades than Canada. Everything seemed outdated but still functional, nonetheless. There were no hologram ads...but they had print ads that were on the walls behind glass cases. It was nice to be removed from technology. I could see why people would come here for vacation, you'd spend more time focusing on others rather than flashy electronics that kept you distracted.

Our bags finally arrived, and mine was deep underneath six others. Ed was able to get his luggage with ease while I tried to get mine as the conveyer belt kept moving. Ed set his bag down and reached to get mine. He gave it a good yank, sending the other baggage soaring off the conveyor.

"Ed, you didn't have to do that. I could have gotten it."

I could see other people behind us waiting for their bags, giving Ed an irritated look. It was clear he couldn't handle his liquor. As he handed me my bag, he noticed the tag on mine that specified I had a weapon inside.

Ed gave me a sharp look and said, "I wouldn't have pegged you to carry a gun, that's actually pretty cool. Remind me not to fuck with you."

"Yeah, long story," I replied with a cynical look on my face.

We continued on our way to the exit. I could hear Ed let out a loud "Oye" to the cabs that passed by us. One finally stopped and popped its trunk open. Ed tossed his bag in, and I placed mine in carefully. I knew the gun wasn't loaded, but I always had a fear of it going off by accident. We got in the cab, and Ed sat in the front seat and gave the driver the address of the hotel. We took off, and I could hear Ed talking the driver's ear off and decided it was a good time to call Liam. I pulled out my phone and dialed his number.

The phone kept ringing and went to voicemail. Okay, that's odd.

"Hey, babe. It's me, I landed not too long ago. This place is so beautiful. I wish you could have come now because I think you would've loved it. Oh, and thanks for booking me the fanciest hotel out here. You didn't have to do that. I should only be here for a day, if that. I'm heading to the hotel now. My flight buddy is staying at the same hotel I am, so we are taking a cab together. Anyway, I'm going to let you go. I'll let you know if I get any leads on Colden. I love you. Bye."

Ed broke from his conversation and turned back to me, "How is the wife?" he asked with fascination in his voice.

"Well, I got voicemail, so I'm not sure. But it's probably fine." I quickly turned the conversation back to him. "What about your girlfriend? Any word from her?"

"Yeah, she messaged me before the flight. I told her I would stay here for the night and then make my way to her. Dude, I'm so excited to see her."

I just nodded my head and smiled. His focus was all over the place because he started to talk to the cab driver again. I opened my pack and pulled out the letter my mom received from Colden. I wondered what he would say when I showed up. Probably be shocked that I came all this way to see him. I took another look at the address on the letter. I entered the address on my phone to see how far away it was from the hotel. I only had a day, but that should be plenty of time. My phone pulled up a route from my hotel to a post office from where it was sent. The distance was only a twenty-minute drive. The path notified me that the post office would be closing in less than an hour. I thought it would be plenty of time to check-in and find a ride there. I kept the route open on my phone and asked the driver how long until we would make it to the hotel.

"Fifteen minutes."

"Okay, thank you," I said politely.

The driver was starting to get frustrated with Ed. I wasn't listening to the conversation that much, but it sounded like Ed was beginning to get aggressive, or maybe just more annoying. I think it was the fact that Ed was telling the driver where to turn when the driver clearly knew how to get to our destination.

"Man, you are taking the long route. Are you just trying to get money out of us?" Ed shouted furiously.

"Ed, just relax. I'm sure he knows where he's going," I said, trying to calm him.

"No, fuck that. All these cab drivers around here are always trying to milk money out of all their passengers. It's bullshit." The alcohol was talking now, because a little over six hours ago, he wasn't like this.

"We should be there in no time," I said, hoping it would settle his mood and not direct his aggression toward me.

"All right, fine. It's still fucking bullshit, though. You cab drivers are scum bags."

I could tell the cab driver was trying everything he could to hold it in, but at last, he couldn't.

"Fuck you, man. I'm out here day and night trying to make ends meet. You and your fucking boyfriend can both kiss my ass." The driver yelled with hatred in his voice.

"Are you fucking kidding me right now? Fuck you, dude." Ed shoved the driver, causing the car to swerve into oncoming traffic.

"Ed, what the fuck! Calm down, man. You're going to get us killed," I yelled.

The driver swerved the car back into his lane. After that, he shoved Ed back, causing him to hit his head against his window. He pushed him pretty good because the window cracked and I could see that Ed was bleeding. He was asking for a fight now, and the driver came to a screeching halt in front of our hotel. Ed held his head to stop the bleeding and spit in the cab driver's face.

The cab driver clenched his jaw and got out of the car, slamming the door behind him. He quickly opened the trunk and started to throw our bags out onto the ground. I stepped out and closed my door. I went over to the passenger door and opened it for Ed. He stumbled out, holding his head still and began swearing at the driver. They both exchanged some very interesting words to each other, and the driver got back in his cab and peeled off. I went over to Ed and tried to examine his head. He pulled away from me and went to grab his bags.

I felt a little embarrassed because others staying at the hotel saw the commotion, even the valets at the hotel were laughing, and some of them were shaking their heads in disapproval. Ed took his bags and stormed inside. I went to get my bags and wiped the dirt off of them. I suddenly understood why South America had a high homicide rate. If this was my first encounter in Santiago, I'm sure it wouldn't be my last. I lifted my bag and made my way in, keeping my head down and apologizing to anyone I crossed.

I made my way through the revolving doors and entered the hotel. It was exquisite. The hotel had dazzling marble flooring all throughout. There were intricately designed white pillars that resembled the Colosseum, with many exotic plants that were growing in every archway. Along with an extremely tall cylindrical fish tank that was at the center of it all. I felt like rock climbing again because that fish tank was probably the same size as the rock wall in my gym back home. The aroma of freshly baked bread could be smelled in the distance along with the scent of flowers nearby. My eyes found their way to the registration desk where I spotted Ed, who was still holding onto his head while he checked in.

I rolled my eyes because he deserved what he got. In an effort to offset his rudeness, I greeted the person who was going to check me into my room as pleasantly as I could.

"Hi, I'm here to check-in. My name is Alec, Alec Everly." I said with a tinge of hesitation in my voice.

I had a feeling of 'this was too good to be true' and almost felt like I was at an exclusive club and didn't think I made the VIP list.

"Yes, I have a reservation for you right here. You are in room 408." She handed me a key card along with a device that said, 'Belmon' on it. "You can press this button on the device that will grant you access to our hotel's map. It will give you your current location in the hotel, along with how to navigate to your destinations. All you have to do is speak into the device, and it should be able to guide you to where you need to go. Also, there is something of a surprise for you in your room. Compliments of your fiancé, Liam Brooks. Congratulations on your engagement, by the way," she said with a smile.

I could see Ed eyeballing me out of the corner of my eye. I guess my secret was out because I could hear him scoff to himself. I didn't pay him any attention. He seemed like a decent guy, at first, but after his actions, I think it was best I kept my distance from him.

"Thank you," I politely said to the employee.

I turned around and pressed the button on the device. A layout of the hotel was in front of me in a pale white hue. I asked, "Route to my room, please?" The hologram zoomed into my location with a direction of where to go. Liam always told me if I had a compass, the needle would be spinning around in circles because I never knew which way was up.

I sprang in the direction with my luggage trailing behind me. Some other employees asked me politely if I would like someone to assist me with my luggage and I politely said, "No, thank you." I was perfectly capable, no need for someone to put in work that I could do myself. The device led me to a stunning chrome elevator that had a reflective mirror-like surface. Looking at myself, I was surprised my curly hair wasn't frazzled after all the sleeping that I did on the plane. I smiled because I felt so much better after resting. I took the elevator to the fourth floor.

My room was eight doors away from the elevator. As I approached my door, the abbreviation "PH408" was noted on the door.

I spoke aloud, "No, he didn't." I used my key card to open the door. As I entered, the feeling of pure bliss coursed through me. "Liam, no you fucking didn't!" I screamed in excitement.

The room was amazing. Marble floors all throughout, a living area with a fireplace and an eighty-inch television. Enormous white pillars lined the frame of the room, just as they did downstairs in the lobby. A full-blown kitchen with all the latest appliances. The back wall was lined with eighteen-feet-tall windows that had beautiful long curtains, making the room look even more significant than it already was. I set my luggage and pack down and went over to the window. It was more than a window, though, it was a sliding glass door that went out to a balcony that wrapped around my entire room. I stepped out, and in the distance I could see four amazing waterfalls that separated in their own way as the water flowed over the edges of the mountains. I leaned over the chrome railing and sighed as I cradled my face with my hand and just admired the view. Liam really outdid himself. I wish he had come with me.

I started to make my way inside and turned one last time to look at the falls. "I think I could live here," I thought to myself. I took a deep breath as the warm breeze whipped around me. The sky was a perfect pink and purple haze as the sun was starting to set. I took a breath as I went back inside because the distance from the sliding glass door and the entrance was probably sixty feet or more. I don't know why Liam had to upgrade me to such a big room, but it was glorious. I went down the hall and opened the bedroom doors to find very cliché rose petals in the shape of a heart on the bed. On the nightstand next to the bed was a bottle of chilled champagne, chocolate, a bouquet of flowers, and a card.

Smiling, I went over to open it.

"Today, all of your dreams will come true."

Love,
-Liam Brooks

I knew it wasn't Liam's handwriting, but I felt like he was here with me. I could feel my phone vibrating, and it was Liam. I answered.

"You just had to spoil me with sweets and champagne, didn't you?" I told him this while attempting to control my smile.

"I see you got my gift," Liam replied in that sexy voice of his that I loved so much.

"Yes, I did, and I love it. And this room is amazing, I can't believe you did this," I told him, unable to wipe the smile off of my face.

"Only the best for my future husband," Liam replied with a coquette tone. "How is it there?"

"Oh, it's beautiful. Part of me wishes you were here now. The weather is warm and the people... well, some are a little fickle, at least the ones I've met."

"What happened?" Liam asked with vigilance in his voice.

"Well, my flight companion Ed had a few drinks and was getting aggressive with the cab driver on the way here. It ended with him getting his head cracked on the car window."

"Shit. Are you okay? The cab driver didn't hurt you, did he?" he asked, an air of his military background tingeing his voice.

"No, no. I'm fine. He didn't touch me. It was Ed who was doing the provoking. The guy was asking for a fight," I said, trying to cool him down.

"Do you have your gun on you? Please tell me you do," Liam demanded more than he asked.

"No, I don't, but I'm going to take it with me when I leave here soon. I'm heading to the post office where Colden mailed the letter. They should be closing soon. I'll call you when I get back, okay?" I said in a hurry.

"Okay, just be careful. And stay away from that Ed guy at all cost."

"Okay, I will. I love you. Bye."

"I love you, too, bye, Mr. Future Brooks," Liam laughed as he hung up the phone.

I put my phone back into my pocket. I walked over to my luggage and pulled out some clothes that covered the gun's case. I opened the chest, and my handgun and mag were placed in a black foam cut-out. There was also a gun holster that was made to conceal it on my lower back. I took the gun out, and it seemed heavier than I remembered. Holding it didn't feel right, and I prayed that the day would never come where I would have to use it. I took the mag and slid it into place. I didn't cock the gun because there wasn't a need to.

I still wanted to look like your everyday person, even though I was walking around with a gun hidden under my clothes. I needed something heavier to hide the bulge of the gun and I stumbled upon a dark green plaid button-up shirt. More fabric to cover it up? I also saw a pair of dark brown combat boots that I thought would be a little more fitting. I left my nude-toned tank top on and strapped the gun around my waist. I then slipped on a pair of navy blue pants, and the boots. I could feel the gunmetal through my tank top against my skin...it gave me shivers.

I took out my phone and brought up the directions to the post office. The information showed that the office would be closing soon. I started to make my way down the hallway and out the front door, snagging my key card, translator, and Belmon device. I walked down the halls of the hotel while other visitors were coming and going from their rooms. All eyes were on me, or at least it felt that way. No one could tell I had a weapon, or at least they didn't want to say anything about it.

I clicked the elevator button and waited for it to make it to my floor. It opened, and no one was inside. I entered and pushed the lobby button. I waited for the doors to close so I could have some privacy. After they did, I clicked my Belmon device. "Driver request, please," I said, and shortly after a driver service was requested to meet me at the front of the hotel. The elevator dinged and began to open. There were a group of people making their way in the elevator as I was trying to get out.

"Hey, Al," Ed's voice boomed.

Ed was standing near the elevator. His head was cleared of blood and patched up, and he seemed to be in a better mood.

"Oh, uh, hey," I said, and I continued to walk across the grand entrance.

I could see Ed out of the corner of my eye start to follow me. I figured he would go up in the elevator like the rest of the group, but he didn't. I was on a mission, and I needed to get to the post office in a hurry.

"Hey, Alec, wait," Ed said as he reached for my arm and tried to hold me back.

I could hear him lose his footing as he tried to keep me from leaving. He was either still drunk off his ass or underestimated my strength. I stopped in my tracks because I didn't like being touched.

"Can I help you with something, Ed?" The annoyance in my voice was evident.

"Hey, man. I wanted to say I'm sorry. I didn't mean to make a scene. Sometimes I have a temper. My girlfriend says the same thing, and when she's around me, she usually is the one to calm me down. I'm really sorry, Alec." His voice was riddled with guilt, or regret...maybe both.

I could tell he meant it because he had a look in his eye as if he were humiliated.

"It's fine. We all make mistakes. I don't mean to cut the conversation short, but I kind of have somewhere I need to be," I said as I slowly started to creep toward the door again.

"Okay, well, maybe we can get a drink later? I'm going to head to a bar called Locos. Maybe we can catch up there?" he said with high hopes.

"Yeah, maybe, Ed. I'll see you around," I yelled as I continued to walk out through the doors.

I'm sure he meant well, but I didn't think a bar hangout with him would end well. Once outside, my Belmon device lit up, displaying a projection of a black 2060 Bentley that was pulling in to pick me up. I looked up and could see the car pulling around the valet. Such a fancy car for a hotel to use. I raised my hand to gesture the driver to me. He pulled up, and I opened the back passenger door and got in.

"Onde você está indo senhor?" he asked.

I could hear my translator in my pocket starting to go off. Lucky for me, I could pick up on some phrases and knew he was asking me where I was going. I pulled out my translator and said the address of the location. The translator started to speak in Portuguese, and I held it up so he could hear. The driver smiled and nodded his head, and we began our drive. I opened my map to make sure we were heading in the right direction, and it seemed like we were. I checked the time. Crap, the post office was about too close. I was a little worried that I wouldn't make it in time, but didn't want to rush my driver. As we continued to drive, the beauty of my surroundings began to fade. It seemed like the farther we drove away from the hotel, we were making our way into the... ghettos of Santiago. A little worried, I looked at my map and we were almost to the address.

The buildings outside were ancient and outdated. There were people outside walking barefoot, and some had hoods on that almost concealed their faces. The sun was set now, and it only made the environment look dingier. I could see some cars that had windows broken into, along with shattered windows in buildings that we passed by. I was definitely feeling less safe in this part of town. Liam would have his military radar on high alert if he was with me right now.

"É isso," the driver said.

Outside my window was a small post office. The windows looked like they were broken into, but were then covered with plastic. Part of the building was made of old brick, and other parts were pieces of scrap metal. There was an overhead light above the dingy green entry door that flickered ever so softly. Some lights were on inside the building, and I could see shadows of people moving inside.

"Could you wait here? I will only take a minute." I spoke into the translator and held it up to the driver. He turned and nodded his head. He obviously understood that I shouldn't be left alone in a place like this. I thanked him and stepped out and made my way inside. After I entered, the door swung shut behind me, causing some boxes on a shelf to fall to the floor.

A young girl who was probably in her mid-twenties walked over to pick them up. She had very dark hair, almost black. Her eyes were a chocolate brown, and her skin tone was a rich honey. I noticed a scar on her left cheek that resembled a knife wound. She seemed anxious and afraid in my presence. She quickly took the boxes and walked around the front counter of the store. My eyes followed her, and I could see a slew of metal mailboxes that lined the back wall of the post office.

There was an old woman who looked like she was in her sixties behind the counter staring daggers at me. She wore a simple yet dirty t-shirt. She was a tad overweight, with long salt-and-peppered hair and wrinkles that made her expression look angry. One of her eyes was dark brown or black, and the other was a fog of grey. I made my way to the counter and pulled out the letter from my brother.

"Ugh, hello?" I said as my translator went off. "I'm here to find the person who wrote me this letter. He is my brother. Have you seen him?" The translator was slightly delayed but spoke in the proper dialect for the woman to understand. I set the letter on the counter and pulled out my phone to show her a photo of my brother.

"Have you seen him?" I asked with an uneasy cadence in my voice.

She looked at the photo and looked back at me with the same angered expression on her face. She spoke while my device translated, "You have no business here." The rage in her voice startled me.

"I'm sorry?" I said, "I'm just trying to find my brother. My mother and I think he's missing. Could you help me find him?" I asked politely.

Out of the corner of my eye, I could see the girl with the scar come out from the back room. She did a double-take at the photo. She obviously knew him. I turned to her and asked, "Have you seen my brother? Do you know him?"

The old woman started to yell at me. "You have no business here. No members of Los Furiosos are welcome here. GET OUT!" she screamed at me.

The young girl started to argue with her, yelling back at her, saying something along the lines of, 'It's not him, we can help.' The old woman reached under the counter and pulled out a double-barreled shotgun and took aim at me. I immediately put my hands up and took a few steps back from the desk. I didn't know what the hell was going on or what I did to deserve being threatened at gunpoint. The young girl continued to yell at the old woman and tried to take the shotgun from her. I got down on the ground as soon as I could because the gun could have gone off at any moment. My heart was beating erratically in my chest. The young girl managed to get the shotgun from the old woman, and she set it on the floor. The woman continued to yell at me to get out, and I did as she ordered, but not before I accidentally dropped my translator on the floor, causing it to shatter behind me. There wasn't any point in going back. I went through the door, and it slammed shut behind me.

Outside, my car was still waiting, and I could hear the woman yelling at the young girl through the shattered window. I tried to calm myself and catch my breath. So many questions were going through my head. Who are Los Furiosos? And what was my brother's involvement with them to cause such a reaction? I quickly walked to the car and opened the door. The entrance to the post office swung open. It was the young girl who saved me.

"Hey," she yelled in English, but with a heavy accent.

She started to walk toward me, and my gut reaction was to panic because I didn't know if she was out to get me now. My hand slid behind my back, and I could feel my gun handle in my palm. I gripped it, ready to pull it out if I needed to.

"I'm sorry about that. My mother can be protective after her experiences," she said in her defense.

"Yeah, okay, I guess," I said. Like how do you respond to an experience like that?

Pointing a gun at someone because of past experiences seemed like the logical thing to do, said no one ever.

"Who are Los Furiosos, and what do they have to do with my brother?" I asked, trying to get straight to the point. I didn't want to be there any longer than I had to be.

"I read your brother's letter before he sent it," she said. "I haven't seen him since, but if he messed with Los Furiosos, he is definitely in danger. Their group visits a bar called Locos. That's the only place I would know where your brother would have gone."

That name sounded familiar. Oh, holy shit, I remembered that Ed was heading there tonight.

"Thank you," I said because I think I had enough information than I needed, and part of me wanted to get the hell out of here because I'd had enough excitement for one day.

She yelled out again, "If you are going there, be careful. Those men are not like others. Their eyes are different...and they are very dangerous."

"Okay, thank you," I said with a nervous tone in my voice.

I told the driver to go. I didn't care about the direction, just as long as it was far from here. As the driver left, I looked back to see the girl watching as we drove away. What did she mean about their eyes? The clock was ticking, and I needed to take every chance I could to find my brother. I pulled out my phone and looked up Loco's Bar. It was ten minutes away from here. I was nervous, but if my brother's life were in danger, I would do whatever it took to save him. I could feel the cold metal of my handgun on my back as I shifted in the seat. I had to make a choice. Go and find out more, or leave and possibly never see my brother again.

"Loco's Bar, por favor," I said to the driver.

He looked at me through the rearview mirror, and I could see his eyes widen. He must know of the crowd that hung out there. He nodded his head with hesitation, and we continued to drive. All I could think is that Ed was in trouble and Colden could be in deep shit. With how long ago the letter was written and the Los Furiosos...yeah, they could have possibly taken him. My only option was to keep going. The rush of adrenaline was coursing through my veins. I needed advice, and quickly grabbed my phone and dialed Liam's number.

Shit...voicemail.

"Hey, it's me. Look something happened. I'm not sure how to explain it, but my brother might be with or probably taken by a group called Los Furiosos? But I have a lead on where he could have been seen last. There's a bar called Loco's, it's a long story, but I'm heading there now. I'm a little nervous, Liam. I don't know if I'm making the right decision about going there. But I have a feeling that something could have happened to Colden. Either I stay and try to find him, or come home, and he could be lost forever. Please, call me when you get this. I love you."

My palms were getting sweaty, and you could see my handprint on my phone. Everything would be okay, it had to be. Ed would be there, and maybe I could have a drink with him to calm my nerves. I could use one after a night like this. I thought I should send Ann a holo message. I held my phone away from me and said, "Begin holo-screening, please." My phone started to tick, and a light next to my camera lens started to flicker and cast a blue projection over the upper half of my body.

"Hey, Ann. I'm in Santiago right now trying to find my brother. I didn't want to tell Liam this, but I was threatened at gunpoint a few minutes ago."

I paused and looked at the driver in hopes that he couldn't understand me.

"I'm not sure what my brother was into out here, but he didn't seem to have many fans. I'm okay right now, but I'm a little shaken, Ann." I stopped in fear, thinking about the possibility that something terrible happened to Colden. I continued, "I'm just apprehensive, Ann. Don't tell Liam about this, it would only make him upset. I'll talk to you later. Bye."

The projection over me faded and sent the message to Ann. We were driving back into a more populated and well-kept area. But the neighborhood still had sketchy vibes, but at least some people were walking outside carrying groceries. I could see children walking with their parents while holding hands. The area didn't look nearly as dangerous as the last area. I looked back at the map on my phone, we were only a few blocks away. From a distance, I could see a red sign that flickered in the dark.

The sign that flickered was indeed Loco's Bar. Outside there were some cars, but the parking lot was empty. The driver pulled into the lot where you could see some vagrants huddled near the door, asking for money as patrons exited. The people carried on, and they were stumbling a bit because they must have been intoxicated. Maybe I was overthinking this place and allowing one incident to taint all of the other moments.

I thanked the driver and stepped out. The air was hot and humid as I left the air-conditioned car. I took a breath and reached toward my lower back to make sure the gun was still there. I put my phone in my pocket and started to walk toward the door that was very sturdy because you had to put some effort into it when opening and closing.

One of the homeless men approached me and asked, "Could you spare any pesos?" His English was broken, but I could understand.

He had an overgrown beard, his hair was very scraggly with some grays in it. His breath was sour as he spoke through broken teeth.

"No, I'm sorry. I don't." An apologetic tone lacing my voice.

The bar smelled of cigarettes and spilled beer. The walls were painted a maize yellow and had small cracks near the base of the floor. As I looked around, I could see about a dozen people inside, including the bartender. One of those people was Ed, who sat alone at the bar. I walked over to him while a Spanish song played on a jukebox in one of the corners of the bar.

"Ed," I said, a little frantic.

"Oh, hey. You made it." A drunken smile on his face. "Yeah, I'm okay? Why wouldn't I be?" He questioned while he looked around.

"I don't know," I paused, trying to make up an excuse to cover up why I was worried. "I read the reviews about this place online and heard that it wasn't that great?"

"It seems cool here, the alcohol is cheap, too. Can I get you a drink?" he asked and flagged the bartender to come over to us. "Hey, can I get a cerveza for my friend here?"

The bartender nodded and looked at me with his head cocked for a moment. He walked off to grab a beer and uncapped it before handing it to me. I thanked him and reached to grab it out of his hand. He held onto the bottle before he released it.

"Don't I know you?" A resentful look clouded his face.

"No, I'm sorry. I've never been here before," I said, and he finally let the bottle go.

I took a few drinks from the bottle and turned back to Ed as the bartender walked off, giving me a dirty look as he picked up a phone.

"Hey, have you noticed anything... strange here?" I asked Ed in hopes that I wasn't the only person who knew something was up.

"No, this is a cool place. The bartender is kind of a dick, though, but other than that, I haven't had any issues."

I continued to drink my beer and looked around. I could see out of the corner of my eye a man sitting at the bar not too far from me. Was he looking at me? I couldn't tell because he had his hood up and it hid his face. I tried to ignore him, but it was the strangest feeling of déjà vu.

"Not used to a bar like this, I bet," Ed said as I noticed the bartender getting loud on the phone.

"Wh... what do you mean?" I asked, trying to keep my focus on the bartender, but also giving Ed some attention as I tried to look inconspicuous.

"Well, I'm sure a gay bar is a bit different. You should have told me your fiancé was a guy. I mean, I have nothing against it. My uncle is gay, and we are cool."

"Sorry, it must have slipped my mind," I said as the bartender hung up the phone.

Ed stood up, "I need to take a piss. I'll be back, and we can take some shots." Yeah, that was the last thing he needed.

He walked to the bathroom door near the side of the bar and bumped into a man as he was coming out.

"Hey! Watch where the fuck you're going, man," Ed yelled as the guy scoffed and continued to walk away.

Ed went into the bathroom, slamming the door behind him. When he did, the bartender started to walk over to the bathroom with a pissed look on his face.

"Excuse me." I called out to the bartender to stop him from heading into the bathroom. He turned back and came over to me.

"What?"

"I'm sorry to bother you, but have you seen my brother?" I took out my phone and showed him a photo of Colden. He looked at the picture and then back to me and noticed that we were identical twins.

"What the hell do you want with Los Furiosos?"

I played dumb. "Los Furiosos?"

Out of the corner of my eye, I could see the hooded man glance my way, clearly I'd sparked some interest with my inquiry.

"Trust me, you wouldn't last one minute on Candelario. Stay out of our fucking business." He grunted as he continued to the bathroom.

I scoffed and said to myself, "What the hell is Candelario?" The hooded man turned more toward me.

"Do you need help getting to Candelario?" he said with a shallow and cautious voice.

"I'm sorry?" I said as I moved closer to him. "I'm trying to find my brother Colden." I showed him the same photo, and he just nodded his head. "Have you seen him?" I asked.

"I can get you there, but it won't be easy."

"What is Candelario?"

"It's an island controlled by Los Furiosos. Most people who are missing from around here end up there." He said all of this so quietly to make sure that no one else in the bar was listening. I couldn't see his face as he kept his head down, almost like he was hiding from something or someone? Suddenly I could hear a loud commotion coming from the bathroom. Ed must have let his attitude get the best of him again.

The sound was then eclipsed by a loud truck that pulled up outside. I could see through the bars of the windows that a multi-passenger, military-grade truck came to a stop. The engine was shut off, and two men stepped out of the front cab. Then others stepped out of the back. Grungy and carrying guns.

The door swung open and the first two men to exit the truck entered the bar. The first thing I noticed were their eyes. Both of the men's eyes were lit up by a bright silver halo that surrounded the outer rim of their iris. The remaining patrons in the bar got up from their seats and started to walk toward the back exit.

One of the men quickly raised his assault rifle toward the people leaving and yelled something in Portuguese that I couldn't understand. Of course, a raised rifle and the authority in his voice was enough to give me pause. I took a step back and bumped into the bar. The other men who had exited the vehicle started to pile in. I counted at least ten of them. All of these men had the silver halos in their eyes.

The closer the men got, the more I started to notice scars all over their bodies. Every single man who came in had a branding on their left shoulder in the shape of the letter F. Some who turned their backs toward me had a tiny black device on the lower part of their neck.

Interesting...

These devices flashed different colors. Some flashed green, and others flashed yellow and red. The men started to yell at the other people in the bar. They must have been demanding money from them because people began to take out their wallets. Others who refused were forced to their knees and held at gunpoint.

I gradually started to reach for my handgun as the bathroom door abruptly swung open and Ed was led out at gunpoint by the bartender. Ed looked like he had taken a few punches because his eye was slightly swollen and his lip was bleeding. My heart was pounding, and for a brief moment, I wish I would have just gone back to my hotel. Ed was soon forced to his knees by the bartender.

"What the hell is going on?" Ed yelled.

The two men started to walk toward Ed. The bartender kicked him to the floor, causing him to slam his face on the concrete. One of the men grabbed Ed and brought him back up to his knees, keeping his hands behind his back. The other man stopped when he looked at me. Immediate recognition dawned on him and he pulled out a handgun and pointed it in my face.

"Please," I pleaded, my hands raised higher.

The man started to yell at me, and I couldn't understand him.

"I don't know what you're saying," I said with a shaky voice as he continued to wave his gun in my face.

He stepped closer to me, demanding that I answer him. I could recognize bits and pieces, he said something about 'being dead' and I assumed that he wanted to kill me. He quickly grabbed my right arm and twisted me around, slamming me against the bar and pushing my face down against its cold surface. I could feel him touching all over my body, checking for weapons. He found my handgun and pulled it out of my holster. He must have pocketed the gun and continued to search me. He took out my keycard and threw it over the bar. He continued to frisk me and found my phone. As he pulled it out, it began to ring. It was from Liam.

I started to raise my face up from the bar, "I NEED TO ANSWER THAT." The man pushed me back down aggressively, causing me to hit my cheek on the lip of the bar. I was pretty sure I was bleeding.

"I have to answer that, please," I said again, and the man laughed and showed me my phone, almost toying with me.

He smashed it down on the bar over and over again until it stopped ringing. He laughed and threw the pieces of the phone across the bar. I could hear him cock his handgun and he pressed it against the back of my head. I could feel the cold metal through the curls of my hair.

"Leave him the fuck alone," Ed yelled, defending me.

Ed got loose from the man holding him and started to charge at my attacker. The man turned the gun from me and quickly aimed it at Ed. A shot was fired...hitting Ed in his right shoulder, causing him to fall to the floor. People in the bar let out screams, and the men yelled at them. They must have told them to shut up.

"Don't do anything stupid, Ed," I said, frantically. "Stay where you are."

Ed was clenching his shoulder now as blood ran down his shirt.

He began to scream in pain. "Fuck you, motherfuckers."

I started to raise up again, and the man pushed me down by my head. He turned my face in Ed's direction as I had tears welling up in my eyes. He pointed the gun at Ed again and started to laugh.

I whispered, "Edwardo." He had one hand up trying to shield himself from the gun.

A tear rolled off my cheek as the man squeezed the trigger on the gun again. I tried to close my eyes because I didn't want to witness something so horrific. Ed was shot in the head, causing blood to spray on the bartender. Edwardo's body fell to the floor. Blood began to seep into the cracks in the concrete. The men were snickering to each other like this was a fun game. I wept for Ed as I watched the life leave his body. The man holding me down let off two more rounds into Ed's body. There was a ringing in my ears from all the gunfire. The leader raised me from the bar and tucked the tip of the gun under my chin. I could see a woman in the bar, screaming and crying, but her sounds were silenced by the ringing in my ears.

I couldn't move. There was a dead body in front of me. Ed's eyes were still open. I was in shock. Why are these men doing this? I was beginning to come to, and I could feel the heat of the pistol on my skin. I knew it was my turn to go. He pressed the gun deeper into my skin while he stood behind me. I could hear the trigger engaging. This was the end, and I would have never thought that I would die this way.

"I love you, Liam," I said in a whisper.

"STOP." The man standing in front of me yelled as his glowing eyes pulsed.

"You look familiar," he said as he got closer to me.

His English was understandable but forced.

"Where do I know you from?" he casually asked as if there wasn't a dead body that he'd just stepped over.

I was frozen and couldn't form words. He got closer to my face, trying to look at my features. Something about his eyes seemed almost animatronic.

"What is your name?"

"My name is Alec Everly," I said with spite in my voice.

"Everly?" A hint of remembrance in his voice as he looked at the man holding me, and then back in my direction.

"Well, Alec." He paused and gave me a cruel smile. "It's your lucky day."

He took a step back and started to yell at the men in Portuguese. The men began to exit the bar, taking drinks with them and money that they received from the patrons. I could see two men walk up to Ed's body and pick him up by his arms and legs. They started to carry him out the door.

The man who 'saved me' looked at the bartender before he spoke, "Clean this up." As he pointed at the puddle of blood on the floor.

The bartender nodded. The leader started to walk toward the door, and the guy behind me shoved me in his direction. I turned back and gave him a dirty look. He pushed me again and put the gun to my back. I looked at the people in the bar, and some were holding one another, and others had their hands over their mouths in fear for me. I turned back to look for the hooded man and noticed he was gone. The man shoved me out the door, and I could see the two men who were carrying Ed's body load him into the back of the truck.

"Where are you taking me?" I demanded of the man who I assumed was their leader.

"Why would I tell you that? Get in." He demanded with a stern look.

I looked back in hopes that someone must have heard or seen the gunfire. One of the men grabbed me by my arm and began to pull me into the truck as they zip-tied my hands behind my back.

In the back of the truck, I could partially see through holes in the fabric of the roof. The inside was lined with two benches on both the left and right sides of the truck. All ten men began to take their seats, and I could see in the back of the truck that the homeless men who were in front of the bar earlier were also zip-tied with their mouths duct taped. The truck had dirty floors and garbage all around. In the middle of the aisle, Edwardo's body rested. I couldn't look at him. He was just thrown in here like he was nothing. Some of them had their dirty boots resting on his body as if he were a new footstool. I simply stared at his lifeless body. The man who tied me came back and duct taped my mouth shut.

He placed the tape on my mouth and said something in Portuguese about a bag. I could see the men in the back of the truck rustle around and pull a knapsack out and pass it back. The truck started to pull away, and the lights from the bar began to fade. The back of the truck was dark now, but the silver halos of the men's eyes were glowing. It was beyond eerie. There was moonlight coming through the holes in the roof...just enough that I could make out Edwardo's silhouette.

A tear streamed down my face as I looked at him. The man began to place a knapsack over my head.

One of the men said, "Put him to sleep."

Suddenly I was struck on the back of my head, slowly losing consciousness. I didn't know where we were heading, but my fear for Candelario and all of the unknowns grew as I lost consciousness...

3: CANDELARIO ISLAND

A SPLASH OF WATER splashed across my face. I jolted awake in a panic. I looked around and could see other men around me, all had their hands tied behind their backs, their ankles shackled. I realized that my mouth wasn't taped before I spoke.

"What's going on? Where are we?" They were shushing me and telling me to be quiet.

"Why are we here? Who did this?" I said louder.

"Quiet. They'll hear you." One of the men spoke in clear English.

I noticed that it was the homeless man who had asked me for money at Loco's. As I continued to look around, I felt a sharp pain in my head from where I was knocked unconscious. It was still night outside, and the stars were shining radiantly. I don't know how long I'd been unconscious, though. As I continued to look around, there were armed guards with silver-haloed eyes walking back and forth on the deck. We were on a boat, and it seemed to be an old one at that. The ship looked rusted and had a lot of algae and seaweed on it.

Alongside us were other boats that appeared to hold other captives. My emotions began to get the best of me. I didn't know where we were going or if Liam would come looking for me. I hoped that Ann would have told Liam what happened because I soon regretted telling her not to say anything to him. The boat continued to sway, and I saw one of the men starting to puke. One of the guards began to yell at him. He walked over and began to kick the man in the ribs, saying something along the lines of 'clean up your mess.' He then threw a dirty rag down on the floor and had the man cleaning it up. My head was pounding, and the cold breeze wasn't helping. I pulled my legs into my chest to keep warm.

One of the men yelled, some of it I could make out from my limited knowledge of Portuguese. Part of what he said was, "Hey. We are almost there." The other members of the group all started to yell at each other, letting everyone know. By this point, I could see beyond the fog that we were approaching an island. Torches lined the island's shore, and more groups of men awaited our arrival on the dock. Silver-haloed eyes were like beacons, glistening in the moonlight. I whispered to myself, "Candelario." A guard heard what I said and walked up to me with a smile on his face. His smile faded into a malicious stare, and he swiftly hit me in the face with the back of his rifle.

I fell to my side, shaking my head. My mouth was bleeding. I could feel the excruciating pain in my mouth, but with my hands tied behind my back, there was no way to defend myself.

"Shut your fucking mouth," The man yelled as I was on my side.

I tried to bring myself back up slowly as the man walked away. The guy beside me attempted to help me up as much as he could. As I finally sat upright, he asked me, "Esta bien?" I shook my head because I wasn't okay. I should have never come to Santiago, and I could feel tears of regret leaving my eyes because I knew I had made a big mistake. These men, Los Furiosos, were out for blood and they would kill anyone who got in their way. Our boat was starting to approach one of the docks near the beach. The closer we got to the island, the more massive it looked.

"Get up. Everyone. Get the hell up." One of the men began to bark at us.

Other Los Furiosos walked up to us and grabbed us by our arms and pulled us to our feet. One of the men did the same to me and put his rifle to my back, nudging me forward to the edge of the boat. Our vessel was near the dock and shortly after I could see that the ship that was trailing us was pulling up, too. The boat on the other side of the pier seemed to hold more prisoners than ours did. The ship came to a stop, and Los Furiosos' members started to throw planks off the boat.

"Start walking." One of the men ordered as I was shoved to move.

I was behind five other captives as we slowly started to get off the boat. The first two men had difficulty crossing because the waves were causing the planks to shift back and forth. The third man was pushed into position. He began crossing the plank, when I noticed a big wave advancing.

I hollered, "Watch out."

The captive lost his balance and fell into the ocean. The men started to laugh at him as the man struggled to swim with his hands tied behind his back and his feet shackled.

"Help him," I roared. "He's going to drown."

One of the men stopped laughing and approached me.

"You want me to help him?" he said, "Okay...as you wish."

He then walked to the edge of the boat and lifted his assault rifle and took aim. He commenced unloading his semi-automatic toward the captive who fell in. My eyes widened as he hit the man a few times. You could see red in the water as it reflected in the moonlight. The firing ceased, and the silence caused me to shudder. I looked down and could now see the lifeless body start to float on the surface. The man who fired his weapon walked up to me, lowered his assault rifle, took out his handgun and pointed it at me.

He looked at me as his glowing eyes pulsed, "You wanted to help him." He paused, looking at the body, then back to me, "You're next," he said with a thirst for blood in his voice.

He pulled me by my arm to the edge of the boat. He nudged the plank slightly farther off the ship with his boot heel, so it had more of a chance of staying on the dock. He pushed me into place, and I looked back with terror in my eyes.

"Begin..." He was impatient, you could see it in his jerky arm movements.

I took small steps forward and could feel the plank rattle as I slowly made my way across. I could sense every wave as the plank moved up and down with the tide and I continued forward, timing my movements just so.

I continued doing this all the way across the plank. As I neared the edge, I vaulted onto the dock before the tide could knock me off. Once on the pier, the plank unbalanced and fell into the ocean. The man on the boat scoffed at me and grabbed another plank and threw it across. Someone came up to me and untied my shackles, allowing me to walk freely.

Once finished, he raised his gun at me, "Get moving," he said.

Each of us made our way down the pier and onto the sand. Los Furiosos grabbed torches and lit them. Apparently we weren't at our final destination. We were soon led through the jungle.

After a ten-minute walk, we came to a clearing. Tall lights were standing at least twenty-five-feet high. Many glowing eyes, surrounded us, almost like lightning bugs. There must have been hundreds of Los Furiosos in our midst, all performing different tasks. I could hear many voices in all different languages and I could see a giant mountain that had a trail of lights leading into a cave. We were told to keep walking, none of us knew what was going on. As we advanced, many of the workers paused and gave us glares.

"Look, fresh meat." One of the laborers said as he continued to walk away while carrying a pickaxe.

I noticed that there were workers along with military personnel who barked orders at them, all with similarly glowing eyes. The military marshal's wore deep navy blue uniforms, with accents of neon orange. Many of them sported wool beret hats that replicated their neon orange accent colors. I noticed that the hats they wore had a meniscus patch in the shape of a shield. Surrounding the shield was what appeared to be silver lions, but the shape of the animals was peculiar. What stood out most were the words, "Los Furiosos" in silver.

We proceeded to shuffle forward as Los Furiosos' workers were opening crates that were full of weapons and ammo. Others were unboxing some kind of drugs. More men trickled down the hill, pushing wheelbarrows that were filled with rocks with possibly gold flecks in them. Others that trailed behind them were pushing gold bars that they must have gotten out of the cave. Los Furiosos was obviously not your average third-world gang. More men passed reeking of oil and gasoline, pushing large barrels of oil, maybe? We were forced further through the maze of workers.

The sounds of a screeching animal could be heard in the distance. As we continued forward over a hill, we came upon a group of Los Furiosos who were huddled around a fire, watching and cheering in delight as the sounds of the animal's cries grew louder. The closer we got to the fire, I heard what sounded like a taser.

Beyond the flames, I could see a man holding a long black rod that sparked.

We were all told to surround the fire and were pushed into place and forced to our knees. The man with the rod walked over to a cage where a panther had recoiled into a corner. The panther snarled at the man as he grew closer. The man started to ignite his electric rod with a cruel smile on his face. The rod sparked as he maneuvered it in between the bars of the cage. The panther let out a roar, and the crowd started to go wild. The rod came closer to the panther as it clawed at it in defense. The man quickly drove the rod into the panther's side, shocking it as it let out a significant cry. All I could think was that poor panther shouldn't be here and nor should I. I winced as its roars grew louder.

The man stopped when another member of the group spoke in his ear. He handed the member his device and slowly walked over to a tree stump. Looking through the fire, it was hard to make out what he was grabbing. It almost looked like a branding iron. He began to make his way around the fire, giving us all a look as if he were inspecting us. He placed the end of the iron into the fire and stood with his hands on his haunches.

"My name is Erico. Welcome to Candelario," he said as Los Furiosos applauded and cheered.

Erico was fairly tall, and just like the rest of Los Furiosos, his hair was buzzed short, with a perfect hairline. A vertical scar cut through the end of his left eyebrow. His eyes glowed with silver-halos, and his muscles flexed as he raised his hands and motioned for Los Furiosos to silence.

"Now I see most of you wish not to be here. And by all means, feel free to leave." Erico paused to see if any of us would get up.

"Well, just know you are surrounded by one-hundred miles of ocean, a dangerous jungle and an army of men who follow orders to the letter." He stopped and smirked at the crowd as they all seemed to bulk up for a fight.

He carried on, "So if you want to leave or try to escape, I wish you the best of luck getting out. We are everywhere, even in places you would have never imagined."

We were surrounded by men who carried every weapon imaginable...bows, handguns, knives, axes, assault rifles, the list was endless.

"Although there are many of us, we love strength in numbers. However, we need strong and capable men. By the looks of it, most of you make the cut," he paused and looked to his right, "but some of you are a bit too old for our taste." He eyed an older man who must have been brought on the other boat. A member of the group approached Erico with a handgun. Erico took the gun and walked over to the older man. "Fate has brought you down the wrong path, old man, and I am not sorry to do this, but unfortunately for you, you just don't meet our strict criteria."

Erico instantly executed the man in front of us.

I placed my hands over my mouth to stop myself from screaming and turned away as the man's body fell to the floor. What the fuck is happening? Why are these people doing this? Erico holstered his gun and continued his speech.

"Now that our loose end is taken care of, we can start with your initiation." He raised his hands and then crossed them over his chest as everyone cheered.

"We need you to look the part, but don't worry, we have a very skilled hairstylist on staff and a brilliant scientist to make sure that you won't remember a thing. But first, you must bear the mark of Los Furiosos. We want people to know who they are FUCKNG WITH!" Erico's voice raised like he had a point to prove. The men surrounding us shouted, agreeing with him. Erico revealed his left shoulder, showing a burned scar in the shape of an F.

"This is who we are. And anyone who crosses us will suffer the consequences. Our methods aren't the most conventional; however, we need a lot of members to carry out our mission. And since you aren't volunteers, we have ways to work around that." He smiled and turned around to reveal his implant. The small black square at the top of his spinal column that I'd noticed earlier on the men at Loco's. It resembled a computer chip with a flashing green light. Erico turned back around and continued.

"This implant will allow you to make choices — to a certain extent. But know that any choices you make to harm your device, harm your comrades, or even try to take down our operation will be immediately stopped. These devices are monitored by higher-ups and continuously pumps a low-grade hallucinogen into your brain, allowing us to control what you see and...what you don't see." A sinister smile told us he had it all figured out.

"Once these devices are implanted, they must be calibrated every so often to ensure that you are still under our full control. A flashing green light indicates that the device is fully functional. A yellow light means you are due for calibration. And flashing red means you need to report to Dr. Jericho immediately. And let me be clear, these devices will make you do what we say when we say it. There is no way around it; if your lights begin to flash red, you will return to us no matter what."

"What if we don't?" One of the men questioned with a tone of rebellion in his voice.

Erico smirked and replied, "Well, you better be a fast runner, but I doubt that even you could outrun bullets. Which brings us to Josè." Erico's piercing eyes darted toward one of his men who was holding one of the new recruits down. Members of Los Furiosos got silent, and everyone stared at him. When their voices quieted, there was a faint sound of continuous beeping. Josè removed his hands from the recruit and turned around, reaching for his implant as it was flashing red and beeping like an alarm. A member approached him quickly, pulling out a handgun. Josè turned around with haste, shouting, "Erico, no. Esta bien, Erico. No." Erico nodded to the member as if he were giving him the go-ahead. The member put his handgun to Josè's temple and pulled the trigger.

The sound of the gunfire echoed through the jungle as Josè's body fell to the floor and blood from his skull leaked into the sand. The member who shot him then took his place and held the recruit down who had asked the question. The newbie had his eyes closed and was trembling in anxiety while I found myself shuddering, too. These men were very unforgiving, and the killing seemed to be second nature. Erico gazed over at all of us.

"Let this be a warning if you're feeling like 'a bit too much of yourself.' Get to Dr. Jericho as soon as you can because you wouldn't want to end up like Josè, would you?" He looked for us to respond while most of us shook our heads. "That's what I thought," he replied, satisfied that we were all on the same page.

"Now, gentlemen," he looked over to the fire and back to us. "It's time for your initiation." As he spoke, Los Furiosos erupted in excitement. Erico raised his hands in the air like he was a game show host. Each of us looked at one another, uncertain of what to do. There were so few of us and so many Los Furiosos that we would never make it out alive. I began to pick at my zip-tie with my nails in hopes that I could break free. I realized that it would be impossible, but I continued anyway. Erico approached the fire and pulled out a glove from his pocket. He placed the glove on his right hand and reached for the steaming handle that was laying in the flames. He pulled out the branding iron and raised the end to his eyes. It was red hot.

He looked back at us. "It's ready," he said as the crowd of men continued cheering.

Erico seemed a little unsure who he wanted to start with. He suddenly stopped not too far away from me.

"What? No volunteers?" he asked us all.

Some of Los Furiosos began pushing us forward, trying to volunteer for us.

Erico laughed, "How about we play a game. One that the Americans do. I'm sure some of you might know of it." He continued. "One, Two, Sky Blue?" he asked to see if any of us knew it. Now he was toying with us. I was trying to pull away from my captor because I didn't even have a tattoo, and the thought of being burned and scarred made me wilt. Erico giggled and raised the rod in the direction of us. He began pointing at each of us. He landed on a man who was to my far right, about three guys away from me.

"One..." he said, and continued down my way.

"Two..." While he kept making his way down to me.

"Sky blue..." As he pointed at me, his head cocked to the side and one of his eyebrows raised. He shook his head and continued.

"All..." He Proceeded down the line.

"Out..." With pause, refusing to continue to my left.

"Except..." Erico began, coming back my way, cheating his own game.

"You." While he pointed to the man to my left, he paused.

"Well, this game could take a while, and this will only stay hot for so long." He laughed because he found his first sacrifice. He raised the rod back up to the man. "Hold him down," he demanded as Los Furiosos grabbed the man's shoulders and arms to make sure he couldn't move. The man struggled. One of the members ripped the sleeve of his shirt off. The man spoke in Russian, I'm sure pleading with Erico. He continued to struggle, shouting as he kicked and screamed while Erico got closer and closer with the branding iron.

They continued holding the man down as Erico pressed the brand into the man's skin. The man let out a horrific scream that echoed in the distance. I could hear his skin sizzling as if he were being cooked alive. He tremored in place while one of the members reached around and held his mouth shut. The smell of his skin burning caused me to almost retch.

Erico finally removed the brand from the man's arm while the members released the man's mouth. He tried fighting the men off, clawing his way toward Erico. The man spat at Erico's feet and stared daggers at him as his lust for revenge grew.

"Welcome to Los Furiosos," Erico said to the man. He then turned to me, and I quickly looked away.

"You?" Erico said toward me. "Look at me," he demanded.

I resisted, but my captor forced my face to Erico, pulling me by my jaw. Erico cocked his head again.

"Colden Everly, isn't it?" he asked, "You look different from the last time we saw you." My eyes focused on Erico now. Holy shit, Colden must still be around.

"Your tattoos are gone? And I don't see our mark?" he questioned.

One of Los Furiosos' spoke, "His name is Alec Everly. Colden Everly's twin brother."

Erico's eyebrow raised. "Wow, I guess this is a family affair now. I think we remember Colden mentioning something about you before."

"Faerie," Erico said as he laughed. Los Furiosos began laughing, too.

I look around as they giggled at me. What did he mean, Faerie?

Erico continued, "You just might be the first Faerie recruit we have ever had. Now your brother was a bit of a disappointment to us. I have a feeling that you might be, too, but I'd like to give you a fighting chance. Don't think you will last too long, though. After all, how much damage could someone like you do?" He laughed and so did the others. I gave him a disgusted look as everyone laughed at me. Erico raised the cattle brand to my face. The rod was still surprisingly red as the heat radiated across my skin.

Erico looked around to Los Furiosos, "Have any of you ever heard a Faerie scream before?" he asked as the men got riled up.

Erico smiled and continued. "Well, today is the day. You're up next."

I began to struggle as the men started cheering. I pulled away from Los Furiosos as three men tried to hold me back. One of the men grabbed my left bicep, and I shifted my body forward, pulling the man to the front of me as he flipped onto his back. Another member grabbed me by my shoulders, and I threw my head back, breaking his nose. Five other men approached me, quickly forcing me to the ground.

Erico took a step back, pleased. "You've got some fight in you. That's good." One of the men had his knee to my back as my face was being pressed into the sand. The man whose nose I broke came to my side, clenching his face in anger. He swiftly kicked me in the ribs, knocking the wind out of me. I struggled to catch my breath before he went in to kick me again.

"That's enough!" Erico shouted. "Hold him still."

Erico approached me with the cattle brand. One of the men grabbed the back of my shirt and yanked it, causing my buttons to pop off. Shortly after, someone used a knife to cut the rest of my shirt free. My breathing intensified. Erico came closer with the branding iron, and my eyes started to water. I tensed up my body as if it would help, but I knew it wouldn't. I clenched my eyes shut as the red-hot rod approached my skin.

The iron touched the surface, and it was an immediate burst of pain. I let out a scream as I instinctively pulled away from the brand. The iron was pressed deeper into my skin, and I was quaking in place while I had the urge to vomit. The men chanted in pleasure from my pain. Time nearly stopped as I stared at the brand. It looked like it had been on there for minutes, or maybe even an hour.

Finally, Erico removed the brand. I could see on my shoulder that I was now one of them — a slave for all eternity. The symbol of a red F was now forever on my shoulder, and I no longer belonged to myself anymore. I knew that I would never see Liam again, and I would never see Ann or Issac. No one was coming to save me, and this was my new life. The men raised me from the floor, and I could feel my shoulder pulsing in agony.

"The sounds you made while screaming got me going," Erico said, sexually, "I bet you'd like to see that, wouldn't you?" He continued to taunt me.

"How does it feel, Faerie?" he asked.

I took a moment to find my words. I was paralyzed and felt violated beyond comprehension. The only thing I felt now was anger and rage toward Erico.

"Fuck. You." Words I knew I'd regret erupted but I shouted them anyway and spit in Erico's face.

Erico wiped his cheek, pulled back, and started to laugh. "Fuck me, huh?" His smile instantly faded as he backhanded me, causing me to fall over to my side.

"You're mine now, Faerie. You should be grateful I'm letting you live. Your brother wasn't so lucky."

"What have you done to my brother?" I shouted.

"You don't fucking ask questions around here. I do."

"Take him and the others over there out of my sight until we are done with the rest."

The men lifted me to my feet and brought my Russian companion along. We were forced to form a line in front of the panther's cage. As we were standing near the container, I could see scars on the panther where Erico tased her. She was pacing back and forth in her cage, eyeballing Erico as he continued to brand the others. The men's cries carried through the island, and I could see behind us that the workers just carried on like nothing was happening.

While the panther continued to pace, I noticed that the padlock on the cage wasn't secure. The only thing keeping her in was the hinge that held the gate closed. I thought she could cause some damage if she were let loose. As Erico continued to brand his next victim, my captor's attention was on the show rather than on me. I wasn't that far from the enclosure, and I was sure that I could lift the hinge up with the heel of my boot if I was quick enough.

I slowly started to raise my foot behind me so no one would notice. I could feel the hinge beginning to lift as the panther let out a roar, and my captor's eyes darted back over to me as I quickly lowered my leg. He gradually turned back to watch Erico's brutality. I saw out of the corner of my eye that the Russian man knew what I was trying to do. I glanced over to him, and he nodded his head calmly. I began to raise my heel again, feeling around for the hinge. This time I hoped that the panther would keep quiet as I attempted to free her. She started to growl again, and my captor turned back swiftly. Suddenly, the Russian man rammed into him, causing everyone to look in our direction. I quickly raised my heel, hitting the hinge and releasing it.

The Russian man was kicked at the back of his knees and brought down to the floor. Erico turned around and screamed at his men, "Keep them under control."

One of the men sucker-punched the Russian man in the face. I looked over to see if he was okay. He nodded to me, almost saying 'good job' without voicing it. I slowly nodded back and kept my lips sealed. Erico finished branding the rest of the men, and he tossed the rod over to the side of the fire. The men were moved in line over near us.

"Take them to the stylist. And when you're done, come back here and move this panther to TreeTop." He ordered to one of the Los Furiosos members.

I was shoved to move, and the men behind me followed. I looked back over to the panther in hopes that she would break free. If anyone could outrun Los Furiosos, it'd be her. As we continued onward, we passed by many workers and marshals who continued to work. Many of them looked at our brands, as if they were excited for us to join. We were ushered up a small hill that was isolated from all the noise of the power tools and the murmurs of the workers. As we reached the top of the range, I could see a small building that had been forged from scrap metal, mud, and rusted materials.

My captor approached the door first and opened it. He motioned with his head for me to go in. I looked back at the crowd of recruits behind me who were ready to follow. My captor jerked me by my arm, forcing me inside. The recruits followed behind me, as well as Los Furiosos men. As we entered, we noticed five barber chairs that were all set along the left side of the building. Each had a set of sheers and a mirror. The floors were a dirty black and white-checkered pattern while the sound of Spanish music played in the background. The foulness of cigarette smoke was in the air. To the right side of the building was a tiled shower room. However, there was no separation between the two. It was just one great room with a series of drains in the middle. I looked down at the floor and could see different shades of hair, both long and short that collected in the cracks of the tile. The lighting was very dim and had a green hue just like the one outside.

Suddenly, a deep voice sounded from beside us. "Are these our new recruits?"

On our left, in the darkness, you could see five sets of silver-haloed eyes. The pairs of eyes came closer, as did the cigarette smoke. Emerging from the darkness, one particular man revealed himself.

"Yes, these are our newbies, Alejandro," my captor proclaimed.

As he spoke, the four other sets of eyes came out of the darkness. All of the men looked similar. All of them had buzzed hair, and their clothes were filthy with multiple rips in them.

"Well, you know the drill, one per chair, and have the others wait. We will hose them all down at once to save time. How many do we have?" Alejandro asked.

"There are fifteen."

"Okay, five of you step forward. Don't be scared. It's like ripping off a Band-Aid, let's go." Alejandro ordered as his cigarette-smoking comrades walked over to their chairs, waiting for us to sit down. I was pushed forward at gunpoint, and four other men followed me. Alejandro gestured me over to his chair and had me sit down. Weapons were still pointed on all of us, and I could see my Russian friend two seats down from me. I noticed he was staring at a straight razor on the countertop, most likely debating if he should reach for it or not.

Once I was seated, I saw my reflection in the mirror. I was a mess. I could see that my lip was sliced open, and cuts were littered across my face from being hit so many times. My left eye was slightly swollen, and I could see a reddish-purple pigment forming in my eye socket. I didn't look like myself anymore, not to mention the brand on my left shoulder. The thought of Colden popped into my head. I thought of him dead in a ditch somewhere, having no resemblance of what he used to look like. With how these men acted, I'm sure they would have left anyone unrecognizable. My lip started to tremble because the thought of Colden being dead, almost crippled me.

"So you're the Faerie?" Alejandro asked but already knew the answer. I just nodded my head. It seemed like the name 'Faerie' was a reputation that proceeded me.

"Well, you are the spitting image of your brother. Think he would have looked better without tattoos now. Nonetheless, after

I'm done, the two of you will look even more identical than before." He continued, "Now I know your kind is more 'fashionable', but I'm sure you will still be pleased. I'd rather have you fitting in than standing out. But, I'll leave a little to keep your sanity."

Alejandro reached for a set of sheers on the countertop. He quickly switched them on and turned me around, away from the mirror. I could hear the other sets of sheers from the others starting. I looked over and saw that the other newcomers were having all of their hair buzzed off. Alejandro grabbed my jaw, and I could feel his gnarled hands on my cheeks. His hands were cold as he blew cigarette smoke into my face, giving me a headache. He took the sheers to my head and began cutting.

I could hear the blades. I could see my curls rolling down my tank top and hitting the floor. My scalp felt bare as the cold air hit it. I looked over and saw that most of the men were close to being bald. The other men had some facial hair, and Los Furiosos were taking sheers to that, too.

The sounds of the blades clicked off.

"Want to see the new you?" Alejandro asked, pleased. I shook my head because I wasn't going to see me anymore. I was going to see them.

"Don't be impolite, you little shit. I did great work," Alejandro said, almost offended. He turned me around to the mirror. The haircut made me look very sickly, especially with the new wounds that I now had. He left enough hair so I wasn't completely bald like the others. I exhaled while shaking my head. Alejandro looked into the mirror with me.

"Look at you now. We could pass as brothers, too, don't you think?" he said with a smile as his cigarette was hanging from the side of his mouth. "You are one of us now. You have one more step to take." He blew smoke into my face, and I turned away, holding my breath.

"Get an implant, and those tears will dry up real quick. You won't even remember what you were crying about to begin with," he said as he wiped a tear from my cheek while taking another puff.

"Now, get the fuck out of my chair and send the next recruit, Faerie," Alejandro said as if he were making commissions off of every haircut he did. He seized me by my arm, yanked me out of the chair and flung me to another armed Los Furiosos. Alejandro motioned for the next trainee to be seated in his chair. I was shoved to the corner of the shower-side of the room and was told to stay put. Guns were being aimed everywhere, and locks of hair were falling to the floor left and right. I could feel drops of cold water trickle down from a pipe that was above me. The water was frigid. I wrapped my arms around my upper frame, trying to keep warm while slowly nudging away from the drips.

More nearly hairless men were directed at gunpoint to where I was standing. The last remaining men were nearing the end of their haircuts, and joined the rest of us as we all huddled together.

"All right, boys, hose them down," Alejandro shouted as Los Furiosos started to wheel out water hoses and connect them too showerheads. One of the men turned on the water, and Los Furiosos spread out, making sure everyone got their fair share. I prayed that at least the water was warm.

Los Furiosos pulled their triggers, and water began spraying across all of us. Hitting my head and chest, it was brutally cold. Some of the men tried hiding behind others because the temperature was too cold to bare. Those who hid were pulled out from behind and forced to be sprayed head-on. I was hit with more water than the others. The fact that my brother was here at some point probably had something to do with it, or it was the fact that I was the 'Faerie'. My clothes were soaked, but the bloodstains on my tank top remained. The cuts on my face and my branding stung as the water passed over my skin. I licked my lips in hopes that the water was clean enough to drink. Saltwater? Rinsing us down with saltwater didn't make sense to me?

The hoses came to a stop as we all shivered in place. The rivers of saltwater poured into the drains of the room, and you could see locks of hair float down along with it. Los Furiosos rolled the hoses back up, and others laughed at us, pointing their guns in our direction. We were soon directed to exit the building. We exited through the door like cattle, and I was almost excited to be back outside in the heat. I was the last to leave the building, and before I stepped out, Alejandro shouted at me.

"See you around, Faerie." I stared daggers at him before I left.

I started to walk forward, following the rest of the men up a mountain, when I was suddenly struck in the back.

"What the fuck?" I screamed.

The man escorting me hit me in the back with his rifle, knocking me to the floor. He then kicked me in the ribs while I was down. Facedown in the dirt, he grabbed the back of my tank top and lifted me up and spoke into my ear,

"Your kind makes me fucking sick. Do you think you'll survive Los Furiosos? Not while I'm still breathing, bitch." He then pushed my face into the ground.

His parting gift for me...he kicked me in my thigh with his steel-toed boot. I let out a shriek, and the men who were ahead looked back.

"Get up, you fucking faggot."

"Neil, that's enough." One of the men yelled.

A few of them ran down to stop him. I grabbed at my thigh and ribs, trying to catch my breath. The Los Furiosos who came down promptly raised me to my feet, as I began coughing uncontrollably.

"Neil, take a fucking hike." One of the men shouted at him.

Neil stormed off up the hill and began shouting at the other men ahead of him to keep moving.

"Are you all right?" one of the guys asked. "You can still walk, right?"

I started to walk and had a slight limp. "I'm okay." I motioned for them to keep moving. I wasn't sure why they were asking if I was okay. It seemed like the majority of them wanted us all dead.

"Don't pay attention to Neil. He has a thing against Faeries like you. Once we get you implanted, you will become a brother just like the rest of us." He reassured me.

I didn't want to become a brother. I just wanted to go home to Liam and be free of this place. They let me walk but still had their guns on me. We continued up the hill, and I could see the men trickle into another building. This time the building was more put together than the last. It almost looked like a miniature emergency care facility. I made it to the door, and there was a plaque on the front that read 'Optic's #1' The door was made of steel that had a small window. I opened the door and could feel the difference in weight.

As I walked in, the other newbies were being taken left and right into different rooms. The entrance of the building was set up like a lobby, complete with a female receptionist. The room was so clean, and I felt out of place because of how filthy I was. It was definitely a medical facility because even the woman in the front was dressed in a white lab coat. I still couldn't get over the silver-haloed eyes behind her glasses. Her dark hair was up in a ponytail as she held a silver clipboard.

As I was escorted to the front of the desk, I could see one of the doors was open that went into a room where my Russian comrade was taken. He was lying back in a chair that was reclined. Another man in a lab coat was examining his eyes. The man in his lab coat pulled out a syringe that had a clear liquid in it. He held the Russian man's arm and injected him with the needle. I wasn't sure what they were putting into him, but it couldn't have been good.

"Alec Everly is his name," he told the receptionist.

She went to the computer and started to input my information. As she did, I was focused on watching them implant the Russian man. I could see his eyes droop and the man in the lab coat pulled out a silver cylinder device and placed it behind the man's head. The woman behind the counter noticed I was looking into the room. She quickly walked out from behind the desk and went over to close the door.

The woman spoke softly, "He's entered into the system now, but there was a notification that Dr. Jericho wanted to see him before he is implanted. One of you must escort him to a secure location and wait until Dr. Jericho arrives."

"Where do we take him exactly?" the man asked, obviously wondering why I needed to be seen by Dr. Jericho first.

"Dr. Jericho prefers somewhere private. He will be able to find you with geolocation. He requested that Neil escort him and they both wait for his arrival."

"Why Neil? That's probably the worst idea."

The woman interjected swiftly. "I take orders and don't ask questions. It's per Dr. Jericho's request. If there is an issue, you can take it up with him. Just know it will be your head on the chopping block, not mine. Carry on." She motioned us away and took a seat at her desk.

The man looked annoyed and then whistled using his fingers, motioning for Neil to come out of the room. Neil walked out and gave me a disgusted look before he responded to the other man, "What?"

"Dr. Jericho ordered you to escort the Faerie to a private location. It doesn't matter where, but you must wait for him to arrive. Keep your shit under control, that's all."

I had a bad feeling about this. A huge homophobe must wait with me in private? I started picking at my zip-tie hoping that it would loosen. Neil looked at me with no hesitation and yanked me by my arm. My leg was still in pain, and I tried to keep up with him without straining myself. Neil shoved the door open and pulled me through. The force of him yanking on me was doing a number on my ribs. I resisted, causing him to fall back. He landed on his ass and quickly got back up, aiming his rifle at me. I took a few steps back, inhaling deeply.

"I'm sorry...you're just hurting me. Could you please lay off a bit," I asked politely.

"I don't take orders from you, Faerie. Keep moving or I'll execute you where you stand." The level of seriousness in his voice as almost terrifying.

I knew he wasn't lying. He had a taste for blood, and it showed in his silver-haloed eyes. He motioned with his rifle for me to move. I nodded my head and continued in his direction. I knew this would end badly. My gut was telling me to watch my back with him. He had me hike up a hill nearby. There was a small cave in front of us. He nudged me forward. As we continued, I could hear the sound of a phone. Neil pulled out of his pocket a combination of a satellite phone and walkie talkie. He silenced the phone and put it back into his pocket. We were at the entrance of the cave now, and Neil pulled out a flint attached to a torch and struck it. The spark lit his torch, and he pulled me into the cave behind him.

Inside the cave was a firepit in the center and you could see a skylight at the top of the ceiling as moonlight poured in. Neil grabbed some wood that was near the firepit and placed it in the center. He held his torch to the wood as it began to catch fire and forced me to sit down on a rock. He walked to the entrance of the cave and stood to wait. While he was standing guard, I felt a sharp edge on the rock I was sitting on and I started to rub my zip-tie against it. Neil pulled out his combination device and radioed out.

"This is Neil, what's the location of Dr. Jericho, over?" he asked as he spoke into his device.

While I tried to cut my zip-tie in two, I could see Neil was carrying a makeshift axe that dangled from his belt on his right side. The shaft had a red wooden handle that had a laced grip that must have been white at some point in time, but now it was a dirty, dingy color. The blade of the axe was created from an old bike cassette, the 'teeth' of those circular discs that the chain of a bike switched between when shifting gears were perfect for this type of weapon, guaranteed to inflict a lot of damage. It must have been split into two halves and then welded back to back and placed at the handle's end. The cassette blades had at least ten to twelve rows on each side, and every tooth of the axe was sharpened to a point. As I continued to rub my zip-tie against the rock, I could feel it snap, and my hands were finally free from each other. I kept them behind my back to make it seem like I was still tied. While I continued to admire Neil's axe, he caught my gaze and quickly placed his device back into his pocket.

"What the fuck are you looking at?" he demanded, as he slowly started to walk toward me. "Why are you looking me up and down? Keep your fucking Faerie eyes off me because I don't like that shit." His voice got louder and echoed in the cave.

"You know it could be a while until Dr. Jericho comes. I don't see why I can't at least enjoy myself while we wait." His silver-haloed eyes began to pulse as he stepped closer to me.

This was my moment. I knew if I waited any longer, I would be implanted or even worse, killed.

Neil continued closer, flinching at me. I leaned back, and Neil started to laugh. He suddenly swung a punch at me. I ducked and threw my weight at him, wrapping my arms around his waist, tackling him to the floor. Neil got the wind knocked out of him. I swiftly straddled him and began to throw punches into his face and ribs. Neil reached up and started to choke me. I could feel my airway closing, and I grabbed his wrist, trying to loosen his grip. Neil shifted his weight to the left and rolled me over. He had me on my back now and began whaling on my face with his fists.

"You think you can fucking take me, bitch?" Neil yelled as he continued punching me in the face.

I could feel the impact of every punch he threw as my head was being tossed left and right, over and over. He stopped and began to strike me in the stomach. My head was pounding now, and I was losing my breath from every blow. Neil wrapped his hands around my neck again and started to choke the life out of me. Neil was enjoying himself as my eyes started to roll back into my head.

This was the end. I was losing too much oxygen. I only had one shot...I reached for a nearby rock that was almost lodged into the fire.

"Die, you fucking faggot!" Neil was shouting as his grip around my throat got tighter.

My hand was on the rock, and I could feel it burning as I grasped it. I grunted as I raised the stone into the air with what energy I had left and struck Neil on his head. His grip loosened as I took in a gulp of the much-needed oxygen. I raised my left leg up and over his chest and pulled him back, slamming his spine onto the floor. I dropped the rock because the heat of it was burning my hand. Neil was on his back, and I could see he was clutching his head as blood was rushing out of it. My breathing quickened, and my heart was racing as I crawled over to him. I reached for the scorching hot rock again and pressed it against his face. Neil began to scream in distress, as did I because the stone was not only burning his face but also my hand.

I couldn't bare the heat any longer. I raised my arm and used all of my strength to bash Neil in the head with the rock. Neil lost consciousness. I dropped the stone instantly. What have I done? Did I kill him? He can't be dead, I thought to myself. But better him dead than me. I was straddling him now, and I started to shake his body, trying to keep my wits about me.

"Neil?" I said, "Neil, wake up."

You can't be dead. I don't kill people. I'm not a killer. I told myself this over and over again.

"Neil, wake up." I yelled as tears started to form in my eyes.

My heart was racing because I think I killed him. I would never kill anyone. He must be unconscious, I told myself. I stood up from his body. The fire was dancing near me, casting a silhouette of my body in the cave. My hands were shaking. Someone was going to find him here, and they would come after me. I looked down at his axe and cautiously approached it. I stopped as I reached for it, taking a deep breath in and looking at Neil's body. I grasped its handle.

Neil suddenly awoke.

He reached for my ankle, throwing my balance off, causing me to fall to my knees.

"I'm going to fucking kill you, bitch!" Neil yelled.

I swiftly raised the axe into the air. I shut my eyes and screamed. I brought the shaft down with full force while gripping the handle with both hands, plunging the blades deep into Neil's throat. Blood sprayed onto my face as Neil's screams stopped and turned into gurgling. I opened my eyes and pulled the axe out of his throat. I quickly backed away from Neil as he wrapped his hands around his neck. I shook in fear as he struggled to breathe while twitching in place. He stared me in the eyes as he struggled for air. Every inhale he took bubbled in blood. I dropped the axe next to my knees and held my hands over my mouth and nose. The sounds of him trying to survive made me quiver in place.

The sounds he made began to silence. His eyes were still open. The fire in the background crackled and continued to dance. The tears in my eyes grew, and I continued to clench my mouth shut. The sight of Neil's dead body began to haunt me. A life that I took to spare my own. I saw a man take what was his last breath because of me.

I killed someone.

The proof before me caused me to lean over and vomit.

4: EXECUTIONER

FORCEFUL WINDS SWEPT INTO the cave. The air had a hint of sea salt as it swirled in the obscurity of the cavern. The fire that Neil had started was stagnant now, and the ash began to trickle down fluidly as if it were snow in the moonlight. There was an intense iron smell while the air circulated back and exited the cave. Remnants of the blood smell tinged the air as it flowed toward me. I held my knees to my chest with my back against the cold cavern surface. My mind was playing tricks on me. I almost anticipated that Neil's body would move and he would attack me again, but he laid there entirely still as flies began to hover over his body.

I couldn't help but shiver as I stared at Neil. Seven years of working in the Peace Corps, promoting and maintaining peace is what I stood for. Everything I was known for doing, in a snap, was destroyed in a split second of self-defense. Would there be an understanding jury as I pleaded my case in front of a judge? Would Liam look at me the same? Would my mother stand by her son knowing that he is a murderer? How could Ann stand the sight of me after learning, what I was capable of doing? I sat there, numb. Who was I kidding? I was never getting off this island. My life was laid out for me now, surrounded by other men who have also killed. Some, like me, could have said it was self-defense, and others would say that they did it because they just wanted to.

I turned my eyes away from Neil, conflicting emotions taking over. I could hear the voices of my loved ones, telling me about all the good that I had in me.

"If your father were here now, he would be so proud of you," said my mom.

"It just gives me hope that there is still love in this world," Ann said.

"But I feel like you could've been bigger than you thought," said Issac.

Then Liam's voice spoke to me. My Liam.

"This is about us now."

"Us?" I said to myself. If Liam saw me now, there would be no us. I fought back the tears, what the fuck had I done? I put my face in between my knees and began to break down when suddenly, the silence was broken.

"Neil, what's your location? Over."

My head shot up as I pressed my back against the wall, trying to hide behind a boulder.

"Neil, the location of your implant has stopped. What's your location? Over." The man voiced again.

I peeked around the rock I was hiding behind. I didn't see anyone, my only company was Neil's body, and I could hear the crackling sound of a radio. The voice spoke again.

"Anyone have Neil's position? Erico and Dr. Jericho need him for the gathering. Over."

The voice was coming from Neil's corpse. Right then, I remembered the satellite phone he had been using earlier and crawled over to Neil to search for it. I felt nauseated as I got closer, but I had to see for myself. I rustled in his pockets and pulled out the phone. The device had a small screen with a set of numbered buttons.

"Thank God." I exhaled. "I need to call for help."

I looked at the phone's interface. It was an unusual device — both a walkie talkie and a phone? Definitely wasn't familiar with this device. I went through the call history and saw that there had been no calls made or received. Interesting... The signal bars indicated that there wasn't a strong connection, and that's probably why calls never came in or went out. The bigger question is, who would I call? The police? I knew that the number for the police in this country was different, and for the life of me, I couldn't remember what it was. Of course, I remembered that Neil's dead body was underneath me, so I certainly didn't need the police finding me. I needed someone who could help, someone who knew me and would come to help no matter what. I needed Liam. The thought of him rejecting me because of what I'd done —what I had no choice but to do — disintegrated into thin air. Liam knew I wasn't a murderer, and he knew I would never do something like this unless I was clearly provoked. I had no choice, I had to call him.

"Please pick up. Come on, Liam, pick up," I repeated.

"Lost connection, please try again later," an automated voice said.

"Shit."

I started to pace around the cave, hoping to find a stronger connection. The bars weren't moving at all. I began to walk toward the entrance of the cave. As I stood in the entrance, the wind whipped around my face. I could see lights not too far down below, along with many people gathering and others continuing to work. It was hard to make out because they were so far away. I saw people coming and going from Optic's #1 and I swiftly hid behind the wall to make sure they couldn't see me. I looked back at the phone and it had two bars. I immediately started to call Liam again. The phone was ringing longer this time.

"Liam, please," I said with tears in my eyes as I continued to check around the corner to make sure no one was coming. The tone stopped ringing.

"Hey, it's Liam."

"Oh, my God. Liam, it's me. I need help. I..." I stopped.

"I can't make it to the phone right now, but leave a message, and your number and I'll get back to you as soon as possible. Thank you. Bye."

It was Liam's voicemail.

The sound of a beep went off.

"Liam, it's me." I began to sob, "Baby, I need your help. I'm on an island somewhere that's overrun by a gang called Los Furiosos." I hesitated because I wasn't sure how to tell him I killed someone. "They tried to kill me, and... I had no choice but to fight back... I'm not okay..."

The phone cut out.

"FUCK!" I shouted into the cave.

I had a feeling that the message would be choppy because the phone kept skipping while I was talking. All I hoped was that Liam would get the message and that hopefully he would be able to figure out where I was.

"Everyone report to Island Pointe. Erico is welcoming our new recruits. Over." The voice spoke over the walkie.

This could be the perfect time to escape. If everyone was meeting at Island Pointe, wherever that was, then maybe it would make it easier to get a boat and get the hell out of here. I looked back at Neil. I wouldn't get far without weapons. They made that inherently clear. And if these people were out to kill me, I knew what I would have to do to survive.

I walked over to Neil's body, his eyes were still open, and that tell-tale silver halo in his eyes was gone. His natural eye color showed, and it was now a lifeless golden brown. He certainly didn't need these weapons any longer, so I started taking them. He carried a handgun that looked similar to mine. Holy shit, it is mine. When they brought me back to the island, he must have somehow gotten his hands on it. I removed the clip, and it was still fully loaded — eight bullets in the mag and one in the chamber. I lifted Neil's body so I could remove his holster, that allowed him to carry the gun under his left armpit, and under his right was a pouch that held one magazine. I noticed the mag was full of ammo, too. Perfect.

As I was gearing myself up, I realized that Neil's implant was no longer flashing. Did him being alive serve as the power source? Very strange, I thought. After arming myself, I continued to search his pockets. I found a knife that had a flint screwed in at the bottom of the handle. I removed it and placed it behind my back, underneath my belt. A pair of tiny binoculars were in his back pocket, so I took them and put them in mine. All that was left was the assault rifle that laid next to him. I grabbed it and stood up, slinging it over my left shoulder.

I looked at Neil one last time, shaking my head as a rush of guilt washed over me. Resigning myself to the fact that I'd killed this man, I turned and walked toward the entrance of the cavern. A reflective item caught my eye. The axe was still in the same place that I'd dropped it. I walked over and grabbed it. The feeling of my first kill rippled through my body as I gripped its handle. I controlled my shaking hands and started to walk back to the entrance. As I stood in the cave opening, I looked over what Los Furiosos had built.

"You can do this, Alec," I whispered as the fresh air blew against my scalp.

I pulled out the binoculars from my pocket, needing to get a handle on my surroundings and best means of escape. As I looked through, I realized that the binoculars were more high-tech than I thought. The lenses allowed me to see incredibly far and displayed a distance and elevation setting in the upper right-hand corner. I turned my head and faced Optic's #1. Some men were leaving the building and heading down toward what must have been Island Pointe. Erico was pacing back and forth on what appeared to be a stage made of timber. Someone was also on the stage with him wearing a lab coat. I was just barely able to make out a name tag on his white coat.

"Dr. Jericho," I whispered to myself. "Hmm, you were the one who separated me from the group. Why?" I inquired as he began to walk past the panther's enclosure.

"I guess she didn't get out," I paused while admiring her. "I hope one of us does," I said as I could see her bare her fangs at the doctor. I turned toward where the trail was that I needed to take to get to the beach to escape this island. I couldn't see the path because from my vantage point, the trees concealed it. I couldn't even see the beach from here. Lowering the binoculars, I knew I had to get closer. It was the only way for me to make sure the coast was clear on the beach. Putting the binoculars away, I grabbed the assault rifle. The weight alone made me feel uneasy. After checking the mag, I placed it back and cocked the gun. The sound was loud, and it made my stomach turn. I took a breath and started to make my way down the mountain. As I walked, I could feel the axe graze my right leg as it dangled. It was slightly annoying, yet also comforting, because it steadily swung while I walked, reminding me it was there.

I wasn't far off from Optic #1, and I wanted to remain unnoticed as I hid amongst trees the closer I got. I was at least fifteen yards from the building now and my heart quickly elevated. Stalking through the trees, I made sure my steps were weightless. Hiding in the shadows, avoiding any moonlight that streamed through the leaves, I crouched while I walked, remaining hidden in the darkness of Candelario's wilderness. Suddenly the front door flew open, and three men walked out, obviously in good spirits as they laughed with one another. I stopped in my tracks and squatted behind a tree, peeking out, hounding Los Furiosos. I held my breath as if they could hear my exhale if I didn't.

"Hey, have you guys seen Neil?" one of the men asked. My anxiety ramped up ten-fold because I just knew that my ability to escape was a on a fast countdown.

"The last I heard, he was taking the Faerie to a private location to meet Dr. Jericho," another faceless man answered.

"Wait, isn't Dr. Jericho at Island Pointe?" He paused. "Neil was ordered to take him somewhere private? And that's far from private. You don't think Neil and the Faerie are...you know?" He started to make sexual motions with his hands while laughing.

"Oh, my God. You are a sick man. Neil would never. He probably took him up the hill, and maybe Dr. Jericho is going to meet them up there later."

"Dr. Jericho wouldn't have made them wait this long. Something isn't right. I'll check to see if they are up there. I'll meet back up with you guys at Island Pointe. Tell Erico what I'm up to because I don't want him bitching at me later."

"All right, don't take too fucking long," one of the men replied as both of them started to walk down to Island Pointe.

The man motioned them away and turned in my direction. I moved slowly around the tree, trying not to make a sound as he walked past. He didn't see me, but I could see him. I gently started to exhale as he began to make his way up the hill.

"Shit," I whispered, my escape had to be now or never.

Once he found Neil dead and I was nowhere around, they would come looking for me. As he continued to walk, I checked behind me to make sure no one was around. I tip-toed after him, attempting to catch up. I reached for my axe, it needed to be a silent kill. I was two steps behind him now, and I raised the axe as I stepped closer, A twig snapped underneath my boot and he stopped in his tracks. Damnit.

He instantly spun around as I brought my axe down full force into his skull. He grunted and fell to the floor. His body was twitching as he laid there. I looked around to see if anyone had spotted me. It was terrifying to me how easy my second kill was. I felt myself becoming callous to the noises he made. I put my foot to his chest for leverage and gripped the handle, yanking it from his head. Blood streaks were on my pants, and I had a feeling of gratification, or was it the victory of survival? He was done for while the adrenaline coursed through my veins, causing my eyes to well up.

Another man dead, but at this moment I knew it was better him than me. I started to pull the man's body into the trees as I began to advance past Optic's #1, heading toward the Stylist shack, where Alejandro had buzzed all my curls off. Voices talking in the distance gave me pause, and I took shelter in the trees. I continued moving forward, looking behind me to make sure no one followed. The closer I got, the louder the voices became. The odor of cigarettes so strong as I went around the back of the shack, seeing two men outside. Their voices were almost drowned out by the sound of a machine in the distance. A generator? There was a dim green light, just like the one at the front of the shack, near the back door.

I leaned against the wall while I attempted to peer around the corner without being noticed. Alejandro and his comrade were both taking a drag from their cigarettes. Alejandro had a gasoline tank in his hand and was talking to his comrade. I had nothing but fury in my eyes for him. They laughed and joked about something that was hard to hear over the sound of the generator. Alejandro walked over to the machine and filled it up with gas.

"Stupid," I said to myself because he had a lit cigarette in his mouth as he poured the gasoline, and small embers fell from the tip of it and landed in the dirt. The asshole could've blown this whole place up. Alejandro set the can down, and he and his comrade went back into the shack. My resentment for Alejandro and what he'd done to me back at the shack only grew as I continued to listen to him chuckle indoors. I marched over to the gas can. I didn't want to make a scene, but enough blood had been shed. It was clear that Los Furiosos had a particular way of running things around here, and I was picking a fight now as I looked back at the shack and then to the gas can.

"You messed with the wrong fucking Faerie," I said as I seized the can of gas and walked over to the shack. I was frightened, but

I also knew that I had to fight back. Who would be executed next if I didn't stop them? I thought of Liam and knew if he were in my situation, he would probably do the same. I started to drench the back of the shack with gas and made a trail of gas from the back steps of the shed and continued to walk toward the generator. There wasn't much gas left at this point as I poured the remains around the generator.

"There are consequences to all of your actions," I said as the last few drops fell from the container.

I set the can back where I found it and began to make my way back to the shack. The back door of the shed opened abruptly, hitting the scrap metal wall behind it and causing the green light to turn off for a moment. I hid on the side of the shack as the sickening aroma of tobacco drifted through the air. They came outside and started sparking up their lighters. I knew it was time to get the hell away from the shack. Within a few minutes, I'm sure whoever was smoking would be tossing their cigarette into the now gasoline-soaked dirt. I quickly moved to the front of the shack, getting as far away from the building as possible.

"Where are you going, Abraham?" A jeering voice came from behind me.

I stopped in my tracks. Had I been caught? I continued looking forward as he spoke again.

"Are you going to Island Pointe?" That sounded like Alejandro.

I didn't say anything. Speaking would blow my cover. Alejandro thought I was some guy named Abraham so I just nodded my head, avoiding any reason to talk.

"All right, well, meet back here so we can find Neil," Alejandro said as he opened the door and went inside.

Taking a large inhale, I knew I was pushing it. I could see Island Pointe, and there were hundreds of men down below circling the wooden stage that Erico and Dr. Jericho were standing on. I could hear Erico's voice echo as he spoke, he must have been using a microphone for the sound to carry this far. Running down the hill, crouching behind old crates, I reached for my binoculars so I could see what was happening.

Erico continued to speak, "We have vast plans ahead of us, which is why we have been recruiting so much more. If you didn't already know, our financial success has hit its peak, and with our implants being spread across the world, it's only a matter of time before those who are implanted will soon be under our control." Erico paused as the crowd started to applaud.

He walked over to a silver suitcase and opened it. "Now we know we have numbers, but we also need strength. And with Dr. Jericho's recent discoveries, he has finally fabricated something that will bring us all up a notch." Erico eyed Dr. Jericho.

Erico removed a silver vile from the case and started to walk toward the edge of the stage. He was looking at the panther that was still in her cage.

"Take her away," he ordered the men who were near her enclosure.

The men began to place bamboo sticks through the cage and started to lift. Erico turned his attention back to the crowd, "Without further ado, I present to you Chromosome H." Erico held the silver vile in the air as if it were some holy grail.

"What the hell is that?" I said quietly as I viewed it from afar.

A silver protective barrier encased the vile. Then the barrier soon split into two and retracted into the top and bottom of the case. The vile now looked like it was made of silver liquid that glistened in the moonlight. The men in the crowd started to cheer, and I could see Dr. Jericho was slowly clapping his hands with the group. Inside the vile was the shape of a V that glowed from within, which made me question why it was called Chromosome H when it looked like a V? Erico began to speak again.

"Once injected, Chromosome H will bond with your genetic structure, changing your DNA as you know it. Giving you incredible speed, strength and agility." The crowd started to get overly excited, and all were looking at one another very enthusiastic. "We will be unstoppable. And with our newfound abilities, no one will stand in our way. It is our time to reign." The crowd went wild in agreement.

Suddenly, my walkie began buzzing.

"Alert. Alert." A voice repeated over the walkie.

I lowered my binoculars and held the walkie up to my ear, trying to hear over the group of men.

Erico continued to speak on the stage. "This may be our holy grail; however, Dr. Jericho believes that there may be more to our salvation at hand. Someone whom we have recently brought to our island on this very night holds such promise. Dr. Jericho, please let them in on the news." Erico took his earpiece out and handed it to Dr. Jericho.

My walkie went off again.

"Alert. We have a major alert." The voice continued over the walkie.

Dr. Jericho began to speak to the crowd.

"Thank you, everyone. Chromosome H is just a taste of what we will become. However, we can grow into something much greater. We have recently captured an extraordinary recruit. And I believe this recruit is the missing link to increasing Chromosome H's effects." The crowd started to cheer again.

My walkie sounded once more.

"Neil is dead. I repeat, Neil is dead. And the Faerie has escaped. I repeat. The Faerie has escaped."

"Shit." Time to go.

I looked back through my binoculars and could see Erico look up from the metal case. Dr. Jericho continued.

"Our recruit's blood could be the key to our evolution. The Faerie's blood..."

Dr. Jericho was interrupted as Erico snatched the earpiece from him.

Suddenly, a loud explosion dulled everything else around me. The Stylist Shack erupted as fire and smoke filled the air. Debris began to fall as scraps of metal rained down around the crowd of men. The explosion was so violent that the men carrying the panther lost grip of the cage, causing them to drop it. The cage flung open and the panther finally ran out. She began to claw at one of the men who transported her as she fought for her freedom.

A large portion of metal landed on the crates that I hid behind. The sound of the crates breaking was enough to cause stares.

Suddenly, all eyes were on me.

The silver haloed eyes staring at me all began pulsing. The men grinned at me, almost ravenous, waiting for the order. I was in deep shit, and I could see Erico from the stage place the earpiece back in his ear.

"TEAR THE FAERIE APART!" Erico screamed as his voice reverberated over the panther's roar.

Dr. Jericho grabbed Erico by the arm, and I could faintly hear him saying, "No."

Immediately, I could see the panther begin to run off. The men started to remove their weapons from their holsters. Gunfire broke the silence as rounds began flying all around in my direction.

I had to get the hell out of there.

I ran, ducking behind anything that would shield me in an attempt to avoid the bullets. I continued to run toward the trail that we took from the beach. Men were yelling and breaking off into groups as they scattered to hunt me down. I sprinted through the trees, trying to keep close to the path. I retrieved my assault rifle off my shoulder and carried it in both hands, unhesitant to pull the trigger on the next person I crossed.

I could feel the temperature of the air begin to drop as I began to get closer to the beach. Three men were gaining on me as bullets tore through the nearby woods.

"KEEP MOVING!" One of the men shouted to the others.

I stopped and hid behind a tree trunk, trying to catch my breath. The bullets were shredding through the tree I hid behind. I couldn't stay here much longer. I counted in between the shots that were being fired. Once one of them stopped, I took my opportunity. I stepped out of hiding and held my rifle to eye level. I aimed at one of the men that stepped out. Instantly pulling the trigger, hitting him in the head while his body collapsed to the ground while I swiftly went back into hiding.

"Oh, shit. I hit him," I said to myself, astounded at how natural the feeling of shooting a gun was to me now.

"Move up!" One of the men shouted, and I could hear their footsteps advancing closer. I moved, letting off six rounds in their direction. I shot another man in his shoulder, and I could overhear his shrieks while he cursed at me.

"Damn. He's a good shot." I overheard one of the men say.

"Bring it, motherfuckers," I shouted over their gunfire.

Reaching for my axe, one of the men was coming up toward the tree I was hiding behind. I circled the tree, wanting to get behind him. Shots were fired as I raised my axe into the air and struck him in the back.

"How do you like this Faerie now, son of a bitch!" I yelled, reveling from my attack.

Pulling the shaft, he squealed and promptly hit me across the face with his rifle. I fell to the floor while he aimed at me. As I was down, I swung my axe at his rifle before he fired a shot.

"Not today." His gun flew into the woods as I quickly booted him in his leg, causing him to fall.

I mounted him, using the handle of my ax to crush his esophagus. He struggled to try to loosen my grip while I screamed, pressing all my weight upon the shaft more in-depth into his throat.

"Die, you mind-controlled freak." Suddenly I heard a snap, the man stopped struggling. I must have broken his neck because his breathing shallowed, the silver halos in his eyes evaporated.

I stood up and started to break for the beach again because I knew it was only a matter of time before more of them would be coming. A shot was fired, simultaneously I yelled in pain, crashing to the ground. A bullet had torn through my inner thigh.

I screamed again while holding my leg. "FUCK!" I looked down and could see it was a clean shot, but I was losing blood, and fast.

Relying on my instinct for survival, I took my belt off to make a tourniquet around my thigh. I grunted in agony as I tightened it, but the adrenaline was pulsing through my arteries, and I needed to move. I threw my now-empty rifle into the woods and pulled out my 1911. I was slowly making progress toward the beach now as I could see the flicker of torches through the trees with every stride I took. My leg was hurting, my heart was racing, and I felt the urge to vomit as I kept pushing toward the beach as the scent of sea salt saturated the air.

Once I was free from the jungle, groups of men were surrounding the dock and pacing back and forth on the beach. Waiting. There was no way in my current state that I could make it to freedom. Few boats floated near the dock, perfect for an escape, but I knew that if I stepped foot out of the trees I would be executed.

"What should I do? Come on, Alec," I said to myself.

As I looked over to my left, I didn't see anyone in sight, and there was no way I could go back. I chose to go left, staying hidden in the trees for as long as I could. The sun was starting to rise and the view was breathtaking. I kept moving forward, and as I did, the elevation increased and my walkie began to vibrate.

"Any sight of the Faerie? Over." Erico's voice asked.

"Nothing yet."

"Some of you stay behind and keep looking. He couldn't have gotten far. There's no way he would survive the ocean. He's not going anywhere. The rest of you head back to Treetop and get some rest. We will continue to look later. Over." Erico was determined to find me.

With the combination of the higher elevation and the blood loss, I started to get nauseous. I knew that I didn't want to risk being out in the open, it was too dangerous. I had to find shelter so I could rest and try to figure out what to do from here. Luckily, I noticed that there was an entrance to a cave up ahead.

"Thank God," I said as I quickened my step.

Making my way to the cave as quietly as I could, I noticed that it was empty but that it must have been used by someone because there was a fire pit that had been dug in the ground. There were dead shrubs that were still somehow hanging on between the cracks of the walls that I thought would be easy to burn. I walked over and started to pull them out one by one. With every pull, my energy was depleting. I managed to get a large bundle and limped over to the pit and tossed them in. I used my flint and my knife to make a fire. I lowered myself to the floor, exhausted, hungry, a little bit of every physical and emotional feeling hitting me all at once. I reached down to loosen my belt. Once the belt was off, blood continued to pour out. I took my knife and tore a piece off of the lower portion of my tank top. I placed the blade on a rock near the fire.

I held the material against my wound to stop the bleeding. As I sat in the hollow, my mind started to wander. I thought about Los Furiosos taking over the world. I imagined how it would be if they did — the amount of suffering they had already caused me; I could only envision what it would be like for others. The fire started to turn my blade red hot. I knew what I had to do to stop the bleeding. I felt myself losing consciousness and I needed to hurry before I bled to death. I reached for the knife, with shaking hands, and held the blade into the air. The edge resembled lava while my vision blurred.

"One...two..." the tears were beginning to flow down my face because I knew this was going to be a bitch. "...three."

The sounds of my burning flesh mimicked the same tone as my branding did as it singed my skin. I couldn't bear the pain any longer and lifted the blade. My vision started to fade. The bleeding had stopped as I fell to the floor. I could hear the faint sounds of my heart beating as the fire in my eyes faded into obscurity.

Changing in the locker room of Toronto High School, chuckles of the wrestling team echoed in the distance. Here we go again, I thought, as I adamantly switched out of my gym uniform and into my casual attire.

"Well, well," Grant said, as he and his teammates walked toward me. "Still being a voyeur, Everly?"

"Still being a Neanderthal?" I retaliated.

"Funny, keep your eyes off my jock, cock sucker."

"Not a lot of fruit in those looms to see anyway."

Grant fumed, grabbing my t-shirt and shoving me against the lockers. His teammates flaunted his ego, feeding into his aggression.

"Three against one, that's big of you." Turning my head away from Grant's severe halitosis.

Grant landed a blow across my face, warm blood could be felt leaving my lips.

"I'll show you big...bet you've wanted to suck this dick after seeing me in the showers?" Grant looked back to his boys before saying, "You like taking it up the ass, don't you?"

"Why? Are you interested?" Giving his closeted thoughts attention, knowing my comments would only piss him off more.

"Shut your fucking mouth!" He shoved my back into the lockers again.

"Hey! What's going on here?" Liam stormed into the locker room, making himself look bigger than he already was, towering over the three teens like a giant.

"Nothing, just making sure this queer keeps his eyes to himself," Grant said as he released me.

"Move along." Liam stood in front of me, blocking Grant's view of me.

He scoffed while he and his friends walked out of the locker room.

"Are you okay?" he asked, rubbing my shoulder as he sighed.

"I'm fine, go be with your kind... Liam." Swatting his tender hand off of me.

"Alec," he said, as I stormed off to the bathroom, glaring in the mirror.

My lip was busted as I turned on the faucet, washing the blood that lingered on my lips. Keeping tears at bay was tiresome because I knew that Liam meant well, but hiding his affection toward me was unfair — to me and to him. Gazing at my reflection, my busted lip healed in five minutes' time. Looking around, praying no one was in the vicinity and saw that, I concealed another secret that went beyond my sexuality.

I left the bathroom, nudging into Liam as I walked out.

"Your lip...it's healed up?" Liam questioned, astounded.

I didn't say a word, walking past him instead.

I woke hyperventilating, reaching for my handgun, aiming at the first thing that moved. A silhouette stood before me in the entrance of the cave. Is this a dream? A deer stood before me like a statue, noticed my movements and ran off. I took a deep breath and looked around. I was alone and felt slightly dizzy. I placed my gun back in its holster and tried to get up. I let out a moan of anguish. Once I moved, I could feel the overwhelming soreness in my leg. The cauterized area now looked pink and itched slightly. How long was I out that the wound was beginning to heal already? The silence of the cave was broken as my stomach let out a tremendous growl. I was starving and needed to find something to eat. Soon.

As I rose in search of food, I remembered Erico talking about Chromosome H. Then a flash of Dr. Jericho saying something about the Faerie's blood being the key. My blood? What did they know about me that I didn't? And why did they need my blood to help them? Things weren't adding up, but nothing made sense on this island. All I knew was that I needed to get out of here. I reached into my pocket and pulled out my walkie phone and started to dial Liam's number, praying my call would connect. There was no service as I let out a sigh of frustration.

If I couldn't get a call out, maybe I could get a radio frequency out? I could see that the walkie was set to channel two and I scrolled through other channels. Channel two was hopefully the only channel that the Los Furiosos used. I flipped to channel three and couldn't hear anything. I continued to channel four and five, still nothing. Channel six had some kind of static. The walkie was going in and out. Part of the sounds resembled words, and at times it sounded like music. Maybe someone was listening? I held down a button on the side of the phone, and the static stopped.

"Hello?" I said. "Is anyone there?"

I released the button, the sound of static continued.

"My name is Alec Everly, is anyone there? Over."

The static continued, and there was a slight fade in and out of a voice.

"Hello?" I said with hope. "Hello? Please, is anyone there? I need help. Over." I began to make my way to the edge of the cave.

The static was getting stronger, and the sound of the voice was clearer.

"Hello, my name is Alec Everly. I'm on an island called Candelario. I need help please. Over."

Suddenly the sound of a male voice came over the walkie.

"Alec Everly? Are you there? Over."

His voice had a familiar tone as if I spoke with him before. I was so overwhelmed to hear another person's voice. But then my excitement dulled. After everything, I knew I needed help, but was he trustworthy?

"Alec Everly. Do you copy? Over."

Could I trust him? Was it safe? What if he just wanted to find me and kill me? I held the button down to respond but then let it go. I took another deep breath. The voice on the walkie spoke again.

"Alec, I know you are there. I heard your call for help. I can help you, but I understand that you can't trust anyone right now." He paused for a second.

I remembered his voice.

The man at the bar wearing the hood, it was him. But even still, he was strange, and the fact that he disappeared when all the chaos broke out made me not trust him.

"I've been in your shoes before. Candelario is not a safe place. I've been there before, Alec." He paused again, "I'm sure you are starving and dehydrated. If you trust me, I can direct you to a place to get food and water. But you have to respond, Alec. Over."

Was it worth putting my trust into a stranger? I was starving and thirsty. He was right. Fresh water was essential, and there was no way I was going to find any water around here. I could hunt for food, but I was honestly so damn weak, I wasn't sure how far I'd get. I held down the button.

"What is your name? Over." I asked because if he knew mine, I should at least get to know his.

"I...I can't say, Alec. I'm sorry. Over."

"So much for trying to build trust. Over," I said, annoyed.

This guy was going to get me killed. He couldn't even tell me his name? How stupid did he think I was?

"If your mother knew who you were talking to, I'm sure she would want you to trust me. Over," he replied.

"What the fuck do you know about my mother?" I responded in a rage. "Don't even think about hurting her, you son of a bitch, because I WILL find you," I yelled into the walkie.

"I know about your brother, too...Colden Everly. I tried to help him, but he didn't trust me. I know where you're at Alec. If I wanted to kill you, Los Furiosos would have been there already. But that's not what I'm after. My agenda is to get you off that island alive. But only if you help me in return? Over," he asked as his voice remained calm, and for some reason, I knew I could trust him, but I had questions.

"Help you? And you know where I'm at? How is that? Are you watching me? Over," I said humorously as I started to spin around, looking in every direction.

"I triangulated your position using a satellite feed, and I can see you on my computer screen right now. Nice spin. Over." He responded as I started to walk back into the cave in alarm.

"What the fuck?" I whispered to myself, looking around at my surroundings.

"As I said, I don't want to hurt you or get you killed. But I need your help, and I know you need mine. Over." He spoke with seriousness in his voice.

"Where are you? Over." I asked, still concerned as I pulled my handgun out of my holster.

"I'm far away, off the coast of Chile. I have a boat with food, water, and medical supplies. But there's no way for me to get to you on the island. But I'm sure you knew that already," he paused for a moment. "There is a pond that is northeast of where you are that is safe to drink. And be quiet. You don't want Los Furiosos to hear you. Which, by the way, there are at least ten of them about sixty yards from you, Over."

I put my gun back into my holster and started to slowly walk out of the cave. The deer from earlier was grazing in a meadow ahead. My meal ticket, maybe not? Cooking the deer's meat could potentially alert Los Furiosos so I had to tread lightly. There had to be something else to eat, and I needed food and soon.

"Where is this pond? Over." I asked. If he wanted me to help him, he would have to help me first.

"Turn to your right as you exit the cave and continue for at least thirty yards. The area is clear and should be safe to navigate through. Over," he replied in confidence.

I continued to walk forward. Bugs flew through the air as I got closer to a pond. Through the trees was a decent-sized pond that so looked clear that I could see the bottom. There were some small fish in the water, but nothing substantial that I could eat. I leaned down while cupping my hands as I dunked them into the water, bringing my hands to my lips and starting to drink. It was clean, hopefully. But I was desperate. The water was surprisingly fresh, and I splashed the water over my face. What I would do for a shower right now. I started to splash water on my shoulders and arms and took another sip. I addressed my leg wound, cleaning it with water, hoping to stop an infection.

"How is your leg? Over." I started to find it annoying that he kept talking to me. We weren't friends. I continued to rinse my leg and drink more water.

"It's almost healed, isn't it? Over."

I was grateful that he was willing to help. How did he know about my family? And how did he know that my injury had healed as fast as it did? I pulled the walkie out and clicked the button.

"How did you know my leg was almost healed? Over."

"I...could see with the satellite feed. Over." Hesitation in his voice.

He was obviously lying. He knew about my mother and brother. It made me wonder what else he knew.

"There's no way you could have seen that. What do you know about me? Over," I asked.

He didn't respond.

This man seemed to know a lot about this place, but I didn't even know his name. I started to wrap my leg again and headed back to the cave. Before I entered the cave, I spotted berries growing on a nearby bush. Were they safe to eat? Picking them, the man spoke over the walkie.

"Magellan Barberries, safe to eat, not substantial, but should boost your energy. Over."

I took the berries, entered the cave and almost felt safe now. Whoever this guy was had my best interest, and I felt like I could say he could be trusted. But then again, he did mention that I had to help him, too. He held up his end so far. Scarfing down the handful of berries, my walkie started to vibrate, although this time it had a ringtone. I pulled it out of my pocket. The number made my heart race.

"Hello? Liam. Are you there?" I said, frantically. The phone kept cutting out, and I couldn't hear a single word he was saying.

"Liam, if you can hear me, I'm on an island called Candelario. Liam? Liam." The call dropped.

"Shit." I placed my head between my legs.

I needed to get out of here. All I could do was hope that he heard me. I stood up and started to pace back and forth while I rubbed my neck and shoulders. I didn't want to trust a stranger. But he did help me, and as of now, I didn't have a choice. I had to take control, and I couldn't be scared anymore. Everything I believed in had to be severed. And if I had to kill more people in order to escape, then that's what I would do. I started to walk to the edge of the cave.

"Hey, nameless guy. Are you there? Over," I said into the walkie. There was static.

"Listen, I need to escape from here. And you said I needed to help you, too... So, what do you want?" I spoke with hesitation in my voice.

"I'm here, Alec. I can get you off the island, but it's going to be very dangerous...for you. Over," he said with worry in his voice.

I held the button down and exhaled.

"What do I have to do?" I said regretfully as I rubbed my temples with my hand.

"I have a route set up for you, It's going to be a journey, and you might run into some trouble along the way. Can you handle that? Over." He sounded almost hopeful, like he knew I'd be fine.

I responded, "Let's hope... Where do I start? Over."

"First, you are going to have to pass through TreeTop. It's where Los Furiosos reside. It's the most dangerous area of the island, Alec. And I think you should start your journey after sunset. It would be better to have cover in the dark. Over."

"Okay. So pass through TreeTop? And that's it? Over," I said as I waited for his response.

"Not exactly, TreeTop isn't your conventional living quarters. All living spaces are suspended in the trees, and the ground below is camouflaged with landmines. Los Furiosos knew it would be safer to sleep at night, knowing they wouldn't be ambushed from below, their idea of hands-free security. Over," he said with angst in his voice.

"Landmines, are you serious? Over." Worry tingeing my voice.

I didn't even know what a landmine looked like, and I was to do what? Walk through them and get blown sky-high? So much for an escape plan.

"Don't worry, there are lasers on the ground, indicating where all the landmines are placed. Plus, you won't be on the ground floor... until you're about to leave TreeTop. You can do this, Alec. I know you can." He continued, "Once you navigate through TreeTop, you are going to have to go into the Cimmerian Tunnels. This part is crucial because once you are inside, I won't be able to stay in contact with you. The tunnels are too deep. Over."

I started to worry. "What if I get lost? Over."

"You won't. The Los Furiosos put signs up on the inside of the tunnels so they wouldn't get lost either. And if you do, follow the generator lines. They eventually leave the tunnel at some point. Over."

The thought of being trapped in a tunnel made me feel claustrophobic.

He continued to speak. "When you are in there, Los Furiosos used C4 explosives to carve their way deeper into the tunnels. Alec, I need you to gather as much C4 as you can. This is where I need your help. Over."

I began to scratch my head. "Why do I need C4 exactly? Over."

"Alec, I can help you. But you are going to have to help me. I need you to blow up a lab on the island before I can save you. I know it sounds crazy, but you have to understand... The research these men have gathered is hazardous. If it ever gets out, billions of innocent people will be killed. Can you do that? Over."

I thought for a moment, the fact that I was on a potential suicide mission was more than enough to have me feeling overwhelmed. Now I was to destroy a lab and get away with it scot-free like I was a secret agent? I didn't know what to say. I just wanted to go home to Liam. I looked down at my ring. It had small blood spatters on it along with mud. I wanted to be in Liam's arms again, away from these murderous people on this awful island.

"Alec, are you there? Over," he asked in hopes that I would respond.

The clock was ticking, and daylight was burning.

"I'm here," I said and paused before I continued, still unsure of what I was going to say. "I, umm...I'll do it," I said hesitantly, "Over." My fate was sealed. I rubbed my chin and lips as I looked around. Part of me knew I didn't know what I was doing. And the other part wanted this island and these people to burn to the ground.

"All right... You can do this. Once you have the explosives in your possession, the last steps are to take the Bronze Channel Falls to the lab and place the explosives around the area. I'll walk you through setting a detonation. Then you will be able to make your escape on one of Los Furiosos's boats. They come and go all day, bringing new recruits. I will be waiting for you off the coast of the island, at a distance. Over."

"You won't be here to pick me up? Over."

"I can't, Alec, I'm sorry. It's not safe. I can't get too close because Los Furiosos are constantly circling the island. It's not exactly a search and rescue mission, but it's something. Over."

It sounded simple enough, but even still, Los Furiosos were out there. This was the best shot I had, and I was going to take it. I would rather die fighting than be taken alive.

"Okay, then. I can do this," I said, trying to sound convincing.

The wind blew the trees outside the cave as the sun continued to float across the sky. The more it moved, the more the anticipation grew. I sat down near the entrance of the cave, counting the purple flowers on the trees, trying to distract myself before it was time. My ring reflected in the sun as I looked down at it. Liam. The chance of seeing him again filled me with courage. The time on the island felt like years, and the idea of freedom made me realize that nothing in life was ever free.

Everything came at a price. The sun continued to drift across the sky, and soon it would be my time to pay.

5: TREETOP SHANTY TOWN

SILHOUETTES OF THE TREES outside remained to move gradually throughout the day. The cave was filled with a thin layer of smoke that smelled of tart wood. The temperature sweltered inside while I sat, sweating. Part of me wanted to go outside and get some fresh air, but I didn't want to be spotted by Los Furiosos. Once the campfire started to die I began to panic. I didn't want to give my time to dark thoughts because shortly I would be lurking through the trees of Candelario at night. I sat against a wall, trying to get comfortable, impatiently waiting for the sun to set.

I laid my axe across my thighs, grateful that it saved my life so many times. I felt on edge thinking that way. Some would say that guns kill people when really, people kill people. My axe didn't kill others; I did. Chunks of flesh were in between the teeth of the cassette blades. Blood and dirt streamed across the modules, covering up some of the rust that must have accrued over the years. How many others were killed before I obtained this axe?

I couldn't bear considering taking another individual's life. Los Furiosos seemed horrible, then again, I didn't think anyone should die. I set the axe to my side, attempting to take my mind off the matter. Sweat was developing underneath my ring. I took it off, thinking about Liam. The gold of the ring sparkled in the firelight. I closed my eyes and imagined Liam and I getting married.

Standing at the altar was Liam, in a gorgeous black tux. I wore a tux, too. White rose petals were raining down on us, and I could almost smell the sweet scent of them as they did. Liam came from such a big family, something that I never had. Liam's mother was a concise and petite blonde woman, who dressed very conservative. She had beautiful blue eyes and wrinkles as she aged with grace. Liam's father sat beside her. A very tall man, six foot three, just like Liam. His eyes were dark, salt and pepper hair. He had an incredible build for his age, and I learned where Liam got his figure. Liam's father was very conservative, he was a part of the Emerald Berets, too.

My side of witnesses were minimal. My mother was sitting wearing a lovely white dress. She smiled proudly at us while sitting next to Ann and Issac. Both of them looked incredible in my vision. Ann was glowing in a slinky black cocktail dress, her red hair was down in curls. Issac sat beside her, smiling at her while holding her hand. Issac was sporting a nicely pressed suit and fancy dress shoes.

I could hear the Justice of the Peace asking us to repeat after him. I turned back to Liam, grinning. We were finally going to begin our future together. As the Justice spoke the words 'For better or for worse,' I lost my smile, so did Liam. I held onto Liam's hands tightly because it felt like his grasp was slipping from mine. His face began to express deceit. I tried mouthing the words "I do," but I couldn't seem to get them out. I leaned in to kiss Liam, but before I could, I started to slip. I glanced down, a puddle of blood was underneath my dress shoes. I followed the trail of blood to a pile of bodies of men that I had taken the lives of. My heart accelerated. The scent of the sweet roses began to fade into a vile aroma of iron. My eyes went from the bodies to Liam's side of witnesses. Everyone could see it. Everyone knew what I had done. Liam's father shook his head with disgust, his mother had her hands covering her mouth and nose as she looked at the men I killed.

Mom? She couldn't stand the sight of me. Ann and Issac held on to each other with concern as if I were going to hurt them next. Liam? He let go of my hand. He didn't want me anymore, drifting away from me. I looked down at myself, my dress shoes faded into dirty boots. My dress pants started to peel away into thin air, revealing my bloodstained navy blue pants. My tux jacket was gone, I wore a ravaged tank top with blood and mud stains on it. My curly hair started to fall, bouncing off of my shoulders and chest, hitting the floor, sizzling in blood. I stood at the altar, holding my axe. The walls began to dissolve into rock, a fire pit dancing in the center. Friends and family disappeared, I was alone, back to reality.

My pocket started to vibrate.

"Alec, you there? Over."

I looked to my left and right, making sure that no one was around. I held the walkie up to my lips while my hand trembled. I held the button down.

"Yeah, I'm here. Over." I responded with apprehension in my voice.

"You ready? Over."

I looked up at the atmosphere with anticipation.

"Yes, I'm ready. I can do this."

"You've got this, Alec. No matter what happens, keep moving forward."

He paused, almost as if he hoped my spirits were lifting. They weren't. I just wanted to get the fuck out of here.

"The coast is clear for now. I need you to start traveling northwest. Alec, you must stay hidden within the trees. The route I have you on is going into the heart of Candelario. Over."

"How far am I supposed to go? Over."

"You're going to keep heading northwest for a while, wait until I say otherwise. There is going to be an incline and you will also see a trailhead. Stay off of it. Stay in the trees. Over," he said in a firm voice.

I continued my walk, and the farther I went, the darker the sky started to become. I saw the trail, stayed off of it, kept in the trees. I was beginning to build up a sweat and could feel the incline because my quads were on fire.

"Hey, can I ask you something? How do you know so much about this? Over," I asked with genuine interest.

"I, uh..." he started to respond yet seemed a little hesitant. "Well, I used to work for Los Furiosos. Over."

What the actual fuck? I froze in my tracks for a moment. I didn't know this guy and he could still be working for them, leading me into a trap.

The man spoke again. "I know that's not what you wanted to hear, but trust me, if I wanted anything to happen to you, Los Furiosos would be there in a heartbeat. Over." He tried to reassure me that he was on my side.

I had no choice but to trust him at this point. I wanted to know more.

"So why did you resign? Over."

"Once I learned what the Los Furiosos's agenda was, I wanted out. Over."

"Well, what is their agenda exactly? Over."

"I worked alongside Dr. Jericho. At first, he wanted to help people, but once he made his genetic discovery, he stopped at nothing trying to replicate it. His crusade involved killing anything and anyone in the process." He paused, like he didn't want to continue. "This genetic chromosome created could give individuals great capabilities. So much to the point that they would become unstoppable. Over."

"Capabilities? How do you mean? Over."

"Well, Dr. Jericho had hopes that it would increase a person's speed, strength, agility, and other genetic anomalies. Los Furiosos built a new arms race, and with this chromosome, they would become bulletproof. Their agenda was simple. Recruit as many followers as possible, give each of them these capabilities.

However, with such power, Dr. Jericho's fear was a revolt. Giving people that much power who could eventually turn against him."

Wiping my brow, the incline increased, causing me to sweat.

"Los Furiosos being completely controlled with altered genetics giving them all the power they could ever want. And with the numbers of people they are 'recruiting' they would become a powerful army and eventually take over the world. Los Furiosos believes that the world would be better off with fewer people. So I left. Over."

For some reason, I believed him because I would have left, too. But it made me wonder. Why was Erico showing off Chromosome H to everyone but hasn't given it to them yet? The men I came into contact with were tough, but nothing that appeared out of the ordinary.

"When I was at Island Pointe, Erico was saying something about Chromosome H. I've run into a few Los Furiosos men, and they don't seem superhuman. I don't think any of them have the chromosome yet. Over." I began to question Los Furiosos's logic. I mean, what were they waiting for if they had the magic pill to weaponize their army already?

Suddenly my walkie buzzed. "Alec, hide." The nameless man spoke with urgency.

Off in the distance, I could see signs of light flickering on the trail. The voices of men were echoing through the trees. Los Furiosos were coming, and it sounded like a lot of them. I quickly ran over to a fallen tree trunk and ducked behind it. The moonlight revealed bugs that feasted on the rotting tree as I proceeded to hide. The smell of it made me gag. As I hid, the footsteps and light grew closer. I could hear the men joke and laugh as they approached. As they came around the bend of the trail, I could see six men, all carrying torches and multiple assault rifles. Their silver glowing eyes reflected in the moonlight as they spoke.

"You better get to the lab before Erico sees." One of the men spoke to the man leading them.

The man responded, "I'm only flashing yellow. I should be fine. Besides, it will take forever to make it to the lab, and I'm not going out there alone with that panther roaming the island."

I almost forgot about her. She was free now, and that also meant that I should watch my back, too. I wish she knew I was behind her freedom. If only she did, maybe our possible interaction would not be as brutal.

The man responded. "Would you rather be shot in the fucking head by Erico, or take your chances with the panther?"

The guy leading them replied, "I would take on that panther any day. Erico can suck my fucking dick."

One of the men trailing behind started to laugh and said, "Leave that to the Faerie." They all started to laugh, it pissed me off.

I pulled my handgun from its holster as they continued to walk past me.

The last man walking started to talk to the rest. "Did you hear what Dr. Jericho said about the Faerie?"

The other men all said they didn't know as he continued. "He said if we find the Faerie, we are not to kill him. Some shit about his blood being pure." He stopped while looking around and spoke again.

"Hell, if that fucker comes shooting at me, I'm blowing his ass to bits." He shouted while he held up a shotgun.

I gripped my handgun firmly as rage fueled my eyes. I wanted to kill them all. But there were too many of them, and I would never make it off the island alive. They all laughed and continued to walk. The sounds of their voices and footsteps started to fade. And the light that guided them began to dim as they continued on the path. I wish I could light a torch of my own. My pocket buzzed, and the nameless man spoke.

"Alec? Are you okay?" He was obviously worried.

I pulled out my walkie. "Yeah, I'm fine, how much farther? Over."

"You are almost there. The path is clear. Over."

I stood up, deliberately looking around, the moon was the only light I could rely on as I proceeded to walk through the trees. It was hard trying to decipher which way was which because it was so vague. I just kept moving, I knew if I was heading the wrong direction that he would have said something to me by now. As I continued to hike, I began to wonder about Dr. Jericho's fascination with me. 'My blood being pure?' What did that mean? Part of me wanted to ask the man who was helping me. With his experience, I'm sure there was an answer. But with everything that was happening, I thought it best to stay quiet about the subject. Dr. Jericho wanted my blood. For whatever reason, he valued my life. I shook off the idea and focused on the task at hand. Before me, I could see a large black wall. It was hard to make out in the darkness, but the closer I got, the more detailed it became.

"What do I do now?" I asked myself and pulled out my walkie. "Hey? Are you there? Over."

I didn't know where I was, and I didn't want to risk being out in the open for too long.

"I'm here, Alec. I believe you are near the wall now? Over." He questioned but he knowingly had an exact location on me.

"Yes, I'm here. What now? Over."

"Well, I know you aren't going to like this..." He paused and continued. "Alec, you are going to have to climb from here. Over."

"Climb. Seriously? This wall is probably eighty-feet high." I responded loudly and quickly silenced myself because my voice echoed around me. I began to turn away from the wall. I wasn't sure I could do this, I mean, a vertical freaking wall. "There has to be another way. Over."

"Alec, I know it appears dangerous, but I've done this climb before. I know you can do it, too. If you take the trail into TreeTop, Los Furiosos would see you for sure. It's safer to climb. Over."

"Safer?" I scoffed. "Falling to my death? That's safe?"

"I understand, Alec. But it's either that or have an army of Los Furiosos after you. Over." He granted me no other choice.

I began to hear movement in the woods and the bushes nearby. I could feel the adrenaline coursing through my veins while my breathing started to get heavy. My palms were beginning to sweat, I could feel a tingling sensation in my limbs. There was no other choice, this wasn't like the climbing gym. There weren't safety harness and people to look after you if you fell. One slip and I would be done for.

"I don't know..."

I wanted to trust him. He got me this far, but could I trust myself? I needed to clear my mind because my hands were shaking now as I gripped the walkie. I needed a distraction before I lost it.

"Wh...Why won't you tell me your name?" I asked, while my voice shook.

"I, uh..." He paused with a tone of worry. "It's better if you don't know it for now."

I was about to face a life-or-death situation, and I thought knowing my helper's name would put me at ease. I couldn't continue to call him 'nameless guy'.

"What's the harm in a name? You know a lot about me and my family, it seems. Why is keeping your name a secret so important?"

"Alec, you must understand. If you knew who I was... I intend to help you make it off the island alive. You need to stay focused. There is a lot I want to tell you, but I can't...yet. I take responsibility for you being there."

I could hear regret and sorrow in his voice. I didn't understand. When I saw him at the bar, I was questioning Candelario, and I was bound to make it here regardless. It wasn't his fault I was on a mission to find my brother.

"Hey, if you can't tell me your name, that's fine. I was determined to get here, so it's not your fault." I sought to calm him now.

My hands were no longer trembling, and I turned to look back at the wall. "I'm going to have to give you a name. You've helped me this far and know the area pretty well. How about I call you... Atlas?"

He laughed before he replied, "Sure, Atlas is fine. Over."

I couldn't wait any longer, I had been out in the open for too long and I needed to move.

"All right, here goes," I said to myself and Atlas, there was no turning back now.

I put my walkie in my pocket and approached the wall. The moon was full and was the only light that kept the area illuminated. I reached up to feel for the first rock I could find. I hoisted myself up and began to find my footing.

"Just like the gym, Alec. Nice and easy."

I found talking to myself calming, it was better than climbing in silence. I reached for my next rock and continued to make my way higher up. The farther I climbed, the more confident I was becoming.

"Be careful. Over," Atlas said as I advanced higher in elevation.

I was taking my time because the terror of falling was racing through my mind. Given the situation, I found myself ascending with ease. I continued to breathe and could feel beads of sweat start to drip down my back. My arms and legs were beginning to burn as small pebbles trickled down from above, bouncing off my shoulders.

My walkie buzzed again and what he said almost sent me into a panic, "Alec. Stay where you are."

I held my position on the wall and tried to steady my breathing. I could hear male voices. I looked down below, my eyes widened.

"Oh, that's high, that's really high." I whispered to myself with my face pressing against the cold rock's surface.

Los Furiosos were getting close, and their voices were getting louder as they progressed. I looked back down, and I could see torches begin to come around the curve of the rock wall. Three Los Furiosos members were walking down below, two of whom were wearing dirty clothes, and one of them was sporting their signature military navy blue uniforms. As they passed below me, I could see the light of their torches and it almost revealed my position. My hands, arms, and legs were on fire, working to hold myself up. I was breathing heavily and could feel drips of sweat rolling down my arms.

"It's clear...move, Alec."

My limbs were getting fatigued as I started to climb again. I was nearing the top of the summit but stopped because I could see the edge of the cliff protruding out.

"Shit." I exhaled.

I never had to climb at an angle like that before. I stopped for a moment to relieve my hands, shaking them out one at a time and wiping the sweat on my pant legs. I pushed forward a few more feet, trying to find a suitable position before I had to climb horizontally. Judging by the distance, it was about an eight-foot overhang. The closer I got, the more I could hear my axe clinking against the wall with every move I made. My heart was beating in my throat as my hands were shaking every time I extended my arm to reach for a rock. I was directly under the overhang now, trying to find solid footing. I leaned back to get a better view of the horizontal cliff. Mid-lean I felt the rock under my left foot starting to give way, it broke from the wall and plummeted down below.

I clutched onto the wall, panicking. "Fuck!" I yelled.

My left leg was dangling now, and I couldn't find a good position to support it. Terrified, I could feel tears forming in my eyes.

"Please. Come on," I said as I trembled to find a position for my left foot.

After a moment, I raised my left knee almost to my chest and placed my foot on a sturdy rock to my left.

"You can do this, Alec. Come on. I know you can," Atlas spoke in support with a hint of worry.

I took a minute to rest while clinging to the wall. I shook my hands out once again. I couldn't believe how far I made it up.

Most would have fallen to their death by now. Then I started to tell myself to stop thinking about death before I had another panic attack. The breeze came over me, and I could smell petrichor in the air. A storm must have been coming as there were signs of dark clouds and sparks of lightning off in the distance.

I turned back to the wall and could feel the tension in my arms and legs begin to settle. It was time to move before the rain started to fall. That would bring another level of anxiety to an already-shitty day. I tilted my head up, finding my route for the horizontal climb. I reached above out past my head behind me and grabbed onto my first rock. I kept my breathing calm and began to twist my hips with every reach I made. The overhang of the wall was incredibly steep, and with every move, I could feel the overhang shake. I sprang to move faster now in fear of it breaking off. I was almost to the ledge, pleased with myself. I placed my right leg back on the wall and let my left leg dangle this time. I made one last twist of the hips. One last reach.

"Yes, Alec. You're doing it," Atlas said, cheering me on.

I let both legs dangle as I grabbed the edge of the overhang with my left hand. The wall started to buckle. I could feel it shake as I latched on with my right hand. I as much strength as I could to pull myself up. The ledge began to break. Cracks formed on the surface. On my knees, crawling as fast as I could, the shelf broke underneath me. I scrambled to my feet, the rest of the overhang began to crumble. I jumped, landing on my feet, then falling to my knees, rolling onto my left shoulder while I tumbled until I came to a stop. I could hear the sound of the overhang falling to the floor down below. It was so loud that I was certain Los Furiosos heard it, too. I was panting as I finally let myself fall to the ground kissing it, thankful that I survived.

With every breath I exhaled, I could see clouds of dust float into the air. As I laid there, I could hear the sounds of thunder echo over the island. There was a sharp object pressing up against my left side as I watched the clouds roll in while lightning from the storm struck the ocean in the distance.

"Alec, I can't believe you made it. Over."

I started to laugh as I forced myself up from the ground. I was on my knees now, inhaling the smell of the petrichor as it stung my throat with every gasp. I reached into my pocket to pull out my walkie.

"I know," I said in shock because I couldn't believe it myself. "I mean, if you could do it, I guess I could, too. Over."

Atlas responded with a mischievous tone, "I actually never did that climb before...but at least now I know that it can be done. Over."

I tilted my head up, "Oh my fucking God," I said to myself while shaking my head. I brought my head back down and started to rise to my feet. I could still feel the sharp object to my left, and I used it to raise myself.

"Are you serious? You lied to me?"

Once I was on my feet, I looked at the sharp object I held onto. It was a gigantic pillar made of metal that stood at least twenty-feet high that had been bolted into the ground. The post was wrapped in ropes that circled it to the very top.

Atlas responded, "Well, I knew you could do it. You have a gift, Alec, didn't you know? Over."

As I looked at the pillar, I could see others just like it that went all around the mountain top. Each component had multiple ropes that all went in different directions, but all led into a valley down below. While looking down into the valley, I could see a light fog that rested within it. The trees, however, looked strange, I could see palm leaves on some, but I could also see something like scraps of metal underneath them, as well. It was hard to make things out in the moonlight, though, and maybe my eyes were playing tricks on me. I reached into my pocket and pulled out my binoculars. I was astounded at what I saw. I raised the walkie back up to my lips.

"What is TreeTop, exactly? Over."

Looking through the binoculars, I could see blue and green lights that flickered in between the palm leaves. The majority of the trees were real, but upon closer inspection, I could see that they were more than just trees. TreeTop was an enormous shantytown; the treehouses were all supported by ropes and had wooden bridges that went from tree to tree. TreeTop was a village of treehouses made of wood and pieces of scrap metal. The entire living area was suspended above the ground within the tree lining. Every treehouse had a different design, but all were connected through the webbing of bridges that went from one another.

"This is Los Furiosos living quarters," Atlas replied. "Most of the lower-level Los Furiosos's members reside here. I'm not sure if you noticed that each member has a different level of ranking. Over."

I continued to look down below. The webbing of ropes that went from the pillars was used as support for the treehouses down below. I could see many members crossing bridges and going into different houses. Some were drinking alcohol, and others were smoking cigarettes. Their eyes flickered with silver halos. Everyone was under control here, the only person who wasn't was me. I noticed what Atlas was talking about. Most of the Los Furiosos were dressed in relaxed clothing. Other members wore the military outfits. The deep navy blue suits with the neon orange trim must have been a higher ranking. They seemed to keep the other men in check. Some wore lab coats. I'm guessing their attire had something to do with the implants and Chromosome H.

Nonetheless, Atlas wanted me to pass through this area on foot...with landmines. This would be far more dangerous than the climb. Passing through the valley of hell as it were, with Los Furiosos at every corner of TreeTop, there was no easy way around it. Even with the order to spare my life, I doubt that any Los Furiosos would think twice. I started to consider how I was going to get down into the valley. There was no way I was going to climb again. I barely had any ammo left. A makeshift axe, handgun, and knife didn't seem like it would be enough. Many questions were circling my mind. Once again, my heart started to race.

"Why does Dr. Jericho want me alive? Over." I asked in curiosity.

"I'm not one-hundred percent sure. But I think that Dr. Jericho believes that some rare few individuals would have a better compatibility rate with genetic testing. Over."

It sounded like he was lying. I got the feeling he knew something was up. He knew about me, my brother, and my mother. I always had a feeling I was different. Being gay was one thing, but I still noticed something physically different about me. Injuries healed faster than normal, always being faster and stronger than the next guy... Los Furiosos wanted to make super-humans, and of course, I would be the perfect candidate.

"So how do you expect me to pass through this place? Over." I asked.

"As quietly and stealthy as possible, you need to make it to the edge of TreeTop. There is an entrance to the Cimmerian Tunnels. That's where the C4 is kept." He paused in hesitation, "But remember, once inside, I won't have contact with you. Over."

Atlas was my guide. And to not be in contact with him put me on edge. I continued to look down at TreeTop. I noticed the ground had blue-green lasers that were laid out like a grid on the floor.

"Hey, Atlas. What are those lasers for? Over."

"Those are the sensors for the landmines. If you fall to the floor, Alec, you must be very wary of these. One mistake..." he paused in worry. "And you could set one off. Over."

"Great," I said in sarcasm.

Atlas continued, "Once you make it into the tunnels, you're gonna need to head to the heart of the mines. That's where they keep everything. It might seem confusing at first, but the tunnels have maps, it should be okay...I think. Over." Well, that was reassuring, said no one ever.

"So how do you expect me to make it down? Over." I asked in hopes that he wasn't going to say the word "climb."

"Those ropes that lead into the valley, that's your way in. The fastest way to get down is to zip-line. They all lead into TreeTop, but you are going to have to pick the right moment to let go. You need to make it onto one of the treehouse landings. It's either that or you'll land on the ground and possibly not in the right spot... and you don't want that. Over."

"Shit," I said, "How will I know which way to go once I'm down there? Over."

"From where you are now, continue straight directly through the town. You should be able to see the shape of three mountain peaks up ahead. The entrance to the tunnels is located at the center of them. But that means you are eventually going to need to make it to the ground floor. Over."

"This just keeps getting better and better," I said while exhaling. "All right, let's get this over with."

I put my binoculars back into my pocket. I pulled out my 1911 and made sure the clip was full before I put it away. The winds carried the smell of rain as it whipped around me, caressing my skin. I could see the waves from the ocean begin to ripple as the storm was approaching. Flashes of lightning were close, and the sound of thunder rumbled.

I grabbed onto my axe, approached one of the ropes that led into TreeTop and placed my axe on top of it. I held onto the handle of the hatchet with my right hand, the neck of its shaft with my left. I made my way to the edge of the cliff. I could see the trees down below shake from the winds. Before I pushed myself off the ledge, I could feel drops of water land on my head and shoulders. I prayed that the rain would aid me tonight. The sounds of the thunder and lightning from the storm would help silence the screams of the men I was afraid I would have to kill. I dangled my left foot off the edge as Atlas spoke,

"No matter what happens, Alec. Keep moving. Good luck. Over."

I made it this far because of him, but once I reached the tunnels, I would be on my own. I leaned into thin air while gripping my axe as I started to propel toward TreeTop. I was sliding into the belly of the beast as drops of rain pelted me in the face. Picking up speed and descending fast, I found myself raising my knees to my chest to avoid other ropes and tree limbs that blocked my way. Small branches hit my chest and face as my speed increased. The closer I got, the more I could see Los Furiosos walking around on bridges. I began to worry that some could see me, but the rain was beginning to come down hard, and although their treehouses had blue-green lights, they were still dim to the point of low visibility. I must have been moving fast because the raindrops were pelting me so hard that it felt like they were cutting into my skin.

I could see that my rope led to a small treehouse that was at the center of TreeTop. Unable to slow down, I needed to quickly let go to land on the small walkway that surrounded the treehouse. I started to count down in my head the closer I got.

Letting go with my left hand while my right was clinging onto my axe, I landed with a loud thud while rolling toward the edge. My axe flew out of my hand as I slid off the side, holding on to the ledge for dear life. The sound of thunder rumbled as I screamed.

"Hold on, Alec," Atlas winced.

I could feel splinters in my hands as I gripped onto the ledge. My legs were dangling, and as I looked down, I could see beneath me the thin layer of fog that revealed the blue-green laser grid form down below. Thank God I didn't fall because the landmines were directly below me.

I was out in the open and needed to get to a hiding place. I saw my axe a few feet away and scrambled to grab it. Picking it up, I could see through a small opening of the treehouse I was near, someone was inside. The rain was coming down hard as I ran over to the treehouse and rested my back against its wall while holding my ax against my chest. The roof of the treehouse was fabricated of palm leaves and scrap metal that looked like it came from a shipping container. Rain continued to fall, creating a light fog that concealed me from eyesight. The more I studied the treehouse, the more I started to admire Los Furiosos creativity. Assuming they created them. The walls of the homes were created out of mud, wood and scrap metal. Cutouts for windows, doors, and ventilation. Los Furiosos men walk across a bridge from across the way. Thankfully they couldn't see me, seemed focused on not falling because they were stumbling as if they were drunk.

The sounds of footsteps were coming from inside. I needed a weapon and fast. Los Furiosos didn't expect me to be here, I was outnumbered. Making my way around the treehouse, I could see branches protrude out of the tree houses walls. I stepped over them slowly as thunder echoed through the valley, advancing toward the window. Peeking in, I could see a man standing over a small fire, cooking something. His home was disgusting. He was unarmed but had a muscular build. His implant was blinking green. I could see a small bed made of tree wood and cotton, along with a double-barreled shotgun that was propped up against his bed.

There was no need to hurt him unless it came to it. I reached for the shotgun. The man quickly turned around, I pulled my hand out and hid behind the wall. He walked over to his bed to grab a cloth that hung over a tree branch that protruded into his house. He walked back, focusing on his dinner. I reached for it again. My hand was shaking this time, hoping he wouldn't hear me. I had my hand on the fore-end of the gun as I started to pull it from the window. The sound of thunder caused the man to wince. I used the pitch to my advantage and pulled the gun through the window.

"Two bullets, but anything counts."

I held the gun against my chest, kissed it, I knew this would pack a punch. I let my axe dangle from my belt and held on to the gun with both hands. I could feel my pocket buzzing. I reached down to grab my walkie.

I whispered into it, "Atlas. Where do I go?"

Atlas whispered back when he spoke, "There is a bridge to your left, take it to the next treehouse. But be careful. There are six men inside. Over." He spoke with haste.

I listened to his commands and made my way over to the bridge. Every step I took, I could feel the bridge sway beneath me. The rain was still coming down, and now the winds accompanied it. I ran across the bridge quickly because the more I stood out, the worse it would make my case. I made it to the next treehouse, resting my back against its wall. The smell of meat being cooked filtered from the makeshift windows and made my mouth water.

"Damn. It's coming down hard. I wonder when Erico wants us to meet?" one of the six men said from inside.

"I don't know, but let's eat before he calls us," someone responded.

I whispered into my walkie again, "Atlas?"

I knew where I needed to end up, but the way TreeTop was set up was confusing. The webbing of the bridges led in different directions. There didn't seem to be a straight shot to the center of the mountain.

Atlas replied, "There are another two bridges that connect to the treehouse you are at. Circle around the house. You'll see them both, and when you do, take the one to the left. Over." Atlas spoke quickly and quietly to avoid compromising my position.

I started to make my way around the treehouse and stopped when I came to another window. Some of the men were standing, and others were sitting at a table. It wasn't safe to pass unless I crawled under the window. I got down on my stomach and began to army crawl past. As I stood, I could see the two bridges and started to make my way to the left one. While crossing the bridge, I stopped halfway.

"Shit," I whispered to myself.

A member was crossing the bridge to my right. He was covering his head with his hands while the rain pelted his skin. I needed to keep moving, but he would definitely see me. He looked over at me, and I continued to walk almost mimicking what he was doing. He came to a standstill and then thankfully started to walk again. I kept my head down so he couldn't see my eyes. He kept moving without hesitating, and he seemed to want to get out of the rain rather than try to speak to me. I made it across the bridge and on to the next treehouse. As I rested my shoulder against the outside wall, I looked inside and didn't see anyone, except more filth. I entered in hopes to scavenge something beneficial.

Inside were some .45 handgun bullets and three sticks of flares. Hell yeah, I took them, but I couldn't carry all of them. I looked around the house and spotted a backpack hanging from the center tree trunk. I opened the pack and immediately put the ammo and flares inside.

I found a container that would be useful to carry water, put it in my pack as well. A set of voices approaching across the bridge that I just came from made me come to a standstill. I quickly hid behind the tree trunk as the footsteps got louder...shit, they were coming inside.

"Keep an eye out for him. Stay here until I say otherwise." Erico's voice spoke.

Erico exited the treehouse as the other man began pacing around. He started to approach the tree trunk I was hiding behind. Shit, shit, shit. I looked down and could see my wet footprints led to where I stood. I clenched my hand over my mouth to silence my breathing. He began circling the tree. I needed to do something and fast. I started to take steps mimicking his while he continued to circle the trunk. Then with every step he took, I took two more so I could make it behind him before he caught me. I pulled out my axe. I got behind him and placed my hand over his mouth, slicing my axe blade across his throat. As he struggled to let out muffled screams, I could hear thunder boom in the distance. Blood poured out of him, I gradually lowered him to the floor.

"Alec, you need to keep moving. Over." Atlas spoke as I stood over the now-lifeless body, his implant stopped blinking.

I pulled out my walkie. "Where do I go now? Over." I spoke frantically while my hands were still shaking from my kill.

"You need to cross two more bridges in order to make it to the entrance of the Cimmerian Tunnels. But be careful because you have to pass through Erico's house to do so. Over."

"How do I get there? Over."

My adrenaline was pumping as I headed to the entrance of the treehouse. I stopped in the door frame and looked back at the body. I was so close to making it out of here, and I had no time to hide his corpse at this point. If I could make it to the tunnels without being seen, then no one would know where I was or how the dead man came to be. I had to keep moving.

Atlas whispered, "The next bridge you have to take is near the window of the treehouse you are in. Go left when you leave the doorway. Over."

I looked outside to see if the coast was clear. The rain was beginning to slow, my cover was diminishing. As I looked outside, I could see the bridge I was supposed to cross. The bridge led to a treehouse that was different than the others.

Erico's treehouse was more upscale than the rest. I would imagine nothing less because it seemed like he was Los Furiosos's golden boy. I could see a man standing guard on the bridge that I needed to cross after I passed Erico's house. The man was pacing back and forth between Erico's home and a wooden landing that was placed directly in front of the entrance of the tunnel. I thought it'd be safe to cross unseen right when the man started to pace back to the landing. I began to run, pushing myself off the wall as if I were in a race. I could feel the bridge ripple underneath me.

When I made it to Erico's treehouse, I realized that there was a large gate that went from the bottom of the deck and up to the roof of his home. Barbed wire, great. It completely separated me and my chances of circling his house and making it to my last bridge. Another bridge was across from me, a gate led to the landing the pacing man stood on. Locked. A thick chain and padlock kept the gate secure. Damn it. I rested my back against the wall as the man pacing the deck started to make his way back to Erico's. I could see a large entrance to the Cimmerian Tunnels. My mood began to brighten because I could taste freedom.

Looking in Erico's treehouse window, no one was inside. I approached his door, reaching for the door handle to see if it was open. It's unlocked? I looked behind me, twisting the handle, entering Erico's domain.

The rain was starting to weaken while I closed the door behind me. Erico had curtains that were mounted above his windows so I shut them to conceal me. I felt a little out of place here. My now rugged and dirty clothes seemed to stand out as I stood in Erico's home. I called it home because it felt like one. It felt safe when the curtains were closed because I could no longer see TreeTop or the landscape of Candelario. I began to get enraged. Seeing how he lived after everything he had done made me nauseous.

The interior was a lot cleaner compared to the other treehouses I'd seen. Candles were flickering on a dining table with four wooden seats that looked like they were made from scratch. I could see a sink that was placed in a wood countertop. A built-in stove and refrigerator, stainless steel. There was a flat-screen tv mounted on the drywall, a bed that looked like it was made of memory foam. Off the back of the treehouse was a walk-in shower. Erico had it made here, obviously. I was a little envious of him because I would kill every Los Furiosos to be able to have a decent shower, a good meal, and sleep on an actual bed.

He had a plush and cushy set up while he murdered innocent people. Los Furiosos obeyed him without hesitation... to an extent. Erico seemed to keep the majority of Los Furiosos in check, but I had a feeling that he wasn't in complete control. He too, was implanted, so someone had to be above him? Someone had to be giving him orders.

I could see a second door near the back of his treehouse. I assumed this door led to the bridge outside where I eventually had to come face to face with the pacing man. Striding toward the back door, I stopped, something caught my eye as I passed by his desk. I turned back and could see a laptop and official-looking documents. Blueprints of how implantation was done. I walked to the table and picked up the papers. I couldn't understand it because it was written in a different language, Russian, maybe? I thought this was valuable. If I ever did make it off this island, someone had to hear my story, and I knew that they would want proof. I slid the papers into my backpack.

Other documents laid out on his desk. My hands were trembling because I knew I had to hurry, but there was so much information here that I couldn't pass up. I shifted the papers around and came across a few maps. One titled Candelario, although it didn't look like it was professionally done, someone took the time to create it, adding detail, and my best guess was Erico.

I began to trust Atlas even more as I viewed the map because everything he told me about what my journey was right. TreeTop, Cimmerian Tunnels, Bronze Channel Falls, and the Lab were all there. I came across another plan called Isle Onocastel. My eyes widened because this island was bigger and more populated then Candelario.

"Jesus," I whispered to myself. "How many islands do they have?"

I hit the mother-load of information. This map was just like the other, handmade, detailed. It seemed like no one had a clue about these islands except Los Furiosos. Isle Onocastel had an array of buildings. Multiple implant locations along with a train that went through the entire island. Significantly scaled buildings seemed to be more modern and sophisticated than where I was now. Docks went around the whole island. Cars and motorcycles were used as transportation. Many things were going through my mind, and Los Furiosos was more influential than I had ever conceived. I took the map and put it in my pack. Finally, I came across the last sketch of the Cimmerian Tunnels.

"Thank God," I said aloud.

I knew I wouldn't have contact with Atlas when I was down there. I was worried when I saw how many tunnels Los Furiosos created because of how deep they all went. The map looked like spider webs but also had many markers of specific locations within the mines. I slid the sheet inside my pack as my pocket started to vibrate.

"What's taking so long in there? Erico will be back any minute. Over."

I knew I was extending my stay, but I needed more information.

I answered back, "I'm sorry, Atlas. I just found a bunch of maps that could help me out. Did you know Los Furiosos has another island under control? Over."

"Yes, Isle Onocastel. That's where they keep most of Los Furiosos families. That island is perilous. Even more threatening than the one you are on now. Just get out of there, okay. Over."

"Okay, just a few more minutes. Let me know if anyone is coming. Over."

I proceeded to look over Erico's desk. Some papers listed names and positions of each member. I didn't think it was that important but I could see that most of the names were crossed out. Maybe they were dead or had been killed? But there was one person at the top of the list, but for some reason, instead of the person's name having a line through it, it was blacked out, like someone took a Sharpie to it? Interesting. Someone was obviously in command, though. Erico was number two, at least on Candelario. Number three was Dr. Jericho. The names continued to go on for pages, some crossed out and some not. I paused when I came across a specific name.

"Colden Everly," I said aloud and could feel my stomach turn.

His name was crossed out, and I could feel tears welling up in my eyes. Was this proof that he was gone? He was just a crossed-out name on a piece of paper kept on the desk of a murderer. I held my hand up to my mouth as a tear rolled down my cheek. Furious, I threw the papers across the room, accidentally hitting the laptop, causing it to wake from sleep mode. On the screen was a diagram of Chromosome H. I wiped the tears from my eyes and leaned in to look. There were a lot of medical and technical words that I couldn't understand. I noticed a blinking red word underneath it that read "failed." Chromosome H wasn't ready to be used just yet.

I clicked the touchpad and moved the diagram across the screen. I noticed another chart was open behind it. I clicked on it to get a better look. It seemed odd because this diagram looked similar to Chromosome H. The difference between the two was that the V within the vile was turned upside down and there wasn't a list of how it was created. The liquid inside wasn't silver, but it was more of an emerald green. The title of the diagram was called Chromosome A.S. (Accrual Synaptic). As I continued to look, I noticed another blinking word. "Stolen." Was Chromosome H a replica of Chromosome A.S.? I scrolled down and could see that there were notes written.

Subject Colden Everly was tested for Chromosome A.S. The subject failed. However, the Subject will continue to be experimented on until further notice. High probability of Chromosome A.S. renders the subject incredibly valuable.
- Dr. Jericho

"But Colden is dead?" I whispered. I scrolled down and saw another record.

Subject's relative Alec Everly has yet to be tested. The probability of Chromosome A.S. is higher. Alec Everly continues to show signs of increased strength, speed, agility.

Possible accelerated healing.
The capture of Alec Everly is of the utmost importance.
His blood could be the key to uniting both Chromosome
A.S. and H.
Creating: Chromosome A.S.H.
This may be the key to unlocking incredible power in
creating our army.
-Dr. Jericho.

"What the hell?" I said aloud.

Suddenly, my walkie began to buzz.

"Alec. Get out of there. Erico is coming. HURRY." Atlas ordered as I heard footsteps.

I quickly closed the laptop and reached for my shotgun and my backpack and bolted for the back door. I could hear the front doorknob twisting as I silently closed the back door behind me.

"Shit, that was close," I whispered to myself.

From my vantage point, I could see the entrance to the Cimmerian Tunnels not too far below. The floor was still lined with mines, and jumping from this height would risk setting one off. I could see the man standing on the landing with his arms folded as he watched over the entrance of the cave. I needed to move because I could hear Erico rummaging through his house. I had no time to lose so I broke into a sprint across the bridge. I looked back as I ran and I could see Erico's eyes pierce mine through the parted curtains as they pulsed in ferocity. He had a mischievous smile as I darted across the bridge. He closed the curtains, and suddenly, an alarm began to sound. As I ran, I turned back to see multiple Los Furiosos's men starting to run across bridges that I once crossed. They were after me, and I wasn't going to stop for anyone. The back door of Erico's treehouse flung open as he carried a shotgun of his own. A shot was fired.

I ducked and turned around, firing off a shot as Erico took cover and hid behind his door. The man who paced the bridge started to shoot at me with a pistol. I laid flat on my stomach, taking aim at him. I let off another round, hitting his kneecap, causing him to fall off the bridge. He screamed as he fell, and when his body hit the floor, a loud explosion went off. Mud and body parts flew into the air like confetti. The sight alone was horrendous. My shotgun was empty as I promptly tossed it over the bridge. I got to my feet and turned around and was sucker-punched in the face. I fell on the bridge as Erico stood above me. He started to advance toward me again, and I kicked him in the stomach. He fell back, grabbing onto the ropes that acted as a handrail for the bridge. I could feel the bridge sway as he fell, and I stumbled to my feet while it shook. I started to make a run for it again and was quickly yanked back. I elbowed Erico in the face causing him to let go of me. The bridge swung violently back and forth, and it felt like it was beginning to give in. The sounds of the alarm continued as Los Furiosos all started to trickle over the bridges, making their way over to us.

I could hear them shouting at him. Erico found his ground with a look of rage in his eyes. "You think you can take me? You're just a fucking Faerie," Erico yelled at me with disgust.

I had had enough. The bridge started to slow as I turned around. He wanted a fight, and I would give him one.

"I'll show you what this Faerie can do," I said back to him, raising my fist.

He raised his fist as his silver-haloed eyes pulsed. I quickly swung a punch at him with my left fist, striking him across his face. He retaliated by punching me in the stomach and face. His hits fueled me with rage. The bridge continued to sway. Erico swung at me repeatedly. I ducked past his blows and socked him in his stomach this time. He let out a grunt, I kicked him in the left leg knocking him to his knees. I swung at him, causing blood to fly out of his mouth. I could hear Los Furiosos getting closer, yelling Erico's name as I was beating the shit out of him. My knuckles bled from the forceful blows. Erico could hear the calls from his comrades, encouraging him to fight. He threw a punch, hitting me in my left ribs. I let out a scream. One was definitely broken.

He found his footing as I clenched my side. I lifted my fist again because I wasn't giving up.

"Show me your worst." Tightening my fist, I was prepared for this to turn ugly.

Erico let out a laugh as Los Furiosos were cheering him on. They were getting close to his treehouse now, and I needed to think of something quick. I looked down at Erico's thigh holster, a revolver. I couldn't run, or he would shoot me. I waited for his attack again. He let out a swing. I dodged his punch and snatched the revolver out of his holster and shot him.

Erico let out a loud wail while clenching at his thigh. I kicked him in the face again, sending him flying back. The ropes that held the bridge up were starting to give. Los Furiosos members started to shoot rapid-fire my way. I sprinted as the bridge started to collapse, looking behind me as I ran, I could see Erico scrambling back to the other side of the bridge as it started to give. The bridge ropes snapped from the bullets grazing the fibers. The bridge fell beneath me, and as it did, so did I. I held on to the wooden planks that were woven into the bridge as it swung down, grazing the lasers down below. As the ropes broke the lasers' beams, landmines began to explode as I swung forward. The rapid-fire of bullets continued to rain down on me as Los Furiosos were pursuing me relentlessly. Half deaf from the explosions, I could hear Erico screaming at them, telling them to catch me. As I started to swing forward again, I let go of what remained of the bridge, what had been my lifeline, and landed in a gaping hole the landmines had created.

I wiped my eyes so I could see the entrance to the tunnels and broke out into a sprint, heading directly toward the entrance.

"Run, Alec, Run!" Atlas screamed over the walkie.

I ran as fast as I could, praying that Los Furiosos's bullets wouldn't touch me. As I went, I began to leap over the lasers that were on the ground, trying to avoid the landmines. My throat burned with every breath I took. The Los Furiosos were jumping down and coming after me. Erico trailed behind them slowly while holding onto his leg.

"Get him!" he shouted.

As Los Furiosos chased after me, I ran faster than I ever had before, jumping over the lasers while trying to avoid being shot in the process. The entrance to the tunnel was in front of me. It felt like I was running in slow motion. Running toward my freedom. I told myself to keep going while my body was telling me otherwise because I was so damn tired from exhaustion. I jumped over the last few lasers while clenching Erico's revolver in my hand.

I was at the entrance now while I turned around, attempting to shoot as many Los Furiosos's members as I could. I held my breath as I squeezed the trigger. I could see things more transparent than I ever could before. I aimed and let off round after round. And with every squeeze of the trigger, I was hitting every target, one by one. The sound of the revolver had my ears ringing, almost silencing the sounds of their screams that echoed in the distance. I counted as the bullets hammered out one by one. I could feel tears welling up in my eyes because I knew what I was capable of now. I knew that I had a thirst for blood.

And with every bullet fired...

I wanted more and more of them dead.

I had become one of them.

I had become Los Furiosos.

1. He fell to the floor.
2. The halos in his eyes leave.
3. Blood shot out of the back of his head.
4. He screamed as he fumbled into the mud.
5. He went face-first into a landmine.

I was out of bullets now. I reached for my handgun in my holster, and at that same moment, a voice shouted from behind the remaining fighters.

"STOP."

The voice came from none other than Dr. Jericho. The men stopped their shooting but continued to run toward me. All were jumping over the lasers avoiding the landmines, and I could see Erico stumbling over the lasers as he got closer. He reached for another man's gun, prying it out of their hands. He continued to make his way toward me. He raised his weapon, aiming at me.

"I SAID, STOP." Dr. Jericho yelled again.

I could see Dr. Jericho approaching from behind the men as they all surrounded me at the entrance of the tunnel. I held my hands in the air while clinging to Erico's revolver. Erico stared at me with piercing eyes, just waiting to blow me to bits. Dr. Jericho approached Erico from behind and placed his hand on his weapon.

"That's enough, brother," he said, attempting to soothe him.

Erico pulled his weapon away, scoffing at him. Dr. Jericho turned to me and smirked. Dr. Jericho stood in front of Los Furiosos wearing his white lab coat. He seemed very out of place as he spoke to me. His stark white lab coat rippled in the wind as he continued to talk.

"Alec Everly. Surrender now and come with us."

"Don't listen to them," Atlas said over the walkie.

Dr. Jericho cocked his head to the side, showing an interest in who was helping me. "Friend of yours?"

"There's no way in hell I'm going with you," I said furiously.

Dr. Jericho walked closer to me, and I raised the revolver at him, knowing I didn't have any more bullets, but maybe he didn't know that. He stopped in his tracks, putting his hands up. Los Furiosos all had their weapons pointed at me now. Dr. Jericho continued to speak.

"Alec, please. We don't mean you any harm. Besides, we can make you even better than what you are now. Don't you want to become more amplified than you already are? To become even stronger and more powerful than you could ever imagine?"

"What the fuck are you talking about?"

Dr. Jericho continued. "Oh, come now. Haven't you always noticed something a little off about you? Your childhood? Things that you've done that you could never really explain?"

"Get into the tunnels now, Alec," Atlas spoke over the walkie again.

Dr. Jericho recognized his voice, his reaction was almost instant.

"Be careful whom you trust, Alec," Dr. Jericho said, smiling. "Come now. Surrender and join us. You will become so magnificent. Your abilities will become astronomical. I promise."

I knew there was no way of getting out of this. I was outnumbered, and I only had so many bullets in my 1911. Then I thought about why Dr. Jericho valued me so much. He thought I was the solution for Chromosome A.S.H. He just wanted to use me for his own personal gain. He knew how important I was, whether it was true or not. If I did have Chromosome A.S., how useful would I be if I were dead?

I raised the revolver to my head.

Dr. Jericho gasped. "Alec. Don't do that," he said in desperation.

I scoffed. "No point in going with you. You want me alive, right?"

Dr. Jericho nodded, looking around at his army of silver-eyed men like I had him by the balls.

"Then let me go," I demanded.

Dr. Jericho shook his head. "You can't get off that easily, Alec."

I scoffed. "Then no deal."

"Hand over your weapon," Erico shouted.

"Alec, don't do it," Atlas pleaded with me.

I was being coerced from every angle.

Dr. Jericho knew I wouldn't pull the trigger. Even if I could, there were no more bullets in the revolver. Erico cocked his gun and aimed at me once again.

"I said to hand over your weapon. NOW!"

I lowered the revolver, nodding my head. As I looked down at the ground, I could see flashes of blue-green lasers. My eyes darted back up to Erico.

"Okay," I said, defeated.

"Toss them over to me," Erico shouted.

"Okay, I will." In a split second, I knew what I had to do. "I'll toss my weapon to you..."

I said, then I whispered, "right next to the landmine."

I threw the revolver over to the closest laser. The two-toned gun split the laser in half, setting off a landmine. I turned and darted into the tunnel as I the men screamed while more landmines began to detonate. The entrance to the tunnel started to sway and crumble. The rocks began to rain down, barricading the entrance.

The silver-haloed eyes that continued to watch me began to trickle away as the entrance became nothing more than a dead-end. I coughed as particles kicked up into the air and prayed that where I was would remain stable enough as the tunnel continued to quake.

6: CIMMERIAN TUNNELS

THE TONE OF STATIC from my walkie was the only thing I could hear. I continued to cough, gasping for air as a nebulous of dust surrounded me. I faltered as I shuffled over stones underneath me. I held my arm out, attempting to feel in front of me. My breathing began to quicken, and I could feel myself starting to hyperventilate as the darkness of the tunnel raised my anxiety. I pulled my walkie out of my pocket.

"Atlas. Can you hear me? Over," I asked, begging that a signal would get through.

But nothing.

"Atlas, do you read? Over."

The silence broke as Atlas tried to respond, "Ale...are you..." While he spoke, the connection continued to break up.

"Come on." I said aloud to no one.

I held up my walkie using its screen light to see what was in front of me. Everything was difficult to make out. I stopped in my tracks, knowing that I was officially alone, and I only had a matter of time before Los Furiosos would find a way down here. There had to be more than one way in and out of here. I could hear unusual sounds in the distance, not sure if that was residual explosions moving rocks or something else. I put my walkie back in my pocket and took off my pack. I lowered myself to the ground while opening it. Fumbling, trying to find my flares in the pitch-black tunnel. I pulled one out and tried to remember how these things work. I could feel the cylinder shape of the flare along with a cap at one of its ends. The lid must have been the igniter? As I removed the lid, I felt it with my thumb. At the end of the cap, I could feel a rough surface that had the same texture on the flare itself. I placed the cap and the tip of the flare together, attempting to ignite it.

Success. The red light it cast revealing my location. As I looked up ahead, I could see a shadow quickly run off into another tunnel. Who the hell was that? If it was Los Furiosos, I knew that their eyes would glow and give them away.

I reached into my pack again, trying to find the map of the tunnels. While I rifled through my bag, I could feel the papers that I stole from Erico's house. I finally came across the Cimmerian map. My breathing started to slow as my flare continued to flicker in the bleakness. Getting my bearings, I noticed that there was a generator near me. There was a marker that had a small note that read,

"Generator lasts 1 hour. Refuel with gas if needed."

An eerie feeling washed over me. I felt like I was being watched and wondered if the person who ran off moments ago was back. Knowing that I had to keep moving, I picked up the flare, holding it in my left palm, along with the map in between my fingers. Suddenly a roar sounded in the distance.

I pulled out my 1911.

"What the fuck was that?" I said.

I wasn't alone. Something was in here, something big. The boom of the roar sounded again within the tunnels, making it hard to pinpoint where it was coming from. If anything, I wanted to know where it was because I didn't want to head in that direction. I pointed my handgun in front of me, shaking. It was one thing to fight Los Furiosos, but whatever was down here didn't sound human. I had no other choice but to start moving. As I put one foot in front of the other, I started to notice wires and cords that were mounted on the ceiling of the tunnels. The more I continued, the more I realized that the cables were connected to small light bulbs that were caged in metal casings. I needed to find that generator. I came to a stop when I reached a small clearing.

As I glanced around, I could see three other tunnels that all forked off in different directions. The marker on the map indicated that the generator was inside the tunnel that forked to the left. I looked around and noticed markings on the walls that looked like arrows. I approached one of them, a neon orange arrow pointed to the right cave. Underneath the indicator, it read "Gen." I glanced back down to my map, and it said that the generator was to the left. I was confused.

"Fuck," I whispered to myself.

The silence split again as I could hear noises that was coming from multiple directions as it ricocheted off the walls. I was anxious. I needed to get out of here, but I wouldn't get far if I couldn't see. I tucked the map underneath my armpit and holstered my gun. I knew if I were to get lost, I would be screwed. I pulled out my knife and set my flare down. While the red light of the flare cast on the walls, I held the blade to my left palm. This was a matter of life or death at this point, I needed to know where I had been and where I needed to go. I took a few breaths, anticipating what I was going to do next.

Three...two...one.

I thrust the blade into my palm, dragging it along, penetrating deep enough to create a decent amount of blood. As I slid the blade across my palm, I let out a small grunt. I could hear the sounds I made echo as it left my lips. Roaring sounded again. The pitch bounced off the walls, left and right, leaving me with no direction of where it came from. I frantically put my knife back into my belt. Back to the tunnel I came from, I rubbed my palm against the wall.

"Just follow the blood, Alec," I said to myself.

I winced. After everything I'd been through, I would imagine overcoming the pain. Even still, a knife wound is a knife wound. I turned back and walked back to the flare that was slowly starting to die out. I picked it up and decided to follow the map. If I could trust anyone at this moment, it would be Erico and his map-making abilities. After all, what choice did I have? If he was as efficient as Los Furiosos thought he was, then I had no doubts about it. I began to make my way into the tunnel that forked to the left. While I walked, I thought it would be a good idea to keep tabs on Los Furiosos. I knew that Atlas couldn't get in contact with me, but Los Furiosos were closer than he was, and I had a feeling that it would be better if I didn't run into a dangerous surprise. I pulled my walkie out of my pocket and viewed its interface. I suddenly stopped in my tracks and noticed that there was a new voicemail sent from an unknown number. I was curious to hear what the message said as I opened it and held the speaker to my ear. As the voicemail played, it continued to cut out.

"It's m...Coming to yo...Tr...stay safe....I will come to yo.... Lov....Alec."

The message cut out before I came to the realization that it was Liam. I could feel a surge of emotions rush over me. He must have been looking for me, and I had only hoped that he would be able to retrace my steps to find me. Part of me wanted to weep, but my mindset had changed. Liam may be coming to my rescue, but he would never make it in time to save me. I wiped more of my blood on the wall of the cave as I continued to walk. I switched my walkie back to channel one, hoping I could hear Los Furiosos's plans while underground. There was nothing but silence for now. I began to think about Liam actually coming here. Would he make it past Los Furiosos? The concept of him getting hurt made me unsettled. I would rather have him safe and as far away from this place as possible. I was barely making it by myself, and with Liam by my side, I started to think that he might slow me down. Los Furiosos were after me and would kill whoever stood in their path, including Liam. I couldn't let that happen.

I paused at the fork I'd come up to and could see to the right was a large boulder wedged in place with signs of moonlight streaming in. I thought that maybe this could be my way out. As I approached the boulder, I couldn't see around it. I thought about what Dr. Jericho wrote about me in the Chromosome A.S. files. The speed, the strength, the agility, the accelerated healing. I scoffed to myself because it couldn't have been accurate. I never stole Chromosome A.S., and there was never a moment in my life that I remember someone injecting me with something like that.

"There has to be another way out," I said to myself.

I walked back to the tunnel I came from and continued on course. I went to wipe my hand against the wall again and realized that there wasn't any more blood coming out. I held my palm up to my face as the flare flickered. The wound I had created was beginning to heal. Half of it was turning into a pink scar while the rest of it was still somewhat bleeding. I shook my head because I didn't want to believe it.

I came to a stop when I reached a dead-end again.

"Shit," I whispered with frustration.

The sound of gravel moving behind me had me frozen in my tracks. I squinted as I looked in the distance. A dark shape slowly approached me on all fours. My hands trembled as I dropped the map. The flare went out. Perfect timing. The sound of footsteps continued to advance.

Whatever it was stopped right in front of me. Digging into my bag, I pulled out another flare. I pulled the cap off the flare, shivering in fear. I had a hunch I knew what it was, though, but I didn't want to accept it. I held the cap to the end of the flare and quickly ignited it. A spark of the light rippled throughout the tunnel. As the light filtered, it exposed its vivid green eyes, jet black fur and razor-sharp teeth...the panther.

Her nose was a foot from my face as she released a ferocious roar. I yelled at the top of my lungs as she lunged at me. Pouncing on top of me, she raised her jagged nails into the air ready to rip me to shreds. I screamed louder than I ever had before and slung my hand across my face in protection. As I did, my flare accidentally hit her in the face, causing her to wince and pull away from me. I struggled to get away, using my elbows as support while kicking my legs out at her. She roared again while swinging her claws at me.

As I managed to get myself off the ground, I reached for my axe while waving the flare at her, attempting to keep her back. She paused her attack but stood her ground.

"Stay back. STAY THE FUCK BACK!" I shook the flare back and forth, lunging at her with my axe, attempting to strike her.

There was no way I was going to win against her. She started to approach me again, and was on the hunt as she continuously tried to lunge at me, baring her claws while she swung at me. I didn't want to kill her, but if it came down to me or this animal, I wasn't going to be eaten alive. She seemed to be more concerned with the flare than my axe.

"Don't like flares, do ya?" I approached her again, shaking the flare at her as she continued to back away. I gripped my axe, anticipating her every move. She roared at me when she found herself backed into the wall as she retreated from the burning flame.

She knew she wasn't going to win this fight as long as I had my flare and quickly turned around and broke into a sprint, leaving the tunnel we were both in. I stood there, shaking, while trying not to pass out.

"I have to get out of here," I said to myself, trying to steady my breathing.

I only had one flare left, and I didn't want to run into this predator on my way out. I picked up the map and broke into a run in the same direction she did. I made my way to the tunnel that was labeled "Gen." To my surprise, I could see the wires and cords on the ceiling leading into this tunnel. If only I had paid attention to that before.

The cords I followed began to run from the ceiling of the walls down to the floor and turned into a clearing where I could see the generator.

"Thank God," I said as I approached the generator, hopeful that there was gas to power this beast.

I had no idea what I was doing and wished that Atlas could walk me through this. The generator was enormous. The red light my flare cast revealed multiple buttons and levers all over the machine. To the side of it, I could see containers of gasoline. Without hesitation, I ran over to them, picking them up and shaking them with the expectation that they were filled with gas. The ones I shook were empty.

"FUCK!" I screamed, looking around, relieved that the panther wasn't making her way back.

I went to the other side of the generator and checked beside it. One canister left. Who knows how old the gas was but I silently prayed that it would work. Picking it up with a shake, I had just enough, I hope.

The sound of the panther's roar boomed through the tunnels, causing me to move even faster. I noticed my flare was starting to dim as I found a cap located on the side of the generator. I twisted the lid off and took a whiff. The smell of oil and gasoline filtered into my nostrils. I hoped this was at the right tank, as I poured what was left from the canister into it. I threw the can off to the side as it bounced into some crates nearby that began to fall over. The sounds of them crashing to the floor reverberated into the tunnels. As it did, I could feel my pocket begin to buzz. I pulled my walkie out to listen.

"Estamos nos aproximando. A fada não pode estar longe."

I couldn't understand most of what he said, but I had a feeling they were in the tunnels with me. I put the cap back on and examined the generator. There was a label that read 'Pull on and off lever to power up the machine.' The stamp had an image of what the lever looked like as I continued to search around to find it. I came across the switch and immediately gripped it and pulled it. As I did, the lights on the generator started to flash on and off. I found a light that gleamed green that had a keyhole underneath it. 'Turn key to start the generator.' I looked back at an empty keyhole.

"Goddamn it. I can't ever catch a break,"

Suddenly, the sound of a voice reflected off the walls. Someone was close. I swiftly threw my dying flare off into the distance and hid behind the crates that had fallen over. As I hid, I could hear a man's voice continue to grow more boisterous. The tunnel was dark where I was now. I could see hints of a torch illuminating the walls of the tunnel as the stranger got closer. I began to worry because I could see the generator's lights continue to flash. Los Furiosos would know that I was here recently. The man finally emerged from around the corner, alone.

He pulled out his walkie as he approached the generator.

"I'm here. It looks like the Faerie tried to get it started," he said as he made his way to the generator.

This was my chance to take him out. The man glared at the machine. Soon the engine started ticking and suddenly revved to life. I gasped because he didn't even use a key. The sound of the generator was like an old Chevy engine finally starting after several years. While the machine rumbled, bright lights began to turn on and illuminate the tunnels. I was thankful for light and knew I had to make my move because I would no longer be hidden. The man started to leave as I began to walk from behind the crates. Instantly, the sound of the panther's screech echoed... she was close.

"The panther is in here. Watch your back!" he said into the walkie.

While I was hiding behind the crates, I noticed writing along the side of one of them. I cocked my head to read because the container was flipped upside down. The box read,

"Property of Los Furiosos: Capitol Optics"

I felt like I heard that name before. Capitol Optics. Suddenly it came to me. The airport. Before I left, there was that ad. Capitol Optics and the people with the white-haloed eyes. It suddenly began to make sense. Everything Atlas said about Los Furiosos was right. They had worldwide reach, and it was all through this new technology.

"Oh, my God," I whispered to myself.

Suddenly I could hear the man start to scream. "Holy shit." As he quickly pulled out his weapon and began to fire it off into the distance.

The panther was quickly approaching as the man fired his weapon. The panther let out awful shrieks as I peeked out from behind the crates. The man threw his torch at her and started to run in the opposite direction. I stood there, wide-eyed, as she continued to hunt him down. My mood improved as I heard the screams that the man cried out while he was being mauled to death. I needed to make a run for it. Los Furiosos were inside now looking for me, and I didn't want to become the Panther's next meal.

While trying to find an escape, I came to the crossroads again. Only this time everything was lit up, making it much easier to navigate. I knew I only had so much time before the generator would run out of gas.

My heart hadn't stopped racing since I entered the Cimmerian Tunnels, searching for C4. The feeling of trauma and fear, of never making it out alive, with Los Furiosos entering from every entrance made me push myself even faster. The lights began to blur as I ran, and I could feel the incline increasing with every step. I came to a stop to catch my breath and found myself at another tunnel crossroads. Only this time there were four different shafts.

Two that went left and right and another two that had steps that led down deeper.

The Cimmerian Tunnels must have gone on for miles, and it was difficult to tell which direction I needed to head. With no time to waste, I choose to take the left entrance and as I ran, I realized the right side of the wall was no longer there. Instead, the wall became pillars that were created of stone and formed multiple archways. I could see spotlights flutter as I passed each arch. Coming to a stop, I looked out over an enormous cathedral that led downward into a pit filled with lights that lit up the entire cavern. My eyes widened trying to take in the massive amount of space. I could see trickles of a waterfall plunge down into the base of the cathedral and into what looked like a pond.

Multiple floors of walkways and arches had somehow been created. I looked up to the ceiling and could see an opening that allowed moonlight to shine in. I counted twelve stories that spiraled down to the ground floor. It was astonishing.

I looked at the shimmering on the walls and wondered why they reflected so vividly. Bring my binoculars to my eyes, I began to investigate. Gold. Now I understood why they had the funds to keep an operation like this going.

The thought of Los Furiosos having so much revenue made me sick. They had access to one of the most profitable natural commodities in the world — and a lot of it. Not to mention Capitol Optics, which was my leading cause for concern. I knew I recognized the haloed eyes from before, but this was much worse than I presumed. In this day and age, everyone was more technologically based than ever before. Everyone had become so wrapped up in the newest and hottest gadgets, and now with Capitol Optics coming up in the world and Los Furiosos being the primary source of ownership made me wonder. Why stop with Candelario and Isle Onocastel? Why not society as a whole? Near the stockpiles of gold were the explosives I needed to get my hands on.

"There you are," I said to myself. "How do I get down to you?"

I stepped toward the edge of the archway. I looked out to my left and right and could see ropes dangling down to the lower levels beneath me. I was on the ninth floor of the cathedral and had a long way down. My heart was racing because I knew I had to propel down the ropes that may or may not be sturdy enough to sustain my weight. Slipping my binoculars in my pocket, I placed my hands on both sides of the archway looking down. After the climb to TreeTop, this height didn't seem too bad. I felt my walkie buzz in my pocket as I reached out to my left, grabbing onto one of the ropes.

"I found Grant's body. He's dead. It looks like the panther got him. All of you keep your eyes peeled." Erico sounded pissed.

I grasped onto the rope, wrapping it around my right hand while holding onto the arched pillar with my left.

Erico continued, "Any signs of the Faerie?"

Another man responded, "Nothing yet, we found traces of blood along some of the walls. He must be injured. We will keep looking."

Erico replied, "As much as it pains me to say, Dr. Jericho wants him alive. Capture him if possible. Terminate him, if necessary." Erico spoke with an appetite for blood in his voice.

I let go with my left hand, grabbing onto the rope as my feet dangled, slapping against the wall. Finding my footing, I propped myself up vertically. I gradually started to lower myself, walking backward. My palms were sweating, lungs were on fire. I tried to hold my weight while gently repelling down. The rope was coming to an end. At the end of the line, I could feel my right foot touching the edge of the eighth floor. I was scared to let go because I was on the edge. I began to swing back and forth, letting go at the first opportunity. I disembarked, striving to slow my breathing. A roar emitted through the cathedral. The panther was around here somewhere, and the sooner I got out of here, the better. I approached the edge of the archway again.

"There has to be a faster way," I said to myself, seeking to figure out a way to make it down safely. I looked to my left and right, the ropes were all different lengths. The archways were only five to six feet apart. I saw to my far right that there was a rope that was long enough to reach the floor. It was three arches away from where I was.

"Great," I said, feeling depleted.

I took a few deep breaths, then I reached out to grab onto my next rope. I grasped the line and stepped off the ledge and began to lower myself. I came to a point just under the arch's shelf and settled. I wrapped the rope around my right hand. I could see the next cable I needed to grab only six feet away. I planted my feet on the wall vertically. I used as much of my core as I possibly could to hold myself up. Suspended in the air, I started to push off the wall attempting to swing across. I used my feet as leverage so I was able to run across the wall. As I quickly approached the next rope, I reached out with my left hand and snagged it.

"Take it as they come, Alec." I reassured myself.

Suspended between the two ropes momentarily, I got a good enough grip with my left hand to release myself from my previous line. Once I let go, I could feel the momentum of my body begin to swing again. I used it to my advantage while pushing off the wall. Mid-swing I went to reach out to seize onto the next rope. My blood was pumping at this point as I extended my arm as far as I could to clutch the next rope. Suddenly, the pulley gave way.

"Oh, shit." I shouted as I began to plummet.

The pulley dropped me down three floors until it snagged on to a latch from above. The momentum of the drop swung my body full force toward the wall. I held onto the rope with all my might, bracing for impact. The side of my head crashed into the wall, ringing in my ears, vision clouded.

"Just hold on," I said to myself as I gripped the rope while my hands continued to sweat.

The pressure in my head began to get worse as I dangled there, holding on for dear life. I could feel my pocket vibrating as Erico spoke.

"Did any of you hear that?" he asked.

Immediately, someone responded, screaming.

"THE PANTHER'S IN HERE. ARGHHH." The man shouted while you could hear the roar of the panther echoing throughout the tunnels and into the cathedral.

"WHERE ARE YOU? JOSEPH, WHERE ARE YOU?" Erico yelled, trying to reach out to him.

He was done for.

"Good riddance," I scoffed to myself because it was one less enemy I had to deal with.

I had to keep going, letting go of the rope, holding on to the ledge. As my legs were suspended, I began to shimmy to the left, making my way to the last cable. I could feel a stone protruding from the wall below and rested my left foot on it. I extend my arm one last time to grab onto my final rope.

"Got you." The rope rippled all the way down to the floor.

Trying not to make another mistake, I yanked the rope to make sure that it was secure. It seemed safe, but then again, all my weight wasn't being supported by it. The risk was too high, either being captured by Los Furiosos or having another run-in with the panther. I took my chances with the rope. I let go of the ledge and was thankful that the line didn't budge. I could hear the sound of voices echoing as I repelled down the wall. There was no telling where the voices were coming from. The sound of footsteps drifted throughout the tunnels as I continued to lower myself. I heard voices again so I steadied my breathing while trying to listen.

"Split up and search for him in teams. There's only one of him and multiple of us, don't fuck this up." Erico spoke loudly while his voice bounced off the walls.

"What if we don't find him?" Another man questioned.

I could hear the man being physically choked.

"We will fucking find him. And when we do, he's mine. He'll wish he was fucking dead after I'm done with him," Erico said, and then I could hear the man suddenly gasping for air.

"Yes, sir."

I could hear steps approaching a ledge from above, and I tried to press my body against the wall in hopes that I wouldn't be seen. I looked up and could see Erico at the edge of one of the archways. He was looking out over the cathedral in admiration. I held my breath. Erico had it out for me, I would willingly be killed by the panther than allow him the pleasure of taking my life. He finally turned and walked away from the archway. I released a deep breath while my arms shook from holding myself up. Moving with more agility now, I descended to the bottom floor. From below, the cavern looked even more beautiful than it did from above. Now that I was on the base floor, I had a better view of what was down here.

I made my way across the cavern and could see many crates and boxes. As I crossed, some of them had gold that was already packaged and placed neatly into wooden boxes. Other containers had what looked like drugs. One of the boxes was labeled "Property of Los Furiosos: Capitol Optics." Just like the one near the generator. Out of curiosity, I had to open it and see for myself. I pried the box open with my axe. The sound of the nails being ripped from the box echoed within the cavern, I was worried that someone would hear, but I didn't care at this point. Once the box was open, there was shredded paper covering boxes underneath. As I pushed the shredded paper away, inside were multiple packages of Capitol Optic implants. Each box was white and sleek. The packaging had a futuristic font that was very appealing to the eye.

I shook my head in disbelief, "This can't be happening." I said to myself.

I pulled out one of the boxes and read it aloud.

"Capitol Optics first personal implant. The first step to controlling the surroundings near you."

My stomach turned as I continued to inspect the case. I looked around and didn't see just one crate, but several. I winced while looking back at the package I held. I flipped the box over and could see directions of how the implant was installed, along with diagrams of what you could control.

"It's a scam," I said, "Los Furiosos don't want to give people control. They want to control others."

With how modern and sleek the packaging looked and how fast consumers hopped onto the next biggest and best thing in technology. Everyone would soon be implanted, utterly unaware that Los Furiosos were responsible. If I was right, Los Furiosos could simply flip a switch, and the entire world would be under their control.

I threw the box to the ground. I knew why Atlas wanted me to destroy the lab now. If Los Furiosos could have multiple people under control, who would stop them once they were all given Chromosome A.S.H? Los Furiosos would have an army, and not just here, but globally. I looked around at all the crates and became enraged. I was at a crossroads between helping myself or helping the world. Everything Los Furiosos touched needed to be destroyed. Starting with this cathedral. I put my axe back on my hip and began to head toward the C4 pile. I walked over to the pond that I had seen from above. Under the water, I could see moonlight reflecting throughout a cave that led to the surface outside.

While I studied the water, I could see my reflection. The branded F on my left shoulder was completely healed but still left a scar. My reflection left me petrified. I was no longer myself, and I couldn't remember what I looked like before all of this. I knew things were never going to be the same as I progressed. If I were to still be me, I knew that I was on the right side of this battle. I couldn't let Los Furiosos change me forever. I left my reflection in the water and continued to make my way over to the C4.

There was a stone staircase that led to the golden infused wall. While walking up the stairs, it almost seemed like the C4 was placed perfectly at the center. At the top of the stairs, rows of golden bars stacked up from the ground up. On the landing of the stairs was a wooden table that held even more bars of gold, ready for the taking. I approached the table and set my pack down on the ground.

I picked up one of the bars and held it close to my face. The reflection of its golden hue cast crossed my eyes. Fascinating, I never held something this valuable before. I looked at my ring and thought otherwise. My ring was gold too, and its meteorite material complimented the golden bar beautifully. The thought of taking a bar never crossed my mind until now. The concept of it being Los Furiosos's gold made me nauseous. I didn't want anything from them, except to bring their entire administration down.

Voices broke the silence as men began to walk on the second floor. I dropped the bar of gold, hiding behind the table. The steps and voices reproduced as they spoke. Los Furiosos entered into a tunnel, and their sounds evaporated. I knew that I needed to make this quick before I was detected. Once the coast was clear, I made my way to the pile of C4, grabbing a few bricks.

I wasn't sure what I was doing. All I knew was that in movies, C4 just blew things up. I needed Atlas's help. I reached into my pocket and pulled out my walkie, praying for a miracle. I stood up, flipping through the interface of the walkie phone to get to channel six. I held down the button.

"Atlas, are you there? Over," I asked, trying to keep my voice low, but any sound or movement I made echoed. All I could hear was static. I started to move around and clicked the button again.

"Atlas, do you read? Over." I said, and I could hear a voice in the distance that wasn't mine. The static started to break, and I could overhear Atlas trying to speak. I kept circling around until the signal got stronger. I came to a standstill when the static of the walkie stopped.

"Atlas?"

"Alec, can you hear me? Over." Atlas's voice was muffled by the connection.

"Oh, my God. Yes, I'm here. Can you hear me?"

"I can hear you. I thought I lost you, Alec. Are you hurt? Are you okay? Over." Anguish in his voice.

"Yes, I'm okay. I'm banged up pretty good, but I'll live for now. I found the C4. What do I do now? Over." I spoke swiftly as I had the feeling that Los Furiosos would find me if I kept the conversation going.

"Thank God. Way to go, Alec." He praised me and then continued, "Okay, so you must be careful arming such explosives. Alec, make no mistakes because it could be your last. Over."

"Okay, but hurry because Los Furiosos are close to finding me. Over."

"Find the detonator. When you find it, there will be prongs attached to it. Over." He said as I quickly went over and grabbed the detonator. I could see a small case attached to the handle. I opened the case, and there were small prongs that all flashed green simultaneously.

"I have the detonator. And I see the prongs. Over." As I spoke, I could hear the panther roar in the distance.

"Okay, good. Be very careful, Alec. Those prongs are linked to the detonator, when the trigger is pulled, it will cause the prongs to release a shock wave that will set off the C4. Over."

Butterflies in my stomach started to flutter. I didn't want to blow myself up.

"Okay, so what do I do? Over." I could hear the sound of footsteps running through one of the tunnels as the roar of the panther rippled throughout the cathedral.

"All right, to arm the C4 place the prongs into it. When you depress the trigger that means the C4 is live. Once you let the trigger go is when the shock wave will be released from the prongs. You're going to want to be as far away from it as possible. Over," Atlas said, tensely.

"Tremendous."

Suddenly the sound of the running footsteps darted out of one of the tunnels on the sixth floor. I could see a man resting against the arched pillars above, trying to catch his breath. While standing there, he looked out into the cavern. His silver haloed eyes caught my gaze as he took in a gasp of realization. His eyes widened as he reached for his walkie.

"Shit. Atlas, I've been spotted," I said as the man yelled into his walkie almost simultaneously as I did.

"I FOUND HIM, HE'S IN THE CATHEDRAL. HURRY."

"Fuck," I said as I put my walkie into my pocket.

I could hear Atlas muffle the word, "RUN."

The man pulled out a handgun and started to unleash fire in my direction. The bullets tore through the wooden table, causing gold bricks to fall to the ground. I took cover, reaching for my 1911. There was no way I was getting the C4 out of here safely. As I took cover behind the table, I waited for my moment. The man continued to fire in my direction, and I paused for him to reload so I could step out. I could hear him begin to click his trigger now with no success. I came out of hiding and took aim, firing my weapon. My heart was racing. I unloaded my clip in his path and managed to strike him in his calf, causing him to scream in pain.

I ran out of ammo and released the empty clip. As it fell to the ground, I reached for my next clip in my holster under my right armpit. I quickly reloaded and cocked the gun. I stepped out from behind the table and could hear the man scream. As he did, the sound of the roaring panther echoed. From where I stood I could see the man crying on the floor, and abruptly the black panther came out of the tunnel nearest to him, latching her teeth into his shoulder while pulling him back with her. He squealed as she dragged his body deep into the mines.

I scoffed to myself, "Good girl."

My position was compromised. And the sound of Los Furiosos' footsteps rumbled throughout the cathedral. I quickly ran over to the C4, taking the prongs out of the detonator and placing them into six different explosives that were accumulated in a pile.

"This should definitely go boom."

I knew I wasn't going to make it out of here with the charges now. This was the only time to use it. I would have to think of something else to destroy the lab with. With Los Furiosos on their way to find me, I started to run down the stairs with the detonator in hand. As I began to pass the crates of drugs and implants, I could see the men beginning to appear out of the tunnels on the ground floor as they all flooded in. I started to back away, but no matter where I turned, they were everywhere. I could see them point their guns at me, smiling while their haloed eyes pulsed.

"We got him, you guys."

More and more started to pour into the cavern. I was fucked, there was no way around it now. The men took aim, but none fired, finally obeying orders. Either way, I was outnumbered as they proceeded to surround me. I counted how many men there were and lost tally after I reached forty-five. There must have been one hundred of them, all here to get me. I could hear them talk to each other in different languages, some in English, others in Spanish and in Portuguese. All entrances were blocked at this point. Most laughed at me as I spun around, desperately searching for a way out. A voice promptly shouted, telling them to move aside. Through the crowd of men stomped Erico.

"Get out of my way," Erico demanded as the men began to separate, forming an aisle for Erico to walk through.

Erico met my gaze as he forced his way through the crowd. He smiled sadistically as he approached me. I noticed that he was walking a lot better since I last saw him and his leg looked like it was treated and patched up as he got closer. His face, however, looked like he had taken a beating. I knew I had wailed on him during our last encounter, but his fresh wounds didn't look like they came from me.

"Well, well," Erico spoke as he stood in front of his men.

I concealed the detonator behind my back.

"If it isn't the infamous Alec Everly. It seems like you won't be getting the fairytale ending after all, huh?"

I scoffed, "So how's the leg?" I smirked.

Erico started to make his way toward me, he was pissed, but his men held him back while he tried to fight them off.

"You're so fucking lucky, Faerie," he said as he continued to pull their hands off of him. "Dr. Jericho said he wanted you alive. But he didn't say anything about beating you to near death."

"Calm down, Erico," said one of the men who was holding him back.

"Yeah, listen to your friends, golden boy."

I was untouchable at this point. Dr. Jericho made his position clear now as Los Furiosos stood their ground. Erico began to calm down and pulled away from their grip.

"If it weren't for Vincent, you'd be dead right now if it were up to me."

"Vincent?" I questioned. "Is that who is in charge of you?"

Erico gradually started to approach me, keeping his distance because he seemed like something was holding him back? I had a sneaking suspicion that it was Vincent who had given Erico a beating.

"You have become quite an inconvenience for him and for us," Erico said, "No one has ever made it off this island alive."

"Yeah, except for Atlas. Wouldn't want to disappoint Vincent again, would you?" I spoke confidently now.

I was testing Erico as much as I could. If Los Furiosos were really under control, I wanted to see how far they were allowed to go.

"Atlas? Who is that? Your little friend helping you?" Erico laughed to himself, and Los Furiosos did along with him. "Oh, Faerie. Haven't you noticed that none of us can be trusted?"

I glanced around at all of them. It felt like I was looking at a cult...all of them dirty and equipped with weapons. So far, I trusted Atlas with my life. I gripped the detonator behind my back as I gazed around.

"Never say never, because I will make it off of this island. And before I do, I'll have the pleasure of killing you myself."

"In your fucking dreams, Faerie," Erico shouted as he quickly ran up to me, eager to throw a punch. I clenched my eyes shut, waiting to feel the impact across my face.

But there was nothing.

I opened my eyes, and Erico stood in front of me with his fist clenched near my face. His eyes were wide, in shock, maybe. He leaned back and tried to throw another punch again. But he couldn't hit me, a force was stopping him. I laughed in Erico's face as he looked at me, flustered.

"Looks like Vincent has all the power," I said smirking, "That's right, Erico...obey."

Erico pulled away from me.

"Well, 'I' might not be able to do you harm. But my comrades can," he said as he tapped one of Los Furiosos's members on the shoulder.

The man raised his shotgun at me, taking aim. I quickly showed them the detonator from behind my back.

"I don't think so," I said, drawing the detonator's trigger while a beeping continued to sound while it was depressed. Los Furiosos began to take steps back. Erico looked to his left and right as his men edged back more and more.

"Silly, Faerie. I doubt you even have the balls to blow this place up. If we go...you go," he said as he smiled, testing my threat.

Suddenly, out of the corner of my eye, I could see something moving on the second floor. I glanced back at Erico and started to wave the detonator in the air. The other men continued to back up even farther. Some were gasping, and others were whispering to each other, worried that I actually might do it. There was no way I was going to release the trigger without killing myself in the process. I glanced up again and could see the figure that lurked on the second floor. She trudged quietly enough not to be heard. Her black fur glistened in the fluorescent lighting that the generator produced. The clock was ticking, and I knew that at any moment, the generator would eventually stop working. The panther stalked back and forth as I waved the detonator in the air, trying to catch her attention. Los Furiosos backed up to the point where they were all underneath the edge of the second floor. The only person holding his ground was Erico.

"You won't do it," Erico said confidently, opening up his arms, having nothing to fear.

I could see her vivid green eyes lock onto Erico, and the flash in her vision showed that she recognized who he was. I smirked as she slowly approached the edge in a crouching manner. Her focus narrowed as she watched his every move.

"Los Furiosos will reign, Faerie. Soon we will consume the entire world, and there is nothing you can do about it," Erico said, lowering his arms.

When he did, she tilt her head out of the corner of my eye. She was beginning to steady her paws on the floor, preparing to jump. I beamed in delight and looked back at Erico, who was completely unaware of her presence.

"I don't know what you have going on here..." I said, pausing just before she sprang to attack.

"But it's over."

She leaped through the air. Roaring as her claws tore into Erico's back. Erico let out a loud scream. The other men all shouted in terror as they began to scatter in different directions while the panther dug her claws into Erico. I laughed to myself and quickly broke into a sprint, hiding behind the Capitol Optic's crates.

The men all frantically ran in different directions. Some darting through tunnels and others running behind other crates hiding from both the panther and from me. I reached into my bag and pulled out my flare. I slung my pack back on and pulled out my 1911. I held both the flare and my gun in my right hand while I continued to keep the trigger of the detonator depressed in my left. The rush of adrenaline was flowing as I took aim at Los Furiosos. Shooting off rounds, hitting anyone I could. The more of them I killed, the better. Some stood their ground, firing back. I ducked behind the crate, taking cover. My eyes darted toward the pond, the only way out. I could see containers that made good cover along the way. The sound of the panther echoed into the cathedral, so did gunfire. I made a break for the next crate, shooting at Los Furiosos as I moved. I managed to hit a few in the process as I took cover once again behind a container.

Suddenly the lights flicked off as the generator died. I could hear the men yelling frantically because they couldn't see. The roar of the panther continued to sound as she was on to her next victim. Signs of the sun filter through the ceiling. Just enough light to see. Gunfire continued, running to my next crate. Mid-run, I popped the cap off my flare and ignited it. The panther was on my trail. I used the flare to my advantage, waving it at her, causing her to run off toward other Los Furiosos. She leaped and attacked them as I continued to the pond. I could see two Los Furiosos men go after Erico and begin to carry him away. I took aim at them as they quickly ran into a mine shaft. I let off a few rounds, damnit, missed them. The panther came back to me, and I waved the flare at her, sending her running off toward Los Furiosos. Silver-haloed eyes floated in the dark.

I smiled and took aim as I fled, shooting as many people as I could. I was thankful that the panther was here to save me. However, she would soon meet a bitter end because there was no way I could keep the trigger pressed for much longer. As I ran for the pond, I continued to fire my gun until it was empty. I slid my

1911 back into its holster as I made my first step into the water. It was freezing, but the rush of danger made me push through it. I had water up to my knees as I continued to move deeper into the pond. I looked behind me, Los Furiosos were preoccupied with the panther, paid no attention to me anymore. I knew this was my perfect opportunity to blow the place to bits. With how many Los Furiosos' members were in here, I would definitely make a dent in their so-called army. I continued forward and came to a point where I couldn't touch the floor anymore. I began to swim like my life depended on it, trying to get as close to the end of the pond as I could. My flare was still sparkling as I plunged it underwater while I swam. I could hear the panther roar in pain as one of the men took an axe to her leg.

I approached the end of the pond and could see sunlight flicker from the other side. I looked back to the C4 along with all the gold that they had acquired. I attempted to steady my breathing as I took a final deep breath before I went under. I swam until I was deep enough to where I thought it would be safe. I released the detonator and could hear the sound of the C4 exploding behind me as I continued to swim using my flare for light. I could feel the vibration of the explosions. The entire cathedral was crumbling. I swam quicker now, holding my breath for as long as I could. There was sunlight at the end of the underwater cave. I could see that the surface was nearly ten meters from where I was.

Panicking now because I was running out of air, I swam as fast as I could. I sprang up out of the water, gasping for my first breath of air.

The pond came to a shallow point as it continued to form into a small stream that led down a hill. I swam until I reached the shallows. I pulled myself out of the water, dragging my legs behind me until I reached a meadow of grass. I rolled onto my back, taking in air as I stared at sky. My eyelids began to get heavy as every breath I took reminded me of the utter exhaustion I was feeling. While the sun shown above me, I shook my head in disbelief that I had survived another night on Candelario Island.

7: Bronze Channel Falls

THE WEIGHT OF SOMETHING pounced onto me, jolting me awake. Instantly, I lifted myself up, gripping my axe and glancing around, ready to attack. My breathing was rapid as I looked around in all directions while I winced from the sunlight. The lapping sounds of water was all around as I sat next to the pond, clutching my weapon. The trees were billowing in the gusts as a cool breeze wafted through the air. I raised my hand to my ribs, the soreness reminding me of the battles I'd fought not that long ago. I stood up slowly, the pain reminding me I was actually human as I observed the pond. In the depths, I could see that the entrance to the Cimmerian Tunnels was completely blocked off. I used the C4 to destroy what I wasn't meant to.

Remembering I was still wearing my pack, I slowly took it off which required a feat of strength because of how sore I was. I laid it down and worked to unbuckle its clasps. My papers were completely wet, and the legibility of them was almost nonexistent. I gently removed the papers, trying to keep their shape without damaging them any more than they already were. I spread the sheets out in front of me to dry. I could somewhat make out the outlines that Erico had created. I dug deeper into my pack and pulled out the canteen I had salvaged in TreeTop. I set the bag down and went to fill it up. I didn't know if the water was safe to drink or not. But I wasn't sure there was another option. As I approached the pond, the sound of mosquitoes zipped by, along with dragonflies that hovered over the water. After filling it up, I raised the container to my lips as I watched the insects fly in every direction. I took a whiff of the water before I drank and couldn't detect any strange smells. Guess it was as safe of an option as I had at the moment.

I sighed in satisfaction with every gulp I took. It seemed like weeks since I last had any type of food or drink. My mind went back to the tiramisu I ate before I left Toronto. How I missed the simple pleasures of food. I walked away from the pond and reached for my pack as my ribs reminded me again that they were incredibly sore.

"I'd kill for some morphine right now."

I reached into my pack and pulled out the small cartridge of bullets. I rested my back against a rock wall near the pond and lowered myself to the ground. I set the rounds to my side and pulled out my 1911. I kept my eyes on the insects and birds in the trees and thought of them as my own personal alarm system. If they fled, then so should I. The clip released and I reloaded. There weren't many bullets left, and I hoped that they were still functional after being saturated. As I loaded the clip, I thought of Liam and wondered if he would think to bring his Glock with him since I assumed he was on his way to find me. Knowing him, though, he never left the house without it. Finishing loading the bullets, my reality was that there were eight rounds left.

I holstered my gun and looked back at the soaking wet maps.

"Nearly home, Alec," I said to myself. "Just two more stops and you'll be out of here." Trying to find the positive and the confidence for another battle.

My pocket vibrated. Oh, my God, the walkie. I reached in my pocket.

"Damnit," I could see that it had taken a lot of water damage.

The screen had water drops behind the glass. The interface of the phone was fading in and out, and there were lines that flickered in different colors as it strived to stay on. I could relate.

I shook the walkie violently as water flung out of it. I could hear Atlas speak, but the sound was less audible than ever before.

"Alec, are you okay? Over." He was probably wondering if I was still breathing.

I clicked the button and could hear the walkie going in and out of static.

"I'm here," I said while I could feel my ribs tingle in pain with every breath I took. "Can you hear me? Over."

Atlas sounded relieved when he responded, "Jeez, I was beginning to worry that you..." He paused because he didn't want to say it. "You're breaking up very badly. What happened to you down there? Over."

I scoffed to myself, "It's a long story," I said. "I blew up the tunnels to escape and swam through a cave to make it out. My walkie was damaged by the water. Over."

"Were you able to get the C4? Over."

I responded, "Yeah, about that..."

Atlas interjected, "Damnit, Alec. That was the one thing you needed to do."

The amount of trauma I had been through was torture enough. Now I was being scolded because I wasn't able to do what he asked? Fuck that.

"Excuse me. I just barely made it out alive. And because I didn't get your precious C4 and made one mistake, yeah, I'm sorry that it bothers you." I responded in anger, mainly because I was in pain, but I was also pissed at the situation.

"Alec, I know you are upset, and I can only imagine what you've been through. But those explosives were the only..."

I interrupted. "No. You don't understand, and you can ONLY imagine. I almost died multiple times last night, and I'm lucky to still be fucking breathing. This isn't me, Atlas. I'm not a fucking 'super-soldier' who was trained for something like this. A few months ago, I was part of the Peace Corps. Saving and helping people. And now I'm fighting for my life on some godforsaken island. Killing people, I might add, of an army of mind-controlled men. Oh, I'm so sorry, Atlas. I wasn't made for this. All I want to do is go back to my life in Canada. Back to where it's safe. Back to Liam..." I said, holding back tears of pain, and from the thought of my perfect life that I had back home. Everything was different now. Things would never ever be the same again.

"I apologize, Alec. I know it's hard and I know you don't think you were built for this, but you are. You've come so far, and most men couldn't do that."

I peered around at my surroundings and the emotions that flooded my mind were overwhelming. The sight of the trees and birds, being on foreign soil, my injuries. Thirst and hunger. I was exhausted from it all. I held onto the wall near me, trying to gather myself. Because this wasn't over.

Atlas interjected my thoughts, "I'm sorry for losing my temper. And I know that you had a life before all of this. Can I ask? Who is Liam? Over."

I lifted my shirt to examine my ribs. They were black and blue, and the outline of the bones were questionable. They were definitely broken. I lowered my shirt and responded to Atlas.

"He's no one," I responded because I wasn't ready to share that part of my life with a complete stranger. "Just tell me that you are still going to help me. Tell me that there is another option to take down this laboratory so I can go home. Please. Over," I said, gasping for air as I started to walk back over to my maps.

"I'm not going anywhere until I get you off of that island. Do you hear me? Over." Atlas spoke like he had a substantial investment in me. Something about him seemed overly protective.

"Okay. How do I navigate the Bronze Channel Falls? The maps I have are all wet," I said as I kneeled down over them. I looked at the Bronze Channel map, analyzing it carefully to decipher what I was looking at. By the looks of it, it seemed like the channel split into two. Both of which led to the ocean. I could see the outline of a building that was slightly blurred. I could make out the name: Genetic Research Facility. I'm assuming that's where I was headed.

Atlas responded to me, "There is a path that is close to you. Your best bet is to stick to the path, but be careful. Just as before, Los Furiosos will be lingering. Once you reach the Bronze Channel Falls, you're going to have to board a boat of some kind and take the channel directly toward the lab. Over."

"Okay? That sounds simple enough." I grunted again.

"Are you okay? You don't sound too well. Over."

"I'll be fine. I just want to get out of here." I said this as I worked to control the pain in my voice.

"Okay, well, when you reach the channel, I think you should try to raid the Los Furiosos' supply shack. They have a small dock where they keep their boats and supplies locked up nearby. There should be some medical supplies and food there. Over." Atlas said, trying to convince me that I really needed medical attention. I didn't hesitate. With how bad my ribs were, it would only slow me down.

"All right, I'll head there. Over," I said as I began to pick up the maps, shaking them slightly, trying to get what water was left off of them.

I walked over to my bag and placed the papers in it. As I did, I noticed there was something glowing inside. I reached in and felt a heavy, rectangular item. I pulled it out.

"Holy shit," I said as I held onto a golden bar. "That's why my bag felt heavier."

I remembered I had been holding onto one of the gold bars and dropped it when I was in the tunnels. It must have fallen into my bag. I laughed because this was most likely the last piece of gold that remained after I destroyed the mines. I placed the bar back into the bag and the blueprint of the implant process caught my eye. I pulled out the wet paper, wanting to get an idea of how these implants worked. Although the article was wet and smudged, I could still make out most of what the writing said. It seemed like Los Furiosos found a way to have the implant attach itself to the significant areas of the spinal column. Giving them control of the person's body, temperature, motor skills, blood pressure, breathing, and even their brain functions.

"This is why Erico couldn't hit me," I said while looking at the diagram. There were notes that stated that the implants needed to be continuously calibrated. With every calibration, there was a small amount of hallucinogen placed and stored inside the implant. Allowing the person in control to be able to make the individuals see and hear whatever they wanted. Other notes said that if the implants were not calibrated regularly, the subject would begin to regain control of their functions again.

But my question was, how could it be removed? Once the implants were flashing red, the person would return to normal, having complete control over themselves. But with how adamant Los Furiosos were about keeping tabs on their implants, it seemed nearly impossible for one of them to ignore the fact that it needed to be calibrated. It also seemed very dangerous to remove something like that without possibly paralyzing the subject. Perhaps even killing them.

Of course, I needed to get a move on, so I slipped the blueprint back into my pack and put it on. I winced in pain and prayed that this supply shack had narcotics because I desperately needed them. Down below, I spotted the channel. I reached into my pocket and pulled out my binoculars and held them up to my eyes to get a better look.

Through the binoculars, I could see the channel up close. It seemed to go on for miles as it forked in different directions. It was beautiful yet I knew it would be dangerous.

"This is going to be a hell of a ride but it's almost over, Alec," I whispered to myself, continuing to look.

I could see a trail that led down into the valley and connected to the channel. At its end was a medium-sized shack where the supplies must have been stored. A dock stretched from the cabin and into the water where I could see three boats lined alongside the pier...one of them was leaving. I lowered my binoculars and placed them into my pocket. Looking to my left, I could see the trees open up, creating a path. I took a few deep breaths and started to walk toward it. I kept off the path so I wouldn't be seen. There wasn't much cover to hide behind because the sun was shining brightly. While I walked through the trees, I admired the beauty of it all. The thought of vacationing on an island after all of this made me feel sick. But then I realized that I was actually feeling sick to my stomach. Maybe I shouldn't have drunk that water.

I continued to make my way down into the valley. My stomach started to roil while I hiked, and I felt feverish. God, this wasn't good. I fought off the sensation and kept moving forward. Almost done. I just had a little bit more to do here and then freedom. I hid behind a boulder, trying to catch my breath, I knew it was hot out, but not to the point that I should be feeling the way that I did. I could hear voices echo through the trees as a group of men were advancing. I pulled out my walkie before Atlas spoke.

"Good looking out, Alec," Atlas said. The men stomped by, talking to each other while I listened.

"Hurry up. We need to get as many of them out as possible. There are a lot of them who are injured. We need all the help we can get."

Another man responded while he was running, "How did it happen?"

"That fucking Faerie set off a bomb. Some were lucky to make it out alive. Others, not so much. I swear, for a Faerie, he's been doing a lot of damage."

"Did the Faerie make it out?" one of the men asked. I laughed to myself, but the pain of my ribs cut me off along with the knot I could feel in my stomach.

"We don't know. Some think he did, and others think he could still be stuck inside. Just keep an eye open." They continued to run off into the distance.

I had to get moving. With every step I took, I knew I was sick. I continued to ignore my symptoms. I didn't have a choice. Beads of sweat continued to drip off of me as I kept pushing myself through the trees. I stopped next to a tree and rested my hand on it, holding myself up. My pocket vibrated. I listened while I panted in place.

"Alec, how are you holding up? Over."

"I don't know, Atlas, I'm not feeling too well. I drank water from the pond earlier, and I think it was a mistake."

"Shouldn't have done that, those waters are teeming with parasites. Over." He could tell I was off my game.

"I feel like I have a fever, my stomach is cramping. I'm feeling really nauseous, and my vision is starting to blur. I don't feel right, Atlas." I spoke, working to hold myself together.

"Alec, try to make it to the supply shack as soon as you can. I know they have medical supplies inside. Probably nothing to help with your symptoms, but there is definitely something for the pain. Over."

There was a cold breeze that felt gentle against my skin as my temperature proceeded to rise. I began walking through the trees again, holding onto my stomach. The more I walked, the louder the sound of the current of the channel rippled in the distance. I came to a clearing and could see the water stretch out in front of the trees. I held myself up against a nearby tree and looked over the water. It was beautiful. My eyes floated across the channel, and I realized why it was given its name. The rocks that were scattered at the bottom floor were reflective, as if they were made of bronze. The water was crystal clear, and silver fish were swimming all around. The channel had a calming sound, and it made me want to fall asleep. Or maybe that was the fever talking. At this point, I felt like it wasn't a bad idea. My head was beginning to pound as the fever worsened.

I looked to my left and could see the supply shack up close. There was a small group of Los Furiosos carrying boxes in and out of the cabin, loading up one of the two boats that remained. I brought my eyes back to Los Furiosos and could see that the crates they carried displayed a red and white cross on them. I noticed one of the men drop a box, and I could see a can of food roll out as he hurried to try to catch it before it rolled off the dock and into the water. I was getting a little worried because I knew it wasn't going to be a simple task to take one of the boats. I held down the button before I talked.

"Atlas, I'm near the channel. What do I do now? Over."

Atlas started to respond, but my walkie kept going in and out. I shook my head and slowly tried to walk around to get a signal.

"Al...can yo..me" Atlas voice kept breaking up.

"Shit," I said to myself.

I looked at my walkie and could see the screen flickering. I put the walkie back in my pocket and started to make my way through the trees, heading toward the shack. As I ran, my fever only continued to get worse, and the pounding in my head grew more substantial. I needed whatever medication I could find in that shack.

I could see two men start to walk toward the shack, and another three of them exited and walked across the dock toward the boat they were filling up. Darting across the trail and making it to the side of the shack, I rested my back against its walls and tried to catch my breath. My stress was through the roof, and my heart raced with every beat. I found a small set of wooden stairs that led to a little porch. I reached for my axe as I slowly walked up the steps. I looked through a window and suddenly a man entered the room, I quickly hid from view, peeking into the window. Another man entered behind him.

"Did you find it? We need all the medical supplies to help them."

"Yeah, we have some more here." The man responded as he pulled out some first aid kits from the cabinet.

My heart quickened as I heard them talking about the supplies, either that or because my sickness was getting worse.

The two men exited the shack. I began to open the door as it creaked loudly. Wincing, I tried to open it even slower. I slipped into the shack, gently closing the door behind me. I approached the entrance to the right and gripped the handle.

I twisted the handle ever so slowly, cracking the door open just enough to see inside. It looked clear, but then again, my eyesight was beginning to blur. I could feel my head pounding, and I reached out, steadying myself on one of the cabinets. Stumbling to keep myself upright, I headed directly to the cupboard that the men were taking supplies from. I opened the doors and found multiple pill bottles, syringes, bandages, and peroxide. It was nirvana in a cabinet as I rummaged through the containers trying to find something for my symptoms.

In desperation, I began to toss anything I thought would help inside my backpack. I didn't know how much time I had until Los Furiosos would be back. I knew I couldn't fight off anyone in the state I was in. I was also able to find a supply cabinet full of canned food and bottles of water.

"Thank God." I whispered to myself as I grabbed water and canned food, stuffing it in my backpack.

I closed the cabinets and put my pack back on. A tv continued to sound in the background. I was curious as what the news said. I slowly approached the archway that divided the room full of cabinets and a small lounging area. I was breathing heavily, feeling faint. As I stood leaning against the wall, I could see the television. The newscaster was speaking in Spanish with subtitles in English. The newscaster was raving about the newest technology to hit the market... Capitol Optics. I started to cough quietly to myself as I watched the tv. The newscaster stated that Capitol Optics would soon be released into different parts of the world, everyone was waiting to get their hands on it.

I pushed myself off of the wall and stumbled back to the door I came from. I slipped out, striving to hold my breath to stop myself from coughing. I trotted down the steps and quickly rested my back against the wall of the shack. I slowly slid down to the ground, coughing.

Clouded vision, I wasn't sure what was wrong with me. I had never felt like this before, and have never experienced repercussions from ingesting a parasite. I took off my backpack and dug inside.

"Alec, are you feeling okay? I can see you on my feed. You don't look too good. Over." Atlas spoke with apprehension.

I pulled out the meds, food, and water and started to read over all of them. I found a bottle that read 'Codeine' and opened it. Took two of them. I came across a bottle labeled 'Penicillin.' I dug until I found a clean and sterile syringe. Is this the right dosage? I was dwindling fast, anything would help.

"This better work."

I held out my arm, I never injected myself before as I held the syringe at an angle, penetrating my vein, pushing the solution inside of me. I removed the needle, put it back in my pack. I took my knife and opened a can of food. Green beans. Scarfing them down, followed by a bottle of water. I reached into my pocket to radio Atlas.

"Atlas?" A boat started its engine.

Atlas didn't respond.

I peeked around the corner. I could see one of the boats was taking off.

"Shit," I said to myself, holding down the walkie button again. "Atlas? Are you there?"

"I'm here, Alec. What's... on? Ov..." he answered with another choppy connection

"One of the boats is leaving."

I felt better, pain pills would only suppress my throbbing.

Atlas was silent.

"I'm going to try to take the next boat. How do I destroy the Lab? Over."

Atlas replied, distracted, "I found a plan B. The lab has a self-destruct system.This won't... the tunnels. It... bigger." Shit. The connection kept cutting out.

"Okay, how do I activate it? Over." I asked while I began to stuff the items back into my bag and made the decision to get moving.

I made it to the edge of the front of the cabin and spotted three men boarding the boat. I radioed Atlas again.

"Atlas? What's going on? Why aren't you responding?" The lack of response and poor connection left me petrified.

I needed to make a decision and move fast. There was no way to get onto the boat without being spotted. The dock extended out far into the water, and my only chance of sneaking onto it was to swim underneath the pier and somehow climb onto the boat. Not sure that my walkie could survive another submersion, though.

"Come on, Atlas. Respond,"

The sound of the boat's engine revved to life. One of the men began to untie the rope that kept the vessel stationed at the dock. My heart was racing because I was running out of time. There was no way I was going to be able to swim to the lab in my condition. Plus, I knew once I hit the water, my walkie would be done for.

"Alec, I'm here. I need to tell... omething." His reluctance caused me to worry.

Shit. I had to make my move. I took off in a sprint once I saw Los Furiosos looking away. I kept moving, trying to stay low enough so the dock would keep me hidden. My pocket vibrated again as Atlas spoke.

"Alec, if... hear me, listen ca...fully. When you make it to the lab, whatev... do, don't let them take your bloo... Alec. Do you understand? No matter the cost... let them... ake a sample of your blood. Do you hea...me?" The walkie was fucked.

"Son of a bitch," slipped out of my mouth.

Those instructions made me panic, but I didn't have time to respond. I submerged myself in the ice-cold water and soon enough, I could no longer touch bottom as I swam underneath the dock. I could hear footsteps moving back and forth above me. The shade of the pier made the water feel even colder as I continued to swim closer to the boat. The base of the craft rocked back and forth as the men continued to talk to one another.

"Here. Take the rope. Hurry, we need to leave."

I shivered as I held onto a piece of wood supporting the dock. Terrified about what Atlas said, I was heading into the deepest and most dangerous part of Candelario. Atlas knew more about me than I estimated. So many questions ran through my mind as I waited for my moment to grab onto the boat. The footsteps above me quieted as the last man stepped onto the vessel. I held the walkie in my hand, trying to keep it from getting wet. I could see the propellers from underneath the boat suddenly spin at full throttle. The sound was incredibly loud, and the wake from behind the craft caused me to drop my walkie.

"No!" I screamed.

The sound of the engine revving muted my screams as I quickly dove into the water to recover the walkie. The depth of the water must have been at least fifteen-feet deep. My ears began to pop once I reached the bottom as I grabbed my walkie that had landed between two rocks.

The pressure of the water made my ribs hurt as I pushed off the bottom, quickly broke the surface and began swimming as fast as I could. The boat was about to clear the dock now, and I risked the chance of being spotted if I stayed above the surface.

But I was in luck. There was a fluorescent yellow bumper line that was being dragged behind the boat while it rippled from the current. I kept swimming and was a foot away from the cord as I reached out, kicking my legs even faster. I snagged the yellow line with my hands and relaxed the lower half of my body while gripping the rope, trying to pull myself closer to the boat while the craft picked up momentum.

The force of the current made it difficult to pull myself closer. But when I looked up, I could see a ladder that was attached to the back end of the boat. I grabbed onto it and held on as the craft continued at full speed.

While I hung onto the stairs, I began to think about what Atlas said about the self-destruct system. If I were to complete my mission and be saved from this island, I had to do whatever I needed to take the laboratory down. How would I activate it, though, I had no idea? I was alone now. Atlas knew where I was, and I only hoped that he would be ready for my escape. They killed my brother, and I knew they would do the same to me once they found out that I wasn't what they were looking for.

The engine turned off, and I could see the propellers begin too slow. I started to panic because I didn't know if something was wrong with the motor and maybe they would head to the back of the boat to check it out. I stayed where I was as the sound of bubbles slowed from the propellers. Shivering in both fear and from the frigid temperatures of the water, I shuddered in place as the natural current of the channel started to cause the boat to drift down the canal. I peeked out from behind the boat to see what was happening. I could see two men sitting on either side of the deck. The third man was steering the boat from inside the cockpit. As I viewed the vessel, I noticed how beautiful it was.

The men began talking about taking a route that would get them closer to the Cimmerian Tunnels. I knew that was the opposite direction of where I wanted to go. I needed to board the boat, or I would quickly become hypothermic. I didn't have time for a detour. As the men remained to debate, I watched their every move. I could see that the man steering the boat had a handgun mounted on his hip. The other two men had weapons, as well. I only had my handgun with limited ammo. I had my axe and my knife, but my weapons were no match against guns.

I had to make a move and quick, as I gazed around the boat, I could see the channel fork off into three different directions. The map had shown that the channel forked off into two directions, not three. I was beginning to think Erico wasn't as bright as I thought. Either that or his leader Vincent didn't want him seeing things that he shouldn't. I needed to make a decision. I pulled out my gun, shaking the water out of it.

"Only eight bullets, Alec. Make them count."

I pulled myself out of the water and onto the back edge of the boat and stayed crouched while looking around. Suddenly, one of the men appeared. He said something to the man steering the boat, and they began to argue. The man who was sitting outside shook his head and glanced back toward the end of the boat. His eyes met mine. I stood up from my hiding place and aimed my gun at him.

"Shhh," I whispered, as I gradually started to approach him, I could see that he was reaching for his gun.

I pulled the hammer back on my 1911. As it clicked, the man winced and put his hands up in the air.

"Get up and turn around," I said quietly so the others couldn't hear me.

I looked over, and I could hear them fighting about what way they wanted to take. Suddenly, the man I held at gunpoint screamed.

"He's here!"

Quickly, the men who were arguing stopped and looked behind them. I grabbed the man by his arm and twisted it behind him, using his body as a shield.

"Everyone keep calm, and no one has to die today," I said, watching their every move. I could see them reaching for their weapons. I pressed the barrel of my gun against my prisoner's temple.

"Make another move, and I will kill him."

The men began to laugh. The man steering the boat ignored me and kept his focus on the current. The other man held up his shotgun and pointed it at me.

"You think we give a shit about him? Kill him if you want."

My hostage struggled in place as I twisted his arm, harder.

"Don't do it, Allen." My hostage winced.

It seemed he was more concerned for his life at this moment because I had the feeling the man aiming the shotgun at me wasn't bullshitting.

"Lower your weapon and kick it over to me," I demanded, trembling in place.

Just then, I could feel my pocket buzzing. Only this time it was someone calling me.

"Don't fucking move." I yelled as I reached into my pocket and pressed the gun firmly against my hostage's head. I pulled out the walkie phone and answered it.

"Hello?"

The walkie phone was fucked, it kept going in and out from both the reception and the amount of water damaged it had taken.

"Alec?"

"Liam?" I said, as my voice began to break. "Liam, can you hear me?" I said, trying to keep focus on the men from making any sudden moves.

"Alec, thank God. I'm coming for you, okay. I'm coming for you."

"Liam, I..." As I spoke, the phone cut out. "Liam? Fuck!" I screamed, and I could feel tears welling up in my eyes.

"Your friend isn't going to help you now," Allen raised his shotgun with confidence. "No one will ever help a faggot like you!"

Suddenly the man I held hostage elbowed me in the stomach with his free arm. I grunted as the force of the blow caused me to let off a shot accidentally. The bullet I fired hit the man steering the boat, causing him to fall to the floor, pulling the wheel to the right as he collapsed. The craft began to turn. Swaying back and forth, attempting to fight the current. The man that hit me tried to run away as we all began to lose our ground while the boat rocked. I pulled him back as Allen took aim at both of us. I quickly pulled my hostage in front of me as cover. Allen let off two rounds that slammed into my hostage. The blood from the man spattered over my face as he fell to the ground twitching. Allen tried to reload his gun as the boat turned and swayed, making him drop his bullets. While the boat shifted, I lost my footing and began to stumble to my left, clinging onto the railing of the vessel. I used what energy I had and tried to charge at Allen as he fumbled, chasing after his bullets that rolled across the deck.

I immediately slammed into Allen. When I did, the shotgun in his hands flung off the boat. He grunted loudly, backhanded me across my face, causing me to fall to the ground.

"You stupid bitch," he yelled as he pulled out a knife from his back pocket.

He quickly started to approach me as I tried to stand up. I immediately took aim at him while kneeling on one knee. I looked to my left and could see the boat drifting toward a large boulder within the water. The ship slammed into the rock as I pulled the trigger. The force of the crash caused me to fall to my side, sending my handgun over the boat. Allen plummeted to his knees, dropping his knife. The current was beginning to get fast, and the ship was floating down the middle fork of the channel now. I could feel the water splash onto the deck. As it did, Allen's knife started to slide over toward me. Allen could see it move as he quickly raised up from his knees and made a run for the blade. I scrambled on my hands and knees, reaching for the knife. I grabbed it, as Allen charged at me. He swiftly kicked me across the face, throwing me onto my back. Allen straddled me as I tried to fight him off while recovering from the pain in my jaw. Allen held my forearm, working to turn the knife toward me. He gripped my palm, starting to lunge the blade closer to my chest.

"Get the fuck off of me." Preventing the knife from penetrating my heart, I used as much strength as I had left.

"Die, Faerie," he shouted, silver eyes pulsing with pleasure.

The boat slammed into a mountain that framed the channel. When it did, large rocks flung onto the deck, hurdling at Allen, hitting him on the back of his head. He fell to his side. I advanced at Allen with the knife. I raised the blade into the air, stabbed him in the inner thigh.

"You motherfucker!" Allen screamed at the top of his lungs.

I pulled the knife out, sprinting toward the cockpit. I knew that I had to gain control of the boat before it took another blow. Allen clung to his leg, screaming in pain. Massive amounts of blood seeped out onto the deck as Allen bled out. Must have hit an artery.

I slammed the door shut. There was a latch on the side of the door, and I promptly slid it into place. Allen rushed to the door, pounding his hands onto the window, leaving his bloody handprints on the glass as he shouted.

"Open the fucking door, you bitch."

The boat was drifting sideways down the channel as the current carried us at full speed. I looked out to my left and could see that the water was beginning to get shallow up ahead. I grabbed onto the wheel, taking control. The boat roared to life as I started to turn the wheel.

"What the fuck are you doing," Allen screamed. "You're going to kill us both."

"You're already dying. Just get on with it."

There was a throttle lever to the right of the wheel, pulled it back. The engine revved powerfully, fighting to surpass the current. The boat began turning.

"It's working. It's working," I screamed, beaming with excitement.

I looked back at Allen, taking off his belt, tying it around his leg. As he did, I could see him reach into his shirt, pulling out a sterling silver locket. He clenched onto it, kissing it, praying to himself. The vessel made a one-eighty. Scents of oil filled the cockpit. Smoke was coming from the lever as the engine struggled

Glancing back, Allen sat on the right side of the ship, holding onto his locket and the railing. My eyes went from Allen to the edge of the boat. The water faded into nothing...no fucking way. A waterfall awaited our ship.

"Oh my God."

The engine's roar dulled to silence, as it did, the current pulled us back.

"No. NO." Forcefully, I pulled the accelerator up and down.

I twisted the key, over and over again. Useless. Looking back, the current pulled us, shredding the bottom of the ship. The sound of the boat beginning to fall made me shudder. I looked back to Allen, who looked at me as he held on. Bracing for impact. This was it. I was going to die. And the only person here with me during my last few minutes on Earth was a mind-controlled man named Allen who was out to kill me.

I could feel the force of the ship begin to drift vertically; rumbling, shaking, searing, and breaking. Sounds that made my heart beat in my throat. We approached the edge of the world. The boat tipped, and when it did, I could hear cabinets open behind me while items began to fling out onto the floor. I wanted to see everything. I wanted to see the world one last time. I wanted to see Liam. I wanted him to be here so I could tell him how much I loved him. I looked down at my ring, brought it to my face, kissed it.

"I love you."

The weight of my body pressed against the cockpit door. Allen dangled from the railing. Plummeting to the bottom, my perception of the fall seemed like more than a hundred feet. Twisting and turning, hitting rocks and branches that protruded from the waterfall. Allen's body flew off the ship, I was tossed around like a rag doll. Closing my eyes, embracing death.

What met me was a boisterous crash, followed by bubbles of water.

Cold water surrounded me, my eyes shot open. This fight wasn't over.

Water overflowing into the cockpit, my body throbbed as the boat sank. Water filtering in from small chunks that had been taken out from the fall. I was in an air bubble that was losing oxygen, fast. I looked out to my left, trying to regain my vision and could see something fall into the water.

Allen's body plunged into the river, hitting the back of his head on a rock. Trails of red blood were coming out of his leg. Struggling to regain full consciousness, I started to move toward a window. Massive amount of pain all over my body. I looked down, a piece of the steering wheel was broken off in my stomach. I had no choice. I gripped the wooden piece and pulled it out.

"Rrraaahhh!" Throwing the piece of a broken steering wheel as far away from me as I could.

Blood sifted through the cockpit as I pressed my hand against the window. Water up to my shoulders, and it was only getting worse. I tried to muster through the pain and started to punch the window. Useless, the pressure of the water on the other side was too high.

"Help," I screamed as if anyone could hear me...of course, no one did.

Punching the window with no success, the water was at my lips now, shivering from the freezing temperatures. I continued to hit the window over and over until my knuckles bled. I began to cry because it was hopeless. My face was pressed up against the glass as the water continued to make its way in. Choking, inhaling both water and air, the entire cockpit had become consumed.

Struggling, fighting the urge to take a breath. I kept fighting to the end. Bubbles filtered out of my nose and mouth while I continued to beat on the surface of the window. I used my left fist to unleash another blow before I ran out of air. The glass barely cracked from the force of my ring. I gave in. The thought of drowning scared me beyond recognition. As I looked one last time, I could see hands on the outside of the window. The sound of breaking glass rippled underwater. All I could see was the water around me, turning red. My eyes started to roll back into my head. Taking in my first breath of water as hypoxia began to settle in. All I remembered was pressure pulling me by my arm as I slowly lost consciousness...

"Breathe. Come on, breathe damn it."

Water violently spewed out of my lungs. I turned to my side, continuing to choke. My lungs burned as if someone stuck a red hot poker down my throat. With every cough, my body twitched, causing my ribs to hurt even more then they already did. I could feel pain all over my body, pressure in my ears made it feel like I was deaf. Everything was silent as I continued to cough out all the water inside my lungs. My vision was blurry as I held myself up with my hands against the grass. My eyes started to clear as I rolled onto my back, taking in the air. Resting on my back, I opened my eyes, Allen hovering over me.

I instantly started to scramble back, but slipped in the mud along the bank. I tried to scream, but my lungs weren't ready. Allen reached out, grabbing me by my arm. I pulled away from him as he clenched onto his leg.

"Stop, Alec," Allen screamed more clearly now. "Stop, please." Holding up his hands.

I could tell he was close to dying because his lips were incredibly purple and his skin was so sallow. I looked around and saw the carnage of what was left of the boat floating in the water nearby. Allen saved me? But why? So many questions went through my mind.

"Are you okay?"

"I'm okay, I think," I said while coughing. "Did you save me?" He nodded.

"Why?"

"I knew the last thing I had to do before I died was to save you."

"Save me? But why?" I questioned him while getting closer.

"When I fell, I hit my head and could feel myself again, like my vision was clear, and my freedom was back." His breathing was very erratic. "I needed to save you because I know what you are. I know how valuable you are to Los Furiosos."

"Valuable? What do you mean?" I asked again, trying to get as much information as I could before he took his final breaths.

"Alec, your blood is the reason why Chromosome H was created. If Dr. Jericho believes it to be true. You or your brother were given Chromosome A.S. in embryo. But you..." He began to get choked up. "You are different. Different from your brother." He laughed to himself silently and began to cough. "I can see it in you. You're going to the lab, aren't you? When you get there, DON'T let them take your blood. If that happens, Alec, the world, as you know it will fall."

His voice was shaking, "I know you are good, but power like that should never fall into the wrong hands."

"What kind of power?"

"Dr. Jericho spoke of incredible strength. Insurmountable speed. Rapid, accelerated healing. Possible increased brain capacity, giving the individual *psionic* capabilities." He slowly put his hand on mine, trying to squeeze, but he was incredibly weak. "If Los Furiosos were to synthesize it, they will become an unstoppable army. You must not let it happen, Alec." He was starting to fade.

"I won't." I said, shaking my head.

Allen smiled at me as he began to remove his locket from around his neck. "Take this, and make sure it gets to my son. He's on Isle Onocastel. It's all he will have left to remember me." He handed it to me while his hand shook.

I took the locket, and it opened as I did. A photo of Allen, a woman, and a young boy who was probably eight years old was inside along with a compass that pointed north.

"You remind me a lot of my son." He smiled to himself. "He is so brave, I love him and my wife very much. I never wanted them to see me end up like this. Please, Alec, for me. Be sure that he gets it." He pleaded.

I felt strange accepting it. The man that had tried to kill me was begging me to grant him his final wish. I nodded my head as he took his last breath.

Tears filled my eyes. What had I become? What had Los Furiosos turned me into? These men didn't choose to join Los Furiosos. I shook my head and closed my eyes as tears rolled down my cheeks. I had no real way of making it out of here. And Los Furiosos believed me to be the key to their army.

I had no other choice but to keep moving. I took Allen's locket and wore it around my neck. I stood up and reached for my axe. I soon felt like I was destined to be here. An entire part of my life that had been unexplained was beginning to make sense. If I had Chromosome A.S., I would stop at nothing to protect it. Being saved or not didn't matter to me anymore. All I wanted to do was to bring this entire operation down.

"Los Furiosos thinks I'm dead. I'm tired of hiding. It's time I bring the fight to them."

8: INFILTRATION

THE FEVER IN MY body continued to rise as I watched pieces of the destroyed boat float across the lagoon. My backpack was gone. Whatever supplies that had been inside were among the debris of the sunken ship. My walkie was gone. My 1911 was gone. And the only thing I had left was my knife and makeshift axe. I had to see if I could salvage anything so I took a few deep breaths as I began to walk into the water. The closer I got, the more debris from the ship floated around me. Chunks of wood and soaked medical supplies floated off into the distance.

I held on to a broken piece of wood that was made to frame the ship. As I looked down, I could see many rocks that had algae and fish that swam in groups that filtered in and out of the holes caused by the boats battle between the waterfall. I took a deep breath and pushed myself off of the skeleton of the boat, plummeting deep into the water.

Going back inside the cockpit made me apprehensive. I approached the broken glass and could vividly remember taking my last breath before Allen came to my rescue. I could see in the corner of the cockpit that my bag was wedged in between a cabinet underneath the steering wheel. I swam through the shattered window. I could feel myself losing air as I stretched for the bag, working to pull it out from its confined space.

With the pack in hand, I turned around and swam through the window. Breaking for the surface, I burst out from the lagoon, took in a deep breath, swimming back to Allen's body. I kneeled beside Allen, pulling out the shredded papers from my bag. To my dismay, the documents were finally rendered unrecognizable. The amount of water damage left the papers soggy and frail.

"Splendid." Exhaling, I recognized defeat.

I reached for my knife because I wanted to see if I could get the implant off of Allen. I deliberately held the tip of the blade against his skin, pressing it just deep enough to break the surface. I continued to cut around the implant, going deeper with every pass as I began to pry it out with the tip of the blade. I knew if these were to be removed when the person was alive, it would probably kill them or paralyze them for life. As I began to pull the implant out, I stopped, cocking my head to the side as I set my knife down.

I gave one more good yank, and the implant finally gave way.

The implant was made up of silver tentacles that had an iridescent hue to them that whipped around like octopus legs. Like the implant, itself, was a living organism. Suddenly the tentacles began to wrap around my hand, trying to bond to me, I think. I reached for my knife, frantically trying to cut each tentacle off to free my palm. It took some effort but I'd cut each of the legs free from my hand.

"What the fuck was that?" I said to myself as I watched the implant die.

I took what remained of the implant and placed it into my pack. If I were to make it out of here alive, I needed something to prove to the authorities what Los Furiosos was up to. I silently prayed that once I was free of this island prison, someone would believe me. I had to have hope as I pulled out the last can of food and water out of my pack. I opened them both.

I began to notice the streams turning dull as I kept following the traces of water until they came to an end. I looked forward, and through the trees, I could see the ocean.

"Oh, my God," I started to jog through the palms, freedom just within reach.

I could see a building just off in the distance. This building sparkled like it was made of diamonds. I reached into my pocket to get a better look, pulling out my binoculars.

"Damn," I said, one of the lenses was cracked. "Must have happened during the crash."

It was hard to make out what I was looking at through them, but the building looked like it was a hospital. It stood three-stories high and there were multiple docks with massive boats that were four to five times larger than the one I had arrived on.

Some Los Furiosos were on jet-skis, circling and checking on the ships as they passed, assuring that they had the go-ahead to continue forward. No one was coming in or going out without their approval. I sighed to myself as I watched them move around everywhere. I didn't know how Atlas thought I was going to make it off this island. There was an army that floated in front of me. And unless I had haloed eyes, I wasn't allowed to leave the island alive. My gaze went back to the building.

"How do I get in?" I whispered to myself.

Something caught my eye as it glistened in mid-air, hovering over the forest of trees down below. It was an Ariel tramway that went from the lab all the way to the top of the mountain nearby.

"Hmmm, that's how they get around so fast."

My eyes drifted from the tram and followed the lines that supported it. I could see the lines go past a landing nearby, just close enough for me to board the tram from underneath.

"Perfect."

This was much higher than the waterfall, much higher than the climb I made to get into TreeTop. The more I pushed forward, the grander everything was becoming. It was a bit overwhelming. I knew this was bad, but then I remembered the map of Isle Onocastel. This was just the beginning, I could only imagine how big and terrifying Onocastel was. As I kept moving, I could see the tramway beginning to get higher in elevation. I stopped and found a place to hide as it was getting closer. I thought it would be best if I caught a ride when it was going down, not up. There was a small cave that looked like it was manmade. I stepped inside as the tram approached.

I peeked out of the cave, watching the tram suspended in place. Once it began to move again, I sighed with relief. I stepped back farther into the cave and noticed markings on the walls. Realizing it was names and notes to loved ones. I continued reading the names and love notes to their wives and children until I came across one message in particular. I shook where I stood because I knew the handwriting as I read it aloud.

"I miss you, Mom. Not a day goes past that I don't think about you. Soon we will be reunited, and Los Furiosos will reign, bringing us back together. I miss you, too, my brother. Eventually, Los Furiosos will realize that you are strong, too, and we will be together again, fighting side by side."

-Colden Everly

My brother did care for me. I should have been here to save my brother. I would have stood by his side and fought with him until every last Los Furiosos member was dead. I could have saved him, I thought as I wiped my eyes. I noticed something else that was written in brown. As I picked myself up to get a closer look, the writing wasn't in brown ink, but in blood. I read the words aloud.

"Diablo Twins." I knew that name.

Where had I heard that phrase before? It sounded so familiar.

"Diablo Twins, The Diablo Twins." I said over and over again.

I thought of Colden and me every time I said it. My mother never called us that, but for some reason, it rang a bell. I stopped in my tracks as a light bulb went off in my head. A flashback of my mom mentioning it to me came to mind.

"You know he gave you and your brother a nickname. He used to call you the 'Diablo Twins'." My mother's voice telling me that on my last night in Canada.

I approached the writing again, terrifyingly interested. The penmanship definitely wasn't Colden's as I said the words aloud again.

"The Diablo Twins," I repeated, I shook in place as I slowly mouthed the word, *"Dad?"*

I could feel the cave suddenly vibrate. The tram must have been descending now, and I needed to catch my ride before it was too late.

The tram moved rather slowly as I waited for the perfect moment to make a break for the landing. I began to make my way against the wall of the mountain, nudging myself closer and closer to the landing. The wind whipped around me quickly as my right foot slipped off the edge and small pebbles plummeted to the ground below. I held my position against the wall, waiting for the tram to pass so I could make my jump. The tram was a foot away from the landing, and just high enough for me to reach the bottom of it without being seen.

"Okay, Alec." I inhaled deeply. "One…Two…Two and a half… THREE."

I broke into a sprint. Charging at full speed, I flung myself through the air. My hands gripped the rail of the bottom of the tram, causing it to shake as my weight suddenly pulled it down. The tram slowed for a brief moment and continued to move forward. Voices from inside the tram questioned what caused the violent tremor as the tram gradually stopped swaying. I knew that I couldn't ride it all the way into the lab, or my position would have been compromised.

The tramway was going to enter the lab soon, and by the looks of it, it would stop on the third floor. I knew I would have to let go, and had three levels of falling until I hit the ground. My nerves got the best of me as I prayed I wouldn't break anything on my way down. The car kept moving, getting closer and closer to the lab. I could see I was going to pass over a willow tree. That was my only choice for a somewhat softer landing, I supposed.

"This is gonna hurt," I whispered to myself as I hung from the railing.

In free-fall, as my body dropped, I could feel my stomach in my throat as the branches of the tree whip across my face. Hurdling my body down as I hit multiple branches on my way down. With every blow, the wind was knocked out of me. I slid from a limb and fell to the ground. I landed on my back in a meadow of grass, desperately trying to catch my breath and right my vision.

"Did you hear that?" A voice from somewhere said.

Another man responded to him. "It's probably just birds in the trees."

The other man continued to speak as my eyes rolled back into my head.

"I don't know, I have a weird feeling."

"Just keep a lookout. Dr. Jericho said to keep it tight." The man sounded irritated.

The shock of the fall had me out of sorts. I could see the lab not that far away from me. I tried to think of a plan on how I would get in as my head throbbed.

I knew I had to carry out my mission, but the risk was too significant. There were so many of them and only one of me. I reached into my pocket and pulled out my binoculars.

From my vantage point, I could see them entering and exiting glass doors. The men were wearing lab coats and identification badges. The men who exited next were wearing the military outfits. I noticed guards were on either side of the glass doors waving to those who entered and exited. The only way I could get in was if I looked the part. I lowered my binoculars and placed them into my pocket. As I did, I looked down at my clothes.

"Need to blend in."

I looked back up and watched the group of men who left the building. Somehow, I needed to get one of them alone.

The three men walked into the forest, and I began to follow. Hoping that they would eventually drift apart and make it less noticeable if one of them went missing. They made their way onto a trail that led to the mountains. The men slowed and eventually came to a stop. I hid behind a tree as one of them spoke.

"I need to take a piss. Wait up for me," he said as he walked in the opposite direction of where I was.

As the man walked deep into the forest, the other two men continued to talk to one another.

"So how many more recruits do they need?"

"I'm not sure. Vincent said he needed as many as he could get. He's wanting us to head to Chile and ransack homeless shelters for anyone who can be taken without suspicion."

I needed a diversion to separate these two goons. The tree I was hiding behind looked like it would be easy to climb. I climbed it as quietly as possible, trying to get high enough so I couldn't be seen from above. The men continued to talk.

"Why does he need so many all of a sudden?"

"Vincent said that Dr. Everly's son would be the key to all our problems. He knows that he's still alive out there somewhere."

I stopped climbing for a moment. Dr. Everly? What the hell? He must have misspoke and meant to say Dr. Jericho. I crouched onto one of the limbs of the tree and could see from where I was that the man that went to take a leak, was beginning to come back. I needed to think of something fast. I inhaled deeply and placed my fingers into my mouth, blowing out a loud whistle for them to hear. Both men stopped talking and looked in my direction. They couldn't see me. One of them cocked his rifle and started to make his way into the forest. He walked in my direction, looking everywhere but up as he approached

"Where is he going?" The man who relieved himself asked.

The other man responded, "We heard a whistle. He's going to check it out."

The man scoffed, "It was probably just a bird." The man turned toward the direction of the man approaching me and yelled out to him.

"Hey, Dante. Meet us back here after Optic #2."

"All right. Meet back here in ten." He turned back in my direction, holding his rifle up, trying to hunt my whistle down.

As he continued to walk, so did the men on the trail. Their voices carried through the trees and soon began to fade as they progressed to Optic #2. I could see Dante down below me start to get closer to my tree. I reached behind me and pulled out my knife, waiting for the right moment to strike.

Dante nudged closer and closer, as he did, I waited in silence. He continued forward just a little more, and he was in a perfect position. I leaped into the air, pulling my knife up, building up enough momentum to penetrate him. The wind blew into my face as I landed on top of his back, plunging the knife deep into his neck. While I crushed his body, I held his mouth shut as he grunted wordlessly, struggling to fight me off. I twisted the knife within his neck, he gave in.

Dante planted his face into the floor as blood puddled into the soil beneath him. I pulled my blade out of his neck and placed it back onto my belt. My breathing was accelerated now as my head continued to pound from both my fever and the fall from the tramway. He took his final breath, as he did, I could see the implant on the back of his neck stop blinking and turn off. The halos in his eyes disappeared as I took yet another innocent life. I looked around to assure no one was watching. I quickly removed Dante's uniform, fully changing into his attire.

I looked down at myself and could tell right away that the coat was too big for my body but I felt like I made a decent marshal, minus the silver haloed eyes.

"Just keep your head down, Alec. Get in and out."

I kept moving forward, getting closer to my destination. Suddenly a voice called out from behind me.

"Hey. Dante."

I stopped in my tracks. I stood there, frozen in fear, keeping my head down while glancing to my left and right. The voice called out again, as I pulled my collar up, attempting to hide the fact that I didn't have an implant on the back of my neck.

"Dante. Where are you going?"

I couldn't turn around because I knew I would be compromised. I tried to speak in a deep voice, deeper than my voice has ever been.

"I'm going back to the lab." Waving my hand toward the lab's direction. "I gotta take a shit." I spoke, hoping that it was a valid enough excuse. I could hear them behind me laughing, and then one of them responded again.

"All right, well, hurry up. Can't keep Erico waiting," he replied. I nodded my head up and down and started to walk off the trail and toward the lab.

As I grew closer, I only wished that Erico wasn't alive. If he knew I was still around here, I'm sure he would stop at nothing to have my head. I started to veer off into the trees, weaving in between them. I felt myself moving like I usually would and then looked down, forgetting that I was in disguise now. I started to make my way toward the entrance of the lab and immediately got nervous. I looked up quickly and looked back down. I could tell that the guards thought my actions seemed off. I hesitated and turned my head toward the docks. I could hear the men whispering to each other, wondering what I was doing. Although I was wearing their military uniform, I had the feeling that my face was beaten from everything I had been through.

I was terrified about entering the lab. I stood at the place Atlas wanted me to destroy, I stared in the face of freedom and cowered. I could feel a lump in my throat. I was in broad daylight, and the men filtering in and out of the lab paid no attention to me. I had an eerie feeling as I looked at the mirrored glass windows. I was more scared of what I would find inside, and what terrified me the most was what would find me. I came here to find my brother, and although he was dead, I needed answers. I wanted to know where his body was. I promised Atlas I would take this lab down. Even if it meant me dying in the process. So many questions and the answers were right in front of me.

I began to make my way toward the lab. There were a pair of Los Furiosos guards in their military outfits standing on either side of the glass doors. The men noticed my steady demeanor and puffed out their chest as I approached.

"Marshal Dante," I spoke with a firm tone. Presenting my badge while I kept my eyes glued to the floor.

The men glanced at my badge and looked back at me. I kept my eyes to the floor, looking left and right.

"Well... go in," he said, annoyed.

As I walked through, I looked ahead and there was another set of glass doors in front of me. I glanced to my left and right and could see my reflection in the mirrored glass.

My face was very beaten. While I sported their military garb, I looked just like one of them, nothing more than a new addition to their insane cult. I looked away from the mirror in disgust.

Suddenly, blue hologram lights shot out from both the left and right sides of the mirrors. A computer's voice spoke as the holograms moved in on me.

"Assessing implant verification."

I knew it was taking a scan of who I was, and I didn't have an implant. I was screwed.

"Shit," I whispered to myself as the hologram lights began to pass over my body.

The blue scanner passed over me, and after it did, it faded into thin air. I looked around, and suddenly, an alarm started to go off. The sirens continued to sound, and I could see red lights flashing as the computer's voice repeated,

"Intruder. Intruder."

The glass doors I passed through slid open, and the guards quickly stormed in raising their assault rifles at me as they began to shout.

"Drop the weapon. Put the rifle down, NOW."

I yelled back, "YOU PUT YOUR WEAPONS DOWN." I wasn't going to let it end this way. The alarm continued to sound as the men kept shouting at me.

Suddenly out of nowhere, the red lights stopped flashing, and the alarms fell silent. I peered around, wondering what was going on. The men stopped shouting and suddenly froze. My breathing was heavy, ready for another fight. The men lowered their weapons and stood still. They moved like they were robots, and it gave me an unusual feeling. The doors slid open, and they went back to their position of guarding the entrance.

"What...what the hell?"

I stood there, confused as to what just happened. My eyes landed on a camera in the corner of the room. Someone was watching me. They knew I was here and they wanted me to come in? Just before the doors slid shut, one of the guards spoke, "Good luck getting out."

The doors shut behind me and the sound of a locking mechanism slid into place, sealing my chances of ever getting away.

9: Genetic Research Facility

I BEGAN TO HACK fiercely as I squinted my eyes due to the brightness of the lab. My temperature was elevated from my fever, whatever I had, wasn't shaking. I was so out of place. I knew I wasn't allowed in here, and had the feeling that someone let me in. Glancing to my right, I could see a small sign mounted on the wall.

The sign read like a directory with arrows pointing up, left and right.

↑ Calibration Center
↑ Implantation Bay
↑ Elevator
→ Dr. Cooper's Office
← Marshal Erico's Office

I peered to my left and right and saw many doors that were closed. As I stepped forward, I looked into a room filled with Los Furiosos wearing lab coats.

This must have been the Calibration Center. I could see men wearing lab coats filtering around the room, hovering over other men who were sitting in chairs that were lined up in rows. Suddenly, I could hear footsteps. The more I listened, the more the steps sounded like clacks of a woman's heels. The footsteps stopped and started to walk in a different direction until they faded away. I let out a breath of relief, and my eyes went back to the Calibration Center.

I approached the window again while my interest was heightened. I wanted to know how they were kept in check, but I also didn't want to be caught learning about their secrets. I approached the window and peeked in. My eyes were suddenly met with another Los Furiosos member who was in a lab coat. I took a deep breath because he stared me dead in the face. But for some motive, the person who noticed me just nodded his head toward me and proceeded to work. I felt awkward, nodded back at him. The more I looked at the people in lab coats, I began to notice that they wore face masks along with white medical gloves and protective eyewear. Even under the goggles, I could still see the silver halos pulse as they operated. I felt a little at ease because no alarms were going off. I boldly stood in front of the window now and watched in both fascination and animosity. As I resumed to watch, I could see the lab coat personnel reach for tray setups that held multiple tools and syringes. One of them reached for a small instrument that looked like a micro-thin screwdriver. He deliberately took the device and reached under his patient's head. He began to twist slightly, the person in the chair winced.

The lab coat man removed the instrument and placed it back onto his tray. He then reached for a device that had many buttons and a wire that protruded from the top of the mechanism. At the end of the cable, it seemed like there was an adaptor that could be inserted into something. The lab coat man took the adaptor and reached around underneath his patient's head and entered it into his implant. As he did, he turned on the interface of the device, pushing buttons. I could see the other lab coat individuals hover around their patients doing the same thing. They worked in teams. I watched each of them in disgust as they worked efficiently. I counted thirty chairs lined up in rows of ten.

Cabinets of medical supplies and instruments were lined up along the walls of the room. I pressed my hand against the glass holding myself up because I could feel my head pounding. My eyes went back to the lab workers. The patient's irises were flashing with their silver halos and then fading out, back to his standard eye color. They continued to do so, and as they did, the lab worker reached for a syringe on his tray, raising it into the air. The fluorescent lights made the solution inside the syringe reflect onto the lab worker's face, as he pushed the plunger, the solution to ooze out.

My eyes furrow in curiosity. Whatever it was, I had the feeling that it was probably some type of hallucinogen. The man in the lab coat took the syringe and injected the solution behind the man's head, into his implant. I watched in repulsion as he pushed the plunger until the solution was drained. My blood boiled as they all worked quickly like they had a cure for cancer. They all seemed animatronic. I wanted them to stop. All of their patients were people who all had the right to a free will. They had families and loved ones who were looking for them. Los Furiosos were worked like slaves and guard dogs. I reached for my rifle and gripped its handle. A doorway led into the room, and by the looks of it, the door could be accessed from the hallway where Erico's office was. In a rage, I stomped in that direction, circling back to the glass doors I entered to get inside the facility.

Groups of men entered the facility. Hesitating, I turned around, running down the first hall and opening the door labeled "Dr. Cooper's Office." I snuck into the room as I continued to watch the recruits filter in. Los Furiosos' marshals pointed their guns at them, ushering them down the hallway.

I looked away and my eyes passed over the office. Holy shit. Dr. Cooper was a woman, sporting silver-haloed eyes behind her glasses in the photos around her office. One in particular caught my eye...she was shaking hands with Dr. Jericho. A small, petite, Korean woman with black hair that was tied up in a ponytail. Awards filled her room, acknowledging her skill in pregnancy, child birthing, and the reproductive system. Why was she important? Why did Los Furiosos need her? I noticed that she left her ID badge behind. I swiped it. I had Dante's badge, but whoever Dr. Cooper was, she would probably be allowed access to anywhere inside the lab.

I left her office, stalking around the first hallway.

Where the hell was the self-destruct button? I figured wherever Dr. Jericho's office was, was probably my best chance to start looking. I peered around the corner and could see the last of the men walk down the last hallway to the left of the elevator where I could see another sign on the wall beside the elevator that listed all three floors.

Floor 1: Calibration/Implants
Floor 2: Genetic Testing (Authorized Personnel ONLY)
Floor 3: Research Team & Tramway Entrance

I knew I was being watched. With cameras all around, there was no way I was walking freely through this building without being apprehended. Whoever was watching me, I was confident that they wanted me here. Either way, I thought that the less I came into contact with Los Furiosos, the better. Dashing down the center hall, making a left at the elevator, a door to a stairwell was at the end of the corridor.

I opened the stairwell door and entered, quickly shutting it behind me. I led with my rifle as I walked up the first flight of stairs. I came to my first landing and made sure that I was the only one in the stairwell. I started to go up the next flight of stairs reaching the second landing. There was a door with the label to the side of it that read 'Genetic Testing (Authorized Personnel ONLY).' As I read the sign, I looked down to the handle and could see a scanner.

I looked into the window of the door. The lights on this floor were lowered, to the point that it was hard to read the signs and see the doors that were inside the halls. I had a bad feeling. I held up Dr. Cooper's badge to the scanner, and the lock to the door immediately released and I walked in.

I saw a window to my left that had bright lights shining from within. Someone was in there. There were rows of tables that filled the center of the chamber. Each worker had a set of different syringes, test tubes, and beakers. Some of the tables had cages on them that had different species of animals...rabbits, rats, birds, dogs, cats, even a coyote. They filled syringes with different-colored solutions and injected the animals.

Oh, my God. Near the back wall were glass cells that held people. They were ordinary like me, none of them were implanted yet, and they all wore gowns and had medical wristbands on. One of the patients began to beat against the glass, demanding to be released from his cell. Whatever was being experimented on them definitely wasn't Chromosome H. I wanted to help them. But there was no way that I could because I couldn't save them without being caught myself. The man pacing back and forth in his cell began to get very aggressive, ramming his head into the glass. Hitting his head so hard that he began to bleed.

One of the workers went up to his cell, holding a clipboard as she began writing something down while she watched him continuously slam his head into the glass. He soon knocked himself unconscious and fell to the floor. The woman jotting down her notes must have ordered some of the other lab workers to open the cell and remove the man's body. The workers obeyed and unlocked the room the man was in, using a different type of key card than the one I had. The men entered and started to pick the man up by his arms and legs, carrying him into a separate room. The woman who was writing notes held the door open for them as they moved his body inside. I felt nauseous because I could see inside, where rows of multiple dead bodies were on steel slabbed tables.

I looked away.

I had no idea what they were testing, but whatever it was, was bad. Suddenly, a loud shriek sounded in the distance. I quickly turned away from the window and held up my rifle.

The sound came from around the corner. Whatever it was, it didn't sound human. I walked away from the window. The more I walked away from the fluorescent lights, the darker the halls became. Whatever they were experimenting with was on a different level than Chromosome H. As I continued walking, I could see another window just like before, only this time the window was blurred. The light inside was flickering as I approached. And the closer I got, the more I began to notice that the window was frosted that made it nearly impossible to see through. I started to see flecks of red smudges on the window that looked as if it were blood. I got closer to the window as the lights flickered from within. Through the blood smears, I could see someone lying on the floor in a lab coat, and their body was twitching as the sound of chewing could be heard from inside.

I tried to get a better look, and suddenly, the body stopped moving. I took my hand off the glass and pushed my face in closer. A bloody pair of hands slammed against the window. The shriek from earlier boomed from inside, and I quickly moved away from the window as the palms continued to pound against the glass. The shrieks continued. I turned toward the elevator and could hear it ding as it landed on my floor.

"Shit." I ran down the hall that led away from the elevator.

I glanced to my right and could see two doors. One that must have led into the blood-spattered window room and another across from it, that led to who knows where. I didn't want to take my chances with whatever was behind the gory window. I ran to the door across from it, quickly reaching into my pocket for Dr. Cooper's ID badge, frantically holding it up to the scanner as the shadows got closer. I ran inside as quietly as possible, praying that no one was in the room waiting for me.

My prayers obviously fell on deaf ears because I was greeted by the sound of panting behind me. A shriek suddenly sounded, and I jumped. Frozen in fear, I knew I had to turn around and face whatever it was. The panting advanced quicker, and it sounded less animalistic, and more human. Spinning around, I was faced with a gigantic man who had to be at least seven-foot tall wearing a hospital gown. He balled his fists and lunged both of them at me. I anticipated the blows would connect.

Instead, the man's fists made contact with the glass of the door to his cell. I fell back in shock. I watched him as he panted more and noticed that there was blood oozing out from his lips and dripping onto his gown. His eyes were bloodshot, and the color of his iris was a cryptic black. I looked behind him and noticed someone else inside his cell. Only this person wasn't alive because they laid on the floor in a puddle of blood.

There were gashes of flesh missing from the individual's face, neck, and torso. Had he been eaten alive? My eyes went from the lifeless corpse back to the deranged man. I held my hand to my mouth as I watched him continue to pound of the glass window. The man looked like he was hungry and wanted more than the dead carcass in his cell. He wanted me.

"What the fuck is going on here?"

Nervous that someone would hear the man pounding and screaming from behind the glass. To my left was a solid wall, to my right, I could see a small hall that had two sets of doors. One that was in the middle of the passage and to the left, the other was at the very end of the corridor. The man continued to beat on the glass, it cracked significantly. Any moment, he would break free. I made my way down the stainless steel hallway, looking into the double doors to the left. At the entrance, I recognized thick steel leverage locks that latched at the top, bottom, left, and right sides of the door. Why so many locks? To the right of the door was an electronic scanner. I had that gut feeling again. As the vicious man continued to beat on the glass, a clear window looked inside.

Large rectangular boxes made of metal that was welded shut. Green lights flashed on them, too far to read. I noticed multiple

tubes and wires coming out of the tops of boxes that went down to the floor and ran to the back of the room. What is in there? I had no idea that Los Furiosos experimented to the point where their creations needed to be locked up and put under maximum security. Whatever was inside must have been deadly...why else would there be so many locks? I needed to know more, to expose Los Furiosos for what they truly were...savages. The violent man began to ram his body into the glass now, trying to break free to get a taste of my flesh. I gazed at the other door at the end of the passageway. Above it, an 'exit' sign.

I needed to know, it was now or never. Dr. Jericho's office could wait. If only I had Atlas to tell me where to go next. I reached into my pocket and pulled out Dr. Cooper's badge. I looked inside one last time as the sound of breaking glass could be heard from the cell down the hall. I slowly held the I.D. Card to the scanner, and a computer's voice spoke.

"Access Granted."

Locks on the entrance began to release one by one. The man in his cell was so close to breaking free. There were eight locks collectively, and as it reached lock five, the man began to shatter through the glass. I shifted back to him as my heart skipped a beat, taking aim at him as lock six began to free. The man kicked and punched the remaining shards of glass that framed his cell, stepping out of his cage. His bare feet stood on broken bits of glass, it didn't faze him. He stood there, shaking and panting excessively as he stared at me with jet black eyes like a shark's. Foam was drooling out of his mouth as he watched my every move. Lock seven released as he cocked his head to the side. I trembled in horror, keeping my rifle on him. He let out a piercing screech, began to charge at me.

I opened fire.

The echos of the shots caused my ears to ring. I continued shooting until I hit the man in his right shoulder and left leg. It threw him back a few steps. He couldn't feel pain as I proceeded to ignite him.

"Fall down, you freak." Lock eight finally released as he began to charge at me once again. I let off two more rounds into his torso. Empty. I immediately chucked my gun at him and pressed against the doors. The man advanced, I attempted to close the doors behind me. The man let out a high-pitched shriek as he thrust his body against the doors, prying them open. The deranged man had incredible strength, edging the doors open ever so slightly. My fever had made me fatigued as I squeezed sweat from my palms, using every bit of my strength to keep him from entering.

An alarm began to sound, echos of footsteps ran through the lab. The interface of the scanner was sending an alarm because of how long the doors were open. The man continued thrusting against the doors as I fought his aggression. I reached for my knife and rammed my body against the entrance, edging them to the point where they were nearly closed. I immediately placed the blade in between the door's handles and let go, catching my breath. The man screamed as the alarms continued to ring.

"What the fuck is going on in here?"

I looked around. No exits. I studied the ceiling and noticed a large vent that was big enough that I could fit through. I ran up to the closest holding tank, preparing to climb. As I approached the tank, I began to notice that the green lights flashing on it read: "Contained."

The tank stood twelve-foot tall, as my eyes went down to a small window that looked inside. Alarms blared, but the man's attempt to get in stopped. I looked behind me, his eyes were looking to his left as he let out a loud yell and began to run in that direction. I could hear men shout, the sound of bullets rippled in the halls. Los Furiosos were here. I needed to make it to the air duct. I looked back to the window and did a double-take because I wasn't sure of what I was looking at?

My eyes were fixated on the glass as I grew closer. Inside I could see tubes running from the top of the cell down. The conduits then turned into large needles. The tubes were feeding some type of creature, it seemed. The beast was suspended in the air as the machines filled it with a brownish fluid. I took a few steps back and could see that there wasn't just one cell, but multiple. I counted nearly thirty as I stood a pit of them all. The cells were contained...for now. But if one of these things were to get loose, I could only imagine how bad it would be. The sounds of the men's screams and the gunfire stopped as the alarm continued to ring out.

The sound of voices became louder as they got closer to the double doors. Pulling myself up by the tubes, I could feel them loosen with every hoist. The voices began to yell over the alarm as they approached the doors. I was almost to the top of the chamber and could hear Los Furiosos' men at the door. They shouted from the doorway. Uniformed men held guns up to the doors.

"Don't move, or we will fire." One of the men screamed.

"Yeah, like I'm going to stop." I didn't listen.

I kept climbing, and the man ordered the others to ram the door. They obeyed, causing my knife to come loose. I reached the top of the cell, accidentally yanking one of the tubes out from underneath me. The sound of the alarm continued to buzz, causing my stress to rise while Los Furiosos violently continued to crash into the door. I looked down underneath me as I stood over a fence-like material that looked down into the cell. The tube I pulled was torn out of the experiment inside, the liquid it pumped spewed everywhere. Was the creature awake? Panicked, I glanced back up to the vent. It looked big enough for me to fit inside, but not with my coat on. I removed my coat and bag while I swiftly threw the jacket to the floor, putting my backpack back on. I could feel the sweat on my arms, shoulders, and chest begin to cool now that I was free from the uniform's material.

Los Furiosos smashed through the doors and began to make their way in, aiming at me as I stood on top of the chamber.

"DON'T FUCKING MOVE, FAERIE."

I knew they had orders not to kill me, and I knew that I still had a chance to make it to Dr. Jericho's office.

"STOP MOVING." One of them yelled, "SOMEONE GO UP AFTER HIM."

I shook my head as one of the men began to approach the chamber I stood on. I looked down on him as he got closer. I suddenly yanked the tubes with all my might, causing the needles from the experiment underneath me to tear out. The men shouted, and I could feel movement from the chamber beneath me. The sound of the alarm came to a halt. The men began to step back as the sound of snarling came from below me. As I watched from above, I could see the creature's claws reflect in Los Furiosos flashlights. It began to strike its cell, attempting to break free. The men continued to edge backward, their guns at the ready. I didn't want to be in the same room once whatever this was got out.

So I hoisted myself up into the vent above me. The sounds of gunfire continued while my claustrophobia grew. I could see a light near the end of the duct. As I grew closer, I noticed the light shining down through the vent from above. I stopped once underneath the vent, and I sought to pry it open.

The vent wouldn't budge. I laid down on my back and pressed my feet up against the vent. I began to kick the vent over and over. It was hard to breathe while inside the duct, and I could feel tears welling in my eyes because I didn't know how much more my body could take. The vent burst open, I climbed out.

This must be level three, so there was no turning back. I could hear voices as I inhaled deeply.

"Oh God, how many are there?" I stood and held onto the railing on the wall as I continued to move.

I came to the end of the hall and could see a sign on the wall. A directory. It listed the names of multiple doctors. One, in particular, seemed odd because the name of the doctor was scratched off. However, traces of the doctor's name faintly remained. The doctor's name began with an 'S.'

I continued to look at the list and saw Dr. Jericho's name. Room #301.

"Dr. Jericho's room must be around here somewhere." I took a few deep breaths.

A computer's voice sounded from speakers above.

"Attention, Dr. Jericho. Assistance is needed on the second floor. Attention, Dr. Jericho. Your assistance is needed on the second floor immediately."

A door swung open as Dr. Jericho quickly rushed out, running his arms into the sleeves of his coat as he closed his door behind him. He quickly made his way to the elevator, hitting the down button, awaiting its arrival. The silence finally broke when I could hear the elevator doors begin to close, but something stopped them. I listened to the sound of Dr. Jericho's footsteps enter the elevator as I waited for the doors to close again. It felt like an eternity. Either that or Dr. Jericho was holding his hand against the openings, essentially waiting for me to reveal myself.

Finally, the elevator doors came to a close, and I found myself letting out a massive sigh. I made my way to room #301 and looked through the door's window.

I could see papers and files scattered across his desk. I twisted the handle and realized that it self-locked automatically. I went to reach in my pocket to pull out Dr. Cooper's ID badge, unsure if it would grant me access to another doctor's office.

"Fuck," I said because I must have lost the badge on the second floor when I took off my coat. I used the teeth of the blade on my axe to pry the door's latch. It wouldn't budge. I took my backpack off and quickly reached inside because I knew that I had little time before someone entered the halls again. I could feel an empty syringe inside the bag, and I took it out. I removed the cap of the needle and could see that there was a badge scanner near his door. I took the needle and slowly began to wedge the needle into where the badge was swiped. I looked around before I tried to gain access to Dr. Jericho's office. I immediately placed the needle into the card slot, trying to do anything I could to make the lock release. I could feel the needle get caught on something inside the slot as I pressed the needle more in-depth. The needle went as deep as it could, to the point where it stopped at the top of its luerlock. I forcefully wedged the needle up until it broke.

A sound from the interface beeped, and the screen glitched until the words on the screen read, *"Access Granted."*

"If there's a will, there's a way."

I had no idea what I was doing, but I knew I had a will to try, and it had gotten me this far. The sound of an automated lock turned as I reached for the handle again. The suspense grew as I twisted the knob, edging the door open.

I felt strange standing in his office. Photos of Dr. Jericho were on shelves. I approached them to get a better view and could see Dr. Jericho shaking hands with people I didn't recognize. The more I looked, the more I noticed that this was all before he was part of Los Furiosos. I only assumed because, in his photos, I could see that his eyes didn't have the silver halos within them. Dr. Jericho's eyes were gray, and they suited him very well. He seemed a lot younger in these pictures then what he looked like today. My eyes continued to scan over the photos in his office, I began to notice all of his awards and achievements.

Dr. Jericho had one trophy in a glass case that must have had incredible value to him.

"The Nobel Prize," I read aloud.

My eyes widened because I knew that something like that was only given to those who have made an astounding mark in the medical and scientific field. But this signifies peace, which Dr. Jericho seemed to no longer believe in. With the experiments I found on the second floor, and how violent Los Furiosos was, there wasn't a hint of peace on this entire island. There were other photos of him teaming up with researchers in other third world countries. It seemed like Dr. Jericho was very well-traveled and had a sense of peace and accommodating others before all of this.

"Why did you go to the dark side?"

A brilliant mind like his deciding to work for evil instead of good? Either that or he was taken over just like the rest of Los Furiosos.

My eyes suddenly made their way across the rest of his office. I could see a door down a hall that was behind his desk. Unsure of where it led to, I found my eyes wander to papers scattered across his desk. As I peered over the papers on his desk, I skimmed over them. I picked one up and learned that Dr. Jericho had teamed up with other people to seek out a genetic cure for cancer. I set the paper down and reached for another. For years it seemed as if Dr. Jericho continued to fight for a cure as there were news articles of him and his team, researching for the cause. I was beginning to like him, but deep down, I had a feeling something went wrong. There had to be a reason why he became the way he is today. I set the document down and reached for another. The more I read, the more fascinated I became.

The next article I held up began to go on about how Dr. Jericho's research could potentially become deadly. Journalist and doctors alike feared that Dr. Jericho was navigating dangerous territory that could result in death to some of his patients.

"I knew it," I scoffed to myself.

So much information was filling my mind, and I became infatuated with Dr. Jericho's past. His reasoning for keeping me alive only made my curiosity grow even further. The next article I began to read started to reveal a little more of Dr. Jericho's true identity. The report stated that Dr. Jericho had begun testing on animals that led to multiple fatalities. Dr. Jericho insisted that his search for a cure could not be tested on animals, and should be tested on humans.

"You were warned about your research."

I set the article down and found another with a photo of Dr. Jericho's mugshot. I found it strange that Dr. Jericho left all of these articles on his desk perfectly laid out, ready to read. It was like he must have read them to himself every day, almost reminding himself of what he had done. Dr. Jericho had been arrested for the murders of multiple people in the name of research. All of his victims were volunteers, lucky enough for him, they all signed a waiver that stated death was a possible outcome.

Legally he was released.

"Son of a bitch." I said spitefully. "And look where he is today,"

I set the article down and then came across another. My eyes widened because I wasn't sure of what I was seeing. The document had a photograph, a rather large photo at that. My hands shook, I could feel my heart beating in my throat. I rubbed my eyes because I didn't believe what I was seeing. As I slowly reached for the article, my hands trembled.

"You have to be kidding me," I said to myself as I began to get choked up. "This can't be true."

I felt extremely faint as I held the article close to my face. I immediately began to pant and gulp to myself…I started to feel woozy as I stumbled into Dr. Jericho's desk chair. As I sat, I could feel tears welling up in my eyes.

"No. Oh God, please, NO!"

As I looked over the article. The caption below the photo read as follows:

"After Dr. Jericho's medical mishap, he spoke in confidence as he would continue his research in hopes of finding a cure. Dr. Jericho stated that he would be teaming up with none other than the world-renowned Nobel Prize winner, Dr. Samuel Everly."

I rocked in my seat as the photo on the page was of Dr. Samuel Everly shaking hands with Dr. Jericho. After all the years of not knowing who my father was. After all the scenarios I played in my head over and over of what my father really was, now it was finally laid out in front of me. My father, just like Dr. Jericho… was nothing more than a monster.

My hands shook as the information filtered through my head. "What the fuck have you done...Dad?" I whimpered to myself.

Everything was beginning to click. The experiments, and the men outside talking about me being Dr. Everly's son. The scratched-off name of the list of doctors who were here. Colden's letter about our father potentially working with these men. It was something I refused to believe. But the evidence was clear. Whatever my father was doing here, I knew in my heart of hearts that it was all a well-kept secret that he never shared with my mother. He was a dark and twisted soul, and for a moment, I was pleased that he was dead. Could my father have done this to me? Could he have done this to his own unborn child?

There was no real way of telling without giving Dr. Jericho the satisfaction of making me his own experiment. I shook my head in rage. I furiously I grabbed the papers and flung them across the room.

"NO."

My sudden movements caused the desk to shake, making Dr. Jericho's computer screen come to life. I wiped my eyes to clear my vision so I could see what was on his display. I didn't know how much more I could take, but the more I learned, the more I could understand. I reached for the mouse on his desk and used the cursor to navigate his computer. To my surprise, his workstation was unlocked, and I had access to everything. I gulped to myself in fear of what I would learn next. On his desktop, I could see multiple folders listed. I started to click from top to bottom.

The first item was labeled "Capitol Optics Live Feed" I double-clicked on the program, and it opened immediately. Once the application was initiated, I could see a large interface of windows within the program. It seemed like footage, but to my amazement, it wasn't just footage but a live feed of what every Los Furiosos member was seeing. I noticed it looked almost like a first-person video game because, within the small windows, I could see hands and guns moving around. I clicked on the first

RISE OF THE FAY

window, and the video feed opened and filled the entire screen. Audio played as I could hear the voice of a man telling others to work faster. It looked like they were at the Cimmerian Tunnels, trying to maneuver rocks around to gain access to the mines again. As I watched, I could see everything the Los Furiosos member was seeing. While he looked at another member, there was a caption above the man's head, stating that he was not a threat to him. The men continued to maneuver rocks, and I went to minimize the feed.

Once it was closed, I noticed another live feed of a waterfall. I clicked onto it, enlarging the feed. I could see the man looking at the same place I had been. The boat of where I plummeted into the lagoon was there. The man's eyes went from Allen's body to another man. I gasped to myself when I saw who he was talking to.

"Erico," I said to myself in annoyance. "Do you ever give up?"

He didn't look great. I could see scratches across his chest, arms, and face that was left from the panther. I shook my head and minimized the feed. I knew Erico was close and that he would soon make his way to the lab. I knew that I had to be long gone before he made his way here. There were even live feeds from average citizens around the world.

These people were your everyday consumer, and they had been implanted with something that could eventually control them forever and had no idea. It was only a matter of time before soon everyone would be subjected to mind control.

There was also a file labeled Chromosome H Testing. I wanted to know more but was worried that Dr. Jericho would soon return. I hoped I had plenty of time knowing that I had released a mutated creature just a level below. I immediately clicked onto the file to open it. As the file flashed open, I noticed that all the documents inside were video files. I ran my cursor over the first one I was close to. The file title was labeled "Test Subject 026 - Deceased." I clicked the file, and the video opened, taking over the computer screen. The video began to play, as the camera must have been mounted over a medical table where a middle-aged man laid with his mouth gagged shut. A voice of a man spoke, and I could hear it was Dr. Jericho.

"Testing Chromosome H on subject #026."

I could see Dr. Jericho's hand holding a syringe of a silver substance as he began to inject the needle into the man's forearm. Once inoculated, the man started to have a seizure. In the background, I could hear the sound of a heart monitor beeping excessively as the man convulsed on the table. His hair began to change from a dark black to a frosty ash-blonde. The man continued to seize as foam was oozing out of the side of the gag. The man arrested and I could hear the heart monitor flatline. I could detect Dr. Jericho shut off the heart monitor and called the victim's time of death.

He then said, "Subject failed. I had high hopes for this one, he seemed promising." I shook my head in disgust as I viewed the dead man's eyes.

I closed the file and scrolled down to find another. I clicked on a different video file titled "Test Subject 056 - Deceased."

The video initiated and started to play. The video was filmed just like the previous one. Only this time, it was a woman who was gagged and tied down on the medical table. Dr. Jericho once again injected Chromosome H into the woman's arm, and the same result occurred. There were videos upon videos collected over the years as he documented his tests on innocent people. I scrolled down and clicked on another video titled, "Test Subject 462 - Deceased." The footage opened and played. Only this time, the person on the medical table was a little boy who had to be about twelve. I watched as he injected the Chromosome, and I could see the boy's eyes light up in fear as he began to seize. I immediately closed the clip. I couldn't bear another second of this.

"Dr. Jericho, you monster." A chill went up my spine.

I sighed in hopes that I would find the self-destruct system somewhere on his computer, but I failed. As I glanced over the live feed, I began to scroll in the belief that I would find something useful. But then I stumbled upon live footage of Isle Onocastel. The feed was at a prisoners' facility. I watched one feed in particular because I could see a man pacing back and forth in his chamber. His movements were so familiar. I was able to manipulate the camera to zoom in and out.

My eyes instantly grew. It was none other than Colden.

"He's alive."

I wanted to second guess myself, but the feed I was viewing was live. I could see the tattoos over his arms as he walked back and forth.

"Why did they say he was dead?"

All I knew was that he was fortunate to be alive. I wasn't sure how far Isle Onocastel was from here, it could have been miles away and heavily guarded. I remember looking over the map of Onocastel and seeing how massive it was. If Colden had been taken there, it would be a far graver task in helping him escape. I smiled because my brother was still alive. Although I wasn't in the best position to save him now — hell, I needed to save myself — but I knew that I couldn't just leave him there. After all this time, he was alive, and I was looking for him in all the wrong places. However, my work here wasn't done.

Suddenly, the live feed of Colden closed, and another popped open automatically, consuming the entire screen. It was a live feed titled 'Dr. Jericho.' I inhaled sharply as I viewed the footage. While I watched, I could see someone sitting at a desk with their back toward the camera. The camera was moving and I realized that the person sitting at the desk was me. I wasn't alone. Someone was approaching me from behind. I looked to my left, trying to use my peripherals to see who it was. I immediately gripped my axe, waiting for the person to get closer. My heart raced in my chest because I could see in the feed that they were getting closer and closer to me. I could hear breathing coming from behind me, and the sound of footsteps crept along, edging nearer. I swiftly turned around. Raising my axe into the air, eager to strike.

"DROP IT."

As I turned around, I saw who it was. Dr. Jericho walked up, holding a handgun pointed directly at my face.

"Drop it. Now," he said again.

I couldn't win a gunfight with an axe. I did as he ordered and dropped my weapon

"Good boy. Now kick it over to me."

I rolled my eyes, raising my hands into the air. I used my right foot and kicked the axe over to his feet. The weapon slid over to him with ease.

"Now, walk around my desk, Alec, and have a seat. Let's have a little chat, shall we?" He was so pleased with himself.

He caught me. I kept my hands raised as my eyes pierced his. I had a lot of questions, and I wanted answers. I did as he said and walked around his desk.

"Sit." He maintained his cool.

I looked down at the chair and then back to him. He pointed with his handgun toward the seat, directing me to follow his orders. I knew he wouldn't kill me, but he could still injure me. I took a seat and exhaled, leaning my arms on the armrest of the chair. Dr. Jericho kept the gun pointed at me, and his gaze never left mine. I was weaponless and defeated. However, deep down, I knew this wasn't over. I knew what Dr. Jericho wanted from me. My agenda was to prevent him from taking my blood, but also to try to stay alive. Dr. Jericho broke the silence.

"So, if it isn't the infamous Alec Everly," he said with a smirk as he looked down at the article with a photo of him and my father and then back to me. "So, what have we learned so far about your precious daddy?"

"Fuck you," I said with disgust in my voice.

Dr. Jericho let out a laugh. "I'm sure you would like that, wouldn't you?"

I scoffed and rolled my eyes, "You know the whole homophobic rhetoric is getting really old, come up with something original."

"Oh, you want... original?"

He turned his computer screen around to face me and glared at it. With his implant installed, he was able to control whatever technology that was around him. The screen flicked to my brother in his holding cell. I looked at the screen and back to him. He then turned his head back to the screen, and the camera zoomed in on him. An electric shock rippled through his cell. Colden grunted in pain and collapsed to the floor.

"STOP. Please, just stop," I said in regret, trying to restrain myself from jumping up out of my seat.

Dr. Jericho grinned and glanced back at the screen. The electric pulse came to a halt.

"What do you want? Why are you doing this?"

Dr. Jericho cocked his head and took a seat on top of his desk.

"Oh, Alec, my dear son. There is so much that I want." He looked off into the distance and then back to me. "For starters, I want to know what you know about our little operation." He sat in silence, waiting for my reply. I honestly didn't know what I had witnessed over these last few hours while I was inside of this psychotic laboratory. I tried to muster a response.

"I know...I know that you have some type of insane experiments on your second floor. Why you have them, I don't know," I said, hoping he would play along. He began to speak.

"Ah, you are wondering about our new pets, aren't you?" He looked back to the screen, opening a recording of the second floor.

The screen played a clip of me, face to face with the insane man in his cell. My eyes widened because I had no idea I was being recorded. The clip continued to play as I began to open the double doors while the man began to charge at me. Dr. Jericho raised an eyebrow, almost like he was impressed with how I escaped. The footage soon fast forwarded to the marshal's entering the hallway and shooting the man who was taking the shots as if they were no more than pellets until one of the men finally capped him in the head. The deranged man fell to the floor. Dr. Jericho looked back at me.

"You see, Alec. This is one of our most recent experiments. The man you saw on the second floor was merely infected with an accelerated form of rabies... among other things. The mutation we generated leaves its victims alive, allowing them to endure excessive amounts of pain. However, they are rendered extremely dangerous. One bite and the individual bitten will become infected, as well." With a smirk, he seemed proud that he had created a lethal weapon. "They are known as the *Skinfiends*."

"Why?" I asked as I glared from the screen and back to him.

"Well, why not? We live in an age that if something like this were ever to get out, it would be hell on earth. Wouldn't you agree that there are some people in this world whom you could live without?"

He laughed to himself. I looked at him and said, "Oh, yes. I can think of someone I could certainly live without."

Dr. Jericho backhanded me across the face.

"Watch your fucking mouth," Dr. Jericho said in outrage. "Count your blessings, Faerie. You're lucky you have something I want, or you would have been fed to the Cabra while you were still alive."

I held my jaw and responded with a grunt, "*The Cabra?*"

Dr. Jericho calmed himself, adjusting his lab coat back into an appropriate position and glanced back to the computer monitor. Suddenly a clip of me climbing into the air duct on the second floor played. As I vanished into the vent, I could see the cell rip open. Claws started to shred the steel chamber into pieces as if it were paper. A large creature emerged from the darkness. An overgrown creature snarled at the men, its grotesque body crouching on all fours. Its muscles were exposed, and you could see its bones underneath. The beast charged and attacked the men. Hurling their bodies around like they were rag dolls.

I found myself holding my hand over my mouth as my eyes grew bigger. The video cut out because the recording was through the eyes of a marshal who had been killed by the creature.

"What...the fuck...is that?" I had never seen anything like that in my entire life.

Dr. Jericho giggled to himself, trying to control his joy as he nearly fell off his desk with excitement.

"This is one of our ongoing experiments. Most of us have been trying to come up with a name for it, until we recently released one of them onto our sister island, Isle Onocastel." He paused and looked at me, pleased. "The people on the island began to refer to it as the 'Chupacabra.' Most of the residents here in South America have had superstitions for years about this legendary creature, until now. So the name seemed fitting."

I shook my head, "You're fucking sick."

Dr. Jericho stood up and began to walk toward his window. He opened the blinds, letting the sunlight pour in. My axe was still propped up against Dr. Jericho's desk. I looked back to him as he looked out the window and began to speak again.

"Yes, I would agree that some of our experiments are a bit... mmm, outlandish. However, every mutation could result in evolution. Which brings us to you." He turned around and stared at me. My eyes went from the axe, back to him.

"No," I replied sternly.

"Oh, please, Alec. Don't be so naïve. You know exactly what I'm talking about." He turned back to look out the window as he spoke.

"I have been waiting years for your return, Alec. After all, you are Samuel's prodigal son, as it were."

"I don't know what you're talking about," I said, trying to keep him distracted.

"Alec, don't play stupid with me because I know you're not. You've made it this far on our island of 'murderous mind-controlled Los Furiosos'. There is no way in hell that someone like you would have ever made it here alive if it wasn't for your abilities," he said, pausing almost like he was telling me and not asking me.

I looked at him, annoyed. "I don't have any abilities... You have the wrong guy."

Dr. Jericho scoffed and walked back over to his desk, glancing at the monitor again.

"Alec, I've seen you in action." The monitor soon opened up multiple windows of footage of me.

All were recorded from former members whom I had ran into or killed. Some of the footage was from cameras that were hidden around the island. Dr. Jericho had been watching me this entire time. One clip consumed the computer screen. The footage was of me getting shot in the leg. Then it fast forwarded to me at the pond where Atlas told me to get fresh water. The camera zoomed in on my bullet wound healing abnormally fast. I looked away from the monitor and slowly raised my eyes, meeting Dr. Jericho's silver orbs. I had an expression of violation on my face. The thought of him watching me all along made me feel exposed.

"You know your father and I worked together for many years. I find it funny how you two look so much alike. Your expressions, even some of your mannerisms. It's incredible to watch, especially after all these years." He paused and folded his arms. There was a look of revenge on his face. "Once your father betrayed us, I knew what we had to do next. I knew when he was lying, I could always tell from his eyes. Almost the same way I can tell from yours."

"I am not lying," I said, scowling at him. "I am not one of your fucking experiments. And I am definitely NOT my father."

Dr. Jericho cocked his head and looked up to the ceiling and back to me. "You know, when your father left he said what we were doing was wrong. The experiments we created and the technology we developed. Once he learned that I was beginning human trials, he said he couldn't be a part of something of this nature. Such a coward, in my opinion."

"When he fled...he took something from me." He paused and glanced from the ceiling to me. "When your father was alive," he laughed to himself for a moment like he recognized something but continued. "Right 'when' he was alive. We worked on our first-ever genetic anomaly. But for some reason, when we tested it, all of our subjects died. The more deaths that resulted from our testing, the more your father began to distance himself from our work."

Dr. Jericho continued, "I knew he was waiting for his moment to leave. I had the feeling that he had cracked the code as to why our subjects remained to deteriorate. Chromosome A.S. seemed like a failure until your father took the one — and only — sample of it along with all of the research...ALL of OUR research. Did you know that all chromosomes come in pairs?" He paused, waiting for an answer.

I shook my head as he continued.

"Well, Chromosome A.S. was unsuccessful because it needed a pair. I realized that Chromosome A.S. was unable to bond with our experiments on a cellular level. Mainly because our experiments' DNA was already fully developed. So I began to go off of memory on how your father and I created Chromosome A.S., and until now, I believe I have created its pair...Chromosome H. Of course, I would never know if the two would ever bond unless I had Chromosome A.S., So I went to find your father who was with his precious love, Abigail Everly."

He continued. "Yes, I made a little visit to your father and mother. And of course, I brought a few of my friends for...physical support." He laughed because I knew he brought Los Furiosos. Part of me knew where the story was going, but I wanted to hear it from him.

"I demanded to know where our creation was. And your father went on about how he turned it over to the government. But he had that look in his eye. If I knew anything about your father, I knew he would never let something this valuable go to waste. It wasn't until he told me that Chromosome A.S. was something that had to incubate over time, that it would take years for something like that to be able to adapt to a human's DNA. I went into a rage because I knew I had its genetic pair. I'll admit, I tend to get a little out of control when I don't get what I want." He paused and smirked at me, "And I may or may not have had an obsession with fire in the past..." He popped off a sly smile toward me.

"You didn't?" I said in disbelief. "You...you killed my father?"

He smirked, "Well, I wouldn't say killed...they never did find his body."

Everything I had been told as a child. Everything that I was led to believe about my father's death, was a lie. It wasn't an accident, he was murdered. And his killer sat right in front of me. I gripped the armrest of my chair, and it took everything inside of me to not jump up and snap Dr. Jericho's neck where he sat. I could feel my hands shaking, and my body shudder as my eyes pierced Dr. Jericho's. He just smiled at me and continued like it was nothing.

"A few months later, I tracked your mother down to see where she had been. I had no intention of harming your mother. She was a sweet woman until I made a discovery. I followed your mother one day to a supermarket where I watched as she shopped for groceries. It wasn't until I started to see her wandering into the baby section of the store that I saw her baby bump for the first time... I had a feeling of hope. Your father wouldn't let Chromosome A.S. go to waste. What are the odds that your mother gets pregnant? A perfect opportunity to introduce a genetic anomaly into a developing fetus, a developing genetic DNA strand." Dr. Jericho grinned from ear to ear. "I knew soon she would have her baby, and the truth of what your father and I created would finally be unleashed into the world."

I shook my head in disbelief, my stomach turned as I imagined him stalking my mother. Just waiting for us to be born after he killed our father. My entire family was ripped apart all because of a cruel man who was seduced entirely by greed and power.

"The day finally came." Dr. Jericho said, smiling. And it seemed like tears were welling up in his eyes.

"But to my surprise, it wasn't only you, but an identical twin brother, as well. You and your brother, two healthy, bouncing baby boys. I never felt prouder. I have been waiting years for this, and the future that I had planned for the both of you."

He spoke as if he had ownership of us. The way he talked and how he got choked up like he was someone important in my life, filled me with bitterness.

"Now I've kept in the shadows and obeyed Vincent's orders. I continued watching over you and your brother for years. Every birthday I was present...in a sense but kept my distance as promised. For years I waited, and it wasn't until I learned that your brother Colden had an interest in his father's death that I began to feed him clues, keeping it subtle, but giving him enough hints to find his way here. Just as I did for you."

I interrupted, "For me?" I asked because I didn't know what he was talking about.

He responded, "Oh, yes. Capitol Optics has control over all technology, distribution... advertisements." He paused, almost waiting for me to realize.

"The ads...the ad in the airport...calling my name?" I said in realization.

"Oh, and it gets better. We even rigged your application for the Peace Corps, just to free up your time. And that cute little letter we forced your brother to write to your dear mother, it was just something to get you to make a move. And we have...others... who play both sides." He laughed and continued. "But no names I'd like to share with you right now."

I shook my head furiously. He had been playing me this entire time. He stopped and cleared his throat again, and clenched his jaw almost angry, and then continued.

"Unfortunately for your brother, he wasn't blessed by what your father and I created. He found his way here, and I immediately took him in. I ran tests to see if his results were positive. To my disappointment, he did not contain the gift. I eventually told him the truth, as I have told you. He rebelled, but I found him too valuable to turn loose. So, I've been keeping him alive, a sort of ongoing experiment of mine."

"You're a fucking monster!" I shouted at him. "LET HIM GO!"

Dr. Jericho pulled out his handgun and aimed it at my head. I froze in place, alarmed that he would pull the trigger.

"You want him free?" Dr. Jericho asked politely as he held me at gunpoint.

I paused before I responded, "Yes," I replied, clenching my jaw shut.

"Then stay with us...all the evidence is clear, Alec. You have what I want. I have been waiting and watching you for years. I'm not going to let you walk away after all the time I have invested in you." He spoke like he was my father, as if he had a connection with me that ran deeper then I would ever know. But I knew without a doubt that I would never stay with him. I would never become what he wanted me to be.

Dr. Jericho glanced at his computer monitor and spoke, "Send them in."

I could hear footsteps sound outside in the halls. Dr. Jericho's door swung open, and marshals stomped in. There must have been ten of them.

Dr. Jericho leaned in and whispered into my ear, "Welcome home, son."

The men who stormed in soon separated, clearing a path allowing someone to walk through the door. I looked down and could see his black boots slowly walk in with a slight limp. My eyes trailed up, and I began to see a medical wrap around the man's leg. Erico came to a stop right in front of me. He was panting as sweat was dripping off of him. Erico glanced at Dr. Jericho, and I looked behind me. Dr. Jericho nodded and I turned back around as Erico punched me in the stomach.

I doubled over, trying to catch my breath. Erico kneed me in the face, causing me to fall onto my back. The marshals stomped over to me, grabbing me by my arms and lifting me up. They held my arms as Erico continued to pummel me.

Dr. Jericho finally spoke after what felt like forever, "Okay, that's enough."

The men then turned me around to face Dr. Jericho. I could see him walk around his desk and reach into one of his drawers. He pulled out a long tube that had a swab inside. He popped the cap off the container and pulled the item out as he made his way around the desk. I began to lose it. I pulled my arms into my body. Sending the men who held me flying to the floor.

"GET OFF ME!" I screamed.

I started to kick the men in the face and punched anyone who was near me. More men came in and tried to restrain me.

"WHAT ARE YOU DOING?" I shouted. "GET OFF. NO. GET OFF."

I continued to struggle. Yanking my arms free and throwing as many punches and kicks as I could at anyone who approached me. I was outnumbered as they kept reaching out to me, holding me back. Dr. Jericho's eyes pulsed, and his face lit up as he admired my strength. Dr. Jericho approached me as I continued to fight.

"Easy, son. It's just a cotton swab. It's harmless," Dr. Jericho said, trying to coo at me like I was a child.

I thrust my head back, head-butting a man behind me. I could see Erico out of the corner of my eye with his hands folded across his chest. He stood leaning his shoulder against a wall with a look of admiration on his face. Dr. Jericho bravely approached me.

"Just open your mouth, it'll be over before you know it." He tried to calm me.

"FUCK YOU!" I could feel tears welling in my eyes as I continued to thrash in place.

Dr. Jericho held the swab out, nearing my face. I shook my head back and forth, forcefully holding my mouth shut. I could feel the marshal's hands on my neck and head, trying to hold me still. They turned my head toward Dr. Jericho.

"Open."

I kept my jaw clenched shut until Dr. Jericho pinched my nose. I thrashed back and forth as I held my breath. It took everything in me not to breathe. I knew it was futile, though. As soon as the last of my oxygen had been depleted, Dr. Jericho inserted the swab into my mouth and took what he needed. I cried out as the men all laughed at me. The world as I knew it was over. Liam and I would never see each other again. My brother would soon be killed. And the Los Furiosos army would rise and take over the world. I gave up and allowed my body to fall as the men held my weight up. I would be a prisoner forever...or at least as long as I stayed alive.

Dr. Jericho spoke. "Take him to a cell immediately. I will begin testing this. If the test is positive, we will need a blood sample right away."

The men loosened their grip on me as Erico spoke.

"I'll take him to his cell." He sounded almost giddy.

He picked me up and threw me over his shoulder. Feeling his hands on me made me violent. I just couldn't give up. I still had fight in me. Through this whole ordeal, through my love for Liam, my revenge for my father, and the hope of seeing my brother... that is what kept me going. I looked up before Erico carried me out, starring daggers at Dr. Jericho.

"You won't get away with this," I said to him as I was carried out of the room.

Erico continued to walk down the halls of the lab. I continued to punch him in the back, attempting to make him let go. I flailed with all my might as we passed multiple doors that would eventually lead to my cell.

One door in particular caught my eye. A plaque was beside it that read, 'Dr. Samuel Everly.'

Erico stopped in front of a door that looked into a stark white room with bright fluorescent lights. My prison. The doors automatically slid open and Erico carried me in.

He threw me down onto the floor. My head slammed onto the marble flooring, and I immediately felt a knot forming. Disoriented, I felt Erico yank on my left arm and stab me with something. I screamed. Erico held a device that penetrated my forearm. He pressed a button and I watched as an object shot into my arm. Erico pulled the tube out, and I immediately grabbed my arm. I could see something blinking under my skin as Erico laughed at me.

"What is this? What have you done to me?" I yelled at him.

He turned around and stepped outside the doorway. He reached for the door's handle.

"It's a tracking device, Faerie. We wouldn't want you going anywhere, would we?" he said with a smirk on his face as he slid the door shut, pushing a large metal bar into place.

I got up immediately and started to bang on the door. I was forced to stop because my entire body was in pain, from all that I had been through the past two days. It had finally caught up to me.

I began pacing back and forth. I searched for anything that would help me escape.

But I had to admit to myself that I was a failure. I had disappointed Atlas, Liam, and Colden. I needed to get out. But how? Minutes began to pass, and soon, the minutes turned into an hour. The clock was ticking, and there was only one thing that I was certain of.

I was fucked...

10: AWOL

HEAT EMANATED FROM MY skin while sweat forced its way out of my pores. My gaze went up to the camera in the corner of the room, and I noticed that it tracked my every move. My eyes went from the camera and down to the shower. Although a shower sounded terrific right now, I didn't want to miss the opportunity of someone entering the room and offering me the chance to escape. I got up and walked over to the sink. Leaning over the basin, I turned on the knobs for both the hot and cold water.

I cupped my hands together and held them under the spout. For a moment, I dreamed that I was in my own bathroom back home. Water overflowed in my hands, and I raised them up, splashing myself in the face. It felt marvelous to have something as simple as clean water again. I splashed the water onto my neck, shoulders, and arms and reached behind the faucet and pulled the sink's stopper. The water filled up quickly and I lowered my arm into the water, allowing it to clean around the injection site. I peered around my cell once again. There was nothing in here that I could use for defense. Now that I was stripped of weapons, the only thing I had was my fists, intuition, and a will to live.

Looking around, I noticed there was a small puddle of water on the floor that I had made. But it gave me an idea. I stepped farther away from the sink and looked over to the shower. Inside was a small bottle of soap. My eyes went back and forth between the sink and the shower. I had an idea that would probably help me if someone were to enter my cell, or even better, a plan that would get someone to come to my room. I tried to keep my excitement anchored. The camera was still on me, and with my every move, I could hear it swivel as it tracked me. I walked back over to the sink and turned the water on cold. I came to a stop and let the water continue to run, filling the basin as I moved away from the sink and over to the toilet.

I unzipped my pants and started to relieve myself. I let my eyes wander to the right while I used my peripheral to see the sink continuing to fill up. I turned back to the toilet and grabbed the roll of toilet paper that was sitting on top of it. I then walked over to the shower and opened the glass door. As I did, I could hear the water pouring over the sink's edge. There was a smirk on my face as I stepped into the shower. The camera was following my every move. I dropped the roll of toilet paper onto the drain of the shower floor and stepped on it, trying to make it appear like it was an accident. I reached for the bottle of soap and held it in one hand, and with my other I switched on the shower and allowed the water to run. I stepped out of the shower, but before I did, I dropped the bottle of soap onto the floor and stepped on it, causing the contents inside to spew all over the floor outside of the shower.

I walked over to the door of my cell and looked out the window. The floor of my cell began to fill up with water and bubbles. The water crossed the threshold of the cell door and flowed out into the halls. I smiled to myself. I wasn't going to give up. I had the will and the reason to escape.

My thoughts ran amok as I awaited for someone to enter my room. I was thankful that they were stupid enough to leave me alone in a cell to plot my escape and the destruction of this place. Atlas had to be waiting for me, and although I didn't have a chance to find the self-destruct system, my intuition was telling me it was in my father's old office. As I thought about my father, I felt outraged.

The thought of him working here side by side with Dr. Jericho and under the supervision of Vincent made me wonder if he really wanted to help mankind or if he simply wanted to destroy it. As I pondered the reasons why, water continued to run and flood the room. Sitting down on my bed, I pulled my knees into my chest and rested my back against the cold wall. I must have dozed off momentarily because suddenly I heard footsteps. My eyes darted to the window in the door, and I could see a set of glowing eyes peer in.

A woman stood at my door looking at me and then down to the floor. Dr. Cooper. I could see her eyes furrow. She quickly turned away and I could hear her heels click and splash in the water as she stormed off down the hall. I knew she would get someone and have them open my cell. I inhaled a few deep breaths because I knew I would soon have to put up another fight. My agenda was clear, destroy this place...and get the fuck out of here. Los Furiosos had underestimated me for the last time, they had no idea that I was a force to be reckoned with.

A man's footsteps approached my cell door. I mentally prepared myself for who was going to enter. Erico. His eyes pierced mine as he shook his head in anger. I had him exactly where I wanted him, and I had to choose my timing wisely in order to make it out of here. The door opened and he just stood there, flexing and clenching his jaw.

"You are a cunning little shit, you know that."

I gave him a sly smile. "What can I say? If there is a will, there is a way."

Erico pulled out a handgun from his holster and pointed it at me. I held my hands up, pretending to be afraid. I knew he wasn't going to kill me. Erico walked into the room, doing his best not to slip. He reached into the shower and turned the water off, then walked over to the faucet. I laughed.

"What's fucking funny?" Erico was pissed.

"Oh, nothing. You just seem scared."

"I'm not scared of a fucking, Faerie."

He released the plug, allowing the water to drain after he turned the knobs to the off position. I wanted to get up and attack him as he had his back toward me. But the sound of my footsteps in the water would have given my intentions away. Besides, my curiosity had gotten the best of me.

"So, what are my results?"

Erico lifted his head toward the ceiling and sighed. I could see him look up to the camera in the room. His jaw tense before he spoke.

"You think you are something special, don't you?" he said as he slowly turned around, placing his gun back into his holster.

He rested his palms on the edge of the sink, almost like he was taking a seat. He was just sitting there, waiting for my response.

I asked again, "What were my results?"

Erico reached into his pocket, for what, I didn't know.

"What are they?"

Erico sighed before responding. "You know, I've always had a thing for those who rebelled." He paused as he still had his hand in his pocket, "Those who fought against me...against us, for some reason, I was sympathetic for them. Their will to rebel reminded me of when I was younger. You, on the other hand... you're different."

I interrupted him, "What...are...the results, Erico?"

Erico continued with a sly tone, "I've never met someone like you...a Faerie, who had such a strong will to live. And if I were being honest..." He paused and looked at me up and down in a peculiar manner. "Someone with your capabilities, well, it's sort of been a...turn on for me," he said in a flirtatious manner.

I was taken aback, "What?" I asked, perplexed.

Erico spoke again, almost in a soothing tone, "Don't play dumb, you know what I mean." After he said that, I realized what he was talking about.

"Really?" I said as I rolled my eyes. "So you are saying that you're gay...is that what you're telling me?"

Erico let out a small snicker. He didn't respond, but all he did was wink at me. Then he removed his hand from his pocket and revealed a syringe.

My eyes widened as I stared at him. "What were the results?" I asked again, almost terrified that I knew the answer, but I wanted to hear it from him.

Erico smiled, "Don't be afraid. Maybe I can get you to relax a little before we...draw blood."

I shook my head, "Say it...tell me what the results are." I needed him to say it. But it appeared like he was more interested in getting into my pants than informing me of the truth.

Erico set the syringe onto the sink. He then turned his head to the camera and glared at it. I could see the green blinking light turn red and shut off as the camera went offline. Erico turned back to me as he reached for his belt. The man who had been out to kill me this entire time now wanted me sexually? I loved Liam, and no other man was allowed to touch me. Erico wanted both me and my blood. I knew that letting him take my blood was one thing, but taking me was something completely different.

Erico slowly unbuckled his belt and continued to look at me up and down. Unfortunately for him, he had revealed his weakness. My breathing quickened, and I began to play the victim.

"Don't be afraid," he said as he reached out for me and stroked his thumb across my jawline. "We can take it slow, I won't hurt you. And when all this is over, and you become one of us, you won't even remember that it happened." This was the future he had planned for us.

His thumb went from my jawline to my lips. It was hard to tell if Erico was doing this for himself or if it was because he was being controlled. I had no idea how far Los Furiosos free will went. It was strange being this close and personal with Erico. This entire time, he had been my nemesis.

I started to pull away from him as he pulled me into his chest. "Stop."

"You know you want it," Erico said as he persisted, pulling me toward him.

When I looked into his eyes, it was like I was looking into hell. The darkness within them while the silver halo encapsulated his iris filled me with anxiety. I pushed away from him, and my eyes went to the door. It was unlocked and cracked open. My chance to escape was there, but if I ran, I knew Erico would follow. I knew that he would become violent if I didn't give him what he wanted. As Erico continued to pull me into him, my eyes went from the door and down to the water and soap on the floor in front of the shower. This was my moment. Erico was trying to get something from me and I, on the other hand, had a different agenda. I caught him off guard because I started to give in to him. This was something I would never tell Liam, but I would do what I had to in order to escape. Given the situation, I would use this to my advantage.

I turned back to Erico and leaned into him. He let out a breath as I placed my hand on the back of his neck, pulling him closer to me. I could feel the rigidness of his implant, flush against the surface of his skin. Looking at him, I could see the claw marks across his face from where the panther had attacked him. His well-maintained facial hair had small specks of dirt and blood in it, and his left eyebrow had a small scar that split it vertically into two. I decided to play his game. My hand moved from his neck and down to his shoulder. He pulled me into him and began kissing me.

I kissed him back, but I felt disgusted that it was him and not Liam. His entire body flexed as he kissed me while he wrapped his arms around me. He continued kissing me all over as I looked away toward the glass door of the shower while he did. Feeling his hands move all over my body made me shake. I needed to make my move, and soon. I had to take control of the situation. I could feel he was aroused and I tried to distract him by touching his chest, caressing his pecs, and working my way down his abs, even though it made me sick to do so.

Erico was letting out sighs of pleasure. So I continued and he started to moan. His hands went from my waist and down to my ass. He squeezed and continued to thrust against me. He was enjoying himself, and my actions were only making him more aroused. I could feel his gun against my inner thigh. My lips pressed against his chest, and I lightly started to bite his skin, pecking, and biting him as I operated my way down his abs.

"Yes, Faerie. You definitely know what you're doing."

I kept up this act. Erico was silly to give in to me so easily. I started to raise his shirt with my left hand and moved my other hand down his abs, toward his gun. I continued kissing his abs, praising him as I unbuttoned his pants. As I did, my left hand slowly drifted toward his gun. I was ready to end this motherfucker's life. Suddenly Erico opened his eyes and grabbed onto both my hands.

"No, no. Not yet." He wrapped his arms around my waist and flipped me over onto my back.

His movements were quick, and it reminded me of Liam. But he wasn't Liam, and that was a huge problem. Erico straddled me now and slowly edged off the bed and onto the wet floor. He spread my legs apart and wrapped them around his torso. As he did, I leaned up toward him, upset because I was so close to getting his gun, and I wanted this to be over. I grabbed onto the back of his neck and pulled him into me. I placed my lips against his and kissed him. He parted my lips with his tongue and caressed mine with his. Erico unzipped my pants. I couldn't allow this to go any farther. I looked past Erico to the soap on the floor in front of the glass shower doorway.

It was now or never. I pulled Erico off the floor and onto me. He was on top of me as he began to thrust his dick against me while kissing my neck and pulling me into him. I played his game, and my hands went from his back and down to his ass as I aided his thrust. I could hear him laughing in my ear, and it was starting to set me off. This was it, I had to make my move. Suddenly, I pushed Erico away from me. Punching him in the face, Erico got aggressive. I thrust my boot into his thorax, hurling him back.

"You crazy, BITCH." He yelled while he slid back in the water on the floor. He slipped on the soap and fell back into the glass shower door. The glass shattered as he fell. I got up from the bed and could see bits of glass in the water. I grabbed the biggest glass shard I could find and held it in my hand as Erico stumbled to his knees. I grabbed him by his throat with my left hand and plunged the shard into his left shoulder, cutting my hand simultaneously. Erico screamed as my grip tightened around his throat.

"You will NEVER have me...EVER," I whispered to him, snapping the shard of glass, leaving it in his shoulder.

He tried to scream but grunted instead because my grip on his throat was too strong. He reached for his shoulder to stop the bleeding, and I released his throat. Erico gasped before he spoke.

"I...am the only one...who can have you," he said, smiling with a mischievous smile.

I grabbed his handgun, pulling it out of his holster. He tried to reach for me but failed because of the pain he was in. I turned for the door, almost slipping as I did. I pushed the door open and closed it behind me. Erico was climbing out of the shower and looked at me as I slid the lock in place. I mimicked him when I spoke.

"Don't you go anywhere," I said sarcastically.

I pulled my pants all the way up, zipping and buckling my belt.

I was out, and I needed to move fast.

I looked around the halls and could see I was alone. I started to book it, leading with Erico's handgun as I went around corners. I pressed my back against a wall of a hallway and looked at a directory to find my dad's office. I quickly discovered his scratched-off name on a sign with a room that was numbered, #333. I was two halls away. I immediately started to run.

Two Los Furiosos members rounded the corner. I didn't think twice as I ran at full speed, raising Erico's gun at them and letting off two shots, both of which blew a hole point-blank in each of their heads. Their bodies fell to the floor, twitching violently as I bolted to my father's office. I didn't give a fuck anymore. Innocent or not, something finally changed within me. I finally realized I had no one to trust but myself now. No one to say if what I was doing was right or wrong anymore. I quickly shook off whatever I was sensing and opened the door and went inside.

Locking the door, turning around, and anxious to see what a day in the life was like for Samuel Everly. Shocked, the office was ransacked. Everything was destroyed, what a mess. Samuel's desk caught my attention, I headed toward it. Glass broke as I stood on top of a picture frame. A photo of my father and mother, holding each other in an embrace. That must have been taken before I was born. I removed the photo from the frame, folding it, and pocketing it.

As I approached his computer, I could see a thick film of dust cover his keyboard. I blew the dust off to see the keys. The mouse that was alongside the keyboard had a dust coating on it as well. I reached for it, and it felt strange to the touch. The thought of my father once touching it and using it when the computer was up to date and modern back then made me shudder. Being precisely where he was so many years ago gave me an overwhelming reaction.

"Okay, Dr. Everly. Let's hope you can do something for me," I said to myself as I moved the mouse.

The computer came to life, and the screen had an array of colors streaming across it that must have been caused from it being bashed in. The processor was unlocked. Although it was hard to navigate due to the age of the computer. I proceeded, nonetheless. I came across a familiar program that I had found on Dr. Jericho's computer and double-clicked the program as it filled the computer screen. The program glitched and skipped as it worked to process the live feed of everyone and every camera on the island. I shook my head because it was nothing I hadn't already seen.

When suddenly the screen glitched again, and I could see the cursor move by itself.

"What the hell?"

Someone was controlling it. A note memo popped up on the screen, and I could see writing begin to spell something out. I looked at the keyboard and then around the room, thinking that one of the Los Furiosos must have known I was in here and was trying to play a trick on me. The typing came to a halt as I tried to read what was written. I rubbed the screen with my hand once again until the text became legible.

"Alec...is that you?"

I was officially creeped out. I gripped Erico's gun as I looked around the room. I was alone but my eyes went to the door. I looked around to see if there was a camera in the office, but I didn't see any. I shuddered while I was on my knees and could hear men shouting, frantically searching for me outside in the halls. I wanted to write back but hesitated. The text suddenly deleted and started typing again.

"I hacked the computer system but can't access full control. It's Atlas."

I gasped to myself, "Holy shit."

The text deleted, and I slid my fingers across the keys, striving to respond to him quickly.

I wrote, "Thank God. Yes, it's me. How do I access the self-destruct system?"

He quickly replied, "There should be a program within the live feed. It's labeled 'Demolition'."

I quickly ran the cursor over the program and started to click any tab I could open. The computer screen made it hard to read what I was clicking because of the cracked screen. I could see Atlas typing as I kept looking for the program.

"Keep looking. It has to be there. When you activate it, you will have thirty minutes to escape. I'll be waiting for you outside the cape, Alec. I promise."

My stress had reached its peak. I continued to click every tab and could see the text that Atlas wrote delete as he quickly started to write again. I was so relieved that he was still waiting for me. I was hopeful again as I continued my search.

"I'm about to lose connection, Alec. Keep loo..." He wrote just before the text stopped and came to a close.

"SHIT!" I could hear the men searching for me shush one another as they heard my outburst.

"Come on," I whispered as I kept trying to find the program. I finally came across a tab that was barely legible. The application opened and was titled "Demo."

I could hear the sound of the doorknob starting to twist. My heart skipped a beat when I saw the door handle jiggle as someone tried to open it. Screams from Los Furiosos could be heard from the other side of the door. The program began and required a security code. The authorized user was my father, Dr. Samuel Everly. The password had a hint underneath it, it read one word.

"*Fidelity.*"

I sighed, "Really, Samuel?" The sound of pounding could be heard from the door as they continued trying to break in.

My thoughts were all over the place. I tried to think of anything he would have used.

I thought of my mom and entered her name.

"Abigail." The computer read, "*Access Denied.*"

I tried her full name, "Abigail Langston"...denied.

I tried it with my father's last name...denied.

"What the fuck did you use?" I said aloud as the men outside screamed, "He's in here."

I kept trying.

"Colden"…denied.

"Colden Everly"…denied.

"Alec"…denied.

"What an asshole," I said to myself, hoping that my name would have been a dead giveaway.

"Alec Everly"…denied.

"Los Furiosos?"…denied.

"Chromosome A.S."…denied

I heard the bolts on the door begin to give in. I took my hands off the keyboard and reached for Erico's gun. I started firing at the door and could hear the men on the other side scream in pain. My clip was empty now as they continued to pry.

"Fuck. What did you use?" I screamed. "Think, Alec."

Almost instantly, I had the feeling I knew what the password was. The same phrase I had seen in the cave before I made my leap onto the tram. The same nickname my mother mentioned to me, just before I left Canada. I took a deep breath and placed my hands back onto the keys. I whispered as I typed at the same time…

"Diablo Twins."

The computer glitched.

Access Code, Accepted.

Something was telling me that my father wasn't a bad guy after all. The Demo program opened and seemed very simple. A hazard warning displayed on the screen stating that the demolition was not a drill. I could see a red button displayed on the screen. I took a deep breath because I knew that the clock would soon start ticking. I had that rush of adrenaline just as I did when I was climbing the rock wall back home.

I pressed the button.

Suddenly alarms within the facility began to sound. Red lights flickered from the window of the office door. The sound of a computer's voice began to speak, and before it did, Los Furiosos who were beating down my door soon stopped to listen.

"Warning.
The demolition sequence has been activated.
This is not a drill.
All locks have been released to allow full evacuation.
Thirty minutes until Demolition.
Evacuate. I repeat. Evacuate."

The alarm continued to sound, and I could hear a click as the lock on my door soon slid open. My eyes widened because I was weaponless now and my enemies were on the other side.

But they weren't.

The sound of multiple locks could be heard in the distance starting to release. I could hear people yelling in the hallways, and footsteps running in every direction. As I stood at my father's desk, I could see shadows, military uniforms, and lab coats passing by my door. The alarm continued to ring as the computer's voice spoke again.

"Twenty-nine minutes until Demolition...Evacuate."

The hairs on my arms stood up, and as they did, my head throbbed because of the loud alarm. I clenched onto Erico's gun as I approached the office door. I looked out the window as the red lights flickered all throughout the halls, Los Furiosos were scattering like ants in all directions. Every lock was released. I was nervous about stepping out, but given the situation, I didn't have a choice. I reached for the doorknob and thought that I should at least pretend that I had bullets in my gun. I opened the door and led with my weapon. As the door swung shut behind me, I aimed it at those who ran up to me. Shockingly enough, they didn't attack. Men and women in lab coats filled the halls as they all ran at ample speed.

They had the right idea because it's exactly what I wanted to do. I looked around, and even Los Furiosos' marshals were running past me. Some looked at me in anger but kept moving. I knew I had pulled the switch of Armageddon when even Los Furiosos were running for their lives.

I scoffed to myself, "Run, you bastards."

The years of goodwill I had from working in the Peace Corps almost disintegrated as I watched with a smile on my face while everyone scurried away like roaches. It was like music to my fucking ears.

I ran to the elevator as it began to slide closed. There were multiple people inside, and I could see them pushing the button frantically to close the doors. It was probably for the best, it would have been an awkward ride. I turned around and started to run again. Trying to make my way toward the stairwell door. I came to a stop when I approached Dr. Jericho's office. His door was wide open, and he was nowhere in sight. While I looked into the room, I could see my bag and axe still where he had set them. I ran inside, grabbing my things.

"Twenty-five minutes until Demolition...Evacuate."

I inhaled and did as the computer ordered. It was only a matter of time before the facility would be obliterated. Snatching my bag and axe, I darted out of Dr. Jericho's door and headed straight for the stairwell door. As I reached for the door handle to the stairs, I could hear men arguing back in forth from a room nearby.

"I DON'T KNOW THE CODE!"

Another responded, "Try everything. Shut it down."

"The code that was used is old. There's nothing in the system that can be used to override it."

Ignoring them, I opened the door and ran down the stairs. I worried as I approached the second floor. The infected patients.

All the doors were unlocked. I deliberately walked down to the second level and could see that the doorway to the second floor was open. Sounds could be heard from within, along with screams and shrieks of unknown creatures.

"You just need to get to the ground level."

As I walked down the steps, I could see a cluster of chairs, desks, and shelves that barricaded the stairwell down to the first floor.

"Shit." I said to myself, as I glanced at the floor. I noticed bloodstains of hands that seemed to be dragged into the halls of the second floor.

This wasn't good. I couldn't go back now. I was running out of time. Passing through the second floor and making it to the elevator was my only shot. I pressed forward, the alarm continued to ring throughout the facility. As I got closer to the doorway, I could see bloody handprints on the door handle and frame. I pressed my back against the frigid wall and took a deep breath as I pivoted into the doorway, clutching onto my ax as I held it into the air with both hands. I could see that the halls were now filled with sunlight that cast in from shattered windows.

"What happened in here? It's only been five minutes."

The fluorescent lights remained dim. The second floor was chilly. With the wind rippling in form the shattered windows, the scent of iron filled my nostrils. My eyes went down to the marble of the halls to bodies of men and women, both Los Furiosos and patients alike. Fed on and torn to shreds.

"Looks like your beloved experiments got loose."

I could hear the faint sound of something being dragged down the halls. My heart was pounding in my chest, walking down the narrow corridor. I knew from my last visit here, there were two lethal experiments I had crossed, *Skinfiends* and the *Cabra*. Judging by the shattered windows, I could only imagine that some of those Cabras had escaped into the island. Trudging through the hall, striving to avoid stepping onto the broken bits of glass, a shadow moved in the corridors to the left. I froze in place and glanced behind me to make sure I wasn't being followed. Hyperventilating now, clenching my axe, my arms and hands trembled from its weight. Looking ahead, I could see three halls.

"The elevators at the end, come on, Alec. You can do this," I reminded myself, shaking the tension from my soul.

I wanted to run, the clock was ticking. But whatever was in here would definitely hear me. I pressed my left shoulder against the corner and lowered my axe. Before I could muster the courage to look, I could overhear to the sounds of chewing repeating within the hall.

I peered around the bend and quickly pulled away, pressing my back onto the wall as I covered my mouth. In the center of the hall were three patients who had escaped, surrounding a body that they were eating. The sounds of them chewing into the muscle caused me to shudder. I could hear their teeth beginning to bite into bone, the sounds of snapping popped over the alarm as they all fed like they hadn't eaten in days. The alarm and red flashing lights kept revolving, my anxiety to heighten. Looking down the hall, I could see a faint shadow. I prayed that it wasn't the Cabra because I knew I would never make it to the elevator alive.

The shadows were two members who had stepped into the hall, and their eyes pulsed as they came upon the horrific sight of the infected feeding. Suddenly their eyes met mine, they knew who I was. I knew one of them, Dr. Cooper, and a random Los Furiosos marshal. Although he didn't seem to be a threat at the moment, he and I both had an enemy in common. He quickly made a gesture with his hand toward me, trying to tell me something. One of the patients stopped feeding and looked up toward the marshal's direction as he and Dr. Cooper quickly hid behind the corner. The patient's eyes shifted back and forth, and then he went back down and resumed feeding.

The computer's voice alerted once again.

"Twenty minutes until Demolition...Evacuate."

The anticipation was building. Whatever I did, it needed to be quick. I looked back down the hall, and the marshal held out his hand, holding something. It was a grenade. He signaled with his hand telling me to head for the elevator. I didn't trust him, but I had no other option. We were all in a bind and needed to hurry. He held up five fingers and pointed toward the end of the hall again. He then began to lower his fingers, one by one, counting down before he threw the grenade into the corridor. I counted down to myself as his fingers fell.

Five...four...three...two...one.

I instantly snapped into a sprint. He hurled the grenade down the hall, and it slid into the center of the patients. As I ran, I looked down the hall and could see the marshal and Dr. Cooper break into a sprint, too. One of the patient's eyes shot up and met mine. He let out a loud shriek as he rushed down the hall toward me. As I crossed the hall, the grenade went off, causing the entire building to shake and him to be instantly killed. Both the marshal and Dr. Cooper ran toward the elevator. I ran as well, but then suddenly stopped because I didn't know if I was their ally anymore.

The marshal held his gun up, aiming at me as he stood in front of the elevator. I stood frozen, clinging to my axe while I shook from the adrenaline and the constant race against time. His eyes pulsed as he glared at me. Dr. Cooper in the lab coat grabbed the marshal's shoulder and spoke. "Lower your weapon, it's going to take all of us to get out of here alive."

The marshal scowled at her for a moment, and then he did as ordered. I let out a breath and approached them. Dr. Cooper pressed the elevator button, and you could hear it ding. The elevator was on the first floor and was beginning to make its way up. We all waited as the alarms continued to blare. I looked at the marshal as he looked me up and down with disgust. Dr. Cooper stared, analyzing me.

"I've been wanting to meet you. But given the situation, it doesn't seem like the best time for introductions," Dr. Cooper said.

I noticed she was holding units of Chromosome H. My eyes went back to hers, a look of disappointment on my face.

"Your genetic structure is strong, but it seems like parasites can still get the best of you," she spoke swiftly.

"How would you know if I have parasites?"

Suddenly the sound of a loud roar could be heard over all the other noise. Smoke was drifting around us from the grenade that had previously gone off. The marshal and I both looked at each other and then back down the hall. Dr. Cooper hid behind both of us, pressing her back against the wall where the elevator button was. She pushed it over and over. A figure emerged from the end of the corridor. It was exactly what I had feared. And specifically what I didn't want to encounter.

Its eyes were dark black, its muscles almost glistening as it emerged from the smoke. You could see the creature's spine rippling as it walked. Even on all fours, it was still bigger than a human. All I had was my axe to defend myself. The sound of a ding went off from behind us as the elevator doors slid open and Dr. Cooper quickly walked in. The Cabra's head tilted to the side. The marshal exhaled and looked over to me.

He suddenly shouted, "ALEC!" as he hurled his MP5 toward me.

The gun sailed through the air as I reached up and grabbed the weapon. The marshal pulled his other MP5 off of his shoulder. We both took aim as the Cabra shrieked and broke into a sprint down the hall. The marshal and I both began to fire. As we shot, we both stepped back into the elevator as our bullets rippled through the corridors while the sound of every round caused my ears to ring. The Cabra wasn't affected by the bullets as it sped toward us. With the creature's every step, I could feel the elevator rattle in place. Dr. Cooper held one hand against her ear as she pressed the button to level one, along with the button to close the doors. The doors finally slid closed.

"You people are fucking stupid for creating something like that," I told them as I began nudging away from them.

You could hear the Cabra slam its body into the steel doors as the elevator began to descend. I soon heard a loud sound from above. The Cabra screeched and I assumed it was now riding the elevator with us. I raised my MP5 toward the ceiling of the elevator and started to open fire. As I did, so did the marshal. For a moment I felt like we were a team. I finally had some kind of help on this godforsaken island. After a few rounds, I ran out of bullets and so did the marshal.

"Why can't that fucking thing die?"

I threw the MP5 onto the ground and reached for my axe.

Quickly, its sharp silver claws began to tear into the top of the elevator, ripping it to shreds. The elevator came to a stop, and the doors slid open but stopped because of how much damage that was being done from above. The doors were wedged just enough for us to pass through as the Cabra continued to claw its way in. Dr. Cooper passed through the doors first. As she did, the marshal threw down his weapon and pushed me toward the exit. Without hesitation, I wiggled my way through the doors. I turned around, and through the sliver of steel, I could see the marshal get scooped up by the Cabra. The sound of crunching could be heard from above as blood started to drip. Dr. Cooper stood by my side as she watched and finally closed her eyes and shuddered in place. I started to edge back from the elevator.

I glanced over to her, "You're on your own." I began to run away.

She shouted after me, "Be careful, Alec." And she, too, began to run.

The computer's voice spoke once again,

"Fifteen minutes until Demolition…Evacuate."

I pressed forward. The alarms continued to wail all throughout the first floor. It seemed like this floor was just as chaotic as the others. Everyone was running back and forth, trying to gather as many supplies and research as possible. I felt like I was running in slow motion. The horrors of the Genetic Research Facility would haunt me forever as I made my escape.

The double doors slid open as I passed through them, then the second set of doors did the same. I almost found myself screaming as the first breath of the outside air filled my lungs. I looked toward the dock. There were two ships that the Los Furiosos were preparing for departure. I had less than fifteen minutes, and I knew that I had to end up on one of these ships.

Everyone outside was running either to the vessels or deeper into the island to avoid the blast. I could see that the craft to the right was almost untied and I immediately booked it toward that one. As I ran, I could see someone standing off in the sand as his white lab coat tussled in the breeze. Dr. Jericho had made it out alive, taking one last view of the scene before it would soon be obliterated.

As the waves rolled in, he folded his arms as he watched me run. He smiled at me and then waved...his actions caused concern. I was nearing my freedom, and the farther away I got from this place, the better. I would soon be met Atlas. Eventually, be reunited with my friends back home, and soon see my mother again, and tell her the awful things I had discovered about my father. And hopefully, I would be back in Liam's arms, preventing him from ever seeing what I had seen on this island. Los Furiosos were all on the ship I was running toward. I had to board without being seen.

I jumped onto a set of retractable steps before they were pulled back into the ship. I stepped onto the edge of the deck and came across a steel door with a title on it that read, "Engine Room." I immediately wedged the door open, knowing this would be the room my journey followed.

Before I took my steps into the engine room, I thought of Colden. Although I wouldn't be able to save him now, I knew that he was still alive. I was already running scenarios in my mind of how I would go about getting the government to infiltrate Isle Onocastel. Although I was escaping Candelario, Los Furiosos still needed to be taken down. I turned and entered the engine room. I felt calmer than ever before. All I had to do now was wait as the clock continued to count down.

Metal steps led down into the engine room, and the deeper I went, the warmer it got. Fog was at the landing of the room, sounds of multiple machines running at maximum capacity. A table with drawers and two wooden chairs wedged up against compressed tanks of methane gas. Passing by them, pipes that pumped out steam led down a T-shaped landing to the back of the ship. Resting against handrails, I glared out of holes to watch Candelario.

I waited for the explosion, I wanted to see with my own eyes as the facility erupted. The anticipation was killing me just as it did before a firework was about to go off. A dull silence filled the air until suddenly...

I watched as a sonic boom sounded in the distance. A beautiful blue dome erupted over the facility, and I could see it crumbling before my eyes. I gripped onto the base of the railing while the explosion's blue rays reached out in every direction, causing a massive ripple effect into the ocean. I could see the water from the shore being pushed back and begin to create a wave in itself. The water quickly rushed toward the stern, and I held on, closing my eyes as it finally reached the ship. The wave the explosion created aided the ship and moved us even farther across the ocean, pushing us entirely out of the cape. I could feel the ship rock.

The fallout alone was brilliant. I never thought I would see the day where I would be happy about something so terrible happening.

"It's finally over."

The momentum of the ship picked up after the blast. I had completed my mission. Although the results of my DNA test were still inconclusive, Los Furiosos never got my blood, and for that, I was grateful.

"All right, Atlas. Now, what do I do?"

I had escaped Candelario, but still, I had not been rescued. Atlas was somewhere outside the cape and how he would approach a Los Furiosos ship, I had no idea. Either that or I would have to jump. Suddenly the sound of the engines began to slowly dull and come to a standstill. I walked back toward the engines.

"What's going on?"

The engines had come to a halt, and a red flashing light was blinking in the distance. I approached and could see that it flashed because of the lack of fuel. I shook my head and inhaled a deep breath. I knew eventually someone would have to come down. Los Furiosos didn't know I was here, and I wanted to keep it that way until I caught up with Atlas.

Just a little bit farther to go… Suddenly, the sound of the engine room door slowly creaked open.

"When will this end?" I whispered as I shook my head.

11: Spinning Compass

I COULD FEEL THE blood coursing through my veins as I listened to the footsteps and voices from above. Someone was standing in the doorway of the engine room having a conversation in Portuguese with another Los Furiosos. I was nearing my escape, and any slip up would seal my fate forever. While looking out of the window, I could no longer see the island of Candelario, only the vast expanse of the ocean. There wasn't a boat in sight, and I had an overwhelming feeling that Atlas wasn't going to be here in time to save me.

The voices continued and I found myself putting bits and pieces together of what they were talking about. Something about the explosion on Candelario and that their research was secured. They went on about setting a course for their sister island, Isle Onocastel. I had a lump in my throat when I overheard, and it was only a matter of time before they came down to refuel the heart of the ship so we could begin our journey to yet another hellscaped island. Although Colden was on Onocastel, I wasn't in the greatest position to go there now, especially in my condition.

I opened my locket to reveal my compass and could see the needle pointing south. I should have been heading east and back to the mainland of Chile. With no way of contacting Atlas, once again, I was on my own. The pair of voices in the doorway fell silent.

The men were walking down the stairs now, and I could hear them talking to one another, arguing about Candelario. About supplies and that they would restock and start to rebuild the genetic facility after the fallout. I shook my head because Los Furiosos were extraordinarily ruthless and persistent. The men continued to argue back and forth, and their aggressive behavior soon turned into a physical confrontation. They accidentally knocked down some of the methane tanks. One of the tanks began to roll away from them and headed directly to where I was hiding. The tank came to a stop once it hit the pipes that slightly kept me covered.

They both began to pick the tanks back up and place them against the wall near the table. I exhaled slowly because I knew they would have to come and pick up the container that laid at my feet. I only hoped that they wouldn't see it and just fuel the engine and go about their merry way. But it was hard to ignore the tank that continued to clink against the pipes as the ship rocked back and forth. I was about to be discovered, and I reached for my axe, anticipating one of them to approach.

I could see a small boat approaching through the window. I was filled with hope that it was Atlas here to rescue me. The craft outside that floated in the middle of the ocean was very small, but big enough to hold fifteen people. As the boat moved closer, I could hear Los Furiosos talking to one another, questioning who it was. Part of me wanted to charge at both of them and make a break for the stairs. But I held still because there was no guarantee that it was even Atlas on that boat. I guess I assumed that he would have others with him, but there were no other passengers on board. Atlas would be a fool to come out here all alone, and if I knew anything about him after Candelario, I knew that he wouldn't do something so ridiculous. The boat docked. Whoever approached us outside wasn't someone they were expecting.

The man filling the engine told him to get the tank and head upstairs, he would follow behind him after. I held on to my axe as the man came closer. Through the steam, I knew he could see me. His eyes went from my boots, all the way up my body. I stepped out from behind the pipes, kicking him in the stomach. He doubled over and it gave me the opportunity that I needed. Taking the back end of my axe, I struck him across the head, knocking him unconscious. The sound of the tank falling to the platform rippled throughout the engine room. The man who was filling the engine abruptly dropped the gas can and went to reach for his knife in his back pocket. I ran up to him, holding the blades to his face. He began to shout, attempting to alert the others from up above.

I held the teeth of the blades up close to his neck, "SHUT THE FUCK UP!"

I could hear footsteps. They knew I was here and it was only a matter of time before the engine room was flooded with Los Furiosos. I needed to think of something.

"Is there a lifeboat on board?" I asked the man.

He shook his head because he didn't seem to understand me.

I asked again, but in Portuguese, "Existe um bote salva-vidas a bordo?"

My dialect was fragmented but he got the point. I was trying to get information out of him before the rest of the ship's crew came down here. The man continued to shake his head so I got closer to his face and pressed the blade into his skin. He began to shout, and I immediately covered his mouth with my hand. I could hear the door to the engine room open, and multiple voices were talking to one another in Spanish. I leaned into the man's ear and told him not to say a word. I grabbed him by his arm and pushed him in front of the stairs. He stood quietly, shaking in place as the voices stopped, and began to descend the stairwell. I eyed the man once again, shaking my head, gripping onto my axe with both hands, raising it in the air, waiting for the perfect moment to strike whoever came down.

The steps halted, and a voice spoke softly, but just loud enough so that his voice echoed over the waves.

"Faerieeee...." The man spoke as if he were singing a tune, taunting me. An object was thrown through the air in our direction. It was a handgun that the man I was holding hostage caught and pointed directly at me.

"Damn it."

The man aimed the gun at me as I took a few steps back. He directed me with his weapon to move away from the stairs. I did as directed and lowered my axe. The man from the stairs emerged, at least now I could see his boots in the dim yellow lights. I exhaled when I saw his face and rolled my eyes at the same time.

"Well, well," Erico spoke sarcastically. "Did you miss me?"

I scoffed to myself, "Can't you just fucking die."

Erico pointed a handgun at me and laughed. His comrade did the same as he awaited Erico's next order.

"Put down your weapon." Erico spoke in a calming voice.

I could tell he wasn't ready for another physical fight. After everything he'd been put through in the past twenty-four hours on Candelario, he had multiple injuries that were too numerous to count. I did as he ordered and laid my axe on the floor. As I did, Erico approached me and kneed me in the face before I could rise to my feet. I fell back onto the floor, clenching my nose. Erico took his next opportunity to kick me in my broken ribs, causing me to shout in pain. My broken ribs caused more than I'd been in so far.

Atlas wasn't coming for me, and had a feeling that the vessel outside was just an individual who happened to be in the wrong place at the wrong time. I was never going to make it out of here. My hope and faith were starting to dwindle. All I wanted was to curl up into a ball and let Erico do his worst. Sick, tired, hungry, and dehydrated all in one, I wanted it to be over.

Erico spoke to his comrade in Portuguese, "Pick him up and tie him to the chair."

The man nodded his head and approached me, yanking me by my arm, causing me to scream out in pain again. The man pulled me to my feet and reached for one of the wooden chairs at the table. He dragged the chair to the center of the room and shoved me down. Erico continued to hold his gun toward me but it appeared that both Erico and I were on the same level of exhaustion...or injury. He stared at me before he spoke again.

"I want to enjoy this," he said as he exhaled, almost rolling his eyes in pleasure, or maybe that was fatigue.

His comrade appeared with rope and duct tape. He began unraveling the rope and tying it around the arms of the chair and around my body. I wanted to fight him off. I couldn't go on any longer. But the man tying me up didn't seem like he knew what he was doing. The ropes were tied, but were still loose, allowing me a little wiggle room. Erico told him to hurry up because he was becoming impatient. The man moved faster and tied off his last knot around both my ankles. He pulled a piece of duct tape and tore it with his teeth. I pulled back, telling him no. I didn't want that over my mouth. Erico pushed himself off the wall and stumbled over to us, holding the gun to my face. I began to shout.

"HELP! SOMEONE, PLEASE HELP!"

Erico pressed the weapon to my temple and leaned into my ear, whispering. "No one is coming, Faerie. You are finally...all mine," he said and kissed me on my neck.

Erico told the man to cover my mouth. He did as ordered and placed the tape over my lips. It was difficult for me to breathe through my nose because I was starting to hyperventilate. Through my panic, I overheard the man's voice from above.

"Who do you have down there?" the man asked before Los Furiosos spoke over him.

Erico turned to his comrade and ordered him to go upstairs and see what the commotion was about. The man obeyed and ran up the stairs and out the door, slamming it behind him. Erico watched me for the longest time until he finally broke his silence.

"I never wanted to do this to you, Faerie. Through all of our encounters, I've always respected you."

I shook my head, not believing a word he said as the men above us, their voices raised, broke out into a ruckus.

Erico continued, "The branding I gave you was only a taste of pain. By now, you know I have orders to keep you alive. However, I do admire a good barbecue." Erico pulled one of the drawers open at the table and reached inside.

He pulled out two items. One was a syringe and the other was a blow torch. I began to shake. Erico smiled in pleasure.

"You will become one of us, Faerie. Whether you like it or not, you will submit." Rage now filled his voice.

Erico limped over toward me with the syringe in hand. He placed his hands around my neck and stroked my jawline with his thumb as he looked into my eyes with admiration. I could see him look at my chest and shoulders as he licked his lips. He leaned in, inhaling my scent as if he were a wild animal. He placed kisses on my shoulders, chest, and neck. He leaned in to kiss my lips that had duct tape across them. I tried to pull away, but he fought my resistance by pulling me by the back of my neck closer to him. He came to a stop and looked at me again, almost like I was his for the taking. He spoke with tears in his eyes.

"I can't wait for you to be reborn. I can see us together."

I shook my head vigorously. There was no way in hell I would ever be with him. Erico laughed and pulled his face away from mine. The scuffle from above had ended. Erico proceeded to speak,

"You can't see it?" He paused as he gripped the syringe. "Well, maybe this will help." He stabbed the needle into my right leg. Injecting me with what I thought was hallucinogens.

I shook my head back and forth, crying. I wanted to be free. I wanted to be with Liam. In my drugged state, I could hear the voice of the man speak from above.

"Where the fuck is he?"

The tone of the man's voice made me think of Liam. But it was hard to tell because of the effects of the hallucinogens. My perception of reality was starting to go in and out. Erico laughed before he grabbed the blow torch and ignited it. Erico turned back to me to reveal the blue flame of the torch that was pulsing.

"It's nice to have you silent. Usually, you would have some stupid comment, but this...this is going to be good." Erico walked toward me with the blow torch.

The blue flame looked so beautiful to me, it radiated throughout the room. For a moment, I wanted to feel it, but I knew that was a bad idea. Erico stood before me and spoke.

"Although it's nice that you are speechless, I still don't want to hear your screams," Erico said as his eyes went to the engine. I could see his eyes pulse as the motor automatically revved to life. The noise of the engine started to drown out the voices from above. Erico smiled as he slowly edged the flame closer and closer to my right thigh. My eyes got bigger, violently fighting against the ropes that kept me restricted.

I could feel everything. The heat of the flame began to ignite my pants first and soon started to seer through the fibers and made its way onto my skin. The pain was too much. My mind was all over the place. Bouncing back from my family, Los Furiosos, Liam, and back to prison on Candelario Island. I was about to pass out from the pain as I let my head fall back. When I looked up again, my mind was playing tricks on me, I was sure of it. A man was here, and it wasn't Erico or his goon. This man looked like Liam, but when I blinked my eyes, he turned back into Los Furiosos. I looked down at my leg, the muscle of my right thigh was exposed. I shook in place, trying to get free, and I could feel the ropes that held me down start to loosen.

The man spoke in Portuguese, but it was too hard for me to concentrate because of the drugs. Erico broke into a rage and began to yell at the man. He threw the torch onto the table and held his gun to the man's face, demanding something.

Erico shouted at the man, "GO. I'LL BE UP IN A SECOND."

My eyes slowly drifted toward the stairs, and I noticed that the man who came down was already gone. Either that or I imagined he was there but really wasn't. I didn't know anything anymore. I could see Erico walk over to the table again and open another drawer. He pulled out a backpack, similar to the one I wore on the way to Candelario. Erico approached me, but the way he moved made it seem like he was traveling at the speed of light. My eyes were deceiving me. With every blink of my lids, I could see that Erico hadn't even walked toward me to begin with. Reality or not? I didn't even know. I could hear him say, "I'll be back, baby." But when he spoke, I could hear Liam's voice leaving his lips.

I shook my head and blinked, I could see that it was Liam who was in front of me rather than Erico. He stood, holding the pack, looking at me. Was it Liam? Had he come to save me? I blinked my eyes again and could see Erico standing in front of me. Erico placed the knapsack over my head, and I could hear him go up the stairs. I could make out small beacons of light through the tiny holes of the sack. I pulled at the ropes again and continued pulling with all my might, to the point where it felt like I was ripping the skin off of my wrist. My right hand came loose from under the ropes. Heard the voices from above again. I could hear Erico and what sounded like Ann and Issac talking to one another?

I knew that Ann and Issac weren't here. I was the only one who could save myself. I reached for my left wrist, beginning to loosen the restraints. My left hand was free and I reached for the sack covering my face. I removed the knapsack when suddenly, the noise of the screeching Cabra billowed from my right. My eyes darted to see its large body standing on all fours near the window. I quivered in fear and blinked my eyes once again to see that there was no Cabra, but just the ship's engine whining. Untying my ankles, I swore I could hear Liam's voice from above as he asked about me.

Once my legs were free, I stood up and immediately fell down. I no longer knew how to use my limbs. Crawling across the floor, I edged my way toward my axe. After grabbing it, I reached for the tabletop and pulled myself up to my feet. Stumbling as I did, I could almost hear a siren go off just as it did in the Genetic Facility. I began to panic because I knew I only had a matter of time before the facility was going to explode.

"It's the drugs, Alec, it's not real," I told myself, shaking my head trying to regain my vision.

The sirens stopped as I looked over to the pipes that let off steam that whistled in the distance. I didn't like the effects of the hallucinogens, and I now understood why it was so easy to manipulate Los Furiosos. Groaning came off in the distance. I quickly stumbled over to the chair I was tied down to and rested my weight on its armrest.

Behind me, the man I knocked unconscious was waking up. I walked to him, in a split second, I could see the man's face morph from Liam's face and into Erico's. I shook my head, clenching my eyes shut and opening them again to make sure I was seeing what was actually in front of me.

The man was starting to wake up, I needed to stop him. Grabbing him by his limp arms, pulling him toward me, dragging his body to the chair that I was once constrained in. Once I had him close to the seat, I hoisted his body up, trying to support his weight against me. I slouched his limp body into the seat.

"Make him look like you, Alec. Buy yourself some time." I debated with myself, reaching for ropes to tie him down.

I placed my hands on his knees so I could help myself up. As I did, the voices from above got louder. My eyes went the man's wrist, and I quickly used the ropes to tie him down. I looked back to the table and went to reach for the duct tape. I pulled a pieced off and taped the man's mouth shut.

I looked down at the floor and picked up the knapsack along with my axe. I placed the bag over the man's head and stumbled back onto the table. My vision was beginning to sway, and I found myself losing my balance.

"Damn, these drugs are strong," I said to myself as I wiped sweat off my forehead.

The torch that once melted my leg laid on the table. It began to roll backward and hit the methane tanks that stood behind the table. I reached for one of the containers, seeking to twist the knob open and allow the gas to fill the room.

"Come on, Alec, come on," I whispered to myself, and as I did, I could hear my voice echoing over and over.

Furious, I grabbed my axe, watched the tanks, trying to time my swing just right. I swung. The spout of the tank broke off, sending the compressed gas inside to spew out. Absent of breath, I began to stumble toward the stairs.

"I need to get out of here before the ship blows." I clung to the hand railing as my eyes wandered up the staircase.

The dim yellow lights and steam made it appear like I was looking up to the gates of hell. Holding onto my axe, I started to walk. Falling to my knees onto one of the steps, I found myself crawling up the stairs instead.

I reached for the door handle and hoisted myself up. The effects of everything was finally hitting me. My heart pounded in my chest as I raised myself up to my feet. I took in a deep breath and pulled the door open.

Bright lights from outside poured into the engine room. I was temporarily blinded as I stumbled through the doorway. The scent of the saltwater filled my nostrils, and I finally felt like I could breathe again. Unsure of where the voices were coming from, I could see shadows of multiple people coming from the other side of the passageway.

Erico's voice spoke in haste, "Deal with this motherfucker. I'll be back."

The ship swayed in the ocean as the men continued to shout to one another in Portuguese. I made my way toward the front of the boat, stumbling as I did, I could hear Liam shouting in my mind?

"WHERE IS HE? WHAT HAVE YOU DONE TO HIM?"

Was this real? I only imagined him saying those words as if he were here to find me. I hoped Liam was safe, far away from this place. As I approached the head of the ship, I held onto the wired hand railings. In broad daylight, I could hear the men get silent and begin to shout in my direction. Paying no attention, I needed to jump ship. My eyes looked down to the water, its beautiful deep blue abyss was calling to me. I had to swim to the mainland if it was the last thing I had to do. I shook from the thought of the freezing temperatures below, and sharks could be waiting in the water. For some reason, I could hear the men's voices from behind me grow louder.

"Who is that?" Liam's voice asked.

Why was he asking strange questions? It didn't make any sense to me as I gazed into the deep blue. The sound of guns being cocking echoed from behind me, I didn't know if they were real or not? For a moment, the shouting of the men faded and stopped, and the only thing I could hear was the igniting of the torch that once melted my thigh. The silence finally broke as I shook in place.

Liam's voice boomed in the distance as he shouted my name, "ALEC."

It seemed so surreal; it sounded like he was actually here? I slowly began to turn around, as I gripped my axe, awaiting an attack from Los Furiosos. As my eyes gradually drifted over my left shoulder, adjusting to the brightness from outside. Standing from afar and across the deck near the boat that floated in the distance was a group of men. My vision continued to blur from the effects of the drugs and my fever. The men were huddled together, some were holding guns, and others were holding a man hostage? My eyes kept playing tricks on me. The sun's rays blurred my eyesight as I could see the man that was being held looked familiar?

He stood tall. His dark hair seemed to tussle in the wind. His body was built strong, and he stood his ground while he was being held against his will. His features were the same as they were the first moment I saw him the night of the party in high school. The same way he stood in the airport as I waited for his arrival. It had to be a hallucination? It appeared realistic until my vision began to fade in and out. I could see him being to struggle and fight off Los Furiosos, striving to make a break for me. It couldn't be real, because as he fought, there was no sound leaving his lips. No voices were threatening one another as Los Furiosos violently fought back, moving their mouths as if they were shouting. They continued to scuffle as the ship rocked, and Liam's face morphed into Erico's and then back into Liam's again.

Silence broke as two voices rippled in the air.

Erico screamed, "OH, SHIT."

Liam shouted, "ALECCC…"

An explosion rocked the boat. The shockwave sent me and the others hurdling off the ship. My ears were ringing, my body shaking. After breaking the surface and taking my first breath, I watched the ship go up in flames. It was unreal, I didn't know if what I was seeing was real or not, but I felt lighter than I had in what felt like forever.

A piece of debris floated by as I reached for it and rested my body on it. I'd just rest for a moment, and would tackle escaping after I felt better. The waves of the water rocked me back and forth as my eyelids began to get heavy.

But the hallucinations were still there, even with my eyes closed. I began to kick my feet as paranoia started to set in. Los Furiosos were after me. I needed to swim, I needed to get away, and their pursuit was relentless. But it was only the dead Los Furiosos around me, thankfully.

I imagined Atlas's voice and hoped he would find me. Minutes turned into hours. I could feel the sun on my back as I continued to drift through the ocean. The sun trickled across the sky while I floated to nowhere.

I looked off into the distance and realized that my dead companions were no longer in sight. Just the neverending blue waves that danced in place. I rested my face against the wood and waited. Someone would find me: Los Furiosos, Atlas, or the sharks. I began to question if this would be how it ends for me. Never knowing if I had been given Chromosome A.S. Never seeing Liam's face again. My mother would search for me, it was one thing to lose her husband, but losing her children would destroy her. Colden would be experimented on until Dr. Jericho grew bored. And Los Furiosos would rise, and humanity would soon transform into global slavery.

Something moved underneath me. I gasped as I looked down into the dark blue water. I couldn't see anything, but the fear of sharks piqued my anxiety. I began to pant, peering in every direction. This couldn't be how my life ended, I gripped onto my axe, begged that it was another hallucination. The wooden carnage I rested on jolted. A splash of water spewed across my face. Clinging to both the debris and my axe, realizing I was at the bottom of the food chain. Water shot off into the air as if it had been compressed for hours. It rained down on me as I could see a dark object swim nearby.

"Please don't be a shark." My eyes grew when I saw what the animal was.

A colossal blue whale, it wasn't a hallucination. The scale of the whale was vividly clear as it swam alongside me. Shaking on my wooden debris, the whale raised its enormous fin, splashing a tidal wave toward me. The swell crashed over me, sending me underwater. Breaking the surface, I took in a gasp of air, swimming back to my chunk of wood.

Suddenly she broke free from the surface. Her gills, body, and fins had revealed themselves while she floated in thin air like an angel. Alarmed, I kept kicking back, trying to avoid her forthcoming splash. She free-fell back toward the ocean's surface, gracefully floating down as if she were a ballerina. As she slipped under the surface, an enormous wave was created as a consequence. I held onto my wooden debris and axe, bracing myself for impact. The wave sent me and the chunk of the ship flying off into the air. I could feel my hands and legs kicking in the air as I darted across the surface like a skipping stone.

The wave she produced swallowed me whole. Kicking my way back up to the surface, my broken ribs crackled while I reached up above. My face broke free, and I gulped in as much air as I could. When my eyes finally cleared, I was instantaneously greeted by my floaty which slammed into my face. I could feel the right side of my temple pulse and swell, the water around me turned red. I was losing blood, and my worry wasn't for the amount of blood, but sharks.

My thoughts began to turn into a haze while I bobbled in the water like a buoy. I could feel myself slipping away from the amount of blood I had lost. My arms and legs began to get weak, and my vision was fading. I could see my wooden floaty begin to descend deeper into the ocean and soon disappear into obscurity. The sun was just beginning to set as I yelled from the agony. Pain radiated over my entire body, I found myself giving in. I tilted my head back into the water until my ears were submerged. I floated on my back, concentrating on breathing.

The sky was a pinkish purple. This was the end, and soon, sharks would smell the blood and come to hunt me. I was too weak to put up another fight, the moment of giving up finally began to set in as I floated alone in the ocean with no land in sight. I cried to myself. I cried from both the pain and the thought of dying at sea after everything I had been through. My body shivered, with every tremor, it felt like more and more blood left my body.

"Think of Liam. Think of a better place, Alec, better than this," I cried, welcoming death.

I could hear the sound of a loud horn in the distance as I imagined me and Liam in our pool. I thought the horn was music playing in the background while Liam got out to get us a few beers. It felt as if all my feelings of fear, pain, and sight were fading to a dark place. For a moment, it felt peaceful, and I wanted to embrace death because it was so much easier than life. For a moment, Liam spoke.

"Alec..." he said, his voice was low, but as I looked at his face, it looked like he was shouting.

Why? I didn't know because he was so close to me. He suddenly dropped the bottles of beers into the water and shouted again.

"ALEC!" His voice grew louder.

I said his name back, "Liam. What is it?" I laughed and cried all at once.

He shouted once again, *"ALEC, GIVE ME YOUR HAND!"*

Liam grabbed onto my right arm, yanking me aggressively. It felt so real. My eyes shot open.

A man and woman aboard a bright yellow speed boat floating beside me. My eyes were blurred from tears, saltwater, and blood while the man and woman both struggled to pull me onto their boat. After being dragged aboard, the woman was digging through a trunk filled with towels and blankets and ran over to us, wrapping them around me. I didn't know what was happening, and as my eyes began to droop, I saw the woman run over to a first-aid box, grabbing supplies and running back over to us.

Then I passed out from the pain and the exhaustion of everything that I'd been through.

The woman cracked an ammonia vial underneath my nose, and I tried to fight off the man who was cradling me. He stood his ground, holding me tight and stopping my outburst as I was too weak to fight.

"Calm down, Alec. Calm down. You're safe."

I shook in his arms and found myself settling. His body was so warm. He rocked me slightly and rubbed his strong hands over my shoulders over and over again, trying to keep me warm. I could feel my head slouch over and was greeted by the woman. I took in a deep breath because I recognized her. The girl from the post office. I identified her dark hair and honey brown eyes, and the scar on her cheek. Why was she here? How did she find me? I felt safe because I could see her eyes were normal, and I knew she wasn't a threat.

"He's lost a lot of blood. I think I can stitch up his temple. Mateo, keep him warm," the woman said as she quickly walked back toward the first-aid kit.

My eyes went past her, and I could see a man with short salt and pepper hair driving the boat. He remained turned around as the craft took off at full speed toward the sunset. The man driving the boat shouted aloud,

"Is he okay?" he said, his voice sent shock waves through me.

The man shouted again, "Catalina, is he going to be all right?"

"Atlas?"

Catalina answered him, "I don't know, he's not exactly in the best shape."

The boat continued to move, rocking me to sleep.

The man holding me pulled me into him tightly.

I looked up to him, "Liam?" I spoke in confusion because the way he held me was the same way Liam did.

"I'm Mateo, Alec. We're going to help you. You're safe, okay?" he said, trying to calm me.

He looked up to Catalina and spoke, "You need to hurry. He's lost too much blood." He held a towel against my temple, trying to stop the bleeding, as he shouted at her.

"We should be safe until we make it back to Chile," he said, and it was then that I knew it was Atlas.

Before I closed my eyes, I felt like I was looking at an older version of myself when I looked at Atlas. It was right there at the forefront of my mind, but I could feel myself slipping away. Atlas spoke one last time, "We have you now, son. You're safe."

It couldn't be true...this couldn't be real. Was this just another hallucination? I took one last breath as my eyes began to roll back, the sweet relief of unconsciousness pulling me under...

"Dad?"

12: Golden Boy

AS ALEC EVERLY ESCAPED, Los Furiosos stayed behind and began to rebuild after the devastating bomb that consumed a chunk of Candelario Island. Many of those who survived the explosion of the lab had orders to begin helping those aboard the vessel that the Faerie took out. During the ensuing chaos, Dr. Jericho received word that there was a survivor among the remains of the ship who was not one of their own. Dr. Jericho was the first to respond and dragged the man's body out of the ocean and onto their boat. The group set a course for Isle Onocastel. They had received orders from Vincent himself to report to the island immediately. Now that Erico was dead, it was time that they promoted a new leader. Someone who was well trained, highly organized, and knew the ins and outs of Alec Everly's life.

As Dr. Jericho and his comrades sailed to their destination with their new recruit's unconscious body, Dr. Jericho had an overwhelming feeling that Alec's escape would ultimately bring retribution to Isle Onocastel. Dr. Jericho ordered his men to carry the man's body to their holding facility.

Once they arrived, the difference between Candelario and Onocastel were astronomical. There were large buildings across the island that mimicked skyscrapers. The sounds of cars, motorcycles, and trains could be heard in the distance. As Los Furiosos carried the man's body, they passed many ordinary individuals. Those who were the family members of Los Furiosos and were promised a life of protection once Los Furiosos rose to control. Men, women, and children all watched Los Furiosos carry the limp man's body toward a massive building that had many well-armed guards patrolling the facility. The island seemed to be a city, urban and high tech to where it appeared to make Candelario look like a third-world country.

Cars drove throughout the night and halted at street lights and stop signs like any other city. The island was not as chaotic as Candelario was. You could see coffee shops and farmers' markets in the veins of the city. It seemed like everyone had a job on Onocastel, a position that consisted of aiding Los Furiosos in any way possible. Jobs that kept the city and its people afloat. Dr. Jericho came across a woman and a child and stopped as Los Furiosos continued to carry the body into a shiny building that reflected in the moonlight. There were massive tapestries with a modern design that hung from the premise that displayed the Los Furiosos universal crest.

"Hello, Mrs. Valenzuela. Or should I say, Miss Valenzuela? I'm sorry to say I have terrible news." The woman shielded her son behind her, with an expression on her face of worry and a primal instinct to protect her child.

"What? What has happened to Allen?"

Dr. Jericho replied without a hint of guilt, "He is no more. I do apologize. It seems like the Faerie killed him, he didn't stand a chance."

Dr. Jericho eyed the child she hid and smiled sadistically. The woman cried silently to herself, seeking to put on a brave face for her son before Dr. Jericho spoke again.

"Now that he is gone, there is no reason for you two to be here." He paused as he looked at her son again. "Unless, of course, you volunteer your boy for testing. It would be the only reason to keep you here. I will give you some time to give me an answer, but don't keep me waiting," Dr. Jericho said as he reached around the woman and rubbed the child's head.

The woman recoiled deliberately and pushed her son away from Dr. Jericho's hand. Dr. Jericho scoffed to himself and followed behind Los Furiosos into the facility. The woman cried to herself quietly and bent down to hug her son.

"I'll never let them take you," she said to her son, making him a promise.

The boy looked concerned for his mother and held on to her tightly. Holograms projected around the streets of Onocastel. Broadcasting news about Candelario and how the citizens residing here would soon have to become new recruits to replace their loved ones. Those taken and implanted were chosen against their will, and others volunteered. Los Furiosos made it appear like they were drafting individuals to become one of them. Either that or they would become experiments or worse, killed. It soon made sense that those living on Onocastel were only prisoners kept against their will. Pawns that were elected to take the places of their loved ones once they passed in order to keep Los Furiosos agenda alive.

Trains could be heard screeching in the distance of the island. The woman and child quickly ran toward the railroad nearby and boarded. The train tracks filtered into the city of the island. There were no homeless here, no one without a job or duty that didn't serve Los Furiosos. The people living here seemed to have a cushy lifestyle. Modern technology was everywhere. Most who roamed the streets of Onocastel were not implanted, and those who were, retained the peace and balance of the land.

Dr. Jericho entered the facility with his men. Inside were marshals. A woman stood behind a desk and babbled as she released the locks on multiple doors that led deeper into the facility. She went around her desk and approached Dr. Jericho with an update.

"Vincent has been waiting for you. You know how he doesn't like to be kept waiting."

"That man will never be satisfied. Hasn't he realized who the brains of this operation is?" Dr. Jericho said sarcastically as the woman gasped.

"Don't let him hear you say that, or else he will have you killed. You are just like the rest of us, Dr. Jericho."

"Please, honey. I am irreplaceable. How else would he be able to replicate Chromosome A.S.H. without me? He needs me," Dr. Jericho said with a smirk as he continued down the corridors of the facility, leaving the woman behind.

The facility was constructed of concrete, the deeper Dr. Jericho walked inside, the darker it became. The only thing keeping the halls illuminated was high-tech lighting. While Dr. Jericho walked, he came across cells that were framed with bulletproof glass. Dr. Jericho stopped once he approached a cell that contained a man with tattoos who stood tall. The man was wearing a patient gown, just like the other prisoners. His hair was buzzed cut, and he was beginning to sport slight facial hair. His eyes narrowed as he watched Dr. Jericho stand before his cell.

"How is the wonderful Colden Everly doing these days?" Dr. Jericho said with sarcasm.

"I promise you, if I ever make it out of here, I will snap your fucking neck."

Dr. Jericho scoffed to himself, "That's a mean thing to say to someone who has kept you alive for so long." His eyes looked at the cell up and down, an electrical shock wave radiated from within. Colden fell down to the floor as electricity rippled through his body. The moment he began to foam out of the mouth is when Dr. Jericho stopped the lethal voltage. He leaned into the glass window of the cell and let out a small laugh.

"You should mind your manners, it seems like you may not be of any use to us anymore. Consider yourself lucky to still be alive." Dr. Jericho spoke as if he were a god.

Colden gradually raised himself from the ground, clenching onto his stomach and chest.

"Your brother has made quite a stir on Candelario," Dr. Jericho said with a smirk.

"What the fuck are you talking about?"

"Oh, you didn't know? We had the pleasure of meeting, and let me tell you...the guy has a gift. Something that we Los Furiosos have been waiting for for many years."

"Don't you fucking touch him. Stay away from him, or so help me God I'll..." Colden shouted but paused when Dr. Jericho began to look at his cell once again, he immediately silenced.

"Yeah, that's what I thought."

He began to walk away from his cell and continued to follow the trail of water that the unconscious man's body left behind. Colden approached the glass window of his cell and started to pound on the glass.

"DON'T YOU HURT HIM. STAY THE FUCK AWAY FROM HIM."

Dr. Jericho continued to walk away, smirking to himself. He soon approached a set of double doors and glared at the I.D. scanner until its locks released. He stepped in, and inside was a single slab of a metal table underneath a headlamp with dim fluorescent lights that kept the room illuminated. The men who carried the man's body stood silently, awaiting their next order as their eyes pulsed. Dr. Jericho broke his silence.

"Place him on the table."

Dr. Jericho's eyes went from the table and over to a two-way mirror on the wall that was nearly ten-feet wide.

A voice blared over speakers within the room, *"Where is the Faerie?"*

The men started removing items from the pockets of their prisoner...a clip of ammo along with his wallet, passport, and a photo of Alec Everly. One of the men turned the man over and reached for a gun that was holstered on his lower back...a Glock .45, and placed it on a table that was nearby.

"You let him escape?" Enraged that Dr. Jericho didn't answer.

"Yes, he did. And the tracking device we placed on him is ineffective now that our computers on Candelario were destroyed." He paused when he spoke. "However, we have alerted our informant and have arranged to meet him soon to give him the salvaged hard drive we recovered from the Genetic Facilities carnage. I take it you can still trust the informant given your... relationship with him?" Dr. Jericho spoke in secrecy.

"You failed me, once again, Dr. Jericho. Remind me why I keep you alive?"

Dr. Jericho scoffed and eyed one of his men who held on to the wallet that once belonged to the unconscious man. The soldier nodded his head and approached the mirror, opening up the wallet and placing it against the mirrored glass, revealing a photograph to Vincent. Dr. Jericho smiled to himself and looked at the man's body that laid before him.

"Trust me, the Faerie will be back. Now that we have something that he wants."

"That may be true, and we still have Colden Everly. Any chance you got a sample of the Faerie's blood?"

Dr. Jericho turned around and approached the small table, opening a miniature drawer underneath the tabletop. He pulled out a syringe along with a cylinder device used to implant new recruits. He walked back over to the man who laid on the table and reached above to adjust the headlamp.

"I didn't, actually. But as I said, he will be back," he replied with a smile.

"You had better be right, Dr. Jericho. His blood is the key to our army. In the meantime, we must rebuild. And as far as he goes..." Vincent paused, referring to the man passed out on the table. *"You have chosen our new lead command well. His military experience and training will be very impactful to Los Furiosos. You better make sure you keep him under control. If there is even a hint of him remembering the Faerie, it'll be your ass on the chopping block."*

"Hold him down," Dr. Jericho ordered Los Furiosos marshal's in the room, as they all surrounded the man, grabbing his shoulders, arms, and legs.

"We are so fortunate that you came to look for him and lucky that you even survived the ship's explosion at that. Just like him… you are a fighter. And once he sees what you've become, it will be glorious…"

Dr. Jericho implanted him as the man's entire body shook. Jericho disliked this part the most, it was almost animalistic. So he glanced over at the picture in the man's wallet of Alec Everly and Liam Brooks standing on top of a mountain in climbing gear, their arms around each other.

With one final tremor, Liam's eyes shot open as silver halos surrounded his iris.

"Welcome to Los Furiosos," Dr. Jericho said, grinning as he stood over their new golden boy.

Acknowledgements

The moment I finished the first installment of *"Rise of the Fay,"* a sense of gratitude had to be given to those who have supported me throughout this entire journey. I want to give a huge thank you to both Eladia Hernandez and Miguel Resendiz for allowing me to live in their home and accepting me for being me. I want to thank my roommates, Ariadne Perez for reassuring me during my writing and a special thank you to Kiara Perez, who was the very first person to ever read my book. I also want to thank my mother and brothers for mostly being the character inspirations within *"Rise of the Fay."* Next, I have to applaud my entire Launch Team for helping me choose the cover design, website design, and giving me their take on the story. A massive shout out to apple.com for equipping me with a fantastic MacBook where I wrote the majority of the story. I want to give a big thanks to 99designs.com for all of the submissions for the book's cover. A special thanks go to Nicolette Adams who photographed me for my author photo. This next shout out goes to Michael Burton who took the idea of Alec Everly's axe and made it into a reality, a very iconic piece in the *"Rise of the Fay"* series. I'd also like to thank everyone at fiverr.com who helped in designing so much artwork that was all meant for the book. Carolinereverie for characters, Honey_creative for the Los Furiosos logo, Mangasteen for the logo animations, and Exoniensis for the map of Candelario Island.

Last, but not least, I'd like to give a BIG thank you to all the readers...none of this would have been possible without them. I hope that this story touches many LGBTQ+ communities, allowing them to finally see a hero whom we lack to have in theaters, so why not in a book? Thank you so much for reading, and don't forget that we, too, are a force to be reckoned with.

INSPIRATIONS

There are multiple authors whom I would like to give thanks to for inspiration, as well as outside influencers who have kept me going even if they weren't a part of my life. Author Lisa McMann of the "Wake Trilogy" was my absolute favorite. Author Jennifer Niven of *"All the Bright Places"* will always have a special place in my heart. Author Emily Lockhart of the book *"We Were Liars"* took me to a place that almost made me feel like it was my family. Next, I would like to give thanks to my YouTube inspirations whose videos have helped me with self-acceptance and pushed me to continue to be creative. Special thanks to Todrick Hall for being such an iconic singer whose songs made me dance like no one was watching. Kathy Griffin, whose stand-up and overall sense of humor about the gays has left me having a positive outlook on life. I want to thank two of the most iconic influencers, Shane Dawson and Ryland Adams who have always put a smile on my face, especially during the hard times. Another thank-you goes to the gorgeous couple, Mark E. Miller and Ethan Hethcote for helping me find a balance even in my relationships. I want to thank Matt Dallas and Blue Hamilton for helping me aspire to be more creative, primarily while I work in construction. And, last but not least, I want to give a special thank you to Jeffree Star for inspiring me to be just as creative in both writing and makeup. Thank you to all of the beautiful people who have always had an impact on my life and inspired me to keep pushing forward through the difficult times that life throws at you.

About the Author

Andre L. Carr is the author of the first installment of the "Rise of the Fay" series. A novel surrounding a young adult, LGBTQ+ character named Alec Everly, whose journey to reconnect with his identical twin brother shifts into a deadly fight for survival that later leads to a revelation of his father's dark and hidden past. Andre L. Carr was born in 1992 in Stockton, California. However, he grew up in Las Vegas, Nevada, where he  graduated in 2010 from Spring Valley High School. Afterwards, Andre attended Anthem Institute of Technology where he earned his certificate of Dental Assisting. Throughout the years, Andre has participated in multiple careers in the medical field and trade work. Andre L. Carr has dabbled in various areas of work including modeling, YouTube, makeup artist, writing, insurance, and construction. To learn more about Andre L. Carr and the book *"Rise of the Fay,"* please visit: www.AndreLCarr.com.

Lightning Source UK Ltd.
Milton Keynes UK
UKHW010655220820
368637UK00005B/27/J